WHAT
BLOOMS
FROM
DUST

JAMES MARKERT

THOMAS NELSON
Since 1798

What Blooms from Dust

© 2018 by James Markert

Published in Nashville, Tennessee, by Thomas Nelson. Thomas Nelson is a registered trademark of HarperCollins Christian Publishing, Inc.

Thomas Nelson titles may be purchased in bulk for educational, business, fund-raising, or sales promotional use. For information, please e-mail SpecialMarkets@ThomasNelson.com.

Library of Congress Cataloging-in-Publication Data

Names: Markert, James, 1974- author.
Title: What blooms from dust / James Markert.
Description: Nashville, Tennessee : Thomas Nelson, [2018]
Identifiers: LCCN 2017051228 | ISBN 9780785217411 (trade paper)
Subjects: LCSH: Psychological fiction.
Classification: LCC PS3613.A75379 W46 2018 | DDC 813/.6--dc23 LC
record available at https://lccn.loc.gov/2017051228

Printed in the United States of America
18 19 20 21 22 / LSC / 5 4 3 2 1

ACCLAIM FOR JAMES MARKERT

"Markert's unusual story line and compelling characters offer a fresh perspective. Verdict: Readers looking for lighter horror will enjoy."

—LIBRARY JOURNAL STARRED REVIEW OF
ALL THINGS BRIGHT AND STRANGE

"Markert's latest supernatural novel is captivating from the beginning . . . Readers of Frank Peretti and Ted Dekker will love Markert's newest release."

—RT BOOK REVIEWS, 4 STARS ON ALL
THINGS BRIGHT AND STRANGE

"Screenwriter Markert (*The Angel's Share*) conjures an apocalyptic page-turner that blends Frank Peretti-style supernatural elements with the fine detail of historical novels."

—PUBLISHER'S WEEKLY ON ALL THINGS BRIGHT AND STRANGE

"A haunting tale of love, loss, and redemption."

—BOOKLIST ON ALL THINGS BRIGHT AND STRANGE

". . . this magical novel warns us to be careful what we wish for. We may get it."

—BOOKPAGE ON ALL THINGS BRIGHT AND STRANGE

"In *All Things Bright and Strange*, James Markert melds the ordinary and the extraordinary to create a compelling tale. Can miracles be trusted? Are the dead really gone? Can we be undone by what we wish for most? The citizens of Markert's Bellhaven must confront these questions and more, with their fates and the existence of their entire town at stake."

—GREER MACALLISTER, BESTSELLING AUTHOR OF
THE MAGICIAN'S LIE AND GIRL IN DISGUISE

"Mysterious, gritty and a bit mystical, Markert's entertaining new novel inspires the question of 'What if?' Many characters are nicely multilayered, providing a good balance of intrigue and realism. The fascinating glimpse into the process of distilling bourbon—and the effect of the Prohibition on Kentucky and its bourbon families—adds another layer to the story."

—RT BOOK REVIEWS, 3 STARS ON THE ANGELS' SHARE

"Folksy charm, an undercurrent of menace, and an aura of hope permeate this ultimately inspirational tale."

—*BOOKLIST* ON *THE ANGELS' SHARE*

"Distinguished by complex ideas and a foreboding tone, Markert's enthralling novel (*A White Wind Blew*) captures a dark time and a people desperate for hope."

—*LIBRARY JOURNAL*

"Markert displays great imagination in describing the rivalries, friendships, and intense relationships among the often quirky and cranky terminally ill, and the way that a diagnosis, or even a cure, can upset delicate dynamics."

—*PUBLISHERS WEEKLY* ON *A WHITE WIND BLEW*

"The author's ability to weigh competing views against each other, and the all-too-real human complications are presented with a remarkable understanding of conflicting ideas that makes even villains human eventually. The author writes well and reads easily; you'll finish this book in a day or two and wish for a sequel."

—*BOOKPAGE* ON *A WHITE WIND BLEW*

"A tuberculosis epidemic, as seen through the eyes of a sanatorium doctor driven by his love of God and music."

—*KIRKUS REVIEWS* ON *A WHITE WIND BLEW*

"[Markert's] debut novel, *A White Wind Blew* is set in Waverly Hills, that massive Gothic structure that is said to be one of the most haunted places on earth."

—RONNA KAPLAN FOR *THE HUFFINGTON POST*

"The book is at its best when Pike, McVain and their eclectic band of musicians are beating the odds, whether against tuberculosis or against stifling institutional mores."

—CHERYL TRUMAN, *KENTUCKY HERALD-LEADER*

"Markert has interwoven three seemingly unrelated subjects—tuberculosis, music, and racism—into a hauntingly lyrical narrative with operatic overtones."

—*BOOKLIST* ON *A WHITE WIND BLEW*

WHAT BLOOMS FROM DUST

ALSO BY JAMES MARKERT

For David, Joseph, and Michelle.
This one is for all three of you.
As siblings go, I do believe I struck gold.

The nation that destroys its soil destroys itself.
FRANKLIN D. ROOSEVELT

BEFORE

1908

SOUTHERN PLAINS

The train ride out west was free.

Paid in full by the brand-new state of Oklahoma in hopes of encouraging settlement in the land once occupied by bison and Indians. Wilmington Goodbye knew the truth of it. They'd been killed off—the bison, for sure, and too many of the Indians to count. Those that survived the cowboys and Rangers got squeezed together into reservations. The state had earmarked the rest of the land for homesteading. And no place looked more promising than Majestic, Oklahoma.

Wilmington studied the pamphlet for the tenth time in the last hour—glorious pictures of elegant buildings, paved roads edged by flowers, show houses where finely dressed couples wandered about. And that fountain in the town center looked majestic in itself.

With each *choof* of the train, Wilmington and his pregnant wife, Amanda, inched closer to becoming landowners, with fresh soil to plow up and a fortune to be made in a state just one year old.

He folded the pamphlet and slid it back into his suit pocket.

He teased the corners of his mustache and straightened the fresh rose he'd pinned to his lapel that morning.

"Health, wealth, and opportunity, love."

Amanda was bathed in sunlight nearly the color of her hair. She smiled. They'd repeated the slogan often enough, as had the rest of the men and women on the train. He'd met half of them already and was proud to call them future neighbors.

Citizens of Majestic.

He had a notion to look at the pamphlet again but resisted. Instead he watched his wife as miles of grassland flashed in the background. The doctor back east said the air would be better for her out here, away from the city pollution. Her breathing had already become less labored. The swell of her belly pressed tight against her blue dress. *She has to have an entire brood in there.* She'd laughed the idea off at first, but had recently admitted she felt more than one baby kicking around.

Tall prairie grass swayed alongside the speeding train. Miles of velvety blades, moving like something Wilmington couldn't quite put a finger on. *Ocean waves, maybe.* They had to be getting close. But where were the buildings? Where were the roads? And that town center? Shouldn't they see it over the horizon?

Two minutes later the train slowed and then screeched to a halt.

"Why are we stopping?" asked a man Wilmington now knew as Orion Bentley, a fancy gentleman in a suit as sharp as his wit and a bowler hat straight from the newest catalogues. They'd befriended each other minutes after boarding the train and had engaged in meaningful, optimistic dialogue for much of the trip.

"Must be something on the tracks," said Wilmington.

Everyone crowded near the windows. A man in a brown suit and matching hat stood in the shin-high grass holding a clipboard and pen. The doors opened. People hesitated, but then, beckoned by the man's hand gesture, they exited the train.

There were twenty-two of them in all, dressed to the nines in their Sunday best—long, colorful dresses, pressed suits, and polished shoes for the special occasion.

Wilmington stepped in front of the group and faced the suited man. "What's the meaning of this? We're supposed to be escorted to Majestic, Oklahoma." He removed the pamphlet from his coat, as most of the others had already done. "See? Right here." Only then did he notice the rippling white flags spaced out across the prairie land, staked like the homesteading of virgin land instead of one already expertly developed.

The suited man said, "I'm sorry, sir. But there is no Majestic, Oklahoma."

Wilmington showed him the pamphlet, pointed hard enough to crinkle the paper. "There sure is. It has paved roads and buildings and plots of land to grow wheat on."

"Well." The man chuckled. "The land we got." He reached his hand out for a shake, but Wilmington didn't bother. "My name is Donald Dupree. I work for the state government. I'm sorry to say, folks, but you've been swindled, same as the folks just west of here, in what was supposed to be Boise City. Except it looks much like this."

Wilmington pointed to the pamphlet again, this time with a little defeat. "The buildings? The town fountain . . . with all that marble."

"All made up, sir. A horrible fiction, I'm afraid. But I'm happy to say the developers who conned you have been arrested and will be held in Leavenworth until their trial."

The newcomers eyed one another. Tears mingled with the

wind. Husbands held their wives as prairie grass whipped to a frenzy around ankles and knees. All those white flags. Miles upon miles of desolation cut by a blazing sun. The orange sky looked to be bleeding in places, swirling just along the horizon.

Grass as far as the eye could see.

"We want to help right this wrong," said Donald. "We've staked the land, and we're prepared to sell it for next to nothing." He forced a smile, the tips of his mustache fluttering. "Health, wealth, and opportunity. Right at your fingertips."

Wilmington studied the land, inhaled the air, and turned to where Amanda and his new friend Orion stood. "We're out in the middle of nowhere."

The two men locked eyes. Amanda looked from one to the other and knew.

"We're not going back, are we?"

ONE

Old Sparky was supposed to have killed Jeremiah Goodbye.

But here he stood squinting against the hard sun in the middle of the Oklahoma panhandle, at a fork in the road marked by two signs nearly buried in the same dust that covered everything. Mounds of it. Drifts sculpted into hurricane waves, as far as the eye could see. Dust in the air. Dust in his eyes. The dust in his mouth crunched when he'd grind his teeth, and he had no Vaseline to coat his nostrils from the abrasive grit.

When the wind blew, dust stung like bees.

Roads were buried by dust, although there were tire tracks from those who'd recently risked it, braved it as he'd done before the Model T he'd taken back in Guthrie choked out on dust two towns east of where he now stood—back in Woodward, or maybe it was Enid. One town looked like the other—all covered in dust, homes and fences buried.

Two days he'd been walking. If only he had a light for the hand-rolled cigarette in his pocket, it could take his mind off

5

the fact that he hadn't eaten all day. Even the tumbleweeds the Russians brought to the plains years ago looked appetizing. Too many recipes included them now, or so he'd heard.

Russian thistle made into edible gunk.

He'd found the car abandoned alongside the road, probably shorted out on the electric sparks that often accompanied the black dusters. Lucky enough the gas tank had been half-full. That's how he looked at things now—half-full instead of half-empty. That jolt of electricity he'd taken during his short affair with Old Sparky hadn't killed him as the warden had said, but it *had* joggled something loose.

For the first time since he could remember, his nights hadn't been plagued by those night scares—the whirlwind struggle for his life, the dusty figure like a shadow, and then the spot of light that always led to him waking up and gasping for air.

Half-full or not, this wasn't the Oklahoma he remembered. It looked like the end of the world had come and a desert had swallowed what remained. The flat prairie land of his younger days was long gone, the buffalo grass buried under drifts made by drought after the great plow-up of the land.

Land that wasn't meant to be plowed in the first place. Jeremiah covered his mouth with his shirt collar. *Sodbusters getting rich off the wheat boom and never stopping to consider the repercussions.* He had warned them all, having digested the fears of many of the local cowboys dead set against the homesteading. But did the sodbusters listen?

Earth moved over the horizon. Another duster.

He tilted his black Stetson against the wind, low over his brow to protect his eyes. It wasn't a duster after all. The low rumble gave it away, grew louder as it approached.

Jackrabbits.

A thousand of them at least, down from the hills, scrounging for food, starving like everything else. They paid him no never mind, scampering past, kicking up dust in pursuit of the unattainable. The sheer force of them wobbled him in his stance. One stopped atop a dust mound to nibble the prong of a fence poking through. Another scratched at a roof shingle visible from where a dugout wasn't quite buried. A cluster scratched and clawed over a thicket of tumbleweeds. One nibbled on his boot and moved on— too scrawny to cook up and eat even if Jeremiah had the notion.

A minute later the jacks were gone, kicking up dust and heading for Texas.

They'd have no better luck there, unless they struck some oil. There were more ways than one to rape the land.

The air cleared. Blue sky returned like a pot of gold. Until the next black blizzard. Best head on, but this was why he'd stopped in the first place.

Decision time.

Two signs faced him, one pointing south toward Guymon, the other north toward Nowhere.

He reached into his pocket and felt the quarter between his thumb and index finger.

The same quarter he'd taken from the pocket of the prison guard he'd found buried in the rubble. Probably Officer Jefferson, by the look of those boots. Big as boats—the man was tall as a lamppost.

He'd liked Jefferson, who was one of the few guards willing to sneak him off the row every so often for a smoke under the stars. If he'd been right of mind he would've moved some smashed cinder blocks and buried him proper. But with how that thunderboomer

7

had quickly spun into a twister, collapsing the back wall of the execution room five seconds into that first jolt of 2,500 volts, he couldn't expect to be immediately clearheaded. Those were five seconds of his life he'd like to forget. But at least he had two feet to stand on and an unfamiliar warmth in his heart that might could even be described as hope.

He'd thanked the dead Jefferson for the cigarette he'd found in his trouser pocket.

The warden had been buried too. Last Jeremiah had seen him was when he stepped behind the curtain to crank down that lever, triggering something that sounded like a hammer on an anvil just before Jeremiah's body started to dance.

Jeremiah pulled the quarter from his pocket and approached the fork in the road.

Guymon or Nowhere?

For the first time ever the quarter felt like a boulder in his hand, instead of that smooth skipping rock, and he hesitated in the flipping of it.

Blamed that on Old Sparky too.

The Coin-Flip Killer was what the ink-pages had named Jeremiah, and ink stains, once settled, can't be so readily wiped off. He wasn't too sure if the name fit or not. Kinda fuzzy in his mind, those days, everything going down about the same time the earth started peeling off with the wind.

He assumed his daddy was still alive back in Nowhere. He hadn't heard anything to the contrary. But Wilmington Goodbye had a bullet lodged in his head, just over the left ear, a ricochet shot from the day of Jeremiah's arrest, when the badges clopped into town on horseback, flashing tin with their rifles loaded. The shoot-out was unnecessary. He would have come out willingly, but once bullets started flying he had to defend himself. He'd like to think it wasn't one of *his* bullets that found his daddy's head, but something told him otherwise.

As far as he knew, his father was still getting about too, even with the bullet. But he'd never come to visit in the almost three years Jeremiah had spent locked up in McAlester for four murders in which he had no direct hand—*direct* being the key word because, try as he might, there was no way to distance himself from the responsibility of them.

Jeremiah assumed it was the bullet that had kept Wilmington away. Maybe he wasn't supposed to travel with it in there. Or maybe he'd fallen to believe what all the newspapers were saying—though his letters never said as much. And to be fair, Wilmington had the drought to worry about. And money—or the lack thereof. There were probably plenty of reasons he never came. But no matter how grown the man, a father is life-medicine for the son, and those letters, regular as they were, had never been able to give the dosage that was needed.

Jeremiah straightened his Stetson and peered toward Guymon.

A car approached. Another black Model T, throttle-choked and puttering like Josiah used to do with his lips in the bubble bath when they were kids. Seemed the entire country had one of those Fords now. This one was weaving as if trying to find the road. The driver had half his torso out the window so he could see. The windshield was dust-covered and the wipers looked stuck midthrust.

Jeremiah waved his arms to get the man's attention. The car slowed. Chains hung from the back bumper to ground it from the static in the air. The man had goggles on and a gas mask he must have kept from the Great War.

"Careful out," said the man, voice muffled. "You'll choke to death if one of them dusters spins up. It's a graveyard out here. Where you headed?"

"Don't know yet, which is why you found me standing instead of walking."

The man lifted the mask. "Well, for what it's worth, there ain't too many good choices. Ask me, you're heading in the wrong direction. If you're a man on the wander, I'd be wandering east. Wouldn't stop until I hit the coast neither. 'Course we've already had one of these dusters float all the way to the Atlantic, spread gunk all over New York. And the capital. And ships a hundred miles to sea." He squinted at Jeremiah, studying him a little closer.

Jeremiah remembered the rifle propped over his shoulder and lowered it slowly, holding it loosely to the side. He tipped his hat and smiled until he swallowed dust. "Got any more of those masks?"

"Not on me." The man stared a second more, then gulped, his Adam's apple moving like a clot of food down a snake belly. "I best get going. Don't want no trouble."

"Not intending any," said Jeremiah, realizing by the man's perked shoulders that he'd just been spotted. His face was probably all over the papers.

So much for getting a lift.

Jeremiah wished him safe travels, but the man had already puttered off, swerving again as he wrestled the mask back on his face with one hand while the other steered.

Things grew quiet.

Guymon or Nowhere?

The quarter no longer felt as heavy in his hand.

New start? Or return home to a family that once loved him but now apparently no longer wanted him?

He and Josiah had been thick as thieves until suddenly they weren't. Inseparable the instant they came into the world—in Jeremiah's case, two minutes late and gasping for air. *His* birth had weakened their mother. Three years later she died of lung cancer, buried before Jeremiah and Josiah were tall enough to see over the summer prairie grass.

Jeremiah could have chalked that up as his first so-called murder; the hard birth was on him. Josiah had come out first, and easily, rolling like melted butter would, while Jeremiah's had been a breech birth.

Heads for Guymon. Tails for Nowhere.

He studied the signs.

Quit stalling.

Old habits die hard. He flipped the coin in the air. Sunlight dappled as it spun. He caught it in his right palm and smacked it against the top of his left hand. After a deep breath and an exhale that dislodged dust from his mustache, he removed his right hand.

"Tails."

He set out on foot again and did his best not to suffocate. He had a Winchester rifle with one bullet, a coin he'd stolen from a dead prison guard, and a hand-rolled cigarette in his pocket with no way to light it.

The coin had already spoken. The bullet would be for his twin brother. And the cigarette, well, he reckoned he'd find some fire soon enough.

TWO

Unlike the big cities in the northeast, where skyscrapers loomed from miles out, a prairie town gave no prior warning of civilization.

You just stumbled upon it.

Jeremiah knew the land well enough, even if the miles of prairie grass had turned to a dusty wasteland. Nowhere, Oklahoma, grew fast during the 1920s wheat boom, and the folks who lived there saw their bank accounts swell. The wet years made them rich. Nesters moved from dugouts and sod houses and built real homes. They bought cars and farm equipment on credit, and the banks got fat. A hotel sprang up, as well as a theater that showed stage plays, vaudeville acts, and talkie films. Nowhere was a town on the move, and the direction was upward, prospering even more on wheat than Liberal, just to the north in Kansas, and Boise City to the southwest.

Jeremiah couldn't see the Bentley Hotel from where he stood—the dust had started to spin—but he knew he was close when he saw the dugouts. A cluster of nesters had come in right at the tail end of the boom, staking their land four miles east of Nowhere and busting up sod with wheat seed in hopes of getting rich like the rest of them. But then the stock market crashed in '29, wheat prices hit rock bottom, and the sky dried up like their dreams.

Most of the dugouts looked empty now, half-covered in dust, but the third one down had a sign out front that made Jeremiah do a double take.

Child for Sale.

He'd heard rumors of such things during these Depression years. Even one less mouth meant more food for the others. But he hadn't really believed it actually happened.

Black tar paper covered the dugout's plank-board walls, and the roof looked ready to crumble. A dozen or more centipedes crawled across the front—nothing a good pot of boiling water wouldn't kill, if they had any. Ten paces behind the dugout was a wooden windmill that was cracked in the middle and leaning. If it was still able to pull water from the ground, it couldn't be more than a trickle. The woman standing in front, presumably the mother, looked starved. Behind her on a wooden bench sat three boys, all under the age of twelve, dressed nicely enough yet covered in dust. The one on the end, the youngest, probably eight or so, sat smiling while the other two looked as bleak as the land.

A thin-haired gentleman in a white button-down and suspenders stood next to the woman with his arms folded, hairy arms well muscled, and shirtsleeves rolled to the elbows. Under his dirty bowler hat he had dark, beady eyes and a black mustache so thick it covered his lips. Jeremiah didn't trust his wrinkled, sun-beaten face, so he stopped, even though following these hunches was what put him in prison in the first place—his gift that had proven to be more of a curse.

"What's the meaning of all this?"

The man turned from his conversation with the mother. "Just partaking in some business here. So mind your own."

It wasn't just the man's face Jeremiah didn't trust. It was his soul. Jeremiah could feel the blackness of it. He'd always been able to feel it, like he could an approaching norther or thunderboomer. In the past, whenever he stumbled upon a bad one, sensing the evil dwelling within, his mind would show him hints of it as evidence, and ultimately he'd let the coin decide their fate. But today was different. The feeling had an unburdened dullness to it instead of that more familiar sharp blade. That jolt of electricity he'd taken in Old Sparky had turned his clear radio to static—something he'd often hoped for but now wasn't sure he liked.

Jeremiah stepped closer. "I'm gonna make this one my business, pal."

The man ignored him and went along speaking with the mother.

"There will be no selling to this man." Out of hard-grained habit, Jeremiah reached into his pocket for the coin.

"Who says?"

"Reckon I just did." He ran the coin between his fingers until it got the man's attention. "What's your name, partner?"

"The name is scram."

"Funny name, but fittin' for a fool, I guess."

The man turned away from the woman.

Jeremiah stepped closer. "Which one's for sale?"

"The goofy one," said the man. "One that won't stop smiling. He ain't right in the head, and she said he eats too much."

"Then what do you want with him?"

The man paused, dry-swallowed, looked at the smiling boy and then back to Jeremiah. "Need help around the house is all."

"You can't look me in the eyes."

The man didn't deny it, and then tried to but didn't linger. Sun glistened off the coin moving in and out of Jeremiah's fingers.

"I've got one bullet in this rifle," Jeremiah said.

"So?"

Jeremiah stepped toe-to-toe with the man. "You ain't leavin' with that boy. Now I'm gonna ask you your name one last time."

"Name's Benny, but I go by Boo."

"That 'cause you're scary? Or easily scared?"

Boo didn't answer, but he took a step back.

Jeremiah held the coin out and flipped it high, and when it landed in the dust he covered it with his boot. "You know who I am?"

The man jerked a nod, not so mouthy anymore. "I'll just be on my way."

He started to move, but Jeremiah stopped him with an outstretched hand. "Ain't that easy, partner. Done flipped the coin."

Boo looked down at Jeremiah's boot.

"If it's heads you'll lose yours," said Jeremiah. "Something tells me you deserve it."

Boo had begun to tremble, and it showed in his voice. "And if it's tails?"

"You walk. With the knowing that you'll be watched from now until the end of your days."

"By who?"

"By those that do the watchin'."

Boo snickered. "That makes no sense."

Jeremiah moved his boot. "It's heads. Sorry, Boo." He raised the rifle toward Boo's head and fingered the trigger, although he had no intention of pulling it. He made eye contact with the smiling boy, who was shaking his head and no longer smiling. *Don't do it, Mister.*

Jeremiah winked at the boy, then looked at Boo and said, "Bang."

Boo jumped.

The boy, who'd just buried his face in his hands in anticipation of the gunshot, looked up, relieved but still teetering on that line of trust and panic. He hunkered over and started bobbing to and fro while his brothers watched, both hesitating to give comfort, as if afraid to touch him.

The boy caught Jeremiah's gaze again—he had eyes blue as summer sky—and that look jolted warmth back into Jeremiah's heart, having not even recognized if and when it had really gone cold. There was something oddly familiar about the boy that Jeremiah couldn't place, but the look they'd just given each other had bridged some kind of chasm. Back when the Indians ruled the plains, they used sign language to communicate through the wind, and Jeremiah reckoned this wasn't much different.

Then that boy's smile returned, dimpled from cheek to cheek.

She said he ain't right in the head.

Jeremiah jerked his head to the side, in the direction away from Nowhere. "Go on."

Boo took off running, every few steps looking over his shoulder as if afraid the bullet would find his back. A minute later he disappeared in a dust cloud.

The woman cried. No doubt she'd needed the money the man was going to pay her, probably for food for her two oldest. Jeremiah picked the coin up from the ground and blew dust from it. He stopped just before pocketing it, noticing the way the mother eyed it. Not much she could buy with a quarter, but times were hard and he reckoned it was better than nothing. He handed it to her, closed her fingers over the hard realness of it. He'd come across another soon enough. Until then he'd make decisions like most men, from the gut.

Thanks to Old Sparky, the nightmares were gone, and his head was something he couldn't quite put his finger on—fuzzy now, but somehow more clear at the same time.

He tipped his hat to the woman and went on his way.

Five minutes later he'd put a half mile between him and the dugouts, wandering through dust swirls and floating tumbleweeds.

Centipedes slow-crawled through loose dust, and scorpions scuttled over the hardpack. Over the horizon, beyond a dark, coiling line of approaching dust, lay the town of Nowhere. The Bentley Hotel was the tallest building in town and he could barely see one of the two chimneys. He hoped to get there by nightfall unless the duster got to him first. It could have been two miles away or twenty. It was hard for him to tell the distance.

He hadn't experienced the black blizzards like the rest of the plains had—he'd been protected inside the prison walls—so mostly what he knew was what he'd heard from others, inside the walls and out. The monthly letters he'd get from his daddy, chicken-scratch writing that always looked hurried, never touched on what had really happened—questions he was probably afraid to ask. So mostly he wrote about the weather. About the drought. And the dust.

A tarantula scurried across the road and burrowed into a hill of dust. To his left, another cluster of jackrabbits echoed across the land.

He stopped when he heard footsteps and looked over his shoulder.

It was the boy, the one for sale, the smiler. Up close his eyes were even bluer than Jeremiah recalled back at the dugout, and in his arms he held a clunky, black Royal-model typewriter.

"Go on back to your home," Jeremiah told him.

"Go on back to your home," the boy repeated, smiling. "Go on back to your home."

"Don't do that."

"Don't do that."

"Stop repeating what I say, you hear?"

"Stop repeating what I say, you hear?"

Jeremiah scratched his forehead. *Why's he keep smiling like that?* The mother had probably sent him along thinking Jeremiah had purchased the boy with that quarter he'd given her.

"I don't buy kids," said Jeremiah. "I buy smokes. And horses. Food and such."

"Food and such." The boy started rocking slightly on the balls of his dusty shoes, finally looking away toward the ground. "I buy smokes. I buy smokes."

"Quit repeating what I say, boy."

"Boy. Repeating what I say, boy. Quit repeating. I buy smokes. And horses and such." The boy looked up, smiling so wide his teeth showed. He was missing three of them, two on the bottom and one on the top. "Heads or tails. Heads or tails. Quit repeating—"

Jeremiah held his hand up, palm straight. The gesture silenced the boy, but it didn't erase the smile from his face.

It must have been contagious somehow; Jeremiah smiled too as he leaned on his rifle. "Do you understand me when I talk? Nod if you do. Don't be bouncing my words back to me."

The boy nodded. His brown hair was unruly even without the wind.

"You're gonna have to go back home to your mother. Do you understand me?"

He nodded.

"Go on then."

The boy shook his head no.

"You can't come with me. I'm not that good of a person."

The boy nodded, smiling.

The boy is simple, all right. Jeremiah laughed and scratched his head, wondering how long it had been since he'd laughed. "What's your name, son?"

"What's your name?" the boy asked. And then added, "Son."

"I'm Jeremiah. Jeremiah Goodbye. And I just crushed out of prison. Do you understand?" The boy nodded but didn't seem to care. His smile grew. The typewriter looked heavy in his arms. Jeremiah told him to put that thing down for a minute and the boy did so carefully, like the typewriter was a newborn instead of a bulky machine with keys.

"What are you doing carrying a typing machine around anyhow?"

"Anyhow."

That's better.

"You're going to have to return home. To your mother. And brothers."

The boy shook his head no.

"You can't come with me."

The boy nodded.

"Notice I didn't shoot that man back there? I was just trying to put a scare into him. But I do intend on shooting my brother. You understand?" The boy nodded. Jeremiah shook his head and sighed. "Why do you smile so much?"

"Why do you smile so much?"

"I don't."

"I don't. Heads or tails. Heads or tails. I didn't shoot that man back there. Trying to put a scare into him. You understand?"

"You never told me your name."

"You never told—"

Jeremiah held up his hand again, and the boy went silent. "Never mind." He rubbed his hand across his stubbly face and pondered his predicament. The boy had latched on like a tick and wouldn't easily be shaken. He could walk him back to the dugout, but what would stop the mother from trying to sell him again? And what if she sold him to somebody bad, like that man called Boo?

No, the boy might be better off coming along, after all. Even though his family in Nowhere wouldn't want him back, surely one of them would take in the boy and give him some kind of life. Anything was better than what he was living.

Ellen. She'll take him in. She's good with children.

Just thinking her name made his heart flutter. Would she welcome him home or run him off? Were she and Josiah even still together?

Jeremiah moved on toward Nowhere. After a few paces he looked over his shoulder. "Well, you coming?"

The boy smiled, nodded, picked up his typewriter, and hurried to catch up.

Jeremiah walked slower so the boy could keep pace. "That thing looks heavy."

"That thing looks heavy."

Jeremiah stopped. He removed the lone bullet from the rifle and slid it in his pocket. "Trade me."

The boy was reluctant but handed the typewriter over.

Jeremiah handed him the rifle.

The boy seemed leery of the weapon, so Jeremiah told him it wasn't loaded. "It can't hurt anybody." The boy smiled again.

"Pretend to shoot those rabbits or something."

"Pretend to shoot those rabbits." Instead, the boy dragged the rifle barrel behind him in the dust as he walked. "Pretend to shoot those rabbits. Heads or tails. What's your name, son? Pretend to shoot those rabbits."

Jeremiah just let him mumble. No wonder that poor woman had picked this one to sell out of the three. He was liable to drive a person insane. He chuckled, and the boy looked up at him, asking with those big eyes, *What's funny, Mr. Goodbye?*

Nothing, he wanted to say. *Just as far as buying a kid goes, seems I got me a defective one.*

Instead Jeremiah grinned, stuck his unlit cigarette between his lips just to taste the tobacco, and jerked the boy a nod. Together they walked toward the approaching black clouds carrying a typewriter and a rifle barrel carving a meandering groove in the dust.

Making Nowhere by sundown was no longer an option.

Jeremiah guessed they were less than two miles away from the town center, but the duster was nearly upon them and the boy looked anxious. His mumbling had grown quieter but incessant, and instead of dragging the rifle he was hugging it like a blanket.

Fifty yards away stood a sod house, seemingly abandoned. They hurried for it. The rolling black cloud coming at them resembled a thunderboomer, except without the thunder. The black got closer and taller, coiling and rolling like a snow avalanche on its side, silent until the dust started to hit them like tiny glass slivers. They coughed and shielded their eyes. Visibility was suddenly down to ten feet. The sod house disappeared, reappeared, and then vanished in the black dust again. But Jeremiah had seen enough of it to redirect their course. A couple of minutes later he felt the scratchy side wall, a small square window, and, a few paces down, a door.

Something crackled in the air, and the boy jumped.

What at first Jeremiah thought to be lightning strikes turned out to be static electricity, currents of blue and yellow sizzling around the blades on a nearby windmill. Another current shot across the dust like a prairie fire.

Jeremiah pushed the boy inside and closed the door the best he could—a mound of dust had blown inside, jamming it. Black dust still filtered in through the inch-wide crack. They coughed and heaved and spat wet dust on the floor. The boy sneezed black snot and wiped it on his sleeve. Jeremiah looked around. Clearly nobody home.

He found a sheet bundled against the stove and secured it over the door. If only he had water to wet the sheet down. It would have to do. The boy mumbled in the dark corner, holding the typewriter again instead of the rifle. He punched keys even though there was no paper or ribbon in the machine, and it seemed to help keep him calm.

"Keep doing that," said Jeremiah, searching the sod house for any form of light. "Keep punching those keys."

"Keep punching those keys," said the boy. "Those keys. Keep punching those keys."

Truth be told, the melodic snapping of those keys proved to calm Jeremiah as well.

The boy coughed into his fist and then resumed hitting the

keys, as if writing an imaginary letter. How long would the duster last? In prison, although Jeremiah had had no window in his cell, he'd once heard dust scratching the walls nonstop for days.

Twenty minutes later the wind picked up, and the sod walls shifted. Black dust sifted from the roof, sneaked in through the closed window, and continued to blow in around the sheet. The boy typed faster, mumbling under his breath with the hint of a smile.

Jeremiah's eyes adjusted to the dark. A small tin of Vaseline rested on the floor. He blew dust from his nostrils and coated them with the stuff. He called the boy over and helped do the same to his nostrils.

"That better?"

The boy nodded, mumbled. "That better? That better?"

Jeremiah shushed him.

Wind howled, black dust tapped against the walls, and static electricity crackled.

Jeremiah hunkered in the corner, trying to create a pocket where dust couldn't go, but it just wasn't possible. A minute later he felt the boy's weight leaning against him, burrowing into the valley between his chest and shoulder. Jeremiah at first held his arm up as if afraid to touch the kid, but then slowly lowered it in protection against the dust. He patted the boy's back, told him to close his eyes and think good thoughts of blue skies and buffalo grass.

He wondered if the boy wasn't a catalyst of sorts, because for the first time in a long while Jeremiah found himself thinking of the baby boy he and Ellen had been due to have. The one no one ever knew about.

And then his thoughts were interrupted by a voice.

"Peter," the boy said. "Peter."

Jeremiah looked down at the head of hair below his chin. "You trying to tell me something? Is that your name?"

"That your name?" the boy mumbled, nodding. "Peter . . . Peter . . ." He grew silent for a beat or two, and then said, "Pumpkin eater. Had a wife but couldn't keep her. Put her in a pumpkin shell . . ."

Jeremiah, so amused that his heart grew warm, spoke along with him. ". . . And there he kept her very well."

Dust flicked the windows and walls.

"Peter, Peter, pumpkin eater," said the boy. "Had another and didn't love her."

Jeremiah hadn't recited the rhyme since he was a boy, yet it came back easily. "Peter learned to read and spell, and then he loved her very well."

The boy went quiet. Jeremiah could make out the letters on the typewriter keys. The boy punched the letter *P*, then *E, T, E*, and finally *R*.

Jeremiah patted the boy's back again, shushed him quiet, and continued to shield him from the dust. "Close your eyes now, Peter. Get some rest."

THREE

Ellen Goodbye was stubborn.

She was a schoolteacher, and come rain or shine, black blizzard or thunderboomer, she was going to teach the children of Nowhere. Half the town wondered the point of it all. What was the learning for? They were right in the middle of the end of days. What would adding two and two get them besides four?

"It'll get them one step closer," Ellen would tell the naysayers.

"Closer to what?"

Closer to leaving this place, she'd think, unable to shake the sight of her little boy, James, of late, hacking and wheeze-coughing himself to sleep every night. Instead she'd change course. "Better to fill those fresh brains with good knowledge than let 'em harden with all this dust."

It hadn't rained worth a hoot in four years, and when it did, it flash-flooded. Worst drought in history—locals in the southern plains pronounced it "drouth," but no matter how it was said, it showed no signs of going away.

So Ellen wasn't waiting; plus it did her good to get out of the house, especially with how her husband, Josiah, was wallowing of late, sneaking drinks of corn liquor in between his coughing fits, staring out the window at what used to be their wheat field and was now miles of dust.

After kissing James on the head, she'd left the house yesterday as usual, despite the warning from Josiah's father, Wilmington, who'd clutched his head where the bullet had entered three years ago and claimed he felt a duster coming. Like the pressure from that bullet was some kind of weather vane. She didn't believe him; the dusters simply couldn't be predicted. And anyway, Wilmington said he felt a duster coming *every* morning. He liked to hedge his bets and say he told you so.

But with that bullet still lodged in his head, Wilmington was just happy to be alive—tempting fate every day now, trying to see how far he could stretch his luck. Dr. Craven had warned him not to move about too much. The bullet might move. *"And if the bullet moves, it's good-bye, Mr. Goodbye."* The doctor had laughed when he said it, just as Ellen did now remembering.

Three years now, and so far so good.

If she'd listened to her father-in-law yesterday, she wouldn't have gotten trapped in the schoolhouse with all the kids overnight. She wouldn't have worried herself half to death about Josiah not watching their son properly while she was gone. But she was stubborn. Determined was more like it. Determined to teach these kids something. Didn't matter if her fellow teacher had become an exoduster. Mrs. Emory Rochester and her husband had uprooted their family and left town in search of some grass, leaving Ellen alone to teach all the kids. Didn't matter that the banks had frozen up and the state could no longer pay. She was still going to hammer the words and numbers into their heads if it killed her. She'd been working free for the past ten months anyhow. And seeing the kids lifted her heart, which did its best to sink every day under so much dust.

They'd been in the middle of arithmetic when the duster hit, seventeen kids with ages that ranged from eight to thirteen. They were learning pounds and ounces. Ten-year-old Nicholas Draper was telling a story about how their last cow died two days prior. All skin and bones, but when they cut her open they'd found her belly full of black dust.

"I bet that weighed a lot of *pounds,* Mrs. Goodbye."

Ellen was about to agree, sadly of course, when eleven-year-old Rachel Finnigen pointed toward the window. The sun was blotted out. The wind howled. Black dust tapped against the windows, intermittently at first and then in torrents.

Dusters could come out of nowhere. That was the town joke, at least, but when they hit, nothing was funny about it. Ellen and the children knew the drill well enough. There were two buckets of water by the schoolhouse door and a pile of stained sheets that used to be white. It was harder now to prepare for the storms without Emory. Ellen hoped she'd found that green grass, but doubted it. The oldest kids dunked the sheets in water, wrung them out, and hung them over the windows and doors to catch at least some of the dust that got through. Even with the precautions, fat dust motes circulated across the classroom. The students hunkered low. There were tables along the back wall beneath the chalkboards, and they gathered underneath. William Trainer, the oldest—everyone called him Windmill because he was fixing to be as tall as one—carried two wet sheets and hung them from the tabletops like curtains hanging down to protect them from the increasing amount of dust inside the room.

Ellen lit a candle. Windmill lit another; he was the only one allowed to play with fire. He fancied himself an artist. He dripped wax onto paper they kept under the tables and made pictures for the rest of the kids. They sang songs for an hour and told stories for another while dust pummeled the school walls and static electricity crackled like lightning. Ellen passed around Vaseline, and they took turns applying it around their nostrils. Eventually she and Windmill blew out the candles, and some of the kids fell asleep—the ones that didn't miss their mothers and fathers. The ones that did cried. Ellen stroked their backs and reminded them not to worry. She'd never seen a duster that didn't eventually pass, and this one would be no different.

How many days in a row now?

Come morning, the sun was high in the sky. Dust covered the floor and desktops. One window was broken. Windmill knew how to replace the small pane of glass and promised to have it done by lunch.

Ellen said there wouldn't be school today, not after they'd been forced to spend the night together. They'd resume school tomorrow. She couldn't wait to get home and check on James.

Windmill looked sad. He didn't have much of a family to go home to; his father was a drunk and his mother, like half the town, had fallen prey to the dust pneumonia. Ellen knew that Windmill had a crush on her. She'd playfully remind him that she was married, with a three-year-old, but he still followed her around like a lost mutt.

Ellen bundled all the muddy sheets into a canvas satchel to be washed later. She escorted the kids outside, counting heads as they stepped into the warm spring sunshine. Most everyone was digging out—sweeping dust from porches, shoveling dust from buried cars. Ned Blythe pulled dust from his mailbox by the armful and then went into a sneezing fit. Front doors were propped open and brooms whisked busily inside the houses and businesses—Richard Klamp's clothing store; the opera house; Blythe's Food Store, which hardly had any canned food left; Dr. Craven's office, which was constantly full of coughers; and the post office, where Phillip Jansen's mailbags remained empty.

The Nowhere Bank had been closed down since the fall of 1931 and now stood a dilapidated eyesore, broken windows boarded up and painted over with graffiti. It looked like some long-forgotten building ripped from the Old West—swinging doors and all—so inviting for one and all to come leave their money. Some in town wanted it knocked down. It was too painful a reminder of how the bank had fleeced them, like so many banks across the country, backing its promises up with nothing but words, toothy smiles, and greasy handshakes. But Wilmington demanded it stay because it *was* a reminder.

Of what once was, thought Ellen as she walked through town, remembering what Jeremiah had done the day the bank closed its real doors—the swinging doors were just for show—and how the town had cheered him.

Some of those same town folk had now given up, and their doors stayed closed. What was the point in digging out when another black blizzard could rush through as soon as they put the broom down?

Ellen understood both sides of it.

But now the air was calm, the sky clear.

Noise carried; all that coughing sounded like a tuberculosis hospital. Nowhere Hospital, run by the Catholic sisters, was overrun with coughers.

Somewhere under all the dust were paved roads from when

Nowhere had prospered. Every so often, when the wind blew just right, pavement and curbs showed themselves. Not today. Ellen used the buildings as beacons, as well as the telephone lines, although there was no operator anymore inside the telephone office. Mrs. Culver and her husband had left in the spring of 1933, sneaking off in the middle of the night to avoid the scorn, and that luxurious home-to-home conversation they'd once thought magical had gone by the wayside.

Just another exoduster. Another Okie.

Sometimes Ellen wondered, though, if she and the others that stayed weren't the nonsensical ones.

She passed the town square, the courthouse, and then the jailhouse. Sheriff McKinney was taking a break from sweeping. He waved. Ellen politely waved back, but something inside warned her not to encourage him too much. He'd been acting strangely of late, staring when it wasn't proper, like he sensed that she and Josiah were in a rut and he was looking to step in. That thought gave her the shivers. And those dead rattlers he'd hung belly-up from the fence around the courthouse, ten of them right in a row, gave her the shivers too. He claimed it would help bring rain, but they'd been hanging there for ten days now with no offerings from the sky.

Her pace quickened up Main Street, where her house stood two stories tall facing the Bentley Hotel. Orion Bentley was digging out too, cheerful as always, but with that air of falsehood that always bothered her—like on the surface he was sunshine and roses, but a smidge sad within. No one could be so charming and welcoming all the time. It wasn't natural. Orion paused to puff on his cigar. He waved—like he always did with the ladies—then he resumed cleaning. Instead of using a broom, he pendulum-swung a throw rug like it was an elephant trunk, clearing a path up the hotel steps and toward the front door, creating a minor duster of his own.

The Bentley had wooden swinging doors like the bank, giving it the look of an Old West saloon. Its cavernous lobby boasted a piano and a bar that stretched across one side of the room. Back when the town was at full capacity and money circulated like a disease, the entertainment at the hotel had stretched from dusk until dawn, with music and dancing, singing and card playing, billiards and talent shows.

Those things still resonated, but like a ghost would, or the thrum from a recently extracted tooth—echoes more than anything. Still, no one dug out faster and with more gusto after a duster than Orion Bentley. To him two was still a crowd, and a crowd meant a party.

Ellen wished Orion a good day and then headed for her house, which was Wilmington's house really. She and Josiah had planned on building their own but never got around to it. Once Wilmington got hit with that stray bullet the day Jeremiah was arrested, she'd told Josiah they should just stay and take care of him anyway. Besides, there wasn't any money to build their own, and no banks for lending.

Speaking of her father-in-law, he was out of the house again, digging around in what used to be their garden—vegetables, potatoes, and a few rows of corn. Now it was a slanted dust drift topped with thistle. In the past month Wilmington had begun to test the waters of Dr. Craven's instructions, venturing to their front porch when the air was clear or walking across the street to bump gums with Orion, but he certainly had no business with a shovel.

She hurried across the street. James must have survived the

night fine; otherwise Wilmington wouldn't have been outside working. They would have come found her had her baby's condition gotten worse. Unless Wilmington was trying to uncover what lay on the other side of the fence—their family cemetery.

"Wilmington, put that shovel down. What are you doing?"

Sweat dripped from his wrinkled brow. His face was hard-lined from decades under the sun, but still handsome beneath the specks of white in his hair. "You ask funny questions, Ellen. What's it look like I'm doing?"

"Hopefully not fixing to dig a new grave."

"The boy's fine."

"I was referring to you."

"Ah, it ain't moved in three years. It ain't gonna move now." They'd spoken so much of the bullet that they didn't have to mention it by name anymore.

Ellen heard no coughing or crying. Her eyes blinked toward the house.

"Josiah got him to sleep a few hours ago." Wilmington leaned on his shovel. "Coughed half the night." He raised his eyebrows. "The duster . . ."

"You gonna say I told you so?"

He winked. "I told you so."

Wilmington was the same height as his twin sons—three inches over six feet, four depending on the boots. If not for the crow's-feet around his eyes and the hair color, the three of them could have been triplets. He resumed shoveling, attacking that dust drift like there would be no tomorrow. It was only April, but the temperature was already in the eighties.

"Why *are* you shoveling, Wilmington?"

"She's in there, Ellen." He tossed shoveled dust off to the side and went in for more. "Reckon I just don't like all this stuff on top of her."

Ellen swallowed the lump in her throat. The *she* he referred to was his late wife, Amanda, one of the first citizens to be buried in Nowhere, the town Wilmington and Orion Bentley had named after discovering there was no Majestic.

Ellen had heard the story too many times to count. Atop Amanda's grave, in the days after her burial when the soil was still freshly turned, Wilmington started a rose garden. He tended it even more meticulously than his role as a single parent—and he was a good father. Every day he was out there watering or pruning, refusing to wear gloves against the prickly thorns, and often he'd come in sucking blood from a nicked finger. Orion said he couldn't keep those roses alive during the intense summer heat, but Wilmington somehow managed to do it. He built a portable wall out of wood planks that he'd use to shield the rose bed whenever the sun got too bad.

"She's in there, Ellen."

She walked toward the house, grabbed a second shovel from the lean-to, and dug along with him. They exchanged a glance but then worked in silence as the sun beat against their necks, he in his overalls and she still in her teaching dress. *He's in there too*, she wanted to say, referring to the boy she and Jeremiah had conceived, the one she'd lost five months early to a miscarriage. She'd carried small during the winter, and it had been easy to hide under the layers of clothing, so no one had even known.

Ellen bit her lip as she dug, the memory fueling her efforts.

"What's Josiah doing?" Ellen carved the shovel blade into the shrinking drift. "He should be out here helping."

"He's cleaning the rifles."

33

She paused. "What for?"

He breathed heavily against the shovel. "You don't know?"

"Know what?"

"I guess you wouldn't, since you were locked in the school-house," he said. "The newspaper come yesterday, two days late as usual."

"What did it say?"

She surveyed the town. Not only were the residents of Nowhere digging out, but many of them now stood on their porches and stoops, armed with pistols and rifles. Sheriff McKinney paced in front of the jailhouse. "Wilmington, what's going on?"

"That twister that hit a few days ago. Run east across the state."

"Yes?"

"Well, it clipped the back of the prison." He went back to shoveling, probably to hide his emotion. "Jeremiah escaped."

Ellen's hands trembled. She covered her mouth as if to keep her heart from jumping from it. He must have sensed her confusion. "According to the papers, he was only a few seconds into his execution. Lived through it. Now nobody knows where he is."

"And you think he's coming back home?"

He gestured out across the expanse of Nowhere's town center. "Ain't the only one."

Sure enough, more armed citizens had appeared. It was as if the entire town expected Jeremiah.

Even that new man, Moses Yearling, who was staying in one of the top-floor rooms of the Bentley Hotel, was now out on the porch with Orion, watching and waiting, standing next to the hotelier with one of those TNT rockets in his arms. He'd come into town two days ago claiming to be a rainmaker. A cloud-buster. *Successful now in the last three towns,*" he'd bragged, smoothing his orange mustache as the town folk dropped the last of their savings into his white Stetson. He'd been shooting those loud rockets up into the clouds for two days now. Crowds would form to watch, optimistic. Still no rain. *"Be patient,"* he'd tell them. *"Last town took five days, but rain it did."* Ellen didn't trust those fidgety pale eyes of his.

The door to their house creaked open.

Josiah stepped outside with two rifles in hand and a brown shade hat tilted against the sun. Her husband was slender and athletic, just like Jeremiah, but Josiah had brown hair and hazel eyes while his twin's hair was coal black and his eyes cobalt blue.

"Ellen," said her husband without much enthusiasm.

"Josiah," she said, giving it right back.

Part of her craved Jeremiah's return. The other part wished Old Sparky had taken him. Things would have been easier then. But as Wilmington often said, *"Easy breeds contentment. And contentment don't get things done."*

If Jeremiah returned, there would be bloodshed.

Josiah dry-swallowed when he got nervous, and she could hear him from where she stood. Jeremiah would want revenge. His own twin had been the one to call in the law, alerting them to the bodies he'd seen his twin bury in the abandoned grain silo, where Jeremiah had started sleeping months before his capture.

Built himself a private home in there equipped with a kitchen and stove.

"You don't understand, Ellen. It's not what you think."

Those were the last words Jeremiah had spoken to her as the badges wrestled him away. And in the deep nodding of his head, he'd relayed to her without words that she was to marry Josiah and forget about him.

"Josiah is a good man, and I am not."

If he'd said it once, he'd said it a dozen times.

Josiah walked down the porch steps and kissed Ellen's cheek, a gesture that seemed obligatory. "The boy is asleep. Breathing peacefully as of now."

Ellen smiled, then patted her husband's arm.

Dozens of rifles cocked, echoing off buildings.

The three of them faced the road.

Josiah said, "Speak of the devil."

"Don't say that," Ellen said under her breath.

Two figures had blown in with the breeze, one tall and the other half the size. Ellen knew it was Jeremiah by the way he walked, those long, slender legs slightly pigeon-toed.

Josiah held a rifle out toward Wilmington.

Wilmington refused it. "Ain't shootin' my own boy."

Josiah then handed the second rifle to Ellen. After a stern glance she took it, but didn't ready it as her husband had. She wasn't going to shoot Jeremiah either.

Jeremiah grew taller as he walked deeper into town under the watch of so many aimed gun barrels. He stopped. Next to him was a little boy dragging a rifle of his own.

"What's that in his arms?" asked Wilmington.

Ellen squinted. "Looks like a typewriter."

"Harmless enough," said Wilmington.

The rifle shook slightly in Josiah's hands, but he kept it aimed. "Still heavy enough to do damage."

Ellen shook her head. "Who's that boy?"

"And why's he smiling?" asked Wilmington.

Jeremiah bent over to place the typewriter in the dust, and when he straightened back up he held his hands in the air. "I mean no harm."

The boy beside him then said, "I mean no harm."

"Just need a few words with my brother," said Jeremiah.

A pause, and then the boy shouted, "Just need a few words with my brother."

Josiah finally lowered his rifle, looked at Ellen. "Why's that boy doing that? Why's he keep smiling?"

"Only one way to find out." She waved them over.

"I don't like this," said Josiah.

Wilmington ordered everyone to lower their weapons. He leaned on the standing mailbox for support as he paused to gather his balance on the way out to the road. The little yellow flag on the empty box quivered slightly from his weight. Then he stepped toward his wayward son, opened his arms wide, and they embraced in the middle of the dust.

Ellen bit her lip.

Josiah grunted, then spat on the ground.

FOUR

Jeremiah embraced his father, but over his shoulder he locked eyes with Ellen.

Three years of dust living had done little to dull her beauty—those green eyes and sandy curls that hugged her slender neck and accentuated those sharp cheekbones, but even more so the confident way she carried herself, chin upright no matter the bother. He'd always admired her spirit—tough when things needed doing, but soft when they didn't.

Even so, she was the first to look away, right about the time a child started crying from the house. *Hers and Josiah's?* Part of Jeremiah hoped so. The other part—well, he still had the bullet in his pocket. *Must have had it soon after he'd been arrested.* Ellen dropped the rifle she'd been holding and hurried into the house, where the crying turned into a coughing fit.

Wilmington patted his son's back and stepped away with watery eyes and quivering jaw. "Good to see you again, son."

"Not too sure I'll be stayin'." Jeremiah focused on his twin across the way. "Reckon me and Josiah got some business."

Josiah walked out into the open and stopped twenty yards from his brother. Dust swirled. He cocked his rifle and stood straight backed, like he always did when he needed to summon strength. "You're not wanted here, brother." He called out, louder, toward Sheriff McKinney across the road, who approached like a snake would, slithery and not all that straight. "Get on the telephone lines, Sheriff. Call the authorities and tell 'em we caught us a fish."

Sheriff McKinney hefted his belt into his belly. "Fish don't live too long in the dust. Ain't that right, Josiah? Big ol' fish, though. Bigger than that gun-down of Bonnie and Clyde, I'd say."

"Shut your face, McKinney," Jeremiah said without looking at the sheriff, who stopped his approach. Jeremiah stepped away from the typewriter in the dust and said to Peter beside him. "Hand me the rifle, boy."

"Hand me the rifle, boy," said Peter, doing just that as he bounced the words back.

Jeremiah removed the lone bullet from his pocket and showed it to his twin. "No need to get the authorities involved, Josiah. What say we settle it like men? You ready to meet your maker?"

Josiah stepped forward. "Something tells me you've already taken a peek at yours. You like what you seen?"

Jeremiah shrugged, then placed the cigarette in his mouth. "You got a light?"

"In the house."

"I'll have Daddy show me to it, then, when we're done." The cigarette dangled from his lips. "Like the good old days."

"Except these bullets are real," said their father. "Now boys, let's go inside and talk this out. No need for bloodshed. There's been enough dying."

Josiah said, "Daddy, go inside with Ellen. This don't concern you. Go on now."

Peter, now sitting in the dust, clacked the typewriter keys.

"Stop that, Peter," said Jeremiah.

"Stop that, Peter." The boy punched keys. They echoed like tiny gunshots. "Stop that, Peter. Peter, stop that," he mumbled into his chest. "Stop that, Peter. Stop that, Peter . . ."

Jeremiah said to his father. "Take the boy inside with you. Peter, stop the mumbling. Go with Mr. Goodbye."

Peter stood with the typewriter and did as he was told. But Wilmington, other than stepping to shield the boy he didn't know from any danger, didn't move.

Josiah said, "On the count of three."

"Rifles on the ground?" asked Jeremiah.

Josiah nodded. "Rifles on the ground."

They both knelt down, placed the rifles on the dust, and then stood facing each other again. When they were kids, they'd do the same, and on the count of three they'd reach for their rifles to shoot at a turkey buzzard or jackrabbit.

Jeremiah would win every time.

"Don't do this," pleaded Wilmington. "Josiah's sorry. He shouldn't have ratted you out. Let's talk this through."

"I ain't sorry," said Josiah. "He's a murderer."

"One," said Jeremiah.

"Two," said Josiah.

"Close your eyes, Peter," Jeremiah whispered.

Peter closed his eyes, mumbled, "Close your eyes, Peter."

"Three." Jeremiah dropped down, grabbed the rifle, and aimed in one swift motion.

Josiah did the same.

But when Jeremiah put pressure on the trigger, instead of homing in on his brother's chest, which was how he'd been imagining it for three years now, he saw Wilmington blocking the path.

"I'll take the bullet for the both of you," said Wilmington, his posture hunkered in anticipation of possibly taking a bullet from either son, or both. "Enough of this nonsense."

Jeremiah lowered his rifle, but only slightly, enough to see daylight between his father's legs. He fired.

Wilmington jumped.

Peter screamed, covered his ears.

Josiah fell to the ground, cursing and grabbing his boot. "He shot me!"

Wilmington and Jeremiah inched closer, as if approaching a cliff's ledge.

Wilmington, with horror in his eyes, looked at Jeremiah. "You shot him."

"Just in the toe." He watched Josiah writhe in the dust, where blood meandered like the Cimarron River once had. "Get up, Josiah. Show me where that light is inside. I need to smoke this thing before it stales. Plus me and the boy are hungry."

FIVE

H e's really out there. In the kitchen."

Ellen had meant to keep the thought in her head, but it came out as a whisper in her toddler's ear as she patted his back in the hallway, just around the corner from where Jeremiah sat with Wilmington and Josiah at the kitchen table. She'd finally gotten James to stop crying and coughing. She'd pounded his poor back until he hacked up enough black gunk to fill her palm. The coughing fit had lasted just long enough for her to miss the shoot-out.

From the bedroom she'd heard the one shot and then Josiah screaming. A minute later her husband was there on the foot of the bed wrapping his toe in a dusty towel and chugging from a bottle of Old Sam white dog, keeping her away with an extended hand and gibbering about him being fine, with all kinds of embarrassment etched across his red face. Then he'd hobbled ahead of her into the kitchen.

Ellen listened to their voices from the hallway. "It's your uncle Jeremiah in there," she whispered into James's ear, unabashedly now. "Your daddy's twin."

"Daddy's twin." James repeated her words like that boy Jeremiah had brought into town with him, the one she'd only seen from a distance, but was still familiar somehow. James said, "I hungry."

"Well, let's get you something then." Ellen rubbed his back and took a deep breath. *Enough stalling.* She rounded the corner. The three men looked her way. Wilmington had served up plates from a pot on the stove.

She glanced at Jeremiah but then looked away before much could be said between them. They used to claim they could talk with their eyes, and she sensed that might still be possible.

Jeremiah took a drag on his cigarette and then exhaled smoke toward the big hole in the kitchen ceiling.

She could feel him watching her. She balanced James on her hip, got milk from the ice box, and poured some into a cup. James took it with greed. Milk was as scarce as the cows nowadays, and most of what they had went to James to keep up his strength.

Wilmington, who'd taken off his hat and rested it on the table like she'd told him too many times not to do, said, "His appetite looks better."

Ellen agreed. Somewhere deep down was the foundation of a smile, a response lost to the town years ago, sucked up into the same dark void that had stolen the rain.

Before she knew it, James finished his milk and rested his head on her shoulder while she looked around for something more to feed him.

Josiah took another gulp of Old Sam and wiped his brow. He propped his injured foot on the chair beside him. He shot Ellen a glance and read her mind. "Toe ain't blown off. Just nicked it."

"On purpose." Jeremiah, sitting across the table from his twin, spooned in a glob of beans and rabbit.

"You ain't that good," said Josiah.

Jeremiah shrugged, then stared at the ceiling as he chewed. "Want me to fix that hole?"

"I cut the hole," said Josiah. "Put it there on purpose."

Jeremiah asked Ellen with an arched eyebrow.

"Don't do that," said Josiah.

"Do what?"

"You know what."

Ellen said, "The ceiling was sagging. There's nowhere dust doesn't go anymore. Every day Josiah gets up there and sweeps the dust down from the hole."

"That way the ceiling won't collapse," said Wilmington, digging into his beans and rabbit.

"Hat off the table, please."

Wilmington did what he was told, even though it was his house.

"Guess I'll have to get up there now," said Jeremiah, jerking a nod toward Josiah's towel-wrapped foot.

"I can still climb a ladder," said Josiah. "Been suffering through much worse since you been gone, protected by those thick prison walls with food daily. It's us that's been livin' on the nut."

Jeremiah smirked, stole a glance at Ellen that made her heart jump. "Why don't you have a seat?"

"Why don't you mind your own?" said Josiah.

Josiah didn't want her in there with them—that much was obvious. But now that she'd been invited, Ellen at least stepped closer to the table. "I'm fine standing."

Jeremiah looked at his twin across the table. "Looks like you."

"Why wouldn't he?"

"Just sayin'." Jeremiah finished his cigarette and smooshed the butt into the tin plate. The room was silent for a moment, enough for them to hear Peter in the other room, clacking on the typewriter.

Wilmington leaned back in his chair and watched the boy in the other room, where Peter had taken his bowl of beans and rabbit. "Why's he do that?"

"I dunno," said Jeremiah. "I suppose clacking those keys makes him feel calm—he does it when he's fidgety. Boy ain't all there."

"He could have eaten in here at the table," said Ellen.

"I offered," said Wilmington. "Boy just smiled and went in the other room. Came back a minute later to get that typewriter."

Jeremiah folded his arms. "Must just like to eat alone."

"Where'd he come from anyway?" asked Wilmington.

"Yeah," said Josiah. "We never seen you as the fatherly type."

Jeremiah ignored him. "From one of those dugouts a few miles from town. His mother was selling him."

"You bought a kid?" asked Ellen, eager to meet the boy face-to-face.

"Wasn't my intent. I gave the woman my last quarter, and ten minutes later he's latched on like a tick."

Wilmington scratched his head. "Bought a kid for a quarter?"

Josiah took another drink of Old Sam. "You can't stay here. You know that, don't you?"

"Figured."

Ellen said, "That's enough of that whiskey, Josiah."

Josiah took one more drink and then slid the bottle away. Wilmington poured himself a few fingers and offered the bottle to Jeremiah.

Jeremiah watched the bottle for a few beats. Finally he poured himself a finger and found all of them watching as he swirled it. In the past it would have been downed by now. He put his nose to it, dry-swallowed, and then raised the glass to his parted lips. He tilted it, but then paused. He placed the glass back down on the table, untouched.

He took in their curious eyes. "What?"

"What was that about?" asked Josiah.

Jeremiah shrugged, pushed the glass away. "Don't drink anymore."

"Since when?"

"Since the last time I had a drink. I'm a changed man now."

"No longer murderin'?"

"Josiah, that's enough." Wilmington said it just before Ellen, which was probably a good thing due to the already increasing tension in the room.

"That jolt I took in Old Sparky." Jeremiah leaned forward, elbows on the table. He had ropy arms corded with muscle that Ellen knew all too well, and he still kept them covered, the cuffs buttoned tight at both wrists. "That electric chair jostled some things."

"Like what?" asked Josiah. He reached for the bottle again, but Ellen moved it away.

"Would it make sense if I said that blurry is the new clear?"

"You've never made sense," said Josiah. "And you can't stay here. I'll give you till sundown."

"Boys, let's talk this through," said Wilmington.

Josiah winced as he lowered his foot from the neighboring chair and leaned forward to meet his brother's gaze. "I saw you bury those bodies in the grain silo. You didn't know it, but I watched. You killed 'em, didn't you?"

"'Course I didn't."

"Then why'd you bring 'em here and bury 'em under the cloak of night."

"Little birdies need a good nudge from the nest, don't they? And dead bodies need to be buried proper."

"You see? The day he starts making sense is the day this

drought'll be over." Josiah pointed at his brother, then looked at Ellen. "I was *right* in what I did and you know it."

"If that allows you to sleep at night."

Josiah scoffed, flicked a breadcrumb from the tabletop.

James looked up from Ellen's shoulder, and she shushed him back down. She shot Josiah a stern warning.

Jeremiah said, "Don't think you heard what I said, brother."

"Heard 'fuzzy.' That's all I needed to hear."

"I didn't kill 'em with my own hands, if that's what you're asking. Which is what I claimed all along."

"So why'd you bury 'em? Buried 'em right where you were living, like trophies."

For that, Jeremiah didn't have an answer. He might claim to see things more clearly now, but Ellen still sensed confusion in those blue eyes of his, confusion mixed with something akin to guilt. Or maybe it was remorse she saw.

"You can't stay here," said Josiah. "Ain't that right, Ellen?"

There he went, putting her on the spot like she'd hoped he wouldn't. *Should have never even entered the kitchen.* She looked to the floor and mumbled, "You can't stay here, Jeremiah."

Jeremiah smirked. "You don't mean that."

Josiah slapped the table again. This time James didn't stir. He was asleep now and breathing warmth onto Ellen's neck. "I know why you came back," said Josiah. "You ain't fooling anybody."

"Came back to shoot you, plain and simple."

"And that you did," said Wilmington, massaging his temples like he had a headache. "And there will be no more of it."

Ellen said to Wilmington. "You need to go lie down."

"Bullet ain't gonna move, Ellen. Stop your worrying."

Josiah reached into his pocket and pulled out a coin, a nickel.

He pushed it across the table toward his twin. "Go on. I know what you do. Coin-Flip Killer?"

"It ain't like that."

"Then show me how it is. Go on. Flip it."

"Don't think you want me to do that." Although now, after Old Sparky had done away with his urge to drink, would the coin flip still hold that same power?

"If luck may have it, you can put a bullet in my head and put me out of this misery we live in daily."

Ellen choked on a sob. "Josiah, it's the booze talking. Don't say that."

"Dust is gonna kill us all anyway," he said. "Do it. Flip the coin. Let me see how it works."

Jeremiah slid the coin off the table, into his palm, and glanced at Ellen.

Warmth enveloped her heart. She shook her head no, but he flipped the coin anyway. She closed her eyes. Heard the coin rattle to stillness atop the table and his strong hand muffle the sound as it closed down upon it.

"Heads and you'll lose yours," said Jeremiah. "Tails you don't."

Ellen opened her eyes as tears welled. She'd had dreams of Josiah dying and Jeremiah coming home to her. The realness of the moment made her nauseous. *I do love you, Josiah.* The father of her child. *A good man.* "Stop it, Jeremiah. Don't you dare reveal that coin."

Jeremiah kept his hand over the coin and gazed, jaw clenched, at Josiah, but there was a tiny crack in that hardened exterior, and Ellen sensed some doubt in those eyes. Jeremiah always flipped the coin with certainty, but now he looked anything but. Still, he said, "I came back on a coin flip, if you really want to know."

Wilmington looked up. He'd been the one to teach the coin-flip games to the boys when they were little. He'd started it all, and guilt weighed on his shoulders as he watched things unfold between his two sons.

Josiah broke the silence with a nervous chuckle. "He's still off his tracks."

"Ever since I took that jolt in the chair, my nightmares have left me."

Josiah shook his head. "Not the nightmares again. They're excuses. Always have been. Attention seekers is all they are." He pointed at Jeremiah. "You've no idea what I've had to do while you were gone. Things I ain't proud of. Decisions I've made to keep us alive. Those nightmares are real, brother."

Ellen's grip on James grew tighter, more protective. Jeremiah's nightmares were all too real—or *nightmare*, rather, as every one of them was the same in content and duration. How many times had she held him as he told her about them? Describing every detail until she'd had a few of them herself. It'd been that way since they were teenagers.

Jeremiah looked up as if a notion had just popped. "I told you back when. About the land."

Josiah shook his head. "Not again. You was just piggybacking what some of those ranchers and cowboys said. You always did play the cowboy."

"Well?"

"Well what?"

"They weren't wrong, were they? The land is coming back and taking vengeance on account of what we did to it."

Wilmington looked down at the table. Ellen stepped over, rubbed his back, and whispered that it was okay.

Typewriter keys clacked from the other room.

Jeremiah's hand still covered the coin he'd flipped moments ago.

Josiah stared at it, forced toughness. "Go on. Get it over with."

But Jeremiah didn't reveal the coin beneath his palm.

Everything had gone quiet, even Peter's typing. Tiny footsteps approached the kitchen. Ellen's heart fluttered, anticipating the strange boy's arrival.

Peter stepped around the corner with an empty tin plate smeared brown with bean and rabbit juice. He stopped abruptly before Ellen and met her eyes.

Peter smiled, broad and crooked, exposing those missing teeth. Those dimples. And the eyes . . .

Ellen's thoughts slipped out again. She looked at Jeremiah. "It's him."

Her vision wavered. James was heavy in her weightless arms.

She saw black, and then she collapsed.

SIX

Soft piano music carried from the Bentley Hotel.

From the Goodbyes' front porch, Jeremiah and his father watched Peter pace in the dust near the road. The boy mumbled to himself and looked up every time billiard balls collided inside the Bentley across the street, where Orion watched from an upstairs window.

"You think Orion knows we can see him?" asked Jeremiah.

"Doubt it," said Wilmington. "He's not as good at hiding as he thinks he is."

Leaning against a porch column, Jeremiah took in the desert-like expanse of Nowhere. "Like a ghost town."

"About half the town has gone." Wilmington chewed his lip. "Exodusters. Call 'em what you want. I call 'em cowards."

"Even if dying is the only other option?"

"Ah, ain't nobody dying."

"Not what I heard."

Wilmington grunted. He watched the boy pace, kicking up little dust tornadoes as his feet shuffled. "He doesn't say much."

"He's an observer," said Jeremiah. "Says plenty in his head, I bet."

Jeremiah's mind was on Ellen. On how she'd felt in his arms when he'd caught her moments ago in the kitchen—her and the little boy. Somehow he'd managed to gather both before they hit the floor. He'd caught a whiff of her hair and the lavender-scented lotion she'd rub on her neck.

She was inside on the bed now, groggy. Last he'd seen, Josiah was folding a wet rag on her forehead. He'd told Jeremiah to get out and leave them be.

What was it she'd said before she'd blacked out? *It's him.* At first he'd been confused as to what she meant—or *who* she meant— but now it dawned on him. It was probably the reason he'd felt drawn to Peter the day before, or at least aware of the boy's likeness to *somebody.* If he got another chance to talk with her he'd confirm it, but until then he returned his focus on his father and that noticeable scar above his ear.

"Can you feel it in there?"

"Feel what?"

"The bullet in your head?"

"Sometimes." Wilmington leaned on the railing, watching the boy. "What's he mumbling?"

"I don't know. But at least he took a break from the typing."

Wilmington touched the side of his head, where no hair had regrown after the bullet entered. "It's like a weather vane. I can tell when a duster's coming. The pressure around the bullet intensifies."

"I thought the dusters couldn't be predicted."

"I just told you different. Head's been humming for twelve straight days now. A duster has come on every one of them. I could use a break from it." Wilmington glanced at his son and then returned his eyes toward the boy, or maybe it was the buried road. A cluster of tumbleweeds had gotten snagged on a windmill behind the hotel. Peter had stopped to watch a tarantula skitter across loose dust. "Josiah killed ten tarantulas in one day," said Wilmington. "Just last week. Bodies the size of an apple. Legs half a foot long. Get 'em good with a shovel a couple times and they're goners. Faster than you think, though."

"I'm sorry about the bullet. It wasn't meant for you."

"Of course it wasn't. That was a strange afternoon, and you weren't the only one firing." Wilmington coughed three times, hacked up black gunk, and spat into the dust like it was nothing out of the ordinary. "I heard that bullet ping off a lamppost and then thunk. Ping and a thunk, that's how it sounded. Buried deep in a brain that probably needed a jostle. Miracle, I guess. Or the opposite of a miracle. Miracle would have had it thunking into the wall I was standing in front of. Maybe the miracle is that I'm still here."

"Even so."

The front door opened, and little James toddled out with Josiah limping behind him. "She asked for you."

Jeremiah turned. "And you're okay with it?"

"'Course I'm not okay with it, but it doesn't seem time to argue, now does it?"

Jeremiah patted his father's shoulder and brushed past his brother into the house.

"Where's the shovel?" he heard Josiah ask his father as the screen door slapped closed.

A second later, out in the front yard of dust, Peter was screaming.

Jeremiah stopped to look out the window. His brother was out there crunching the tarantula with a shovel, and the action seemed to unnerve the boy. At least Josiah had enough sense to stop when the screaming got too loud and town folk began to gather on their stoops. He then quickly shoveled dirt over the spot. Little James stood by his grandfather, watching the scene in the yard with fascination.

Peter stopped screaming and resumed his pacing.

Jeremiah headed to the bedroom, which used to have two beds belonging to him and Josiah but now had one larger one for Josiah and Ellen. Ellen was lying on her side when he entered, her eyes wide open but not all there. Dust motes floated in the sunray that streaked across the bed. A thin layer of dust coated the floor, the baseboards, the windowsill, and the outline of Ellen's head on the pillow. Jeremiah reached down and brushed some of it off, but it just made her cough, a loose rattle in the chest like Wilmington had sounded a minute ago.

The dust was slowly killing them all.

He sat bedside on the same wooden chair his brother had just vacated. He started to brush the strand of sandy hair that had fallen across her left eye but resisted, not trusting that an innocent touch wouldn't leave him wanting more.

"It's him," she said, stone-faced. Finally she blinked, then blew the strand of hair away from her eye. Dust scattered from the pillow. "You just get used to it after a while. All this dust. The town is trying to cope, Jeremiah. Trying to stay optimistic. But it gets harder every day. Orion across the street, he still has his gatherings each night, with the music and all, but the numbers dwindle." She sat up in bed, rested her head against the wall. "Maybe you can come tonight. We play billiards and cards and sometimes bingo. Those that have the energy sing and dance."

"I don't think anybody here is gonna want me in that hotel carrying on, Ellen." He scooted up in the chair and gripped her left hand, at the moment not caring if Josiah came back and saw.

"I think Josiah is right. I shouldn't have come back. Nobody wants me here."

"I want you here."

"Don't say that." He squeezed her hand and looked deep into her eyes, where half the life seemed to be missing. "Now tell me what caused that fainting spell in the kitchen."

"It's him."

"Who's him?"

"That boy you picked up. Peter. The same boy I've always seen in my dreams."

"What dreams?"

She looked at him, and for a blink her gaze was daggers. "*The* dreams, Jeremiah. You haven't been gone *that* long."

He leaned back, let her fingers slither from his grip. He rubbed a weathered hand across his face, brushing over stubble like sandpaper on wood. He nodded and swallowed over the big guilty lump in his throat. He remembered her hands balled into fists and beating his chest after he told her he'd gone ahead and buried what they'd lost, before she'd even had a chance to look. But she'd been so distraught, her mannerisms suggesting she didn't want to look, couldn't bring herself to. Even Dr. Craven, who was the only other person in town who knew—Jeremiah had run and got him as soon as Ellen started feeling the pains—had said to not let her see the miscarriage. It would be too hard on any mother to see such a thing. And Ellen had been only eighteen; Jeremiah twenty.

"It was a boy?" she'd asked, finally calming, her fists unclenching as she settled into his warm embrace inside the barn that was now collapsed under dust. He'd rubbed her back until the tears dried up. "It was a boy, Ellen. With eyes bluer than summer sky."

But the never seeing hadn't sat right in her head, and within days she'd gotten to wondering. Her mind had conjured up what she imagined the boy would have looked like as a baby and also when he'd begun to grow into a boy. She saw him in her dreams. And those images, as she'd tell Jeremiah after each one of them, never wavered.

"That boy out there," Ellen said now, lower lip quivering. "It's him. Same person I imagined up in my mind, the one in my dreams. He's got those dimples and the same eyes. The exact same tousled brown hair. That smile . . ."

Jeremiah exhaled both cheeks. "Just a coincidence, Ellen." Although he was more in agreement than he wanted to admit.

"No. I don't believe that." She leaned forward on the bed and pointed. "There's a reason you stumbled past that dugout when that boy was for sale."

"I flipped a coin, Ellen. Just as easily could've taken that other road."

"But you didn't. And look what come of it." She leaned back again and folded her arms across a chest he tried not to notice. She'd lost weight. They all had. "Just before I fainted in there, my heart swelled. Literally grew warm, Jeremiah, and that was *before* he turned that corner and stepped in front of me. A part of me knew."

Jeremiah brushed dust that had settled on his trousers. "So what now?"

"I don't know what now." She chuckled briefly, then wiped dry eyes. Tears probably dried up like the land these days. "But you best get back out there before Josiah gets antsy."

He stood. "Long past that."

"Go on."

He did, and she promised to be out soon enough.

Peter stood in the middle of the kitchen, staring up into the hole in the ceiling, grinning. A whisper of dust filtered down from the darkness up there and he raised his arm as if to catch it. A few feet over and sitting on Wilmington's lap, James grinned too.

Jeremiah let them be and joined his brother out on the front porch.

Josiah watched the town as a tumbleweed bounced by. "They're watching us from the windows."

The Bentley Hotel had eight windows on its façade, and three of them showed people watching, as did many of the homes around the town square.

"Sheriff McKinney has no choice but to lock you up."

"Unless I go?"

Josiah nodded, coughed, spat brown gunk over the rail and into the dust, where another tarantula scurried. "The town's afraid of you, Jeremiah."

"Are you?"

Josiah thought on it, then said, "And they're a little leery of that boy too."

"He's nothing to be afraid of. And neither am I."

"They found you guilty."

Jeremiah stared at the massive spider. "Where's the shovel?"

Josiah nodded to his side, where it leaned against the wall.

Jeremiah grabbed the tool, walked down the steps, and stood over the tarantula. Instead of smashing it, he scooped it up inside the pit of the shovel. "We should put it in Mr. Burlough's mailbox."

Josiah grinned, probably at a fleeting memory of the different live things they'd put in that man's mailbox as kids, but then his face went stoic again. "Burlough's dead. Year ago. Got caught out in a duster and suffocated."

Jeremiah rotated the handle in his grip so that the shovel part was inches in front of his face, as was the tarantula.

"Hope he bites your nose off."

Jeremiah grunted, then hurled the tarantula through the air. It landed in the dust across the road and skittered away. He joined Josiah on the porch again.

"You trying to prove you're a changed man now, 'cause you wouldn't kill a spider?"

"Not tryin' to prove nothin'."

"Then what now?"

Jeremiah snickered. *Same thing Ellen asked me.*

"What's funny?"

"Nothing's funny."

They stood silent for a minute as the wind blew dust. Josiah pulled a handkerchief from his pocket and covered his nose and mouth until the wind settled. He folded the handkerchief and then slid it back into his shirt pocket. "Daddy cries every night. He goes out back behind the house, next to the rubble that used to be the barn. He doesn't think anybody can hear him, but you know how the wind carries. Started when he had to trade his John Deere for a milking cow that was mostly skin and bones. Money don't move anymore, but as long as we got a few cows and chickens we can get by."

"I heard about what you did with the cattle," said Jeremiah. "And the government officials."

"Did what needed to be done."

"It was noble, is all I'm saying."

"I don't want to talk about it."

"Fine."

More silence. A black widow sneaked along the porch railing, and Josiah flicked it across the yard. "How'd you know?"

"Know what?"

"About what I done with the cows. When the government officials came."

"Prison walls aren't so thick."

Josiah thought on it. "We were able to fatten the cow a smidge, the one he got for the tractor, but the first pail of milk came out brown. Like chocolate milk. Cow's dead now. So we trade Mr. Mulraney fresh eggs for some of his milk. He's somehow still got two good cows. Also gave Mulraney a nice pair of overalls that didn't fit anymore. For some turnips."

"You remember the day Daddy bought that John Deere?" asked Jeremiah.

"First time he smiled since Mother died." Josiah coughed into his sleeve, watched his brother with curiosity. The sky bled orange over the horizon. "It wasn't the John Deere itself. It was what it symbolized. Prosperity and wealth."

"The American dream."

"Building a town from nothing," said Josiah. "You know, he told me one night over some hooch that during the wet years he and Orion were making more money than the professional ball players. Even Babe Ruth."

"They raped the land, Josiah."

"And the government pushed them into it."

"I suppose they did."

"Well, now he cries every night. No need to cast blame." Josiah nodded across the road. "Here he comes."

Sheriff McKinney walked with a straight-backed gait, forced— his typical walk was more slouched and lethargic.

"He planning on taking me in by himself?"

Josiah shrugged, spat. "I ain't gonna help him. I think he covets my wife."

They shared a glance, and then Jeremiah grinned toward their visitor. "Afternoon, Sheriff."

Sheriff McKinney fingered the rimmed hat that covered his bald head. He puffed his chest out, and the dust-brown uniform nearly lost a button. "I tried telephoning the state authorities, Jeremiah, but the last duster jostled the lines. If you'll come with me, I'll keep you in a holding cell overnight."

"Until when?"

"Until we figure out what to do with you. You're a wanted man."

"And if I say no?"

"Was hoping you wouldn't." McKinley unlatched the cuffs from his chubby waistline and approached the porch. "Come on now."

"Take another step, and I'll whack you in that big noodle of yours."

"Now you've done added threatening a lawman to your list of offenses." The sheriff climbed the three steps to the porch. His jowls jiggled, no doubt trying like the dickens to hold back a victory smile—there was probably some grand reward for bringing in the Coin-Flip Killer.

Jeremiah did as he'd promised. He reared back and punched Sheriff McKinney in the forehead, knocking him down the steps into the dust.

Josiah stepped over to get a better look. "He's out cold."

Jeremiah flexed his fingers. "Wish I didn't have to do that. He left me no choice."

"You could've obliged."

"Nah. Got something I gotta do."

"What might that be?"

"Can't say." Something else stole his attention. Jeremiah pointed toward the horizon, where dark clouds had suddenly appeared. Another black duster was on the way.

"Here we go again," said Josiah, with no life to the words. "They come without warning."

The screen door opened, and out stepped Wilmington, wincing, with his fingers to his left temple. "I feel a duster coming." He looked up, and his eyes grew large. "And there it is." Over the Bentley Hotel, massive black clouds loomed larger than even seconds before, like a big swath of Kansas had been picked up with the wind. He finally noticed Sheriff McKinney in the dust below. "What happened to him?"

"He fell," said Josiah.

"Always was clumsy, like his daddy. Let's get him inside then." Wilmington moved across the porch as if to help.

Jeremiah jumped down the steps in front of Wilmington. "I got it. You shouldn't be lifting anything. That bullet might move."

Wilmington grunted, waved that notion away. "Been listening to Ellen too much already."

Josiah said, "Well Daddy, go on in and warn her now. Get out the sheets and wet 'em down. Seal the windows. And make sure you drape a sheet over James's crib."

Wilmington hurried inside, invigorated simply by being of use.

Jeremiah grabbed the sheriff's legs, and Josiah got him under the arms.

Josiah said, "I don't know where you plan on going. And it's probably not the best idea to come back. But you might as well wait out this duster."

"Don't have time to wait."

"Seen too many people die out there, Jeremiah."

"I'll take my chances."

They carried the sheriff up the steps and onto the porch before Josiah paused. McKinney was easily two hundred thirty pounds of deadweight, and Jeremiah believed he had the heavier end.

"Why'd you stop?"

Josiah gulped. "You know how they say twins have that connection? Well, that jolt you took in Old Sparky, I think I felt it too."

"What are you talking about?"

"We followed the newspapers, and we knew the day they were going to put you in the chair. Knew it down to the hour. Ellen and Daddy, they tried to keep themselves real busy so as not to think about it, so I did too. We all took to cleaning. I was sweeping the kitchen floor when the pain hit and I went down on one knee. Ellen will tell you the same. I felt my arms not just shaking, but vibrating, and my heart thrummed. I looked at the clock, Jeremiah. It was twelve thirty-two. What time did they put you in that chair?"

"About that same time."

"Is it possible?"

Jeremiah looked off into the distance and shrugged. He supposed anything was possible.

The duster had doubled in size. Flecks started to dance across the hardpan ground, and static electricity buzzed like lightning. They again lifted Sheriff McKinney. Jeremiah said, "For what it's worth, before Ellen fainted, I took a peek at the coin under my hand."

"And?"

"It was tails."

Josiah wedged the screen door open with his foot. "Guess it's my lucky day then."

"Don't think luck has anything to do with it."

Josiah paused. "Then what *does* have to do with it, brother?"

"What's meant to be and what isn't."

Josiah scoffed, chewed on it as they carried Sheriff McKinney into the front room and lowered him to the floorboards. Ellen and Wilmington worked together securing a blanket over the kitchen window.

Jeremiah softened his voice and said to Josiah, "Tell the boy I'll be back. If I'm able."

"Bad ol' Jeremiah, always running off. You just love to make people fret."

"You fretting?"

"Of course not. Part of me hopes you die out there in the dust."

"And the other part?"

Josiah sighed. "Make sure you grab one of those masks by the door on your way out."

SEVEN

The duster came and went.

It lasted less than an hour but dropped enough black dust for them to get the brooms and shovels back out.

Most of the porches and stoops had been cleared by sundown. A bell hung down from the middle of the hotel's parlor, where most of the congregating went on. Orion had brought the bell with him from his Catholic church back in New York City, one of the only surviving pieces from the fire that had burned it to the ground three months before he headed west toward the fictional town of Majestic. The bell had a scorch mark on it that some said looked like Tennessee if it stood on end.

Ellen heard the bell but didn't feel much like congregating. The fainting episode had drained her, and cleaning after the duster had all but done her in for the evening. She sipped water at the kitchen table, where the rest of them looked just as whipped—Wilmington and Josiah, James and the new boy, Peter. Sheriff McKinney had come to on the floor twenty minutes into the duster, groggy for a minute until he remembered what had happened, then red-faced, embarrassed, and irate in equal measure.

"Where'd he go off to?"

"Went right into the duster," Josiah had said with an edge to his voice, still busy sealing the last window with Ellen. They hadn't spoken since he'd told *her* where Jeremiah had gone. When the duster started, maybe she'd been too quick to ask. She'd heard the panic in her own voice and then the irritation in her husband's when he told her. Had she shown too much worry? Too much *fret*, as Josiah would have said?

"How could he have just taken off, right into the duster?"

Sheriff McKinney had left as soon as the duster ended, never even offering to help with the cleanup. Said he was going to see if Jeremiah was hiding somewhere, like in the silo.

Now Peter sat at the end of the kitchen table, fingering the typewriter keys but not really pressing them. He'd been clacking the keys minutes ago until Josiah gave him the look, that one where his eyes got big as tin plates. The boy was aware enough to read body language. He'd stopped right away and now only pretended, which, in a way, was almost funny.

Ellen stared at the boy but then glanced away every time he looked at her. Eye contact might bring about emotions she wasn't ready to face. It was surely him, the same boy she'd been seeing in her mind for years now. *How could that even be?* James sat on his father's lap gnawing on a stale hunk of wheat bread as they all watched Peter pretend to hit typewriter keys.

Who are you? She wanted to ask the strange boy, already feeling more connected to him than she ever should. But how could she help it after what happened during the duster, when he started screaming and bobbing, tapping his temples with clenched fists until they'd turned red enough to see even in the dark? She'd done what any mother would do and reeled him in. At first he'd screamed louder, but eventually he'd settled his head against her shoulder and even allowed her to rub his back.

"It's okay, Peter. It'll pass. They always do."

"Peter," he'd said. "It's okay, Peter. They always do." He'd repeated her words back to her until he started into "Peter, Peter, pumpkin eater . . . had a wife but couldn't keep her . . ." And Ellen had found herself mumbling right along with him, even as her own son started crying from his crib because the dust tapping against the house must have woken him up. At that point she'd given Josiah the look. The get-up-and-take-care-of-your-son look.

Across the street, Orion rang the bell again, the third time in ten minutes. Out the window, half the town walked wearily across the dust toward the Bentley Hotel. Phillip Jansen, the postman back when the mail used to circulate, carried an accordion. One of the nuns from the hospital—it looked like Sister Moffitt from where Ellen sat—carried a banjo. Everyone else moved like they were half-asleep or half-dead, most of them coughing and hacking.

She wondered how long it would take a town to starve to death. Most of the excess wheat was gone. Aside from rabbit, meat was now scarce. Most of their milk came out brown from the cow.

Wilmington was the first to stand. He slung the suspender straps that had been hanging loose around his waist to a snap atop his shoulders. "I suppose we should go too. Orion won't stop ringing that bell until the hotel is full. Must have something he needs to get off his chest."

"You suppose?" Josiah stood up with James and headed for the door.

Peter followed with the typewriter.

Ellen walked alongside Wilmington, who offered his arm.

She took it and patted his hand. "You take it easy now."

"I'm not glass, Ellen."

Jeremiah's face hurt.

It was just as he'd heard; black-blizzard dust clipped like glass when it hit the skin.

Maybe he should've listened to his brother and waited the storm out. But something told him he needed to hurry if he wanted answers.

He was thankful for the mask. Without it he could have suffocated. For two miles he'd hunkered into the dark blow with his Stetson tilted low over his brow, knowing the way only because of the power lines in and out of town, following the static electricity as it sparked from pole to pole.

Just when he thought his body might give in, his mind took over. The jolt of electricity had unlocked some doors once darkened by vice and clouded by drink, and good memories found their way to the surface. He and Josiah running through golden fields of wheat, sweating under the summer sun, finding shade from the elm trees that used to exist, and dousing themselves with water from the well. The fruit smells in the house when their mother got to cooking cobblers.

He'd even managed to conjure up a memory of her face—blue-green eyes, hair so blond it looked sun-touched, a smile that made his heart melt. At least that's how Wilmington had described her one day, tending to the rose garden he'd built over her grave. Jeremiah missed those days, smelling the roses as his daddy would water them, warning him not to touch those thorns.

Jeremiah had sworn to Josiah that Daddy would touch those thorns on purpose, kind of like he enjoyed the prick and the spot of blood that followed.

"That makes no sense, Jeremiah."

Jeremiah thought it did, that the blood was some kind of connection to what once was, one of those strange ways an adult has of remembering how to be close to something.

Seeing that blood was something Jeremiah could relate to. He had enough scars on his forearm to prove it too, but he'd always made sure he kept those concealed. Wasn't something he was proud of, and he'd yet to find a logical way to explain them away.

As he wandered through the dust, Jeremiah imagined his mother talking to him. "You didn't kill me, Jeremiah. I lived for three years after you were born, you know. It was my weakened lungs that got me. Not that birth." All things he wished she'd said to him before she died in that bed, a bed that looked to have swallowed her.

He'd been hungry and waddled in to tug on her leg, which hadn't moved. Or maybe it was Josiah who'd gone in first and told him, "Mom don't move." Was it possible for Josiah to feel that jolt he'd taken in Old Sparky? Was it possible for him to have a memory that actually happened to his brother?

Jeremiah plowed on, craving a drink. Not the kind he used to crave—those urges seemed to have been churned under like the nightmares, all because of the jolt. But his dry mouth felt desperate for a cool drink of water.

The nightmares were why he'd begun drinking in the first place, trying that first gulp of hooch behind the barn when he was ten and never looking back, reveling in the realization that he'd found something to help him forget what the nights brought about or at least make them fuzzy. He'd figured out long ago that his ability to sense things in others was somehow related to the nightmare he'd have every night. Like the two were inseparable, one keeping balance with the other.

The wind began to die down, the dust less incessant. What had been black for the entire trip was now flecked with gray sky. The static electricity went away, and visibility returned. It was like it had gone from day to night and back to day again.

He removed the mask and his hat and shook dust from both. He blew wet dust from his nostrils—even with the mask, the granules were so fine they still got in. Then he looked up and spotted it not far ahead—the row of dugouts where he'd accidently bought that boy, Peter. He must have traveled faster than he'd thought, his pace fueled by good memories and by the reason he'd made the journey in the first place. Ellen needed answers, and he'd get them for her even if it killed him.

Problem was, despite his urgency, he was too late. As he approached the dugout where the sign that said Child for Sale once stood, it became apparent that no one lived there anymore. Tire tracks from a vehicle piled heavy with belongings remained even after the storm.

They've all gone. But letting Ellen down wasn't an option. Maybe they left stuff behind.

As he started toward the dugout another memory popped— the day the Maverick family arrived in the fall of 1925. He and Josiah had turned fifteen two weeks prior, and Daddy had recently taught them how to drive the tractor. Josiah had just climbed down from it and Jeremiah was about to climb on when they heard that black Dodge puttering into town, the top of the car just visible above the sway of golden wheat.

"Another suitcase farmer," Wilmington said with a grunt before heading into the house, his neck suntanned the color of leather.

The suitcase farmers would come in for a season, run through a crop, and leave with a suitcase of money, the same suitcase they'd lived out of for the duration of their stay, stealing a quick piece of the wheat boom whose fury rivaled the gold rush out west a few generations earlier. Some of the suitcase farmers would plant in the fall, go back east, and come back a year later to harvest. Those were the ones with whom Wilmington and Orion had the most disagreements. *They can't have it both ways.* Only time would tell what the newest arrival would do.

The Dodge drove into the town square and stopped just outside the Bentley Hotel. The twin boys hurried through the wheat field to get a look at the vehicle with its luggage strapped to the back. Before the newcomers even opened the car door, Jeremiah pulled a quarter from his pocket and thumb-flicked it into the air. He and Josiah watched it spin until Jeremiah caught it and slapped it atop his left hand. "Heads, they end up staying; tails, they go like Daddy says."

The driver's side door opened, and a finely dressed man in a beige suit and matching top hat stepped out. Next, on the far side of the car, emerged a woman wearing a blue and white flapper day dress that swayed like ocean waves just below the knees. Then the back door opened, and a girl in a yellow dress, roughly the same age as the twins, emerged, her sandy hair collected up in a bundle and secured with a red ribbon. They'd learn later that evening that her name was Ellen.

Jeremiah removed his right hand to reveal the coin, which showed heads.

"I was hoping that was so," said Josiah, saying it like he knew most of Jeremiah's coin flips came out in their favor.

They watched the new family walk as a threesome toward

the hotel, where Orion had just emerged to welcome them, cigar dangling like it was part of his lips, probably already starting into his sales pitch for them to throw away the suitcases and come live for good in the glorious town of Nowhere. *"Health, wealth, and opportunity!"* The girl trailed a few paces behind her parents, taking in the expanse of wheat in every direction.

She caught the twins staring and waved.

They waved back.

Josiah smiled. "I'm gonna marry that girl, Jeremiah. What's funny?"

Jeremiah smirked. "Only if I let you."

"Call another number, Orion," said an unenthusiastic Deacon Sipes from across the hotel parlor.

Deacon sat with his pal, Toothache. Toothache had teeth like a horse, and he was always complaining about how they hurt. The two of them wore dusty clothes that smelled of booze, and they both needed a good shave. Together they ran Sipes Automotive, the local fix-up place for cars and tractors on the fritz. Both had hair as greasy as their hands, except Deacon wore his black hair slicked back while Toothache had a deep part down the middle that made him look half-bald.

Ellen sat next to Orion, James on her lap, and repressed a little shiver of revulsion. Those two had given her the heebie-jeebies ever since they came to town during the boom. Of all the folks who might pick up stakes and head west to California, those two would have been first on her wish list to go. But they clung to Nowhere as if they'd been anchored.

People in California didn't like the Okies, anyhow, the two of them liked to point out, turning them away just as they would the Indians and the blacks. "Betteroffstayin'," she'd heard Toothache mumble on several occasions. That's how he talked, a mumbled run-on grumble only Deacon could understand.

Deacon and Toothache now hovered over homemade bingo cards, little piles of beans at their side to serve as markers. Sister Moffitt was the only other one playing, and she was sweating profusely. She never would take that white cap and heavy-looking headdress off, even when the summer temperatures hit triple digits.

Orion nodded toward Ellen, who allowed James to reach into the hat and pull out another cardboard piece. Ellen handed the piece to Orion, who lifted his head with an eager-to-please smile and shouted, "N-47. N-47."

Sister Moffitt raised her hand and said with no enthusiasm, "Bingo." Then she leaned back in her chair, crossed her legs, and took a drag on the cigarette she'd left smoldering on the tin plate next to her card. Wasn't like she got to win anything. Sometimes Orion would give away extra cow chips for the stove, but tonight the game was just for fun. Except there wasn't much fun to be had. Everyone was too worn out, slumping in their chairs like they'd been slung the worst hand life could deal.

"Sister won again." Deacon shook his head, pushed away his card and the beans atop it. One bean bounced on the floor, and Dr. Craven's skinny mutt jumped on it.

"Likesistergotsumhelpfromabove," said Toothache, real fast and all in one big word, like if he didn't get out what needed to be said in one breath it would kill him.

"Shut up, Toothache," said Josiah, standing now in the middle of the cramped room, where the pea-green designer wallpaper was so old it looked jaundiced. The seats, once plush and fancy during the twenties, were now faded and full of dust.

Betsy Finnigen, the town seamstress and hotel piano player, had stopped playing ten minutes into the get-together. She always seemed on the verge of tears nowadays. Phillip Jansen played his accordion in the back corner, but it was low-toned and lazy and sounded like it had dust in it.

Orion clapped his hands together and smiled. "One more game then."

"No more games," said Josiah. He took a few steps in a circle, still favoring that shot toe. "You didn't gather us for bingo, Orion. Now let's get down to the meat."

Where Jeremiah could sometimes speak with his eyes, Josiah liked to talk with his hands, and in the right one he held a bottle of Old Sam corn whiskey.

Ellen's lips pressed together as she watched the bottle wave around. She didn't care for it one bit—neither the whiskey itself nor the fact that her husband drank so much of it. He hadn't been a drinker before. In fact, he'd been against it—not because he thought it was some kind of sin, but mostly because Jeremiah drank so much of it. But ever since the earth started peeling off and Jeremiah went to the big house to pay for his crime—with Josiah being responsible for putting him there—Josiah had taken to the bottle like he was finally conquering some big dream.

Ellen followed the bottle in Josiah's hand, and even though the whiskey was sloshing, she could tell he'd consumed half of it. It was probably what had given him the courage to stand up in front of the town now. It used to be different. Before the bullet, Wilmington had been the one who spoke for the family. Before the arrest, it had been Jeremiah. Lately she had been the one. Now she just wanted to go to bed.

"Jeremiah's gone," Josiah slurred. "Went right out into the dust storm like some hero."

"How's that toe doing?" asked Deacon with a smirk, and beside him Toothache chuckled.

"I'll punch your face off, Deacon Sipes." Josiah gulped, pointing with the bottle. "Don't be interrupting."

Ellen wished Josiah would sit down. He was making a fool of himself. She knew Orion had gathered them to discuss what would be done if Jeremiah returned. And eventually Orion would have gotten to it, but not like this. Beside her Peter sat silently with his hands folded in his lap, the typewriter at his feet. He'd been clacking it earlier, until Deacon said he couldn't focus on his bingo with all that key punching.

"If he comes back," Josiah said. "What are we to do?"

From a chair against the wall next to the bar, Wilmington said, "Have a seat, son."

Josiah held his hand up as if asking for another minute. "We gonna let him waltz back into town like nothing happened? Like we never found four bodies inside that silo." He raised the bottle, tilted his head back, and gulped three swallows. When he lowered the bottle, his stance wavered. "He's my twin brother, but he's also a murderer."

"We don't know that," said Wilmington. Ellen was close enough to put a hand on his arm to calm him down, but Wilmington wasn't having it. "That trial was a bad one. Too much mystery. Too much those jurors didn't know to come up with the decision they did."

Ned Blythe, the food store owner, said, "He is a son of this town. I say we open our arms back up to him and forgive and forget."

Sheriff McKinney stood up. He had a bruise shaped like a walnut on his forehead from where Jeremiah had pasted him earlier in the day. "We can't forget what he's done."

"Allegedly done." Wilmington was on his feet, pointing his index finger like a piston, face red. Orion stood and coaxed his friend back to the seat, where Wilmington shouted, "He was drinking a lot then. Maybe he done some questionable things because of it, and his head wasn't all that clear, but I doubt it was murder."

Richard Klamp, who owned the clothing store and whose hair had gone white since his business went from profit to bartering, said, "I'm sorry, Wilmington. I consider you family, but I've gotta say this. Let me know if I'm wrong," he said to the crowd, "but him being here for just that little bit made us all uneasy. We all seen the bodies they dug up. He admitted to putting them there."

By the head nodding around the room, most of them agreed.

"He's a changed man," said Ellen.

Josiah spun toward her voice. "And how do you know that?"

She didn't like his tone—a tone laced with venom. Josiah had never spoken to her like that. She'd heard it from other couples, but never him.

"Same way you know it," she said to Josiah. "He doesn't drink anymore. His nightmares are gone."

Josiah laughed. "Yes, the nightmares. Here we go." He took another pull from the bottle. "Poor, poor, Jeremiah and his restless nights."

"Sit down, son," said Wilmington, murmuring desperately to Orion. "Please just sit down."

Orion patted Wilmington's shoulder and then stepped out into the belly of the room with Josiah. "Thank you, Josiah."

"I ain't done." He took another swig, staring right at Ellen when he swallowed the gulp.

She pursed her lips and stood with James on her hip. "Jeremiah might have agreed with the cowboys, but he still helped protect this town. He worked the land to help bring wealth to your family."

"She still takes up for him," Josiah slurred. "Even still."

Peter appeared nervous. He'd started bobbing, and the typewriter was back on his lap. He started typing until the clacking keys echoed.

Josiah said, "If he didn't like it, he could've left long before he was forced to."

Ellen said, "No, he stayed for the town. For your daddy and Orion and your mother's memory." Wilmington's shoulders slumped, and he wiped his eyes as she continued. "He stood nose to nose with the judge on the auction block when they started foreclosing our properties. He hijacked that train to stand up for the farmers."

Josiah looked away because he couldn't deny it.

Peter typed faster. Sister Moffitt motioned the sign of the cross and pulled rosary beads from a hidden pocket.

Sheriff McKinney said, "We've got no choice on this. If he comes back, we have to bring him in. He's a fugitive, a dangerous one. Won't be long before the state comes sniffing."

Dr. Craven, from his table, said stoically, "Government don't care about us out here. So what if he comes back? I'll take my chances." Dr. Craven shared a look with Wilmington, and both men nodded. Ellen couldn't help but think they knew something they weren't telling.

Deacon said, "Or he may come back and kill us all."

Toothache added, "Comeinstartflippingthatcoinandwhatnot."

"He's not going to kill anybody," Ellen said to Deacon, eyeing Toothache like she didn't know what he'd just said.

Josiah pointed the bottle. "There she goes again. Always protecting him."

"You can sleep in the living room tonight, Josiah Goodbye."

He mumbled something about that being just fine by him.

"The government is looking after us now," said Sheriff McKinney. "Roosevelt is a man of the people. The common man. And ever since one of these dusters lifted up and dumped dirt all the way to the nation's capital, they're starting to take notice. Those congressmen and such sitting in a room, watching dust fall outside their window. What's that, they said? That's Oklahoma and Kansas!"

"The rain will come." Orion forced a smile. "I can feel it." He motioned toward the redheaded newcomer sitting on the far side of the room, the rainmaker who, after two days of sending TNT into the sky, had yet to lure down that first drop. Ellen couldn't even remember his name. She was still gazing at Josiah with too much angst to remember much of anything. The past aside, how dare he call her out in front of everyone?

Orion wiped his brow, still smiling. "We will get through this. Nowhere will survive. Isn't that right, Wilmington?" Wilmington nodded. Orion straightened the lapels of his sport coat, and he too gave Dr. Craven a noticeable glance. "Nowhere will live on. And if Jeremiah comes back, we'll figure out the right thing to do."

"You need to kill him, is what needs to be done," said an unfamiliar voice.

All eyes shifted toward the swaying doors, which were open to the cool evening air. A tall man stood in the threshold. He wore suspenders and high-waist pants, a white button-down rolled up at the sleeves, and his thick mustache was as black as his eyes.

"And who might you be?" asked Orion, trying to be welcoming, but just plain tired.

The man took off his bowler hat and stepped deeper into the room. He pointed toward Josiah with the hat. "That him?"

"That who?" asked Josiah, stepping closer to the man.

"Coin-Flip Killer."

"No."

"You look just like'm."

"But I'm not."

"Where is he then? Or are you needling me?"

"I'm his brother. His twin. What do you want?"

"I want him to reverse what he's done."

"And what exactly did he do?"

Peter burrowed into Ellen's side as if trying to hide from the man. She whispered, "Do you know him, Peter?"

"Do you know him, Peter?" he whispered back with a couple of affirmative nods.

Josiah stepped closer, suddenly more sober than minutes before. "I'll say it again. What exactly did he do?"

"He flipped the coin, and it came up heads," said the man. "He put the rifle right to my head and was fixing to blow it off."

"Then why are you still alive?"

"I dunno."

"So he didn't pull the trigger?"

"No. Just said bang. Then he lowered the gun."

"He was toying with you," said Josiah. "That's what he does with that coin."

"Putting on some kind of curse is more like it." The man

surveyed the room and spotted Peter half-concealed behind Ellen. "Holy smokes, that's him. He stole that boy right out from under me. I was all set to buy him, and then that killer come along and muddied the waters."

Ellen put her arms around Peter and spoke to the man. "You stay away from him."

Peter trembled. His trousers showed a wet patch, and Ellen smelled urine.

Orion clenched his jaw. "I'm gonna ask you one more time. Who are you?"

The man faced Josiah, watched him like he still wasn't sure it wasn't Jeremiah. "Name's Benny. Friends call me Boo."

"That 'cause you're scary?" Josiah asked. "Or easily scared?"

Boo jerked backward. "That's what he said." He stared at Josiah with narrowed eyes. "You got a coin in your pocket?"

"I don't," said Josiah.

Boo nodded. "Okay, he had different eyes than you, and his hair was darker. So I suppose you ain't him. Okay now, so here's what I need. If you have any idea where he is, I need to find him before . . ."

"Before what?"

"Before he kills me."

"If he was gonna kill you, he would've done it right then and there."

"Well, I need him to unflip that coin."

"That's dumb," said Josiah. "You're dumb."

Wilmington said, "Josiah."

"I can't sleep," said Boo. "Can't even open my eyes without death breathing down my neck. It's coming—just don't know how. I'm changing my ways. Walking the straight. So I need him to reverse it."

"You can't unflip a coin," said Josiah.

Life drained from Boo's face. "Then that's it? I'm just gonna die?"

Josiah raised the bottle. "Never met a man that could undo that eventuality."

EIGHT

Sunlight woke Jeremiah Goodbye.

After a few blinks he remembered where he was—on the floor of a recently abandoned dugout. Only thing the family had left behind was a table they'd probably been unable to fit on their jalopy or truck or whatever had made those getaway tracks in the dust the day prior.

He hoped they found what they were looking for out west, or wherever it was they'd gone. Many of the Okies returned home, unwanted, quickly learning that while there may be greener pastures elsewhere—as in actual grass—the rest of the country was still living on the nut.

Jeremiah pulled himself up from the floor and brushed dust from his shirt. He retrieved his hat from where he'd left it on the table last night before deciding to stay until morning. He still had the coin Josiah had given him in his pocket. He'd need it to see where he'd go next.

Sunlight cut a path across the wooden tabletop, and right in the middle of it was the satchel he'd noticed last night. The dugout had been too dark then to open it up and see what it held. Jeremiah lifted it from the sunlight, and dust motes scattered. He took the satchel outside with him. The morning was warm, the sky as blue as freshly spread paint, the air so clear and clean it reminded him of when Nowhere was alive and fancy, when there was color on the ground and smiles on faces.

"Pinch me," he said, something Ellen used to say on picturesque mornings such as this, when together they'd stare up into the sky and wonder if the blue ever ended.

He opened the satchel and looked inside. It had clearly been packed for whoever purchased the boy, and evidently Peter had left it behind. There was a toothbrush and a neatly folded shirt he assumed was Peter's. A dog-eared book of nursery rhymes rested at the bottom, next to a five-inch-tall wooden statue carved to look like a cowboy with a lasso and a pocket watch with a busted face and no arms for time telling. A red candle burned down to a two-inch nub rested beside a stained brass holder that must have once enclosed it. A smooth rock tucked in a corner would have been perfect for skipping had there been any water anymore.

All personal items, seemingly, packed more thoughtfully than Jeremiah would have supposed from that mother, who'd been so eager to rid herself of the boy in the first place. He was better off with Ellen, anyway, so maybe taking him *had* been the right thing to do.

Wouldn't doubt if the boy had packed the satchel himself.

Jeremiah inhaled the pure air, and his brain cleared. There was no wind to move the dust. He gave the satchel one last glance and pulled out the nursery-rhyme book. On the inside of the front cover was an inscription: "For Peter Cotton, on the day of his birth—August 29, 1926." Which would make the boy almost nine. Jeremiah paused to let the significance of that date sink in, and then he slid the old book into the satchel.

"Pinch me," he said again, although now for a different reason, the date on that page still buzzing inside his head like a bee would. No need to flip the coin now. He knew where he had to go.

"Pinch me," Ellen said as she stared up into the endless blue sky.

James was restless in her arms. Even he had woken with more energy. She set him down on the porch. He walked toward the steps, and she didn't speak out to stop him as he navigated his way down. The wind wasn't blowing, so the dust stayed put. He wouldn't even need a damp rag to cover his mouth and nose.

"Morning, Ellen!" Across the street Orion stood in the dust that buried the front lawn of his hotel, which at one time had been manicured with grass and trimmed bushes and a colorful flower bed. He was dressed to the nines in a tuxedo and top hat, gazing up at the sky with his head tilted back so far she feared he'd topple over like a turtle. "Glorious," he said, puffing his cigar. "It's a sign, Ellen. I do believe the worst may be over."

Ellen nodded with a grin. It wasn't the first time he'd said it, although this morning did seem to hold more optimism than she could remember feeling since the boom. "Morning, Orion."

She didn't know if the worst was over or not, but what she saw in that sky was a calmness she hadn't seen in years, not months.

The winter had been the worst in a long time. February had been the coldest in four decades, with dwindling supplies of cow chips to heat the homes and winds so frigid the town folks were like to never find warmth. In January a duster had piggybacked a snowstorm, and the precipitation had fallen like globs of mud— Orion had called it a snuster instead of a duster, always trying to find some solace in the dreary. March had brought warmer temperatures but stronger winds that knocked men down and nearly toppled Jeremiah's old grain silo. Then there'd been dusters for thirty straight days, many of them blotting out the sun, the static electricity zipping and zapping day and night. They'd had to wrap the doorknobs with rags to protect them from the jolt.

Josiah had sworn the world was coming to an end, and he was in the majority.

To which Orion had responded with a smile, "Nothing in the Bible says the world will end in dust, Josiah. Hardship breeds the strongest of men."

Josiah had found no answer for that, unless a grunt could be construed as talking.

The door opened, and out walked Peter with his hands in his pockets. He must have kicked the screen open with his knee or foot, or maybe he'd done it with his head, which was reddened just over the brow.

"Morning, Peter," said Ellen.

"Morning, Peter." He walked on past her without even a glance, heading for the stairs James had just descended and then following in the younger boy's footsteps. The two of them walked in a circle that would have made Ellen dizzy.

"Walking in the dust," said James, in that rare moment free from the cough.

"Walking in the dust," said Peter, his shadow casting long across the yard and catching his attention as he walked.

Something rustled behind Ellen. She looked over her shoulder. Wilmington waved from the window. He'd just yanked a sheet from the glass. He came out a second later, inhaling the air so deeply his chest expanded.

"You sense a duster coming this morning?"

"Can't say I do, Ellen." He tipped his hat toward Orion across the street.

Moses Yearling, the man claimed to be a rainmaker and cloud-buster, had emerged from the hotel and was standing next to Orion with a box of TNT and rockets in his arms. The man's orange hair and mustache glistened in the sunlight and looked aflame.

"What's he doing with all that?" asked Wilmington.

"Suppose he's going to give his rockets another chance to bring down rain."

"No clouds in the sky, Ellen. What's he gonna shoot into?"

She shrugged, didn't much care. The sun felt too good on her cheeks.

By the second, more and more of the town folk stepped from their homes and places of business to take in the air and stare at the sky. No goggles or masks or anything, just their faces fresh in the daylight. The brooms got to whisking across porches. People unsealed doors and windows and opened them to the air. That man who called himself Boo was still in town, sitting on an exposed patch of roadside curb, elbows propped on his knees, his face tilted skyward like the rest of them. Must be still waiting for Jeremiah to return so he could unflip that coin.

William "Windmill" Trainer walked outside with a baseball and glove, and three more boys followed like ducklings, one of them with a bat dragging through the dust and eyes glued to the sky. Compared to the other boys, William *was* the size of a windmill, especially next to little Nicholas Draper, who looked up to Windmill more than any of them.

Windmill waved and said good morning, and so Nicholas did too.

Ellen chuckled. "Morning, boys. Enjoy the day."

"Oh, we will, Miss Goodbye." Windmill tipped his ball cap. Nicholas did likewise.

Wilmington sidled up to his daughter-in-law. "Haven't seen that smile in a while, Ellen."

"The day is pretty as a painting, and the first thing I imagine doing is washing all our dusty sheets. Let 'em air dry on the line and snap and ruffle in the wind like I remember as a kid."

"Suit yourself, Ellen. I might go for a walk."

Don't walk far, she nearly said. But it wasn't the day to play mother hen.

Where had Jeremiah gone to? Was he looking up into the same sky even now? She assumed he'd survived yesterday's duster, figuring she would have felt a tug somewhere had he not. Josiah certainly would have. Twins just had that connection.

The door opened behind them, and out came Josiah. She imagined his hair askew and his clothes rumpled from sleeping one off on the couch, but he didn't look hungover at all. He wore a clean white shirt rolled to the elbows and his Sunday trousers from back when they used to go to church. His hair was slicked back with pomade, and for once his cheeks weren't sagging from the weight of everything they'd had to endure.

She'd planned on giving him one day of silence from the way he'd spoken to her during last night's meeting—maybe two days, depending on his response. But the way he nodded and said, "Morning, Ellen" and then "Morning, Daddy," she just couldn't help but say good morning back, because that's exactly what it was.

A good morning.

Josiah bounded down the steps with more energy than she'd seen from him in months.

James yelled, "Daddy." It looked like Peter was about to yell it, too, but he caught himself.

Part of Ellen wished he had done it, just so she could see Josiah's reaction. A day would come soon when they'd have to discuss what to do with the boy if Jeremiah never came back. But that day wasn't today.

Josiah patted his son's head and fetched the shovel leaning against the house. At first Ellen thought he was going to start digging into the drift covering what used to be Wilmington's rose garden—they'd barely made a dent in it before Jeremiah showed up yesterday, and what they dug out had already been refilled by the afternoon duster—but instead Josiah walked right past the garden and approached their Model T. The wheels were half-buried in dust, the hood nearly covered in a drift, and the ceiling looked caved-in or at least dented from having too much dust on it for too long.

Josiah crunched the shovel blade into the dirt next to the driver's side.

Ellen said, "Where do you think you're going, Josiah?"

He tossed dust to the side. "Just thought it'd be a nice day for a drive, Ellen."

"By yourself?"

He paused midthrust with the shovel. "Figured we'd all go." He nodded toward Peter. "Even him, I guess."

It took Josiah and Wilmington ten minutes to get that Model T started, and when it did the car coughed enough dirt from the back end to get both Josiah and his daddy coughing.

They loaded inside as the car idled, every few seconds belching out more dust. Ellen volunteered to sit in the back between the two boys, but once back there James insisted on sitting next to Peter, so Ellen sat behind Wilmington. She couldn't help staring at that hairless spot above his left ear and hoping his first car trip wouldn't cause that bullet to move. Josiah was the last one in—he'd decided to remove the chains from the back bumper. There was no static electricity in the air, so nothing needed to be grounded. The car shook when he jumped in and closed the door, almost looking disappointed for a second as he noticed his daddy in the front with him instead of his wife.

At least that's how Ellen perceived it.

Suits him right. I'm no easy mark.

Before clanking the car in reverse he looked over his shoulder. "Now, we can't drive for long."

"Can't drive for long," echoed Peter.

"Ain't got too much gas, and we don't wanna run dry."

"Don't wanna run dry," said Peter.

"Run dry," said James.

Josiah gave his son a queer look, like he was afraid Peter was rubbing off on him in a bad way, but then James said, "Daddy drive a car."

That's better.

Josiah rolled his window down and he and Wilmington rode with their elbows hanging out as they drove toward the town center. Out in front of the courthouse, the sheriff was currying his skinny brown horse, and though the animal's ribs showed, its newly groomed coat shimmered in the sunlight. The horse neighed as they drove by.

Leland Cantain, who owned Nowhere's opera house—where

not a play or musical had been on stage in over a year—had taken a pause from his walk to help ruffle dust from chickens who were out scratching for bugs, and they seemed to like it.

Leland waved, and Josiah waved back.

Richard Klamp from Klamp's Clothing was giving his dog a bath outside his closed-up store. Josiah waved. Richard returned the gesture and said, "I'm getting ol' Harvest here ready for this afternoon."

Josiah slowed the car. "What's this afternoon?"

"You haven't heard? Orion just scheduled a rabbit drive for noon or thereabouts."

Josiah slapped the side of the car like he was excited.

Wilmington said to his son, "I was gonna tell you on the drive back. We decided today would be perfect for a rabbit drive. Get the morale in this town back up."

"Count me out," said Ellen. She didn't see what was so agreeable to everyone about those rabbit drives. It gave her nightmares—the brutality of it, the horror of all those rabbits dying.

"Oh, you have to come, Ellen," said Wilmington. "You're a leader in this town. Not coming would be seen as an act of defiance."

"Which is what it is."

"Peter here needs to see his first rabbit drive anyhow. Ain't that right, Peter?"

"Ain't that right, Peter?" Peter sat stoically, probably unaware of what the two men up front were talking about. "See his first rabbit drive anyhow. First rabbit drive."

"See?" said Wilmington. "He's looking forward to it." He faced forward again as they coasted past a two-story brick building that had housed a tractor and farm-equipment dealership during the boom but was now Nowhere Hospital, run by Sister Moffitt and two other nuns. Most everyone in there suffered from some kind of dust ailment, which Dr. Craven attended to daily. Ten patients now sat outside in the dust, breathing in the fresh air.

"You boys probably don't even know what today is," said Ellen.

"What's today?" asked Josiah.

"Your mother would be disappointed." She gave them another few seconds to guess, but they didn't offer any possibilities. "It's Palm Sunday. A week before Easter. You do remember what that is, don't you?"

"It's when the bunny comes with candy," said Josiah, winking at his daddy. "Ain't that right, James? Bunny comes with a bucket of candy."

"Not anymore he doesn't," Ellen said under her breath. "Perhaps a bucket of thistle."

"Now, now, Ellen," said Wilmington, sounding too much like his friend Orion. "There'll be no negative talk today. Not with a glorious rabbit drive to look forward to."

Josiah focused to make sure he was staying on the road. They'd rumbled over a couple of drifts, and the curb had disappeared. They throttled past a fence line where a dozen dead snakes hung belly-up under the sun, not doing a very good job of bringing moisture down from the sky. The locals were willing to try anything to produce rainfall.

"I'll make you a deal then," said Ellen. St. James's Church stood just to the right of the road, a simple white building with stained-glass windows and a steeple. Father Steven spent most of his time inside the church nowadays, when in the past he'd been a regular in the Bentley Hotel, playing cards and bingo with the three nuns and sometimes Pastor Johnson from Nowhere First Baptist. Father Steven was out now hammering a sign into the dust. He must have just painted it himself because the black letters still looked wet.

"Okay then, Ellen, what's the deal?" asked Wilmington.

She nodded toward the sign. "I'll go to your silly rabbit drive, but—"

Just then the sky exploded, and they all jumped. After a second they realized what the explosion was. Moses Yearling had just fired another one of his rockets into the sky.

Ellen shook her head. How much were they paying that man for producing nothing?

"You were saying?" asked Wilmington.

"I'll go to your silly rabbit drive, but only if the two of you accompany me to Mass this evening for Palm Sunday."

The two men glanced at one another, then each jerked a nod.

Ellen sat back in her seat, satisfied.

Then Wilmington said, "The rabbit drives aren't silly, Ellen. It's one of those . . . what do you call it?"

"Necessary evils," said Josiah, finding Ellen's eyes in the rearview mirror.

She folded her arms and looked away.

Just as she'd figured, the entire town turned up for the massacre.

The dusty wasteland where they now stood had once been acres of golden wheat, and before that, before the earth was plowed, it had been grassland where buffalo roamed and Indians lived in teepees. Now the jackrabbits were just about the only warm-blooded creatures to be found on it. They came out of the hills and mountains out west looking for food, multiplying in numbers not thought possible. And although Ellen would never admit it out loud, they were the town's most obvious source of food. A good rabbit drive could bring them up to ten thousand jackrabbits in only a couple of hours, and town folk could salt and can up enough rabbit meat from that to last the winter.

Orion had already announced that today's goal was twenty thousand, to which the crowd had cheered, pumping their baseball bats and clubs and rifles in the air like a bunch of savages. Now they were already deep into the drive—so many men and their sons, and dozens of women as well, herding thousands of rabbits into the pocket created by those chain-link fences across the way.

Peter and James stood mesmerized, not so much by the sight of it but the sound—the rumbling of so many jack feet pounding the dust, kicking up dust swirls as they sprinted and darted and tumbled over one another in one big pell-mell of panic. Ears and feet and tails and dust, corralled by the dogs and men on horseback. Shots fired, echoed, and the rabbits clumped blindly, funneling into the pit created by the fences.

Peter put his hands over his ears and watched the sky, where birds circled, returning from somewhere. Ellen wondered where the birds nested with no more trees around.

She looked away when they started clubbing the jackrabbits, just as she always did. The sound brought tears to her eyes. She wiped them, tightened her jaw, and tried to not let the boys see. The crying of those rabbits wasn't so different from the sounds the cattle had made when the government men came out to shoot them all for a dollar each. She supposed she'd fallen for Josiah long before that day, but after what he did that afternoon with those dying cows, and right in front of those government men, she'd never again questioned why she'd married him. *Another necessary evil.* The cows were going to die anyway. But she couldn't deny the fact that what Josiah had done had reminded her too much of Jeremiah, which was probably why none of them had ever spoken about it.

The jackrabbits again stole her focus.

Peter pushed his hands harder against his ears and closed his eyes so tight the skin around them wrinkled. His dimples disappeared as he puffed his cheeks out, holding in the air for a few seconds before letting out a loud cry of his own, an ear-piercing ululation that even got some of the clubbers to stop clubbing.

But not all.

Just then the circling birds started squawking, panicked like the jackrabbits, before they suddenly flew south in a cluster.

The jackrabbits that had yet to be corralled began defying the flow, and many sprinted south like the birds. Ellen picked up James to keep him from being trampled. He, too, had begun to cry, although not as loudly as Peter, who trembled now as thousands of jacks followed the birds, dozens of them brushing over their feet and ankles, fleeing in a panic.

More men stopped clubbing.

Nicholas Draper dropped his bat and watched the exodus of the birds as more joined the flight, all headed south. Ellen couldn't hear what Nicholas said to Windmill at that moment because of all the crying from Peter and James and the jacks, but she could read his lips: *What's going on?*

Windmill shook his head, looked around. He didn't know either.

The air felt different, like the pressure had shifted, although there was still no breeze.

The dogs that had been herding the jacks began sniffing the

air, and the horses, tails switching, did the same. One horse bucked his rider. Another spun in a circle, chasing its tail.

Wilmington approached, staggering, and then he dropped to one knee, clutching his temples.

"Wilmington!" screamed Ellen. Had the bullet just moved? She held James against her hip with one arm and coaxed Peter with the other. Peter wouldn't budge. Bringing him had been a bad idea.

Wilmington made it to his feet. "It's bad. Real bad, Ellen. The pressure."

"What pressure?"

"Like when I can feel a duster coming, except ten times worse." He winced, breathing heavy. "Where's Josiah? Where's Orion? We gotta go. Gotta shut this thing down."

The sky was still clear and blue. Nobody would believe him.

Ellen didn't believe him.

The day was too nice. Too perfect.

The rabbits' cries reverberated as if the dust had walls. Josiah was in the mix, beating those rabbits with a fury that made Ellen want to cry harder. Like he was taking out some deeply held rage.

She handed James over to Wilmington. "Hold him." She hiked up her dress and high-stepped into the scrum. Jacks sprinted through her legs and around her ankles. She told Nicholas Draper to head on home, and Windmill too. A big duster was on the way. They didn't question Miss Goodbye. None of the kids ever did. She took a bat right out of Dr. Craven's hands in midswing and told him to start getting people home. He'd started to ask why before noticing the seriousness in her eyes—she'd given him that look.

Ellen plowed on toward Josiah, screaming his name over and over until he finally looked her way.

He must have noticed the blood smear she now felt across her face. "Ellen?"

"Josiah, we've got to go. Something isn't right."

He looked to the sky, where the birds screeched in rhythm with the rabbits.

"Temperature's dropping." Josiah spotted Orion across the way. "Orion!"

Orion wasn't taking part in the actual clubbing—he was still in his tuxedo—but he was deep in the mix and puffing on his cigar. He removed the nub from his mouth when he saw Wilmington not taking part anymore. He was holding his grandson and motioning for him to come.

"We've got to go," Ellen screamed again. "A duster is coming. The mother of all dusters."

Josiah looked to be in a stupor. She grabbed his shirt atop his shoulder and yanked until he fell into a mound of dead jackrabbits. He got to his feet and followed her over the slain animals. And that's when she saw it, coming from the north, from Kansas—what she at first had mistaken to be the horizon because of the sheer width of it. But it wasn't the horizon. Horizons didn't move like that. It was the biggest and blackest duster she'd ever seen, stretching like pitch and tar for what had to be hundreds of miles east and west because she couldn't find the ends of it. It was an inch tall at first, but that quickly changed, growing by the second even though no sound yet accompanied the arrival and no breeze moved the air.

Orion stepped over the dead rabbits with his eyes peeled toward the dark line over the horizon. He dropped his cigar nub to the ground. "Run," he said first to Ellen and Josiah, lips moving with no more words coming out, probably calculating in his head how much dirt from how many states was coming their way.

And then his voice returned, loud enough to reach the town folk who hadn't already dropped their bats and clubs to do so and turn toward what was coming. "Run!"

Ellen rode in the back as she had on the way to the rabbit drive, except now she was in the middle, an arm around each boy as they watched out the window at all that growing blackness.

Josiah pressed hard on the gas, and the car responded, but not without a groan and some rumbling from the undercarriage. Dust swirled from so many cars leaving at once, panicked like Ellen had never seen during one of the dusters. Wilmington slumped forward with his fingers on his temples. She leaned up and touched his shoulder and asked if he was okay. He nodded but said nothing.

It was sunny like the entire day had been, and then all of the sudden it grew darker. The duster had stretched high enough to block out that same sun, like an entire mountain range had lifted from the earth.

Even as they watched it roll in, all was quiet and the air remained still. But that all changed in a snap. The wires connected to the poles began to hum. The temperature plummeted, the wind rushed in, and suddenly their car felt like it weighed nothing at all. Josiah did his best to keep control, but the doors rattled and the wheels shook.

Four hundred yards from town, their Motel T short-circuited and rolled to a stop. Josiah cursed and swore until James started crying again. Josiah hit the steering wheel with the meat of his hand, three times like hammer blows, and then he jumped from the car.

Static permeated the air. Ellen's arm hair tingled. *He shouldn't have removed the chains.*

There was no time to ponder. They'd have to walk the rest of the way. She ushered the boys out and opened the door for Wilmington, who took a minute to hunch over with his hands on his knees.

Dozens of other cars had stalled. Those that were still running had already picked up walkers until there was no more room in them. Those remaining hunkered away from the wind and closed their eyes to slits as abrasive dust began to clip their skin. They were totally unprepared—no masks, goggles, damp rags or nothing. Many of them had left their windows open at home to allow in the fresh air throughout the day, but all they'd be letting in now was what Wilmington had predicted to be the lifted soil from at least four states.

Peter was walking too slowly, stunned by the black, roiling wall preparing to bury them—like a tornado spinning sideways, picking up soil, chewing it up and slamming it back down to the ground as it moved—so Josiah picked the boy up and hurried on with him.

Grown men struggled to stay upright.

Ellen clenched her stomach muscles against the tumult and urged herself onward, trying like the dickens to keep the dust from James's face, which was practically buried against her chest. The main dust hadn't even hit them yet. It was approaching town like a great big wide open mouth, though, big enough to swallow all of Oklahoma and Texas and Kansas and Colorado in one big gulp.

Another car stalled—Dr. Craven's. He practically fell out as the door swung open, and he left it that way as he ran. He spotted

Ellen and their group and then came along to help Wilmington make his way back to town.

Their clothes rippled in the wind. An electricity pole splintered with a crunch and then snapped in half as the buzzing wires pulled it to the dust, the lines flashing with blue-fire current. A stalled car had both doors open on the north side, and a gust of wind picked it right up and overturned it. The Goodbyes avoided it as the car spun clockwise on its roof.

Roof shingles lifted from houses and flew through the air like fleeing birds. A shovel spiraled through the dusty air like a spear, and the blade stuck in Ned Blythe's barn door with a twang and wobble.

"Keep going," Ellen screamed like she was in a war zone. Josiah took the lead with Peter, doing his best to be the windbreaker as the Bentley Hotel loomed near. But the front edge of the duster had already swallowed the north side of Nowhere—First Baptist gone in a blink, the black rolling clouds now a good two thousand feet up into what minutes ago had been the sky.

The darkness grew as if everything it swallowed gave it energy. Every parcel of dirt that peeled away gave it fuel.

Ellen lowered her head as the dust grew heavier. But she had to see. They had to keep going. People were hiding under cars, ducking into sheds and outhouses. A blue Model T swerved into an electricity pole, and the front hood buckled. Steam hissed into the floating dust. The family inside quickly got out and started walking, the father ordering them to link hands like a human chain and hold on for their lives. "Whatever it takes, do not let go!"

It was a good idea, and they were not the only ones to do it. But Ellen needed both hands to secure James in the wind, and Josiah needed both to hold the larger Peter. Visibility was down to only a handful of feet. Finding their home would fall to instinct now.

The rolling dirt at ground level was coal black, and it hit them like a wall. Ellen dropped to her knees. James cried and coughed, but not as loudly as Peter. She could hear the boy but not see him or Josiah, even though she knew they were only a few feet away.

"Ellen," shouted Josiah.

"I'm here," she yelled back, taking in a mouthful of black dust, which she immediately tried to spit out. The void had become so real she couldn't tell if Josiah was in front of her or behind her now. She got to her feet and plowed into the wall, refusing to die like this. "Wilmington? Josiah?" No answer. *Why isn't Peter crying?*

The wind scoured off fresh dirt and slammed it back down as it rolled along, engulfing Nowhere. Static shot through cars, across power lines—lightning strikes that fizzled, unable to illuminate because the black dust was so thick. The duster roared like a tornado. Buildings splintered and cracked. Dust scraped and pinged off every surface as more and more soil ripped from the earth. James's tears muddied his face, but it was so black she could barely make out his eyes. She couldn't see her own hands, so she increased the pressure of her hold.

"Ellen?" It was Josiah again, but he sounded far away. "Ellen?" Closer this time, but then his voice faded.

"Josiah?" She ate more dust and hacked and coughed until her eyes bulged. This dirt was different than the other dusters, like the wind had gone deeper into the soil to lift up what had been dormant for centuries—dirt mixed with the blood and bones from all those buffalos and Indians killed in order for the white men to take over the land.

Where was Jeremiah? Was he stuck out in it like they were

or already dead from yesterday's duster? Dust stung her eyes like bees. A wind gust knocked her down again, but she managed to keep hold of James. She got to her feet and continued on, hoping it was in the right direction. There was no way to tell. No markers. Nothing but roiling, black, coal-like dust.

An arm brushed her shoulder, and then a powerful hand gripped her elbow. "I've got you," said Wilmington. The only father she knew, hers having passed years ago. He knew Nowhere like the back of his hand, had always claimed he could walk the town blindfolded. Now was his chance. But how was he still on his feet? How had that bullet not moved yet?

She heard his voice but couldn't see his face. "I've got you," he said again as they stumbled together through the tumult. "Keep your face down," he said. "Chin to your chest and protect my grandson." She did just that and held on for dear life, counting off the seconds in her head until they formed minutes.

The bell inside the Bentley Hotel chimed, once, twice, three times, but even it sounded dust-muted. Orion must be safe inside. He was ringing the bell to give people an audible landmark. *We must be close.* Her foot hit something hard. Wilmington guided her hand to a wooden railing. The steps up were familiar. They'd made it.

"Ellen!" It wasn't a question this time. She saw the whites of her husband's eyes and the relief they held. He ushered her and James and Wilmington inside and did his best to close the door against the dusty drift that had formed inside the threshold. Coughing resonated like echoes in a cave, not only in their house but across the town as the duster roared through like a train, scraping and peeling and boiling and slamming dirt like fist falls from a God who'd abandoned them.

Josiah lit a lamp as they all gathered in the kitchen, where Wilmington had resealed the windows before they left for the rabbit drive. *Just in case*, he'd told Ellen. But even with the windows covered, so much dirt still spun through the house that all they could see of each other in the lamplight was silhouettes. The walls creaked. The wind howled. Dust clicked and clacked off the roof like dice on wood, except louder, magnified and incessant.

Wilmington found a blanket and draped it over the large kitchen table. Josiah weighted the blanket down with a box full of horseshoes, and then they all gathered underneath, with the lamp. Then, finally, Ellen could make out features from some of their faces—Wilmington's right eyeball. Josiah's hair. Peter's hands—he'd somehow been aware enough to drag that typewriter down with him and was punching the keys. Ellen wiped muddy tears from James's face and cleared caked dirt from his nostrils and mouth. For a second she feared he'd stopped breathing, but he was just eerily calm—or terrified—blinking enough to show he was alive.

The clacking of the typewriter keys took their attention from the horrifying sounds of the duster. Peter's fingers working faster and faster, but controlled somehow, like there were words connected to the key strikes and not just some random punching.

Outside cried a voice, a woman's voice, distraught. "Nicholas! Nicholas. Oh, dear God—where are you? Nicholas?"

Ellen's heart skipped. "Nicholas Draper." She made a move as if to duck back out from under the kitchen table, and Wilmington stopped her.

"No, Ellen."

"Nicholas Draper. He's one of my students. He must be lost. He's out there, Wilmington."

"Nicholas . . . Nicholas . . ."

Without noticing exactly when, she could make out all of their faces now under the kitchen table. They were all coated with black dust, like coal miners.

Josiah sat with his legs folded, rocking slightly forward almost like Peter, staring so intently at the kerosene lamp in the center of where they sat that he almost looked right through it. Had he even heard Mrs. Draper calling for her son?

Just two nights ago Ellen had been locked in the schoolhouse with the students. She recalled Nicholas telling the story about a cow that was full of dust when they cut it open. She imagined him now, lost and alone, swallowed up in the dust and breathing it in like his cow must have before it died.

"I'm going," she said.

But then Josiah's voice stopped her cold. "It's okay, Nicholas. I've got you." He continued to rock, blinking intermittently, so focused on the lamp that Ellen feared it might combust. Josiah was there in body, but it was like the inside of him had jumped clean out and been replaced by someone else. Even the voice was slightly off. He blinked finally. "Stay hunkered down, Nicholas. That's your name, right? Everything's gonna be fine." He pretended to be rubbing something that wasn't there.

"Josiah?" said Ellen. "What's going on?"

He didn't answer. Instead he hunkered down even lower, as if shielding someone.

"Nicholas . . ." Mrs. Draper was out there still calling for her son. Ellen shifted under the table. "I've got to go help."

"He's fine, Ellen." Josiah sounded more like himself again. "He's got him."

"Who's got him, Josiah?"

"Jeremiah."

"What?"

"Jeremiah," Peter repeated, still typing. "Jeremiah's got him."

Ellen gulped. It was like a dream had invaded a nightmare and she was only half-lucid through both. Dust poured atop the house, atop the town. *Must be what it sounds like to be alive in a coffin and buried as the soil is shoveled on top.* The wind howled. A window shattered. Dust swooped across the floor with the shattered glass and skittered under the blanket-curtain. They all started coughing. *How long have we been in the house? How long were we on the road? How long can this nightmare last?*

"He's fine," repeated Josiah in a distant voice, hunkered over like a turtle under a shell, protecting something imaginary beneath him. "Trust me. He's got him."

Ellen closed her eyes and waited and waited and waited until she could wait no more. Then she handed James to Wilmington and rolled out from beneath the table. The air had already begun to brighten, but dust motes still hovered. The duster had not lasted as long as some but had most assuredly dumped more soil than any before it. She could see the front door across the room, a sliver of light beside the sheet covering the window, glass on the floor. She heard crying across the town, more desperate than what they'd heard from the jackrabbits. She grabbed a mask from beside the door and secured it around her head.

"Ellen, what are you doing?" Josiah had slid out from beneath the table. "It ain't safe yet."

She opened the door and stepped outside to the porch, which was covered in dust so black it didn't look real. Didn't look possible. How deep had that wind cleaved into the earth to find dirt that black? Clouds of it still swirled and floated, but the black wall had passed over the town and was on its way to Texas, the sheer size of it nearly as horrifying on the back end as it had been from the front. She had no way to warn those poor souls still in the path, who were probably now out enjoying the sun and blue sky much like they'd been doing before Armageddon had come in the form of dust.

On the ground, so much was covered. Cars and mailboxes and fences and tractors were all mounds of black. Small dust tornadoes spun as the wind swept on and the temperature dropped even further. But visibility increased by the second. Flecks of blue sky showed through the haze.

Josiah joined her on the porch, coughing into his fist.

"Put a mask on, Josiah."

He didn't. He surveyed the town same as she did and probably came to the same conclusion—it was a wasteland, a terrible wasteland that couldn't be real. This was not her country anymore. Not her Oklahoma panhandle. Not her Nowhere.

Mrs. Draper wandered about like a blind woman, covered from head to toe in black. She wiped at her caked eyes.

Ellen slid down the mound of dirt that covered their porch steps and hurried to her. "Don't wipe at them, Loreda. It'll only push the dirt deeper."

"Who is this?"

"It's Ellen. Ellen Goodbye."

"Nicholas? Where's my son? We were holding hands. He slipped from my grip, and I lost him. I lost him, Ellen." Loreda Draper collapsed in the dust, and Ellen knelt beside her, not sure what to do or where even to take her. Her eyes looked buried under an inch of muddy gunk. She couldn't even see any lashes or eyebrows.

More dust cleared, blue sky emerged, and sunlight penetrated, scattered in crisscrossing rays. Those that were willing stepped from their homes and churches and barns and businesses, coughing and hacking and crying in equal measure.

The grain silo that had held the source of so much wealth during the boom had been knocked to the ground, burying that awful place where Josiah had seen Jeremiah bury the bodies.

Ellen peered down Main Street, where a thick cloud of dust broke apart in swirls, revealing what looked like the silhouette of a person kneeling.

The rest of the town saw it too, because many of them were pointing, walking closer to see if it was a live person or some kind of horrid, calcified dust sculpture.

"Stay with Loreda," Ellen said to Josiah. She took off her mask and joined the group walking down Main Street. They stopped their march when they figured out who it was there in the middle of the road, completely covered in black dust.

"Jeremiah?"

He looked up and turned his neck, rooting for her voice. Beneath him lay a dusty heap of clothing and two little shoes that didn't move.

Nicholas . . . Ellen stepped closer.

The shoes moved, a flinch at first and then an all-out slide. A head emerged from the bundle, groggy. It was a boy, all right. Then he coughed.

"Nicholas," said Ellen.

The boy wiped his face. "Mrs. Goodbye?"

Ellen's lip quivered as the boy ran toward her. She took Nicholas in her arms and nearly hugged the life out of him. By that point Josiah had gotten Loreda to her feet, and they were on their way over, a mother reunited with a son she'd thought dead only moments ago. A son she could feel but not see.

Jeremiah looked lost in the eyes, similar to what she'd seen with Josiah under that kitchen table, shielding an imaginary Nicholas Draper just as Jeremiah had been out in the heart of the worst duster ever, protecting the real boy.

Josiah stared at his twin like he didn't believe he was really there.

Ellen stepped closer. How was he still alive? Out in all that black dust without any protection? "Jeremiah?"

He flinched, staggered, and went back down on one knee. He had a satchel in his arms. His hands trembled when he opened it. "Peter's last name is Cotton."

"What's in the satchel?" she asked.

"His things," said Jeremiah, blowing upward to clear dust from his face. "And I may know now when he was born."

Ellen's heart rate sped faster than what was normal or safe, and her legs suddenly felt like melting butter. Her voice cracked. "When was he born, Jeremiah?"

"Same day."

Ellen's jaw trembled, and the lump in her throat made it hard to breathe.

Josiah said, "What's he talking about, Ellen?"

"Summer of twenty-six," said Jeremiah. "August twenty-nine."

Same day.

How was it even possible?

Ellen dropped to the dust on both knees. Then she settled her weight on her heels and cried.

NINE

No one swept out after the duster this time.

They'd been in the ring of a prizefight, and this was the final blow that put them on the canvas. No point getting back up. No point fighting the fight they couldn't win. The land was just too strong and mean and too determined to break them.

Just as they had broken it.

Ellen helped Loreda Draper back to her home and took thirty minutes to clear the muddy gunk from her eyes, removing the dirt in layers, rinsing and sloshing a rag in a bucket of well water Nicholas and Windmill had to change every five minutes. Even as she worked on Loreda, her mind was on Jeremiah and what he'd said about Peter and when he was born.

Orion and Wilmington, soon after the duster moved on, had gathered all that were able to case the town and make sure everyone was accounted for. Both Jeremiah and Josiah had joined them. They'd gone to opposite sides of the cluster of men who'd gathered, every one of them too numb to give Jeremiah's return to town much thought. They would deal with that later, and more than likely it would come to a vote. One thing Ellen knew for certain, and she'd be vocal about it when decision time came—Nicholas Draper would have died out in the duster if not for Jeremiah.

Dr. Craven entered the Drapers' house soon after Ellen found Loreda's eyes. *But what took him so long?* His face was still caked with black dust, and he hadn't even brought his leather satchel of medical supplies. He stopped next to Loreda's bed and just stood there, staring over the patient and toward the dusty sheet flapping against the window across the room.

Ellen snapped her fingers in front of his face. "Dr. Craven?"

"Yes?" he said, his eyes not moving from the window. "What is it, Ellen Goodbye?"

"I got her eyes cleared. Thought maybe you should give them a look."

"All I can see is black," Loreda said from the bed. "Nicholas, where'd you go?"

Nicholas gripped her hand. "I'm right here, Momma. Ain't going nowhere."

"Dr. Craven?" Ellen said again. "Please."

Dr. Craven glanced at Loreda but then returned his gaze toward the window. "She's blind now, Ellen. Can't you see that?" His voice was uncharacteristically stoic and monotone. He'd made a habit of comforting his patients with a bedside manner that made them smile no matter the prognosis. Now he put a liver-spotted hand on Loreda's shoulder, and just when Ellen sensed the bedside manner coming, the doctor said, "You'll probably never see again, Mrs. Draper. Darkness until the end of your days is what I think. Get used to bumping into things and feeling around with your hands. Maybe your boy here will help you about, but I don't know; truth be told, he's never come across as all that bright."

Nicholas stared up at the doctor, the man who'd delivered

him, the man who'd delivered most everyone in town. The boy's eyes filled with tears.

Windmill clenched his hands into fists as if he might strike the old man.

Dr. Craven looked at Windmill next. "You need to stop your daydreaming, son." He gestured toward Ellen. "She's too old for you. Not enough days to close that gap, either. She thinks it's cute, those feelings you have for her, but you're only a boy, Windmill. Her words, not mine." He winked. "Only a boy."

Windmill was the tallest in the room, already three inches taller than the doctor, but he now seemed to shrink and shrivel next to Nicholas. Windmill looked at Ellen, and she looked away. She'd said it, sure as that rain that never fell. She'd said it one day over coffee with the doctor, how she thought it was cute that Windmill carried a torch for her. *"But he's only a boy."* Windmill dropped down into an armchair next to the window and said nothing.

Dr. Craven turned on his heel and headed for the hallway, but then stopped suddenly. "I'll send my bill in the mail."

Ellen caught up to him before he left the house. "Doctor, what is wrong with you? You had no right to say those things."

Dr. Craven raised a crooked index finger and swiped it across his cheek. He showed her the layer of dust on it. "Want to try it?"

"No."

He put his finger in his mouth and licked that dust clean off. "Can you feel it, Ellen Goodbye?"

"Feel what?" she asked, too horrified to think clearly.

"This dust was different. Like it was alive." He tapped the side of his head hard enough for it to echo, like knuckling a wooden tabletop. "It's in there now, Ellen. Munching away." He gripped the front doorknob and flinched from a jolt of static electricity still lingering. "You know what your mother told me right before she breathed her last breath?"

Ellen shook her head. She didn't want to know. She'd lost both of her parents to the white death a month apart, first her father and then her mother. They'd been quarantined in a room with several other tuberculosis patients in what was now Nowhere's hospital.

Dr. Craven told her anyway. "In those last minutes she talked to me like I was her preacher. Your father was intending to be one of those suitcase farmers—rape the land and run with buckets of money."

"Don't."

"But I feel like I have to, Ellen. It's like the dust did something to my filter."

"What filter?"

"The one that keeps the bad stuff in," he said. "This dust—it just seems to make all the truths come out. And it's about time. Just plain old dirty-truth medicine is what all this calls for." *What's wrong with him? Why is he doing this?* He put a gentle hand on her forearm, but it was no longer comforting like it had once been. "Your mother begged your father to stay here in Nowhere, but not because she thought the air was better for her lungs, like she'd told him. It was because she was in love with another man. Another man right here in Nowhere."

Ellen didn't believe him, and at the same time she wanted to know who it was. But she couldn't muster enough air to ask. It felt like she was choking on the doctor's evil dose of medicine.

"What was said was said and can't be unsaid, Ellen. Just like Jeremiah can't unflip a coin even if he wanted to."

"What are you talking about?"

He winked. "I don't know." Dr. Craven placed his dusty bowler hat on his head and nodded. "Good day, Mrs. Goodbye." And he walked right out the door.

She watched, stunned, and then followed him outside, where she shouted for him to tell her who that other man was. But all Dr. Craven did was wave without turning around.

Ellen's legs trembled and her stomach churned, and she suddenly felt panicked about James and Peter before remembering that Sister Moffitt was keeping an eye on them both while the dust settled.

The men who'd gone door-to-door to account for the town folk began to return and cluster in the middle of Main Street, probably ten paces from where they'd found Jeremiah curled over Nicholas Draper. Ellen slid down a slope of black dust until her feet found level enough ground to walk on and approached the gathered men. Josiah and Jeremiah stood apart from one another. Wilmington was in the middle of the men, alongside Orion, who couldn't even fake a smile as blue sky returned.

Ellen caught the gist of their mumbling. Everyone in town was accounted for, which was a miracle in itself, a miracle that on a typical postduster day would have been celebrated with some bingo and beverages inside the Bentley. But all the men did now was stare and mull on unsaid words. Stare at each other. Stare at the blue sky. Stare at all that black dust. Stare at the tail end of the black blizzard that was now a mere sliver of horizontal black in the distance.

Dr. Craven had passed on by and headed for his home. He stumbled twice on the dirt mound covering his front steps, and none of the men made a move to help. Finally Dr. Craven made his way up. He brushed off his trousers and headed inside. The door closed behind him with an echoed click.

Ellen studied the gathered men, studied their faces and their eyes to see if they showed any signs of what had happened to the doctor. Had the living dust entered to munch away on their minds like Dr. Craven said it'd done on him? Had the dust done something to their filters? The men gulped and spat to the ground, each one looking as defeated as the next, and no one spoke.

Ellen's voice was weak, but her words cracked through. "We were all lucky to have lived through it, I suppose."

"Were we though, Ellen?" asked Josiah, grinding the dust stuck in his teeth, his eyes spotting something across the road next to Leland Cantain's mailbox, which was buried except for the tiny yellow flag slanting up as if in surrender. Josiah moved through the crowd, and the men parted for him. He'd honed in on a mound of black dirt that at first looked no different than the rest of the mounds around town—except this one, Ellen noticed as she followed her husband, had three fingers sticking up from the surface.

Josiah squatted as the rest of them circled around the mound. With his right hand he shoveled dirt away from the fingers to expose a hand, then a rigid forearm and an elbow.

Ellen covered her mouth but couldn't look away. If everyone in town had been accounted for, who was that buried beneath the dust?

Josiah had changed course, moving away from the arm, probably figuring they wouldn't know until they uncovered the head, which, according to where Josiah moved, was probably buried a foot or so to the right. After another twenty seconds of digging, Josiah found hair, and soon thereafter a nose and two eyes and a mouth, all open to the dust.

Josiah didn't look surprised at who it was. None of the men did, including Ellen as she stepped closer to get a better look. The only one to look stunned was Jeremiah.

But it was that man all right. That man who had called himself Boo and had come to town hoping for Jeremiah to unflip that coin before death found him.

Too late for that.

One by one they all looked at Jeremiah like they were hoping he'd say something, provide them with some sort of an answer. But all he did was purse his lips and say, "I'll go get a shovel. Suppose we should bury him proper."

TEN

The Worst family had been the first to leave Nowhere when the soil started peeling from the earth, and according to Ellen, folks hadn't been sad to see them go. Mr. Worst and his wife were both as crotchety as a handful of cats in a bag. Their son, William, had been, for lack of a better word, the worst of them all.

Worst of the Worsts, thought Jeremiah, unable to conjure the energy to chuckle at what he and Josiah had once thought funny. William Worst and the twins had a history, one Jeremiah wasn't yet ready to face in light of the latest happenings with that dead man, Boo. Which was probably why Josiah had recommended, if Jeremiah was going to chance staying in town for even one night, that he stay in the abandoned Worst house a few houses down.

"See what kind of memories those walls conjure," Josiah had said, deadpan.

Jeremiah tested a floor lamp next to a dust-covered sofa. As he'd figured, the house had no electricity. The sun was going down, but what bled through the grimy windows showed floors so caked with dust that the inside didn't look much different than out. It would take him days to clean up the place, if he stayed that long. Half the town probably considered that man Boo to be another one of his victims and, with the past being the way it was, he couldn't blame them. But in this case he felt no responsibility or guilt for that man's death, despite the fact that he did indeed flip that coin.

Jeremiah's legs suddenly felt wobbly. He sat down on the sofa without even wiping the dust from the cushions. The fact that he no longer had the nightmares didn't mean he couldn't remember what had been in them, and the memories could hit like a gut punch. Darkness twisted by swirls of light. Rushes of loud noise and muted silence, his body pulled and tugged by shadows. Excruciating pain followed by no feeling at all. Air so thick it was unbreathable.

The darkness swallowed him up—deep and bottomless with nothing to catch him as he fell, sightless, screaming, the unexplainable fear palpable like a heartbeat as it slowed, and slowed. Then suddenly there was a light. A pinprick grew to the size of a baseball, and then his vision filled with brightness.

The gasp of air, like he'd been holding his breath too long underwater.

The nightmare ended the same way every time.

"You can't have me," Jeremiah said aloud, sitting on that sofa the Worst family had left behind, that ray of waning sunlight shining through the window now down to a sliver. He recognized that darkness from his nightmare for what it was, evil, and he sensed the beginning of something spreading about town. From some of the exchanges of words between the town folk as they gathered earlier to search for the injured—meanness when there just wasn't any reason for it—he'd recognized that something was amiss. Then he'd heard from Ellen what Dr. Craven said inside the Drapers' house. Jeremiah knew now that something bad had come from that dust and that it had begun to change the town like his nightmare had begun to change him years ago.

He stood from the sofa and looked out the window, but suddenly the encroaching darkness out there made him antsy. He found a broom in the kitchen and busied himself sweeping in what little daylight remained. He started in the front room, working outward from the far corner next to the window, and found the whisking sound against the hardwood somewhat soothing. He glanced out one of the front windows, half expecting the town folk to be arriving soon with pitchforks and flaming torches. He was surprised Sheriff McKinney hadn't tried to lock him up, especially after they found Boo in the dirt. They all knew he'd flipped that coin. They'd witnessed the fear in the man's eyes the night before, sensing that kiss of death over his shoulder.

Jeremiah shook his head. That man's luck had just finally run out. "Got what was coming to him," he said to himself, using his finger to sweep a clump of dust from the windowsill. Before Old Sparky, when he'd brush up against a bad one, a vision would flash through his mind like a talkie film on speed loop. With Boo there had been no such vision. Just a feeling, a hunch, like a radio voice trying to break through bursts of static. Jeremiah had had to lean in close to catch a whiff of it, which was why he'd ultimately flipped that coin anyway. He'd flipped the coin on those other four men who ended up dead too. But with Boo, the why of it had been fuzzy.

Sheriff McKinney had looked too stunned to bring him in, like his mind couldn't comprehend exactly what had just happened. So he'd turned from that quick burial, entered his house without a word, and closed the door behind him.

Jeremiah could tell even as he swept that this dirt was different—darker, thicker, grittier. The heaviness of it scratched the floorboards as he pushed it along. Before the light faded completely, he'd need to find some candles or kerosene lamps. He went back to the kitchen and looked through all the cabinets. In the first two he found nothing, but in the third he sensed movement. He hunkered down for a better look and found himself nose to nose with a family of tarantulas.

He fell back on his butt and crab-walked away, his fingers digging trenches in the dust covering the floor. And then something skittered over his hand. Another tarantula. He jumped to his feet, found a dented pot on the ancient stove, and brought it down three times until that spider didn't move anymore. By that time the room had turned dark. It could have been his imagination, but it sounded like spiders crawled all over the walls, like the entire home was infested with tarantulas.

Had Josiah known it? Was that why he'd offered up the Worst house? Jeremiah hoped not. Ellen never would have agreed that he stay there if she had known. Luckily the moon was out and a faint glow permeated, enough that he didn't have to feel his way through the house and risk accidently touching one of those tarantulas.

He shook his head. Part of him wished he was back inside the prison walls, where the world couldn't get its claws into him. Wished that jolt in Old Sparky had taken him to his grave.

Someone knocked on the front door, and his heart lurched. Probably Sheriff McKinney coming with his wrist shackles. He still had the dented pot in his hand and couldn't remember where he'd put his shotgun.

"Jeremiah?"

He sighed in relief, dropped the pot to the dusty floor, and hurried to the door. Ellen stood on the porch with a box in her hands. Peter held the typewriter.

"Can we come in?"

He backed away, and in they came—quickly, like they were trying not to be noticed. At least that's how Ellen moved. The smiling boy didn't seem to care.

Ellen put down the box and rooted inside of it. She lit two candles, placed them on the table, and the room hazed with dust motes.

"Josiah know where you are?"

"I can go wherever I please, Jeremiah." He'd always loved her toughness. Nobody ever crossed Ellen Maverick more than the once without a lesson learned, and as Ellen Goodbye she was still no easy mark. No man could tell her what to do.

She said, "He was at the kitchen table when I left, but I don't think he even noticed me. His eyes were open, but all I saw was sleep inside. Like that dust . . ." She paused, chewed on her lower lip like she was wrangling with herself about something. "There was something different about this duster, Jeremiah. And I'm not talking about how big and dark it was. It was something else."

"I sensed the same, Ellen." But he didn't want to get into it either. Peter had just gone into the back bedroom with a lit candle, and he feared the boy might burn the house down. A minute later they heard a broom whisking across hardwood. Dust clouded into the hallway as the boy pushed it out. Dust motes took on another form altogether in that hazy nimbus of light shining from the bedroom. "What's he doing here?"

Ellen folded her arms and scoffed. "Said he wants to stay with you."

"He said that?"

"No, not with his own words. But after we all returned inside, it didn't take but a minute and he was standing by the front door with that typewriter in his arms and that satchel over his shoulder, staring out the window at the Worst house. I said, 'Are you wanting to stay with Jeremiah? In that old, nasty house?'"

"What'd he say?"

"What do you think he said? Said my exact words right back to me. So here we are." She cleared dust from what was once the dining room table and pulled out two chairs. "Sit," she said, like he was a dog and she the trainer. She pulled the nursery-rhyme book from the satchel and opened it to the inside front cover, where that date had been written. Tears pooled in her eyes. "Now, what's this about?"

Jeremiah wiped his seat off and sat catty-corner from her at the table. "I found it in the dugout. The mother left it behind."

"I know that. I mean, what's it *about*, Jeremiah?" Her lip quivered, and her hands shook. Jeremiah moved as if to grab them, but she reeled them back. "The boy was born on the same day we lost ours in the miscarriage." She sniffled, wiped her eyes. "The exact same day, Jeremiah. And don't come back spouting 'coincidence,' because I won't buy it." She pointed down the hallway, where more dust filtered from the back bedroom. "He's the same boy."

"Can't be the same boy, Ellen."

She pounded the tabletop, and for a moment the broom stopped whisking across the floor back there. When it resumed, she said, "It's the same face, Jeremiah. Same eyes and hair and dimples I've seen every night when I closed my eyes and got to imagining what he must have looked like. And when he does talk . . . the voice . . ."

He reached across the table to grab her hands, and this time she let him.

"I don't know, Ellen, but it's why I walked back through that duster when I did. To try to get some answers for you. For us."

At the word *us* she slithered her hands from his and he felt part of his heart drop, but it was a feeling he'd needed to feel because things weren't what they once were. She was married to Josiah now, and they had a kid of their own. *As it should be. As it was meant to be all along.* He put his elbows on the table and intertwined his fingers to keep them busy. "Maybe I was meant to stumble upon him, Ellen. Like a collision course neither one of us had the ability to stop. Two trains rumbling across that same track."

"Like fate?"

"Something of the like."

She fixed a strand of hair behind her ear, and his heart lurched. "I've been thinking," she said. "Ever since when I first saw him and passed out in the kitchen. What if . . . ?"

"Go on."

"You'll think I'm off the tracks."

"Wouldn't ever."

She filled her lungs with a deep breath. "What if, when a couple loses a baby . . ." She shook her head.

He finished for her. "What if that baby is somehow born somewhere else?"

She suppressed a grin at the same time her jaw quivered. "Yes." She gained courage, and her thoughts flowed. "Not the same baby, Jeremiah, but . . . but what if when one dies, something of his life goes into another. Like a part of him is still out there living. Even if it's a small part."

He nodded and wanted to agree with her to the core—Peter had to be explained in some way, didn't he?—but deep down he didn't know. It didn't make much real-world sense, but neither did the life he'd been living since he was born. And truth be told, her theory had formed a ball in his gut that was growing bigger the more he thought on it.

When a baby dies, another is given life . . .

According to Wilmington, his birth had been an arduous one, one that had nearly killed his mother, but whenever he'd questioned him on it his daddy always waved it away, never getting into the details that Jeremiah knew were there. Something had happened that morning that Wilmington refused to tell—as well as Orion and Dr. Craven. And that something had everything to do with the nightmare that had plagued him his entire life, up until Old Sparky put a stop to it.

"What's going through that mind of yours, Jeremiah?"

He looked up and locked eyes with her. "My nightmare was always the same. It never wavered."

"As you've said."

"One night I woke from it, sweating. Me and Josiah were ten, going on eleven." He wiped his face and exhaled. "Josiah asked if I was okay. I told him I was. He said he could tell whenever I was having the nightmare and wished he could be there too. I told him never to wish such a thing and to go back to bed. And I thought he'd done just that. So I settled back into my pillow, craving sleep I knew would come, because I never had the nightmare twice in a night. But then he says, 'Jeremiah, every one of them nightmares lasts the exact same amount of time.' 'How do you know?' I asked him. And he points to the wall clock and says, 'I count the seconds until they're over. That's how I get us both through.'"

"Both?"

"When I woke that night, he was kneeling beside my bed. That's when I first realized what he'd been doing since we were little. When the nightmare would start, he'd come over and hold my hand for the duration."

Ellen teared up again, then covered her mouth. Her hand trembled.

"One minute and fifty-one seconds," said Jeremiah. "Josiah had timed it down to the second, and it was the exact same every night. Even in the heart of my nightmare, I could feel the pressure on my left hand, like something or someone was squeezing it. I learned that night what it was. Who it was." Jeremiah leaned back in his chair, folded his arms. "Some things, Ellen, don't need to be explained, or maybe they can't be. Peter, my nightmare . . . that man Boo we just found buried in the dust. 'Cause sometimes the answers ain't what we want to hear."

They sat silent for a moment. A soft breeze sent dust tapping against the window and then settled. Ellen closed the book of nursery rhymes and the date along with it. She slid it across the table toward Jeremiah.

"You keep it," he said.

She stood from the chair and didn't argue, hugging that book close to her heart.

Peter had stopped sweeping in the back bedroom and begun tapping the keys on that typewriter again. They followed the sounds into the hallway, stepping over the dust he'd recently added to what had already accumulated there.

Jeremiah stopped in the doorway with Ellen by his side. She clutched his arm and rested her head against his shoulder. The floor was free of dust. In the middle of the bedroom Peter sat at a small wooden desk, smiling in the candle glow, and typing away like he was deep into some long overdue clerical work. Around him he'd carefully placed all those knickknacks Jeremiah had found inside the satchel with the book. The broken pocket watch rested to the side of the carved cowboy with the lasso, and every so often the boy would glance at the frozen time as he typed, never breaking stride. He never looked up to see them watching, although Jeremiah sensed that the boy knew exactly what they were doing and exactly what they were thinking.

Taking a moment to imagine what never was and never could be.

ELEVEN

Ellen woke the next morning and fixed a pot of black stovetop coffee.

The sun hung high in a clear blue sky, so reminiscent of yesterday that she dared not go outside yet. She peeked out the window. Nobody else was outside either. Nobody was digging out.

The kitchen was full of dust from yesterday's storm, the duster of all dusters, and now that she got a good look at the particles in the daylight, that dust was most certainly different than the others. It was definitely a darker color, as if peeled from a deeper layer than what had previously been pulled from the earth. It looked thicker too. She rubbed a little between her fingers and remembered what she'd felt on her skin during the blow. It was coarser. Sharper.

She wiped dust from one of the kitchen chairs and sat down with her steaming coffee. What kind of life was this? But maybe yesterday was the worst of it. Maybe from here on out the storms wouldn't be as bad.

She sipped coffee and burned the tip of her tongue but hardly felt the pain of it. Had she become that numb?

She had a notion to walk over to Dr. Craven's house and pour the hot coffee over his old, liver-spotted head. He'd had no right to talk to Loreda Draper like he'd done. *And then what he said to me about my own mother staying in town because she loved another man? What nonsense is that?*

The coffee had already made her fidgety. She left the half-empty cup on the table and stood. A chuckle emerged like a burp. She'd never even thought *half-empty* before today. She'd always been a half-full kind of girl, striving for the sunny-side-up of things, not too unlike Orion across the street. But not now. Half-empty seemed appropriate.

Maybe it was the dust talking, like the doctor had said. She picked up a handful from the floor and let it filter through her fingers to the tabletop. Could it really be alive? Could it have gotten into the doctor's brain and crossed some wires?

She walked down the hallway to their bedroom. James was still in his crib, and she assumed he was sleeping until she walked over and found his eyes wide open, staring up toward the ceiling. He was so still that at first she feared he wasn't breathing, but then his chest rose and fell with a tiny breath. His head rolled toward her. He didn't smile like most mornings when they first locked eyes.

"Morning glory," she said. A blink was his only response. At least he wasn't coughing. "You ready to get up?" He shook his head no and went back to staring at the ceiling. She leaned down and kissed his forehead and told him she'd give him another thirty minutes. "But then you best get up and get something in that belly."

She turned away with reluctance, knowing something wasn't right with her son. She hit the hallway, and finally James spoke.

"Dust to dust, Mommy."

She froze, turned back toward the crib, and waited for more

but none came. *Just your imagination, Ellen. No way the boy just said that.* She returned to the kitchen.

Josiah sat at the table holding the coffeepot by the handle, drinking straight from it.

"Josiah, my lands, what are you doing?"

"What's it look like I'm doing, Ellen? Having my morning pot of joe." He spilled some down his neck and flinched, but that didn't stop him from taking another sip and then a gulp. He put the pot down on the table and wiped his mouth on a white, wrinkled shirtsleeve—same one he'd slept in. "You don't look good, Ellen," he said, deadpan. "The dust is wearing on you. And not in a good way."

It took a few seconds for what he'd said to register, because he'd never spoken to her that way. He'd said some unfavorable things inside the Bentley the other night, but that had been the Old Sam corn whiskey talking. This was flat-out mean and ugly, so much so that she didn't have an immediate response.

Josiah finished off the pot of coffee. "You need some meat on those bones, Ellen. Maybe Jeremiah likes you that way, but not me."

"Hush, Josiah." She brushed the top of her fingers across her smooth cheek and stepped closer to her husband. "You need to shave, Josiah. And change your clothes, because you stink like a garbage can."

She stopped cold and covered her mouth. What had she just said? Her thoughts had just slid out without her stopping them. *With no filter. Like Dr. Craven yesterday.*

"Josiah, I'm sorry."

He waved it away. "It's true, ain't it?" He sniffed his shirt. "I do stink. Hard to come by extra water nowadays though, Ellen."

"Just as it's hard to come by food." She looked at her arms, which were thinner than they used to be. She did need some meat on her bones.

"From dust to dust," he said, staring out the window.

The words made her heart jump, remembering what James had said, or what she'd thought he said.

"You sure aren't the same girl I married, Ellen."

It was something that should have brought tears to her eyes, but she feared that all her tears had dried up. Instead of turning the other cheek she said, "And you're not the man I married, Josiah. Not even close."

He shrugged, patted his knees, and stood from the chair with a grunt. "Welp, I best get to doing nothing today."

She was mentally trying to unsay the words that had just come from her mouth. Like Boo was trying to get that coin unflipped. She thought of Jeremiah and Peter across the way and the conversation she'd had last night about Jeremiah's nightmare, hoping to at some point bring it up with her husband, figuring she'd have to find the right time to do so because he didn't like to talk about things sentimental. But now the words just came right out. "I know you held your brother's hand during his nightmares. You used to time them. Count down the seconds until they ended."

"And then you came rolling into town."

"What do I have to do with it?"

"Everything, Ellen. You coming here had everything to do with everything." He opened the front door, squinted into the sunlight, and tipped his hat. "Now go do something about that hair."

"Soon as you do something about that big nose of yours, Josiah."

He waved without turning.

She bit her lip on the way out to the porch. Josiah was already walking across the street. He took a right down Main and just kept walking and walking until he looked an inch tall. He stopped in the distance, and she realized he'd found the car they abandoned yesterday during the storm. He opened the driver's side door, slid inside, and closed it. She expected him to start it up and drive it back home, but he just sat there. Five minutes he sat there, then ten, and then she couldn't watch anymore. "Sit in that car all day if you want, Josiah. See if I care."

All the windows were open at the Worst house. Inside, Jeremiah and Peter looked busy cleaning. The only two in town who were digging out. The only two who seemed to care about anything.

Ellen craved a cigarette, even though she had never smoked, other than those couple of times she and Jeremiah sneaked behind the Goodbyes' barn and puffed on some rolled butts with the oil smell from the tractor just over their shoulders.

"And then one thing led to another." She smirked, but it was short-lived. The front door banged closed behind her, and James stood barefoot in the dust. She picked him up. "How'd you get out of your crib?"

"Climbed out," he said.

"Who taught you to do that?"

"Daddy."

"Well, your daddy's a fool."

Jeremiah tossed and turned in bed that night.

Dreaming. Surrounded by dust. Chased by scratchy laughter he couldn't locate no matter how hard he tried. But eventually the dust settled, the voice went away, and what remained was a memory from when Jeremiah was a boy. He couldn't recall the exact age but knew he'd been young enough to feel the empty space with his tongue from where a tooth had recently fallen out.

His father had summoned him to the kitchen table, which was where he and Josiah usually got lectured whenever they did something wrong. Jeremiah didn't know what he'd done this time, so he made sure to pay attention to his father's every word.

"Jeremiah, do you know what it means to covet?"

Jeremiah shook his head.

"Means to hunger for. Thirst for. Crave."

"Is it bad?"

"Sometimes can be—if what you covet is for power. If that power you covet starts to change who you are. You see what I'm getting at?"

Jeremiah shook his head.

"That quarter in your pocket, Jeremiah. It's just a quarter. What say you do like the other children and spend it on some gum or a cola."

Jeremiah looked into the other room, where Josiah sat on the couch with his head lowered. "We were just playing a game."

"Sometimes your coin games hurt feelings."

"'Cause I can't lose?"

Wilmington tightened his jaw like he did when he was mad but trying not to be. "I'll give you two options, Jeremiah. One, you hand me over that coin for a few days and give it a rest. Two, you take it down to Blythe's Food Store and buy a couple of colas for you and your brother. Let it trickle into Nowhere's economy."

Jeremiah removed the coin from his pocket and made his daddy think he was about to give it to him. But power sometimes made you do funny things. Instead of handing it over, he flipped it and let it settle on the kitchen table. The gesture didn't please his daddy, but at least Jeremiah had made a decision—or rather the coin had made it for him.

"Tails it is." Jeremiah scooped up the coin and headed for the front door.

"Where do you think you're going?"

"To go get me and Josiah a Coca-Cola."

Jeremiah woke in the middle of the night when he heard dust tapping against the Worsts' bedroom window. The memory of that coin toss in front of his father was still with him.

Afterward he'd walked down the road to spend that quarter on a cola for himself and Josiah. He remembered thinking that it was fine by him to spend that quarter at the food store; he could always get another one. Nowhere was booming in those days, and quarters weren't hard to come by. All you needed to do was walk inside the Bentley Hotel and look down. Locating a coin on the sticky floor was as easy as finding a goldenrod in the wheat fields. He could have done both blindfolded.

He looked out the window. Josiah's car was still parked down the road. Yesterday morning he'd seen his brother leave the Goodbye house and walk toward that car like a drifter, then get inside and close the door. *Is he still in there?* He'd checked a few times during the day, and Josiah had still been sitting behind that wheel, doing a bunch of nothing.

Jeremiah grabbed a spare pillow from the bed, knocked dust from it, and then carried it from the house. He walked down the road as dust floated across the moon. When he got to the car, he opened the door, and there was Josiah, sleeping across the front seat with his head crooked against the inside of the passenger's door.

Jeremiah leaned in and slid the pillow beneath his brother's head.

Told him to sleep tight, and then he closed the door.

TWELVE

The next day, Orion chimed that church bell inside the Bentley.

Ellen's legs were heavy and lethargic from having moved very little since the big storm, and last night's duster seemed to have set her feet in quicksand. Her brain told her to sit down and let another day tick away, but she felt trapped inside their own home.

Panicked and fidgety all of a sudden, she stood abruptly from the kitchen table and looked out the window above the sink. She chewed her fingernail and then headed for the front door.

"Where you going?" Wilmington asked, monotone, from his place at the table.

"I've got to get out of this house." The bell gonged again from across the street. She looked back at her father-in-law. "You coming?"

He pushed himself up from the table with an annoyed grunt. "I'm coming. Matter of fact, I've got some things I need to get off my chest."

This gave her pause. He'd said it like he was angry, which wasn't like him. But the entire town seemed angry now; why shouldn't he be angry too? They'd all been given doses of that dirty medicine.

She carried James outside to where the air was clear and the skies blue, but she'd learned her lesson not to be fooled. Even yesterday, an hour after Josiah walked down the road and closed himself up inside their abandoned car, another duster had come through, not as big and nasty as the day prior or the one that hit last night, but enough to bury them deeper—especially with no one making an effort to dig out.

Almost no one.

Over at the Worst house, all the windows and doors were open. Dust filtered out as Jeremiah and Peter swept. "Only ones in town with any energy," Ellen whispered in James's ear. "Sometimes I wish he was your father."

She didn't realize what she'd said until the words were already out, but luckily James was too young to understand and probably wasn't paying attention anyway. Still, it was a terrible thing to think, let alone say, and she wasn't convinced she even believed it. She never would have married Josiah if she hadn't loved him. But it was true what they'd told each other in the kitchen yesterday: they weren't the same people they'd married. Maybe being parents had changed them, but she didn't think that was it. James just had the misfortune of coming into the world about the same time the earth started peeling up.

If anything, it was the dust that changed them.

The dust and the drought.

Had everyone else not been moving as slowly as she now was toward the Bentley, she might have been embarrassed by how long it took her to shuffle across the road. But the entire town was lethargic and heavy legged, physically and mentally weighed down by all that dust. Her heart beat slowly, like cold syrup stubbornly clinging to the morning jar. She had to remind herself to put one foot in front of the other.

Orion rang the bell again.

"Hold your horses, old man." She whispered to James, "He's an old man—yes, he is. A lonely old man who should know better than to ring that bell all the time. He's never been married because he'd annoy any woman who'd come close with all that constant positivity."

James laughed. Was it because he agreed? Had he taken in a dose of that medicine too? She stopped suddenly and pointed down the road in the opposite direction, where their Model T was now virtually buried in black dust.

Josiah had never come home last night. She assumed he'd stayed all night in the car, was probably there even still. Just then the car door opened. Or tried to. The latest duster had blocked him in. The door would only open to about a foot wide. Josiah tried to shimmy through but wouldn't fit. *If he had a brain, he'd use the passenger door*, thought Ellen. There wasn't a drift over there. But instead the window rolled down, and the next thing she knew Josiah was falling out of it in a slow roll down the drift.

At one time she and James would have found it funny, watching Josiah tunnel through an open window into all that dust, but neither one of them laughed now. James didn't even smile, and he'd been watching the entire thing. Whatever was in that dust had numbed the both of them.

Orion's church bell chimed again.

James said in a monotone, "Hold your horses, old man."

"That's right," Ellen whispered, turning toward the hotel. "You tell him good, James."

"Hold your horses, old man."

They didn't wait for Josiah, who was brushing himself off as he staggered down the road. Seemed like half the town was ignoring the bell. The ones who did come arrived wearing clothes that hadn't been changed in days, their faces covered in dust—too tired even to wash themselves.

Orion didn't even greet anyone on the porch, as was his custom. He was inside, sitting on a chair and gonging that low-hanging bell as if his legs didn't work anymore. He'd taken off his tuxedo jacket. His white shirt was unbuttoned to midchest, where sprigs of white hair jutted. His top hat was on the floor beside his feet, and his wispy white hair was disheveled, recently slept on, pushed out at a tangent that made Ellen wonder if he hadn't fallen asleep with that side of his face pressed against the curve of that bell. When she got closer she noticed indentations in his cheek.

"Orion," said Ellen. "You look like the ghost of something long dead."

Orion looked up, dead behind the eyes. "From dust to dust, Ellen."

He offered no more, so she carried James over to her customary stool in front of the bar and a stone's throw from the piano, which sat vacant. Typically the Bentley Hotel filled within five minutes of Orion's bell chiming, but this gathering took twenty minutes to only half fill it, and those who'd come looked put out, like they'd been rudely interrupted from all the nothing they'd been doing.

Probably just sitting and staring. Ellen had what the rest of the town had. Whatever that duster had brought with it, she'd taken it in too. But by the looks of some of the others, she didn't seem to have it as bad. Her husband walked in and took a seat at a round table occupied only by his father on the other side. The two of them stared like enemies for some reason.

Father Steven sat against the back wall, staring the same way at Sister Moffitt one table over. Sister Moffitt was usually the one who suggested bingo or cards, but today she suggested nothing. She looked angry for even being there and sat with her elbow on the table and her chin resting in her palm. All of a sudden she said to Orion, "You've gained weight."

Without much enthusiasm he said back to her, "You've gained ugly, Sister, especially around the ugly area. Ugly on top of ugly. You know what that equals?"

She scoffed. "You."

Orion let it go, then lazily chimed the church bell again.

Dr. Craven held a dart from the dartboard in his hand, and he was poking it in and out of the tabletop like he was creating a picture in the wood. Windmill was there too, across the room, staring at Ellen, probably still stewing from what the doctor had told him the other day. *But it was true.* "Stare all you want, Windmill," said Ellen. "You're still only a boy." Then she wished she could shove those words back in, but what was said was said and couldn't be unsaid.

Windmill's eyes blurred with fresh tears, and Ellen looked away, not feeling the guilt she supposed she should have felt after muttering something so mean and ugly. She whispered in her son's ear. "Just speaking my mind, James. It's what we need more of, right? Just telling it straight. Giving that boy a good dose of that truth medicine."

Phillip Jansen walked in with an empty mailbag over his shoulder and collapsed into a chair that nearly toppled. He placed the pathetic, dusty satchel on the table and said to Orion, "What's this about, old man? Nobody likes your meetings anymore. Try as you might, there ain't no way we can relive what it was like here in the twenties. So let's get on with it."

Nobody was shocked by what the postman said, because

underneath the ugliness was the cruel truth of it. Orion was always trying to rekindle something that couldn't be rekindled, and finally someone had said it.

Orion lowered his head so low his chin brushed the white hairs on his chest, and he looked to be crying. Wilmington started to comfort him but stopped before he'd even lifted from the seat. Like he just couldn't spare the effort.

Phillip Jansen rested his elbows on the table, atop that dusty mailbag, his eyes darting around the room because everyone was watching him. "What?"

Toothache leaned against the back wall, his right arm peeling a corncob-sized patch of wallpaper from it. "Manyouneverwasgoodat-deliveringthemail." He took what he'd ripped from the wall and tore that in half. "Alwaysputtingstuffinthewrongboxes."

Sheriff McKinney mumbled, "What he say?"

Deacon Sipes had a horseshoe in his hand and made as if to brain Toothache with it. Toothache flinched. He leaned back too far, and one of the chair legs snapped. The room chuckled lazily when he hit the floor. No one moved to help. Deacon Sipes put the horseshoe on the table, and it rattled heavily. "Don't talk no more, Toothache. Ain't nobody wants to try and decipher what you say. It's like fingernails scraping down Mrs. Goodbye's chalkboard. Always has been."

Deacon noticed Phillip grinning. "He's right, though, mailman. How hard is it to put the mail into those boxes? But half the time, back when we used to actually get the mail, I'd end up with Ned Blythe's."

Ned looked up from his slouched position on a stool. "And I'd end up with his. My wife would shiver every time she touched the mail with the name of Deacon Sipes on it, like it was dirty from some virus."

"Least when I talk I don't look like a mouse nibblin' on cheese," said Deacon.

Ned let that go, but he chewed his lower lip like he was wrangling to let something loose. His wife had died four years ago, and he looked to be pondering whether the insult had been directed at him or her.

She did look like a mouse when she nibbled on a corn cob. Ellen was glad that thought had stayed in, because Ned now looked on the verge of crying. And it was bad enough that his food store hardly had anything on the shelves anymore. But looking at Phillip now made her sick to her stomach, and Toothache, as dumb as he was, had made a good point. "I think James here would make a better mailman than you, Phillip Jansen. Orion and Wilmington here, they had so much pride in this town that they handmade every mailbox. Every new resident got one within a week of their arrival."

"Polished and everything," said Wilmington. "Orion, when his mind wasn't too busy wondering what all the women in town looked like under their dresses, attached every one of those yellow flags with the delicacy of one putting the final icing touches on a cake."

Orion still had his head lowered, not denying what Wilmington had said. Instead he was nodding as if he'd just repented and unburdened his sins in front of Father Steven and Sister Moffitt at the same time.

Sister Moffitt said, "I remember the days when I'd look out my window and see that yellow flag sticking up from the mailbox and glowing in the thought of having mail."

"It was a clever idea," Wilmington said to Orion, who nodded in acknowledgment without looking up.

Phillip said, "Wasn't my fault the mail dried up like the Ogallala."

Sheriff McKinney said, "But it was your fault I didn't get my catalogue for three weeks because you misplaced it."

"That was five years ago, Sheriff," said Phillip. "Back when you had hair on your head and a stomach that fit in your pants. How do you continue gaining weight when the rest of us can't seem to keep it?"

"Yes," said Father Steven. "You keep getting fatter, Sheriff. Where are you getting your food?"

Sheriff shrugged. "At the gettin' place, Father."

Richard Klamp said, "Why are we here anyway? Why'd you call this silly meeting, Orion? I need a nap worse than you need a comb."

Moses Yearling said from across the room, "To talk about what to do with your clothing store now that nobody shops there anymore."

"Well, you're not even one of us, rainmaker," said Richard. "You're a rainmaker that can't even make it rain. You need to pack your bags and go."

Maglin Mulraney, from his table in the corner, said, "One of my cows is missing." He pointed toward the sheriff. "I bet he took it and he's been feasting all by himself. That's how come he's gaining all that fat."

Sheriff McKinney turned in his chair. "Your cows are as dumb as you are, Mulraney. Probably went out and got lost in a duster."

Moses ran a hand through his flaming red hair. "I've made it rain in every town I've entered. It's the town, not me." He stood theatrically. "I mean, who names a town Nowhere?"

Orion finally raised his head and then his voice. "I called this meeting to discuss what to do with Jeremiah Goodbye. And the boy he brought with him."

The room sat silent for a few clock ticks.

Orion stood with a grunt. "As we all know, he's taken root in the Worst house with that weird boy. And another man has ended up dead from the flip of his coin."

"Jeremiah didn't kill him," said Ellen. "The man didn't take cover in the duster, and he suffocated."

Josiah shook his head from his chair.

Ellen shot him the look.

Loreda Draper, still blind from that duster, spoke up. "He saved my boy's life. Without Jeremiah Goodbye coming along when he did I'd have nothing to live for. Nothing." Nicholas stood by her side now. He squeezed her hand and rubbed her back.

Ellen noticed a hint of normalcy still residing in Nicholas Draper, as if Jeremiah had shielded him not only from that duster, but also from the ugliness the duster brought with it.

"He's still wanted by the authorities for the murder of four men," said Orion. "Possibly five now. And truth be told, Wilmington, that boy's always made me nervous. Started drinking before he even lost all his baby teeth. I mean, who does that?"

"He's scrappy and tough is what he is," said Leland Cantain, owner of the once-popular opera house. "The way he stood up to the government when they killed our cattle."

"That was me," said Josiah with a grunt.

Cantain stammered. "Well, he stood up to the bank during those foreclosure auctions. And hijacked that train full of wheat to keep it off the market and drive up prices."

Several heads nodded, including Wilmington, who stared across the table at Josiah. It got quiet, so everyone heard what

Wilmington said next. "You know, Josiah, I always liked him more than you. Loved you both, but he was always my favorite. Especially after you went and ratted him out."

Josiah clenched his jaw and jerked a nod like the words hadn't bothered him, but he wasn't so dead that Ellen couldn't see the hurt. She thought of walking over to him in comfort, but that thought passed liked the wind.

It would have taken too much energy to get up.

Wilmington wasn't finished. He faced Orion. "Jeremiah might have a temper that's unpredictable, but if you'd known what he'd suffered through you'd understand." He pointed at his old friend. "And at least he wasn't an actor, a man pretending to be on top of the world when in truth he was becoming buried by it daily. You've been a bachelor all your life, Orion, acting like a lothario on the outside when on the inside you don't know the first words to say to a woman." He looked as if he was finished, but then he went back in for more. "Always finding a certain flaw to avoid getting close, when all along the flaw was in you, my friend. I seen how you looked at my Amanda, too, when she was alive, like she'd have been a luckier woman to have you instead of me—you with your tuxedo and fancy gloves and whatnot. But you know what, Orion?"

Orion's head was still lowered like he was whimpering. He shook his head.

Pour it on him, thought Ellen. *Let him know, Daddy Wilmington, even if it stings.*

Wilmington did just that. "She laughed about it, Orion. 'Poor Orion,' she'd say. 'Poor, poor, Orion. Maybe one day he'll find his match.' And don't forget Ellen over there. Her mother? Hmm? You thought she was in love with you, but she wasn't. It was me she ended up staying in Nowhere for, not you."

Orion had gone white as a sheet, and just as quickly he flipped to red, embarrassment and shame shining in that blotchy skin.

Ellen shot her father-in-law a look that could have made that bullet move by sheer mind power had he the gumption to face her. The truth wasn't so funny now. Her lower lip quivered, and she squeezed James tightly enough for him to start coughing. Then she patted his back harder than she meant to, which made him cry.

Finally Wilmington sat down, holding his head like the bullet in there had begun to hurt.

Maybe that bullet deserved to move after the things he'd just said.

Orion looked like a man who'd just had his soul ripped free, his bones left to flutter like wind chimes. A man the entire town had always thought bigger than life was now slumped over with his back arched like a turtle shell.

On a normal day, Ellen would have been over there in a heartbeat to rub that poor man's shoulder. Instead she did something so mean and ugly it brought tears to her own eyes. "Poor Orion. Poor, poor Orion," she said, but with so much sarcasm Wilmington looked up from the floor and Josiah turned in his chair. "My mother was too good for you, Orion."

Rita Belmont shifted the room's attention from Orion. She stood from her chair in a rumpled blue dress. "Just before we came over here on account of hearing Orion's stupid bell, I asked Ray if I looked fat in this dress, and he said yes."

Ray, her husband, who Ellen had always thought was ugly as a moose, nodded like he was the bee's knees. "Well, it's the truth, ain't it?"

Half the room nodded.

"The truth, Ray," said Ellen, "is that you must have gotten

dropped on your head when you were a kid—as misshaped as that skull of yours is."

Toothache said, "Doeslooklikeananvilfromtheback."

"Enough."

They all looked to the far corner of the room, where shadows dominated the opening of the hallway leading to the first-floor rooms. Out stepped Jeremiah, and beside him was the boy, Peter. "Enough."

"How'd you get in?" asked Deacon.

"Through a door, like most people do." Jeremiah surveyed the room. "Now, if you don't have something nice to say I'd recommend not saying anything at all. And if you're going to take a vote on whether I stay or go, it's best we do it in front of my face."

Josiah stood so fast his chair toppled. He made sure Jeremiah found his eyes, and then he spat to Orion's hardwood floor. "There's my vote, brother."

And then Josiah walked out of the Bentley's swinging doors, the silence so palpable they could hear his boots crunching in the dust as he crossed the street.

"I assume that's one vote for me going," said Jeremiah. "Anybody else ready to show their cards?"

Sister Moffitt stood. "I want you to stay, Jeremiah Goodbye. In a world that's suddenly turned mean, I can't for the life of me think of something ugly to say about you. Not like I can about some others in the room. Like Father Steven over there, who—" Jeremiah held up his hand, and she stopped herself. She coughed into her fist three times and spat dust. "Anyway, like I was saying, I want you to stay. I don't think you murdered those men. And I think I bought you some time with the authorities."

"How so?"

"This morning, before that dust got too deep into my brain, an idea struck."

"Wish it was lightning that struck her," said Father Steven. "Then maybe we could have had some improvement on the otherwise *un*improvable."

"No more of that," Jeremiah told the priest, who settled back into his chair, fingering rosary beads.

Sister Moffitt explained. "I took Father's car and rode into all the neighboring towns."

"She owes me some gas," Father mumbled.

Sister continued. "I got the word spread everywhere that I'd just come from Texas and I'd seen Jeremiah Goodbye heading south with a Bible and a gun."

"I don't have a Bible."

"I just supposed it would sound more authentic," said Sister Moffitt. "But I told all the men in those towns to spread the word that the Coin-Flip Killer was heading to Mexico."

Father Steven leaned back in his chair and folded his arms. "I've got a Bible you can swear on, Sister, now that you're partaking in the sin of being a liar."

Wilmington said, "My son stays."

Father Steven said, "He stays, but I want answers."

"And answers you'll get," said Jeremiah, with Peter standing by his side like a loyal soldier. "As soon as I make sense of things myself."

One by one, everyone in the room raised their hand and voted that Jeremiah stay, either by a few short words or by a nodding of the head. Even Sheriff McKinney, who had been so adamant before, voted he stay, although with a bit of reluctance in his half-raised arm. Truth was, he was probably afraid to vote his heart. He'd always been leery of Jeremiah.

Ellen said, "He stays, and by what I'm reading in all your eyes, I think what you fear more than him staying is him leaving us again." She turned her head toward the hotel's owner. "Orion?"

Orion looked around the room, then gave a slow nod of his head, which looked heavy as a bowling ball. He was staring at the spot where Josiah had spat on his dusty floor.

Then the click-clacking sound of a woman's hard-soled shoes entered the hotel, and Orion's head slowly raised.

Eyes turned toward the doorway.

A pretty woman with hair the color of chestnuts and eyes as brown as mahogany stepped into the room. She was just shapely enough for Ellen to dislike her from the start.

"Are there any rooms available?"

Walking in all put together in a fancy purple dress somehow free of dust.

The woman looked across the room toward Jeremiah, and Jeremiah returned her gaze as if he knew her or at least had seen her before.

Orion straightened from his slouched posture, suddenly looking wide-eyed and lovestruck. He cleared his throat and did his best to regain the boisterous man-of-the-stage persona he was known for, even though the dust had still clearly worn him down. "It's your lucky day. We've got plenty of rooms available."

"Good," she said. "I've luggage in the car."

"You one of them reporters from out east?" Ellen asked.

"I am."

"Then we don't want you here," said Ellen. "Keep to your own. All you'll see here is dust. We don't need any films or stories showing how we failed the plains and the plains failed us."

The woman smiled despite the bluntness. "I'm not here to do a story on the dust bowl."

"The what?"

"The dust bowl." She smiled. Her teeth were pretty and white. "It's what writers are starting to call it out here in the plains. And what blew in two days ago, that massive duster—they're calling it Black Sunday."

Ellen scoffed, folded her arms. "Black Sunday, huh? Fancy name given by those who didn't see it firsthand. If you're not here to report on the dusters, what are you here for?"

The woman nodded across the room. "I'm writing a story on Jeremiah Goodbye. The Coin-Flip Killer."

Jeremiah stepped forward, tipped his Stetson. "Although your work I'm sure is appreciated, the attention accrued from your story will not be."

"It's not that kind of story, Mr. Goodbye." The woman looked around the room. All eyes were on her. "I don't want you to be caught."

Sheriff McKinney said, "I keep waiting for a *yet*. She don't want you to be caught . . . yet. As in, the more stories she writes on you, the more famous she becomes."

The woman smiled. "Are folks always so blunt here in Nowhere?"

Ellen felt a stab of jealousy at the sight of that pretty face untouched by the climate, the dress somehow clean and fresh, the auburn hair that shimmered. "Why don't you want him to be caught then? What do you want with Jeremiah?"

"By the sound of what I heard coming in, I want the same thing as you."

Jeremiah said, "And what might that be?"

"Your freedom."

"I'm already free."

"Then your name untarnished."

"What's in it for you?" asked Ellen.

"The truth."

"And fame," said Ellen.

"I seek only the truth." She locked eyes with Ellen. "If fame comes with the revelation of it then so be it. It's a tough climb for a woman in this business, and I don't plan on being deterred. I do believe the man standing before us is innocent of the crimes leveled upon him."

"Sounds like a lawyer to me," said Deacon.

"If only he'd had one during the trial."

"He did."

The woman smirked. "One who could add two and two?"

Ellen couldn't disagree. Jeremiah's lawyer had been an unprepared slob who'd showed up three sheets to the wind on the final day of trial.

Jeremiah asked, "What makes you so sure of my innocence?"

"Three years of investigating."

"Why?" asked Ellen.

"Every reporter is looking for that breakthrough story. That hint of injustice that could blow a case wide open. I think this here is mine."

"I've seen you," said Jeremiah.

"I attended every day of your trial," she said. "I've been digging into things while you sat in prison. I was there the day they put you in the chair and the tornado came through and tumbled that wall, saving your life at the same time it stole several others. In other words, I've been following you, Jeremiah Goodbye. A lot better than the authorities have, I might add."

Had their brains not been full of so much Black Sunday dust they would have been amused by her words. Instead, most in the room just sat there and stared.

"What's your name?" asked Ellen.

"Miss Buchanan. Miss Rose Buchanan."

For the first time since the woman had entered the Bentley Hotel, Ellen looked over toward her father-in-law. Wilmington had yet to utter a word, and looked like he'd seen a ghost. He slowly stood from his chair and shuffled toward the pretty woman, eyeing her like he wasn't sure she was real.

Ellen said, "Wilmington? What is it?"

He didn't even look Ellen's way. He continued on toward Rose Buchanan and then stopped two feet away from her.

She was a confident enough woman to not step back from him. She seemed as curious about Wilmington's actions as Ellen was, and with his stooped posture, he gave no inkling of being a threat.

"Hello," said Rose, offering a hand with long, slender fingers.

Wilmington gave her hand a glance but didn't shake it. Instead, he stepped closer and gave her a hug.

THIRTEEN

1924

Jeremiah helped Josiah from the ground and told him to run on home.

Josiah wiped his bloody lip and ran a hand through the tuft of hair that had fallen from a thatch he'd slicked back in the morning. He'd been spending more and more time on that hair since Ellen Maverick moved into town, and William Worst had made one too many comments on it.

"I don't need you fighting my fights, Jeremiah." Josiah got back down into a fighting stance, prepared to resume what Jeremiah had seen over the wheat field moments ago—Josiah and William in a violent tussle, and his brother on the losing end of it.

Three days in a row now those two had pasted blows on each other behind Daddy's barn, and Jeremiah just knew it was over the new girl in town, the one Jeremiah had already locked lips with on three separate occasions. Had Josiah been aware of *that* juicy nugget, perhaps it would have been Jeremiah he wanted to fight instead of William Worst, who was mean as a rattlesnake but dumb as one of Mulraney's cows.

William had three inches on both of them and at least thirty pounds of farm muscle disguised as fat. Two months before, Jeremiah had seen him lift the front end of a John Deere all by himself after it got a wheel caught down in a creek he wasn't supposed to be riding over. Josiah wasn't small, by any means, but he was no match for William Worst, who stood with his big legs planted, fists ready.

He had a red blotch the size of a quarter on his forehead, and at first Jeremiah thought Josiah must have landed a blow. But it was only an angry-looking pimple, with a matching one on the left side of William's neck. Those things looked like they hurt, and William seemed to have one brewing at all times. No wonder he was so mean.

But Jeremiah stepped back anyway. If Josiah was determined to have one more go at William, then he'd let him. He just wasn't going to hear him whine and moan about it while they tried to fall asleep tonight. Josiah would find no sympathy from him.

The remainder of that fight took no more than thirty seconds. Josiah got in one good lick to William's five, and soon Jeremiah's twin brother was on the ground again, wiping a glob of spit from his right eye while William knelt over him, his legs jutting right up next to Josiah's ears. After one last slap to Josiah's face, William stood, wiped his bloody hands on his overalls, and walked away with his eyes glued on Jeremiah, practically daring him to retaliate.

But all Jeremiah did was watch, secretly fingering the quarter he kept in the right pocket of his trousers. He'd known William

Worst since they were barely taller than the wheat at harvesttime, and they'd yet to scuffle like William and Josiah seemed to do daily. William knew better than to pick on Jeremiah. He never did anything more than give that stare and walk away.

Jeremiah figured that might need to change soon. But for now he helped Josiah back home, sneaked him in the back door so Wilmington wouldn't see them, and got Josiah all cleaned up, just like he'd said he *wouldn't* do.

That night, as Jeremiah sipped on bootleg corn liquor he got under the table from Mr. Powell down at the pharmacy, he swore he could feel Josiah's bruises. One nasty deep purple one on Josiah's left bicep was perfectly shaped like a clenched fist. Jeremiah touched his left arm in the same place, and although there was no purple mark on his arm, he felt the pain all the same, tender as a bruised peach.

Jeremiah took a heavy gulp of the clear whiskey. He didn't wince like he used to, and he could already feel himself growing numb from the intake of it. He hoped it would help numb the nightmare he knew he'd have that night. He looked over across the room at Josiah, who'd just buried himself under the sheets. "Sure you don't want a drink?"

"I'm sure," said Josiah, his voice all muffled. "And you shouldn't have any either."

Jeremiah took another sip, capped the bottle, and slid it deep under his bed so Wilmington wouldn't nudge it with a toe when he came in to wake them for the morning field work. He knew Josiah was upset he hadn't stepped in and helped fight William Worst. He'd said he didn't need Jeremiah fighting his fights, but deep down he didn't really mean it.

Well, that would soon change. Unbeknownst to Josiah, Jeremiah had flipped the quarter coin when they got home. Heads, he'd go back tomorrow and show William Worst what was what. Tails, he'd let it go.

Jeremiah went to bed preparing for a fight, because that quarter had turned up heads and the sun had even gleamed off it.

He was nearly drunk by the time he fell asleep.

An hour later the nightmare came. Jeremiah woke up in a cold sweat, his heart racing, ending the horror with a sudden, heavy gasp of air. Like always. He looked over at his twin brother across the room. He could tell Josiah was awake under those covers.

Josiah no longer held his hand during the night. Maybe he thought they were too old. Or maybe it was something else.

Maybe someone had seen him locking lips with Ellen Maverick behind Daddy's barn.

Sunlight turned the wheat fields gold the next morning.

Josiah was quiet while they stacked it.

The temperature was already close to ninety, and they were still an hour away from lunchtime. Jeremiah wiped sweat from his brow with his thumb and flung it aside. Across the way, William Worst had been working his family's field for the past hour. When the big farm boy headed toward the grain silo, Jeremiah told Josiah he'd be right back.

"Where you going?"

"I gotta pee."

Jeremiah made as if to go to the outhouse but took a turn at the last second, ducking instead behind a row of elm trees where they sometimes took breaks in the summer shade.

A minute later, after jogging through Dr. Craven's wheat field to reach the silo, Jeremiah caught up to William, who held a pitchfork in two hands and was standing in front of a mound of wheat twice his height.

"What're you looking at?"

"Big pile of nothin'." Jeremiah stepped closer, staring at the tines on that pitchfork. "Why don't you ever pick on me? Huh?"

William shrugged, spat brown chew to the buffalo grass he'd just tamped down with his big fat boots. "Not worth messing with."

"Nah. It's fear I see in those eyes, William. That's how come you don't pick on me. I can smell the stink on you now." Jeremiah continued his approach, fearless even as sunlight glistened off the sharpness of that tool. "You're gripping that handle tight, I see. Like you're afraid you might have to use it against an unarmed man."

"You ain't a man yet."

"Been a man since I was born, William. Seen things a boy should never see, so I figured I'd become one early as I could."

"Stay back now." William readied the pitchfork, pointing those tines like they were bull horns. He chuckled, but Jeremiah could tell from the way his eyes twitched that he was nervous.

Jeremiah struck like a snake would, quick and efficient, and William was down in a blink, rolling in the grass and clutching his throat where Jeremiah had punched him.

Jeremiah grabbed the dropped pitchfork and knelt over William. "Just touching you now makes me feel sick inside, William. I can see the meanness in you, and it gets blacker every day. You've raised a hand to your mother, William Worst. More than once."

"How do you know that?"

"Just seen it when I blinked."

William's eyes grew big upon sight of the pitchfork inches from his jawline. "Don't do it, Jeremiah. I won't pick on your brother again. I promise."

Jeremiah ran one of the points of the pitchfork down William's right forearm until an inch-long cut formed and blood showed.

"What are you doing? Stop that, Jeremiah!"

"It's for your own good, William. Lay still. Gotta let some of that meanness out." A glimpse of his rekindled nightmare flashed through Jeremiah's mind. He pinched his eyes closed to combat it, to block out all that darkness, and when he opened his eyes again it was gone. But that tension had been transferred into a violent two-handed grip on William's neck. He didn't recall grabbing and squeezing, but William Worst was dying under the strength of his grip. Jeremiah let go, and William gasped and spat in the grass. Jeremiah whispered that he was sorry, but he didn't think William heard him.

Jeremiah wiped sweat from his face, sweat mixed with tears, and then he rolled William Worst onto his back like he was a log. That fear in William's eyes had increased tenfold. Jeremiah had a notion to grab the pitchfork and just knew where that notion had come from—that evil from his nightmare rubbing off on him and turning him violent. But instead he reached into his pocket and pulled out the quarter he always kept there.

He'd never done such a thing before—the coin was usually saved for more mundane decisions. But just to put a scare into William, Jeremiah said, "If it's heads I'll finish you off with that pitchfork. If it's tails, you walk away, and you never speak of this day."

William said nothing either way, unless sweating profusely from a hairline that was already receding was a form of communicating.

He stared at the coin like it was the only thing in existence, like he was hypnotized by it.

Jeremiah flipped the quarter high and watched it spin.

Instead of catching it he let it fall to the ground and he immediately covered it with his hand. "Heads or tails, William Worst?"

And then he moved his hand to reveal which it was.

FOURTEEN

Dust spun cyclic—a tornado of swirls that formed what looked like a man leaning against the dining room wall.

A man made of dust with a dust fedora tipped low over his dusty face.

His laugh had dust in it, choked like a clogged car tailpipe.

"You should've never flipped that coin on William Worst, Jeremiah."

Puffs of dust emerged from the dust man when he spoke.

And then that laugh again.

And then he was gone.

Jeremiah nearly startled himself off the couch.

It wasn't that deep gasp of air that used to lure him from the nightmare, but more of a panting and morning sweats like a fever just broke. A new nightmare, something manifested from the evil now spreading across town. The devil from his old nightmare manifested as dust.

You should've never flipped that coin on William Worst.

Was that when things had started to turn and the drinking had gotten out of hand?

No, he knew it had started even before that. And deep down he knew why too. William Worst was just the unfortunate one to take the brunt of the anger that stemmed from it.

Jeremiah sat up on the couch and planted his bare feet on a hardwood floor that was almost dust-free. He and Peter had spent hours cleaning, turning the dreariness of the Worst house into something new. *Why am I even staying here instead of Orion's hotel? Some kind of penance for what I did to William? If I did anything at all.* In hindsight, given what continued to happen in the years thereafter, he knew he'd had more to do with what happened to William Worst than he'd allowed himself to believe back then.

Back when he'd learned to completely bury himself in the bottle.

He breathed into his hands and rubbed his face. Tiny dust motes floated through sunlight that entered the window. No matter how much they cleaned, the dust couldn't be escaped entirely.

Peter was in the dining room, typing every so often, punching those keys in bursts and then going quiet.

That much he expected. The boy had been up early the day before, doing the same thing. But then Jeremiah heard a pen scratching, like someone was writing on a table. He got up to look. Peter wasn't alone. That reporter who'd walked into the Bentley last night sat at the table across from Peter, writing something in sprawling cursive letters.

She looked up and smiled. Sunlight shimmered off that auburn hair. He'd never seen anything so clean. "Morning, Jeremiah."

What was she even doing here, dressed like she'd just walked from a painting? Had the boy let her in?

He scratched his scalp and suddenly wished he'd had time to run a comb through his hair.

Rose Buchanan wore a red dress that was only a shade darker than what she'd put on her lips, the same type of face paint Ellen had used before all the dust started peeling up and making it pointless. She pushed a mug of steaming coffee toward a vacant seat beside Peter, and Jeremiah took it as the invitation it was. The black coffee felt good rolling down, so he took another gulp and rested his elbows on the table.

Why had his father hugged her last night? Hugged her like he'd never seen Wilmington hug anyone before, even Ellen.

"Peter let me in." She sipped her coffee and left an arch of red lipstick on the rim of the mug.

Jeremiah suddenly felt the urge to hug her too. She was beautiful, but he didn't think that's what had prompted it. It was just something he felt like doing, but unlike his father he wouldn't act on it. "Sorry about last night."

"Sorry for what?"

"That was my father who hugged you."

She waved it away. "Oh, that was nothing. It was darling."

Didn't look that way to me. More like he'd collapsed on you and you had to hold him up.

"You know he has a bullet in his head?"

"I heard."

"Who'd you hear it from?"

"Orion. The man who owns the hotel." She put her pen down and folded her arms on the table as if to mirror Jeremiah's pose. "He looks sad, that man."

"Well, he got run through the wringer last night. The town has gone off the tracks since that duster, the one you called Black Sunday."

"So I've noticed."

"I think it makes him act strange sometimes—that bullet." Jeremiah sipped his coffee. Peter typed something that could have been an imaginary sentence. They both glanced at the boy, but then focused back on one another. "Doctor told him if he got about too much the bullet might move. He's been risking it of late. Part of me wonders if that's not his goal. To go ahead and get it over with."

"And the other part?"

Jeremiah shrugged. "Guess he got tired of sitting around." He inhaled the steam and swallowed more coffee. "What'd he say to you when he hugged you? Thought I saw his lips move."

"He didn't say anything," she said. "But truthfully I was so stunned by the gesture that perhaps I didn't hear."

Wilmington had clung to her for twenty seconds before Ellen pried them apart and walked Wilmington home. Jeremiah had stopped by there minutes later, after he'd helped Rose Buchanan with her luggage, but found the front door of his childhood home locked. His knocks went unanswered, so he and Peter had returned home to the Worst house.

Jeremiah finished his coffee and placed the cup down. "Where you from?"

"New York City."

"I seen you at my trial. What brought you from New York City?"

"I'm a reporter," she said. "I follow the news. There were reporters in attendance from nearly every city, if you remember."

"Oh, I remember."

Peter had begun typing again. Rose watched the boy as she spoke. "I heard about those four bodies found in the grain silo, and like most of the country I had to know more."

"Were you horrified or fascinated?"

"Perhaps a bit of both." She scribbled a few words and then looked up. "More intrigued than anything, though."

"By what?"

"How a man could do such a thing. Admit to burying those bodies."

"But I didn't kill 'em."

"I know that."

"How are you so sure? You sit here before me without a hint of fear in those pretty brown eyes."

"Instinct," she said. "If I had something to fear, then perhaps I'd be shaking in my shoes, but I'm not. Why'd you even bring those bodies to the silo to begin with, Jeremiah Goodbye, and then bury them like a guilty man would?"

"No innocent man is completely free of guilt, Miss Buchanan."

"Call me Rose."

"Fine, Rose. Perhaps I didn't kill those men, but I know I sent them to their deaths."

She grinned. "I have files back in my room that I want to show you. I saw you in that courtroom, Jeremiah."

"And what'd you see?"

"A troubled man. A man so deep in the bottle he'd like to drown. A man looking for release from the pressure he'd been under."

"You see a lot."

"I'm good at my job."

Jeremiah pointed at her paper. "What'd you write a minute ago?"

"Notes."

"On what?"

"On you." She scribbled something else, something he couldn't read upside down. Peter was watching from behind his typewriter, taking in their every word. She finished writing, smiled again. "Unlike the other reporters, I didn't return back home after your trial."

"I saw you from time to time at the prison. Why'd you stay?"

"Because although you may have been guilty of being troubled, you were innocent of those crimes leveled upon you." She sipped her coffee, and Jeremiah watched her slender throat massage it down.

For the first time he wondered if he should be talking to her. *What would Ellen think of her being in here with me now? Is she thinking anything at all?*

"I saw the way the others looked at you inside that hotel lobby last night," he said. *Especially Ellen.* "They're leery of reporters. They think you'll write something about all this dust—what'd you call it, the dust bowl? Put us all in a bad light and make us look dumb. They think you're here for your own fame and recognition."

"I'm here only for the truth."

"And the truth shall set us all free?"

"No, Jeremiah, the truth shall set *you* free. For three years now, I've been investigating all four of those men and what happened to them."

He folded his arms, leaned back in his chair, and chewed the inside of his cheek. He'd been thinking about those things too. Dust motes floated in the sunlight. He blew at them, and they scattered. "Why do I feel like we know each other, even though last night was the first time we'd spoken?"

"I don't know."

"What I can't get past is why my father did what he did when he seen you."

She wrote something on her paper. "Truthfully, I didn't spend the past three years hovering around that prison. I returned home on a half-dozen different occasions, usually after the judge would dismiss my findings."

"Tell you to go back home with your tail between your legs?"

"If I had a tail," she said with some bite. "But my real problem was the other parts I was born with, the parts that make me a woman." She pointed at him like he was at fault, but then he realized it was men in general she was pointing to. "The judge brushed me aside every time because I was not a man."

"But then you'd come back?"

"When I'd get tired of my father chastising me about not being married, yes, I'd come back. He doesn't approve of my profession. He and my mother want little grandchildren running through their gardens, like all of their high-society friends, when all I want is to write."

"And chase stories."

"And chase stories," she said with a nod and a quick fist to the tabletop.

Then Peter smiled and said, "Chase stories."

Jeremiah studied her. "There's more to it—you returning time and time again to needle a judge who wouldn't listen."

"If there's more to it, then I don't know what it is."

"Because you just want the truth?"

"Yes, the truth." She leaned forward with her elbows on the table again. "One of those bodies had a cut on the arm, as was stated in the trial. Did you cut one of them?" She'd glanced at his left arm as she'd said it, which made him wonder exactly how much she knew about him. He straightened the cuff at his wrist and made sure it was pulled down all the way.

She was relentless. "Jeremiah?"

He pursed his lips. "Those men were bad people."

"How did you know?"

"Felt it when I got close. Then I saw it when I brushed by them. And now . . ."

"Now what?"

"Now it's just the feeling, and even then it's fuzzy."

"What's fuzzy?"

"When I approach somebody from the wrong side."

"There it is," she said, excited. "You referred to that when you took the stand, which I don't think your lawyer should have let you do. The wrong side?"

"The bad people, Rose."

"As in the wrong side of the coin?"

"I suppose." He looked away and watched the boy, who was focused on typing again. "Ever since I took the electricity in that chair, my nightmares ended. And now I don't see it anymore."

"See what?"

"The ugliness, Rose. The bad stuff that the bad people do."

"Like that man, Boo, you recently buried?"

"How do you know about him?"

"Orion."

"Orion needs to close his hole."

"Did you flip a coin that led you back to Nowhere?"

He sucked in a deep breath and held on to it for a moment. He let it out slowly. "I did."

"And it led you to Peter?"

He nodded.

"And then what?"

"He followed me home."

"You saved his life then."

Jeremiah shrugged, drank from the coffee mug he'd already drained dry.

"What did you see when you brushed up against Boo?"

"Nothing."

"But you sensed something bad?"

"I did. Old Sparky didn't clean the slate, I guess."

"And you flipped the coin?"

"I did."

"And he's dead now?"

"You know he is. No innocent is ever completely free of guilt, Rose."

"So you've said."

"But with those four men, I never should have gone back to them and flipped the coin, like I was playing the role of God or something. Even then I had a notion of what could happen." He thought back to William Worst, but didn't tell her about it. "Part of me regrets that to this day."

"And the other part?"

"The other part needed to know."

"Know what, Jeremiah?"

"If I was flipping the coin, or if it was flipping me?"

"Like the coin was fate?"

He shrugged, then tugged on his left shirtsleeve again.

She leaned back, let out a tired breath, but then the smile returned. "You said something on the stand about releasing the pressure that builds up inside you. What pressure?"

"I don't know."

"Tell me about your nightmare."

"No."

"Why did you make that one cut on the body, Jeremiah?" She spoke like the boy was too jingled to listen, but Jeremiah could tell he was hanging on every word and they shouldn't be discussing these things in front of him.

"Why did I cut that body?"

"Yes."

"Same reason I cut William Worst ten years ago."

Shock splintered her steely resolve. "Who is William Worst?"

"He used to live in this house."

"And what happened to him?"

Jeremiah stood. "I need some more coffee."

She followed him into the kitchen. "What happened to William Worst, Jeremiah?"

He stopped to face her. "He was my first, Rose."

A shiver ran through him. He'd never admitted that to anyone, although he suspected Josiah knew. And maybe Ellen, the way both of them had looked at him on the day it had happened. Some kind of bond had been forged between those two that day.

"Your first what?"

"My first victim," Jeremiah said, his chin sinking toward his chest. "The first victim of the country's infamous Coin-Flip Killer."

He lifted the pot from the stove and filled his mug. She followed him back into the dining room.

Peter watched them.

Rose reached out and grabbed Jeremiah's arm, a move that in the past had caused too many saloon fights to count. You didn't grab Jeremiah Goodbye and get away with it. But now, after a beat, he turned toward her and lifted her chin so that they stared into each other's eyes.

And then he kissed her right on those red lips. Kissed her for ten seconds, and after five he felt her arms around him, her hands and fingers splayed out across his back.

Suddenly she pushed him away. "Why'd you do that?"

"To see what you'd do?"

She wiped her mouth. Her chest was heaving; her neckline flushed nearly the color of her dress. For the first time since he'd met her, she seemed vulnerable.

"Well, don't do that again."

"You sure about that?"

"Not really."

"Well, okay then."

"Tell me about William Worst."

"Tell me why you haven't found a man who'd marry you? You're pretty good at doing what we just did."

Her cheeks went red. "There've been plenty of men who've asked for my hand."

"And?"

"And I just haven't found the right one."

"Yet."

She grabbed his left arm, where the sleeve was still buttoned at the wrist. "It's nearly summer, and the temperature is rising."

"So?"

"So why do you keep your cuffs buttoned when I noticed all these other farmers rolling them to their elbows."

"Just the way I do it."

Before he could make a move to stop her, she ripped at the cuff, and the button popped free. And then just as quickly, she'd pushed his sleeve halfway up his forearm. He pulled his arm from her and turned away, lowering the sleeve back down.

"Where'd those scars come from?" she asked. "I noticed them at the trial. I was watching you. When you'd shift a certain way in your chair, your sleeve would push up and I could see the lowest one there on your forearm."

He reached for the doorknob. "I think you should go."

She didn't move.

Peter had gotten up from the table, though, and was staring out the window. He'd gotten so close to the sill that when he started pointing his finger touched glass.

Sunlight cut a diagonal line across the room, and slowly that line got swallowed up by shade. And then the room turned dark. Jeremiah looked out the open door and then closed it.

"What is it?" Rose asked.

"Another duster. A big one." Jeremiah and Peter moved with purpose from room to room, wetting down sheets and hanging them from every window and door as dust started to tap against the house siding and rooftop.

Rose asked what she could do and proved helpful in securing the house, not at all panicked like Jeremiah had thought she might be. Perhaps it wasn't her first duster. More likely, though, as a reporter, she couldn't wait to witness what the plains had suffered darn near daily for three or four years now. She probably hoped it would be another Black Sunday so she could snap her pictures and do her writing.

He looked for some fear in her, hoped for it, really, just to answer some of the doubt he still carried about her objectives here in Nowhere. And when one of the living room windows shattered and glass blew inward against the sheet, he saw it. Her hand went to her chest and her eyes jumped. He took her by the arm and led her to the dining room table, where Peter was draping a damp sheet like a curtain. The three of them ducked underneath. Dust spun against the floor. Peter lit a candle, and a minute later it blew out. He then calmed himself like he always did, by punching keys on that typewriter.

Any sign of fear had left Rose. She hunkered like Jeremiah, although not as far because she was at least ten inches shorter than him. Gradually their eyes adjusted to the dark. He let her push his sleeve up to the elbow. A shiver swept through him when she did it, and when she ran the tip of her finger with a gentleness only a mother could give over the patchwork of scars he had there, the hairs on his arm stood on end. The only other person ever to touch him there was Ellen, but it hadn't felt like this—like static electricity might feel like if you walked right through one of the strikes. Deep inside he smiled, knowing it was the first hint that what he'd done years ago in regard to leaving Ellen to Josiah was in fact the right thing to do.

"The coin never lies."

"What's that?" Rose asked.

"Nothing." As he reminisced, he suddenly felt the urge to hold Ellen. He hoped Josiah was doing just that, but something told him he wasn't. Maybe that's why he felt the urge now to do what his twin no longer would.

Dust filtered in under the sheet-curtain. He handed damp rags to Peter and Rose and told them both to keep their mouths and noses covered. Peter did what he was told with the one hand and continued to type with the other.

Rose ran her fingers over the fifty-odd half-inch scars on the underside of his forearm, running from an inch below the wrist to where his arm would bend.

"It didn't take much," said Jeremiah.

"Much to do what?"

"To let it out. The pressure. Those images I'd see. I'd cut myself to let it out."

"And you'd bleed?" She traced her finger across the scars again, and his heart sped up.

"Yes, I'd bleed." He rolled his sleeve back down.

"You say that with relief."

"Always felt that way. Seeing the blood reminded me I was real. I tried cutting that one body. It wasn't widely known that I'd done that."

"I've done my homework."

"I was crazed when I did it. Just a little nick before my mind cried out, what are you doing?"

"What *were* you doing, Jeremiah? What were you trying to see?"

"What evil looked like on the inside."

FIFTEEN

No one spoke in the Goodbye household. Coughing and hacking were the only sounds of the day.

Ellen had started a croupy cough of her own that rivaled her son's. In her mind she'd begun to count the days she had left—she felt certain now the dust would eventually kill them all.

Hurry up, then, and get it over with.

She sat at the dining room table by herself. Josiah and Wilmington were in the kitchen, sitting across from each other but not talking. Just staring.

James hadn't slept at all the night before, which meant that Ellen hadn't slept either, and her eyelids grew heavier by the minute. James had finally cried himself to sleep ten minutes ago. Ellen was fighting it, afraid that if she nodded off now she wouldn't sleep during the night, and last night had been horrible. All that crying and coughing had sent her mind wandering to places it only went when hope was gone.

She and Orion had been the only ones in town still clinging to it. Josiah had lost it weeks ago. Wilmington's hope had begun to dwindle the day Jeremiah was taken away. But that big duster, the one that occurred on the day they now called Black Sunday, had buried any hope that remained. The hole was too dark and deep now, and there were no more rungs on that ladder. "No use climbing anymore," she said aloud.

Black Sunday had ruined them, entering their brains like a disease, mean and ugly. The things they'd all said to each other made her sick to her stomach, and it wasn't just those who'd gathered in the Bentley or who lived in Nowhere. Rumor said it was widespread. Folks were acting strange in Guymon to the southwest, and also up north in Liberal, just across the Kansas border. That Black Sunday dust had combed across the plains, churning like the fancy end of a tractor, tilling up dust and slamming it down with a force never seen before, leaving nothing but brain-dead survivors in its wake.

Just about everybody had lost their filters and turned mean and ugly, speaking their minds without any thought of the repercussions. And now everyone had gone quiet, weighed down by all that dust, and no one seemed to have the energy to try anymore.

No one, that is, except Jeremiah and that boy, Peter, the smiler who never said boo. A boy she loved like her own but had only recently met. Come to think of it, Nicholas Draper still managed a smile. Probably had something to do with how Jeremiah had covered him up during all that darkness. That ugly dust had never got to him, and somehow it had never touched Jeremiah. He'd probably spent so many nights under the weight of those nightmares that it had made him somehow immune.

Or maybe it was the five seconds he'd spent in that electric chair.

Yesterday evening she'd gone over to the Bentley to check on Orion. Nicholas Draper had been outside clearing his porch.

Other than Jeremiah and Peter, he was the only one digging out after last evening's duster. And that reporter woman too. She'd gotten dusted in with Jeremiah and Peter inside the Worst house and had grabbed a broom to help them clean up five minutes after the duster moved on.

What does she really want with Jeremiah? What were they doing in that house?

That thought was what had kept Ellen up all last night, wishing more than once that the woman would have gotten lost in the storm. That was a mean ol' nasty thought to have, but truth be told it felt good to have it, like it was all part of the process. *What process?* She stood from the table and walked into the kitchen, where her husband and father-in-law sat like human statues, one dumb-looking as the other. *The process Black Sunday started. The one that turned everybody mean, speaking their minds with reckless abandon, and then turned them quiet. And then what?*

Part of her couldn't wait to know. The other part, well, maybe there was a smidge of something left in her, a little pinprick of light in all the darkness.

When she'd checked on Orion yesterday, she'd found him behind the bar, despondent. He'd stayed clammed up even when she asked him questions. His eyes had been open, but there'd been no light on in there. She recalled hoping that reporter woman would come out of her room, but she never had. Ellen had heard her in there typing though, like Peter, except there was probably paper and a ribbon in her machine and actual words to accompany the clacking.

Had she been writing about Jeremiah or the town?

It was the next day, and Ellen still didn't have an answer to that. She padded barefoot across the dusty kitchen floor. There was a pitcher of water next to the sink. She poured some into a coffee mug, and it came out muddy. They'd forgotten to cover it before yesterday's duster. They hadn't covered the windows either, which was why there were drifts in some of the corners of the room and dust atop the table and counters. Dust filtered down from the hole in the ceiling, and her two men paid it no attention whatever.

Ellen put the mug down hard enough to crack and neither Josiah nor Wilmington flinched. She turned toward the table, leaning with her rear end against the counter, and clapped once. They didn't react to that either. *Might as well be drooling in the madhouse, both of them.* They seemed to be in a more advanced stage than she was. Then again, they'd either dished out or been the brunt of more ugly talk than she had. Josiah, especially, being told to his face by his own father that his twin was the favored one.

"That must have been like a dagger cut," she said out loud. "You know it, Josiah? Like one of those cuts where the knife turns."

Josiah flicked at the tabletop dust in front of him but said nothing.

She wasn't even sure why she'd just said that. Maybe she was still in that mean stage and had some more to say before she'd go quiet like the others.

"And what was that hug about, Wilmington? Hugging that reporter woman last night like she was some prodigal returned. Hugged her just like you did Jeremiah. Now that's not right, you hear me? Neither was all that mean talk you shoveled on Orion."

Wilmington blinked, but his eyes stayed focused on the tabletop.

"Did you ever have relations with my mother, Wilmington?"

Nothing.

She folded her arms and thought of Jeremiah. Tried to think of their good times, but all that flashed was the day before he'd been taken away on the paddy wagon. The day he'd held both her hands in his own and looked down into her eyes like he was fixing to plant one on her.

She'd had a notion he would ask for her hand in marriage that day, just like Josiah had gotten down on his knee and done one week prior, right there in the lobby of the Bentley Hotel with half the town watching. She'd told Josiah she'd have to think about it, whispering in his ear so as not to embarrass him.

"What's there to think about?" Josiah had asked, leading her outside to the sunlight.

"What's there not to think about, Josiah? It's the rest of our lives we're talking about."

"You love me, don't you?"

"'Course I do."

"Then what's holding you back?" He'd said it like he already knew.

"Just need time to think about it is all."

"How long?"

"A week." She wasn't sure why she'd said that, but at the time she'd just needed space.

And then, six days later, Jeremiah had taken her behind the barn, where they'd spent so much time together, sneaking like they always did. Her father, when he was alive, had never approved of Jeremiah like he did Josiah.

"He's got a temper, Ellen. He drinks too much. And the way he's always flipping that coin—I just don't like it."

"But Daddy, he's also got more good than most people I know. It's just that the good keeps getting overshadowed."

Jeremiah hadn't kissed her that afternoon behind the barn, at least not in the context she'd hoped. And he hadn't gotten down on one knee and asked her for marriage either. In fact, he'd about done the opposite.

"I can't marry you, Ellen."

The tears had been immediate, and she'd been too choked up to talk at first.

"You accept that offer from my brother. He's a good man."

"But he's not you, Jeremiah."

"And that's a good thing, Ellen. I've done some bad things. I feel a storm coming, and not the kind from the sky."

"What kind then, Jeremiah?"

"The kind that comes with badges and guns."

She'd covered her mouth and then slapped his chest because she couldn't bring herself to slap his face. "What did you do?"

"I don't know for sure. My mind's been muddled, and I've done some things without the advantage of thinking."

"It's all that drinking," she said. "I'll help you get over that."

"There is no getting over what I've got, Ellen. That's a train track that has no ending." He'd grabbed her arms so she wouldn't hit him again. "Now I know you have feelings for Josiah. Strong ones. And me and you can't be."

"How do you know that? How can you be so sure?"

"I just am, Ellen. You'll have to trust me."

He'd kissed her that day behind the barn, but it had been full of finality, with no hint of future in it. The next day the authorities had dug up four bodies from the grain silo and dragged Jeremiah away in shackles just as a thunderboomer was rolling in.

Even now, as the memory trickled distant, Ellen felt a lump in her throat. Too bad the drought and dust had dried up her tears. Might have been a good remedy right about now.

She lifted her mug of muddy water and hurled it across the

room, aiming for the far wall because she just felt like seeing something break, but the mug went off target and hit Josiah on the right cheekbone. The mug clunked to the floor. Muddy water splashed in a line like a mountain ridge as it mixed with dust.

Josiah turned his head toward her slowly, like the blood now meandering down the cut she'd just put in his cheek. Apparently the drought hadn't dried up his tears—something still resided in there—and they mixed with the blood and dripped together down his cheek to the tabletop.

She looked away, turned toward the window over the sink.

Across the road, the Bentley Hotel looked old and abandoned, the wraparound porch buried in drifts that formed and reformed in the wind. Wearing pajamas, Orion stood in the middle of the Bentley's front lawn—front dust, rather—staring blankly up toward the sky. He looked like a statue, like Josiah and Wilmington at the kitchen table, except Orion was standing. *What are you doing out there, old man?*

Suddenly Orion fell forward like he'd passed out, so unaware that he didn't even brace himself with his hands when his body hit. Just face-planted with a thud right into the dust.

Ellen went out to check on him.

But she didn't go quickly.

No one else was outside when Ellen crossed the road toward the Bentley. Apparently she'd been the only one to see Orion fall.

In a normal state of mind, she would have run outside screaming his name. But things weren't normal anymore, were they? Which is why she casually walked over, no faster than she would have walked to get her mail back when it used to get delivered. Besides, she knew Orion was alive because his arms were moving.

You look like you're trying to swim, Orion. She kept that thought in, and as she crossed the road, she wondered if she'd finally advanced to that next stage from the Black Sunday disease. She was turning quiet, as if the dust had gobbled up her words. She just didn't feel like talking. If she did, it seemed, the conjuring of them might cause more pain than the words themselves.

And then came that reporter, running out the front door of the Bentley in her pretty dress and shiny hair and igniting the air with her toxic screams. "Someone call the doctor," she cried. "Get an ambulance," she pleaded toward Ellen, who just stood there like several other neighbors had begun to do. Even Sister Moffitt did nothing, didn't even finger her rosary beads.

"What is wrong with you people?" Rose Buchanan yelled.

Orion managed to make it to his knees, but he still had his face near the dust, and all of a sudden he put a finger scoop of it in his mouth as if to taste it.

Rose grabbed his hands, and he tried to fight her, but he was old and she was stronger than that slender frame looked. She managed to wrestle him onto his backside, her legs wrapped around his hips in a way that revealed way too much of those long legs.

Hugging Orion from behind, Rose pinned his arms down with her own, and he hacked and coughed out what he'd just attempted to swallow. Rose beat him on the back like Ellen did with James every night.

Jeremiah arrived, and the crowd of onlookers parted for him. Peter wasn't too far behind, flinching every time Orion hacked. He covered his ears and kept his distance.

Jeremiah knelt to the ground to help Rose, but by that time

Orion had stopped fighting her. He looked defeated. His shoulders slumped. His entire face sagged as if he'd just then and there lost all hope that had remained.

Dr. Craven finally arrived, yawning, his shirt buttoned off-kilter and untucked, clearly in no hurry to help.

Ellen looked over her shoulder and saw that Wilmington had made it out of the house too, but he was more focused on Rose than on his pal Orion. Josiah had stayed on their porch, watching from a distance with his elbows on the wooden railing and his fingers casually interlocked, like he was watching the beauty of a setting sun and not the sudden collapse of one of the town's founders. He hadn't even wiped the blood from his cheek.

When Ellen looked back to the chaos—which really wasn't that exciting anymore—Jeremiah's eyes locked on hers. Normally his gaze would have garnered an emotional response, but now it did nothing but make her want to take a nap. They stared at one another. Jeremiah said something that might have included her name, but all she could hear was some warped gobble, his words lost in some void that sounded like when she'd put seashells up to her ears when she was little. Back when her family had lived on the East Coast.

"Ellen?" Jeremiah's voice swooped back into focus like a wind gust. "Ellen, you need to help us here. I think he hurt his shoulder. And maybe broke his nose."

Ellen didn't move. But she did manage to find motivation for some words, as remnants remained from the memory she'd had in the kitchen earlier. "You flipped a coin, didn't you, Jeremiah?"

"What are you talking about, Ellen?"

"On us. You flipped a coin on us. Back then."

He started to say something in denial, but words failed him.

Ellen turned and walked back home, figuring it wouldn't be a bad thing if she'd just spoken her last words.

She heard Nicholas Draper say, "Dr. Craven, you gonna do something for Mr. Bentley or not?"

Dr. Craven answered, monotone. "Life can get heavy, Nicholas. That man there is broken by it."

SIXTEEN

The day after Orion collapsed, another duster rolled in, accumulating on top of the one before it and the one before that. With the citizens of Nowhere refusing to dig out, porches had gone under, fences were no longer visible, and awnings sagged under the weight of so much dust.

Something had to be done before the town was buried.

Jeremiah just didn't know what that something could be.

He and Rose had gone through town knocking on doors and storefronts, but no one had answered. Ellen hadn't even opened up, although he'd seen the sheet move at the living room window. After waiting a couple of minutes to no avail, Jeremiah had moved on.

After yesterday's episode, Orion had locked himself inside his room at the Bentley. They knew he was alive because they could hear him whimpering. Jeremiah had threatened to burn the place down if he didn't come out, but they'd both known it was an empty threat. Jeremiah had even had Peter gong that church bell in the middle of the hotel lobby, but no one had come.

Jeremiah and Rose, after a second afternoon of knocking on

doors, stood in the middle of Main Street surveying the wasteland. "Like something out of a novel," Rose said as a tumbleweed floated by. In the distance, Mr. Mulraney's cows mooed and cried. No doubt starving. Filling up with dust instead of food. He'd found a little bit of hay left in Mulraney's barn loft and forked it down for them, but it wouldn't last long.

The sky was dry, the air warm and humid—more like summer after a thunderboomer than spring. Jeremiah predicted harsh months ahead.

"Might not be any months if these people don't come out of their homes," said Rose. "We don't know what's going on behind those closed doors, Jeremiah."

She was right. He'd feared the same. Everyone had completely given up, and they both feared the town would starve to death like those cows. The windows they'd managed to look through showed neighbor after neighbor just sitting there and staring. The only one to open the door when they'd knocked was Nicholas Draper, and he'd ushered them inside like he'd been hoping for company. His mother, Loreda, was refusing to eat or drink. She'd lost more weight than what Jeremiah thought possible in only a couple of days, and when Rose tried to pour water into her mouth she'd spat it back out.

Rose folded her arms against the wind. After two days of being in Nowhere, she'd begun to wear the look of the southern plains, the look of the so-called dust bowl. Her hair, although combed and gathered in a loose bundle against her nape, no longer shimmered, and on closer inspection it contained little flecks of dust. She hadn't taken the time to make up her face either. The dust had a way of sticking to the makeup anyhow. Her cheeks and nose were burned from the sun. For the moment, she'd backed off on the questions about his past, focusing instead on the town and what was happening to it, and for that Jeremiah was relieved, even if the derailing was only temporary. At least she had her priorities straight.

Something crashed down the road, and they turned toward the sound. With no movement about town, all sounds carried, and this one had come from Dr. Craven's house.

Jeremiah and Rose took off running, trudging through the drifts like they would during a snowstorm. Rose held the skirt of her dress to keep it out of the dust. Jeremiah took a wrong step and sank to his knee. Rose gripped his hand and helped him back to level ground.

No doors opened.

They couldn't have been the only ones to hear it—what sounded like a table overturning. They were just the only ones who cared enough to investigate.

Jeremiah suddenly felt like he was being watched. Last night he'd had another nightmare, the new kind where that figure made of dust was on the prowl, lurking around every corner and laughing. Jeremiah surveyed the town as they moved through it, but saw no such figure, no man made of dust. But he knew now that his mind was sending a clear message.

Evil was doing the town, and the devil was behind those doings.

"Jeremiah, what is it? What's wrong?"

Devil made of dust. Ripped out of my nightmares and covering the town like a blanket. But these nightmares were different than the other kind had been. They varied and had more to do with the here and now, while the recurring nightmare he'd had since birth had been the same every time. Exactly the same. Same duration. Same event. Which meant . . .

"Jeremiah?"

Rose's hand was on his forearm, the same arm as his self-inflicted scars. Together they moved toward Dr. Craven's house. They stumbled up the buried front porch, using the railing for support. The front door was locked, as it had been earlier in the day. Dr. Craven's dog lay next to the door, gnawing on the remains of a chicken he'd either killed or found dead. He didn't even look up as Jeremiah knocked, then called the doctor's name.

After a minute of waiting, Jeremiah kicked at the doorknob until the wood around it splintered. Rose lowered her shoulder and busted the door open. It rammed against the wall, swayed on creaking hinges, creepily audible through all the cryptic silence the house had taken on. Dr. Craven lay in the middle of the living room floor with a spot of blood on his forehead. A rifle leaned against the wall beside the couch. *Was he planning on using it? On himself? On anyone who walked through the door? Surely not.*

The doctor's breaths came out as wheezes, spaced apart and slow as his eyes stared up at the ceiling, blinking just often enough to show he was alive.

He was one of the original settlers of the town, having met both Wilmington and Orion on that train ride to the fictional town of Majestic. He'd delivered Jeremiah and Josiah, along with just about every baby born in Nowhere, even helping bury Jeremiah and Ellen's secret miscarriage. He'd always been a comforting shoulder, a man of reason and patience and hope, and now he'd seemingly lost it like all the others.

Jeremiah moved closer to the body. "Doctor, can you hear me?"

Dr. Craven blinked. Dust flecked the stubble on his face, which was normally clean-shaven. "I fell."

Rose grabbed him under the shoulders. "Let's get you back to the couch."

"Leave me," he wheezed.

"Won't do that," said Jeremiah, noticing how the doc's cheeks looked sunken in. "How many days since you've eaten, doc?"

Dr. Craven shook his head, not like he didn't know, but rather like he didn't care. "We are all dust, and to dust we shall return."

It wasn't the bleakness of Dr. Craven's situation or even the strange words he'd muttered from his death pose on the floor that sent Jeremiah outside with pangs of claustrophobia and shortness of breath.

It was Peter. He felt an urgent need to go make sure the boy was okay. So after they'd helped—practically carried—Dr. Craven back to the couch, propped him up like a doll, and forced half a glass of water down his throat, Jeremiah hurried outside.

Rose followed. "Jeremiah? What is it?"

He didn't tell her about the voice he'd heard as they'd walked the doctor over to the couch, the voice in his head that sounded like wind-blown dust in a paper bag. He knew it was in his head because Rose showed no reaction—no sign that she'd heard the dust man say Peter's name in a whisper.

They found Peter just as they'd left him, at his desk, pecking away on that typewriter. He was so focused, he didn't even look up when they called his name from the hallway. His fingers moved fast, as usual, but without the usual rhythm or sentence-like structure in the pecking. Now Peter typed at a wild tempo that Jeremiah likened to fury or rage, a pressure that needed release, like the pressure that had prompted him to make those cuts on his forearm. Maybe Peter had heard that dusty voice too.

No, those were my nightmares, not his.

Jeremiah let the boy be. He hurried down the hall and grabbed his rifle from the room he'd been sleeping in—realizing now that it felt right staying in the Worst house as some morbid kind of penance for what had happened to William—and headed back outside. The sun had found its way through the moving clouds.

Rose kept up with him. "Where are you going with that rifle? Jeremiah?"

He was too focused to answer. He barely even heard what she'd said, his eyes surveying frantically, flicking from house to house, searching every rooftop and wooden façade for that devil made of dust. Seconds later he stood on Wilmington's porch, banging on the door this time instead of knocking. He rested his forehead on the wood, jaw clenched and breathing like a steam engine.

He gave them a few seconds before banging again, knocking that door until his fist hurt. Then, instead of kicking the door in, he shot the doorknob with his rifle. Rose ducked and covered her face. Wood splintered to a gaping hole. The door swung inward, and Jeremiah stepped inside.

"Josiah? Ellen?" He stepped into the kitchen. "Daddy?"

He heard nothing. Not even James crying or coughing.

He headed for Ellen and Josiah's room first, the one that used to be his room, the room where the nightmares still probably lingered. Ellen was in bed with the sheets rumpled around her bare legs. James was cradled under her arm, and neither one of them moved. Ellen's eyes were open, unblinking, which got Jeremiah's heart racing as he jumped toward the bed and ran his hand through her dusty hair.

Her eyelid moved. She blinked. When he put his finger under her nose he felt air there. James shifted ever so slightly.

Jeremiah's heart settled. He held his face and then ran his hands down his cheeks in an exhale of relief.

Ellen's pupils found him. She stared but said nothing. She looked catatonic.

Rose appeared in the doorway. "Your father is in his bed."

"I'm assuming he's alive?"

"Yes, but unresponsive when I attempted to shake him. His eyes opened, but nobody was there."

"Where's Josiah?"

"I don't know."

"Keep looking."

She ducked back into the hallway, and Jeremiah gripped Ellen's hand, which was hot and rough like the ground would get during the summer.

"Ellen, you've got to get up. You can't just let it have you."

She blinked, whispered something he couldn't understand. She wasn't trying to whisper. It was more like that was all the strength she could muster. He leaned closer.

"Go away," she said.

He squeezed her hand. "Ellen, I'm not going anywhere."

"Dust to dust."

"Don't say that." He swallowed hard and wiped his hand over his face again. "You need to sit up, Ellen. Do you hear me?"

Ellen grinned. "To dust we shall return, Jeremiah."

Footsteps sounded behind him. He assumed it was Rose, but when he looked over his shoulder, Josiah stood in the doorway with a rifle and a facial expression that held no life to it whatever. He wasn't pointing the weapon, just holding it like a soldier would standing guard, butt against his right hip and the barrel angled up toward his left shoulder. Except Josiah was no soldier, and he wavered like he was drunk, eyes miles away and his hair recently slept on.

Jeremiah said, "Josiah, put the gun down."

"Gotta protect my family from all this dust."

"You can't shoot dust, Josiah."

Josiah gave a reptilian blink, as if he didn't understand. "I made you a dust pie in the kitchen, brother. Just like you like it. Put a little water in there to make it muddy."

"Where's Rose?"

Josiah shrugged. "She sure is a looker, Jeremiah. Gotta admit I've taken a few ganders at those long gams of hers." He looked at Ellen. "Sorry, babe." She acted as if she hadn't even heard. He said to Jeremiah. "You gonna flip a coin on her too? Huh?"

"Put the rifle down."

"Put the rifle down." Josiah mocked him, then returned his voice to normal. "You know I seen you behind the barn that day, touching on my future wife. Embracing like she'd just agreed to be yours when she was supposed to be mine."

"You saw wrong, brother. You saw me telling her it couldn't be, to marry you."

Josiah smiled. "Too bad, then, I guess. I was wrangling with calling the authorities on those bodies you'd buried, but when I seen what I seen behind that barn . . ."

"What you thought you seen."

"Anyway, that was the tipping point, Jeremiah."

"And look where we are now."

"Look where we are."

Jeremiah felt like he needed to keep him talking. "Can't always believe what the eyes tell you."

Josiah didn't respond. He closed his eyes as if he'd gone to sleep on his feet. Like he'd just that instant gone from saying whatever he thought to saying nothing at all, a stage most everyone had passed a long time ago—even Josiah, come to think of it. Maybe the burst of conversation was just that, a burst, and the eyes closing was just his way to shut it down again.

Josiah finally opened his eyes, then wobbled like he was going to fall over. He wasn't drunk; he just didn't have the energy—or the willpower—to stand straight. Rose showed up beside Josiah in the hallway, and just as she was about to balance him with her hand, he lurched face-forward.

Jeremiah moved from the bed to catch him, but not fast enough.

Josiah fell straight down, with his finger still on the trigger of that rifle. When he hit the floor, the rifle went off.

Jeremiah's shoulder caught fire.

Rose screamed.

After that, Jeremiah seemed to swim in and out of consciousness. He remembered panting on the floor, pressing against the flow from the wound. He remembered Josiah's left cheek flush against the hardwood, Josiah staring and blinking slowly, eyelids heavy with a mixture of what could have been both remorse and satisfaction.

And then his voice: "From dust we come, Jeremiah. And to dust we shall return."

SEVENTEEN

Jeremiah bit down on the leather as Rose poured corn whiskey over the shoulder wound where the bullet from Josiah's rifle had tunneled clean through and embedded in his childhood wall.

She offered him the bottle. "You need a quick pull?" He spat the belt to the floor and shook his head. Sweat dripped from his brow. The wound burned, and heat waves rolled all over his body as he tried to stay upright on the Worsts' dining room chair. He eyed the bottle but wasn't even tempted to partake.

She studied him and asked for a reason, knowing from the trial that at one time in his life he'd been deeply embedded in the drink.

"It was the jolt I took in Old Sparky," he said, wincing. "Don't have the urge to drink anymore."

"That easy, huh?"

He choked out a laugh. "Nothing's as easy as it seems, Rose."

Once she got the bleeding under control, she wrapped his shoulder with strips she'd torn from a bedsheet. Rose proved herself braver, stronger every minute Jeremiah knew her.

They were lucky nothing more had happened inside that house. The shooting had been an accident, pure and simple, but the bullet could have gone any which way, and Jeremiah was more than willing to take one if it meant saving Ellen and her son.

Peter sat at the far end of the table, peeking periodically through splayed fingers. Earlier, he'd covered his eyes as soon as he entered the house and saw the blood, but then he'd done exactly what Rose told him and hurried to get the bedsheet. And now, the tighter she wrapped the wound, the woozier and more nauseous Jeremiah became, until he suddenly felt sick to his stomach. He closed his eyes for a few beats to quell it. A breeze blew the front door open. Blood trailed from the porch to where he now sat, where Rose, despite her slight frame, had somehow dragged his much larger body and dropped him in the chair.

How much blood had he lost?

He grew lightheaded. His vision swirled, and then it all went black.

Jeremiah and Josiah sat across from each other at a table inside the Bentley Hotel, watching out the window as rain came down in torrents from a sky that kept on giving.

Baseball gloves rested next to plates smeared with remnants of egg yolk, bacon grease, and crust from two pieces of toast each. Josiah liked his eggs runny, but Jeremiah liked his in an all-out sprint, practically drinkable, he'd told Orion upon entering the hotel that morning with his twin and his father. Orion was a fantastic host—everyone loved his hotel and the fancy way he dressed—but many said he was an even better cook.

The boys had hurried through breakfast because it was so good, but also because they wanted to get out to the grass fields, the few that were not plowed for wheat, and toss the baseball around, maybe gather a few of their friends for a real game. Today they'd agreed that Jeremiah would be Ty Cobb and Josiah would be Babe Ruth. But by the time Jeremiah had slurped down his last egg, the one so covered in pepper it made his eyes water, the sky had opened up, and the rain looked primed for a real soaker.

Orion and Wilmington joined the nine-year-olds at the table in an attempt to cheer them up. They'd been behind the bar, cleaning up from a party that had gone well into the night, as most parties inside the Bentley had the tendency to do, but now they took seats on opposite ends of the square table. Now all four sides were full.

Orion pointed out the window to all that rain. "You know what that is, boys?"

Josiah and Jeremiah looked at each other. Of course they knew what it was, but Jeremiah said it anyway. "It's rain, Mr. Bentley. And it's ruining our plans."

Wilmington smiled. "Boys, that out there isn't just rain. Look closer. Go on."

Skeptical, the two boys looked again, squinting this time to see if they'd notice anything different. Jeremiah said, "Still just rain."

Wilmington took a quarter out of his pocket and let it jangle on the table. "This is what's out there, boys."

Josiah said, "That rain's a quarter?"

Orion chuckled, adjusted the lapels on his coat, and said, "Boys, that rain is money. That rain makes the wheat grow tall and fat. That rain helps feed our soldiers fighting overseas, in a war me and your father were too old for and you boys are thankfully too young to fight in." He leaned back in his chair. "That rain is money. Prosperity. And my gut tells me the next decade is going to be chock full of both."

"But you can't play baseball in the rain," said Jeremiah.

Orion smirked and reached across for the quarter. "Here, let me show you something you can do inside when it's raining." Under the tip of his index finger, he held the quarter on edge, and with the middle finger of his other hand he flicked the coin until it got to spinning. The boys watched it rotate like a top and dance across the table, making that same sound the bowling balls made at Nowhere's bowling lane, where the two boys sometimes earned coins of their own as pin catchers.

The coin slowed, started to wobble. And what Orion did next made their eyes grow wide. He blew gently on that coin, and it spun faster again. He blew some more to keep it going, even standing from his chair to follow where the coin had migrated across the table. Eventually he sat back down, and the coin rattled still.

"Wow," said the boys in unison. "Do it again."

"I'm afraid I'm out of breath," Orion said, theatrically patting his chest.

Wilmington grabbed the quarter. "Here's a game me and my father used to play." He looked at Josiah. "First, call it to see who goes first."

"Call what?" asked Josiah.

Wilmington showed his sons both sides of the coin. "Heads or tails. I'll spin the quarter in the air, and you try and guess how it will land. Got it?"

Josiah nodded, said "Heads," and then followed the coin with his eyes as his father flipped and caught it. Wilmington slapped the coin atop his other hand and slowly pulled it away, revealing the tails side. Josiah said, "What now?"

"You didn't get it right. So your brother goes first." Wilmington faced Jeremiah. "Now the rules of the game are simple. You call it in the air. If you get it right, you go again. If you get it wrong, the turn goes back to Josiah. Understood?"

Both boys jerked nods.

"And the first one to call twenty-one tosses wins."

"Wins what?" asked Jeremiah.

"The game."

"And the coin?" asked Jeremiah.

Wilmington looked at Orion, who shrugged. "Sure. Winner gets my last coin."

Wilmington flicked the coin upward and then caught, flipped, and revealed it in what looked like one swift motion while Jeremiah yelled, "Heads."

"Heads it is," said Wilmington. "Well done. You're up one to zero. Now you go again."

"Heads," said Jeremiah.

Wilmington laughed. "Slow down, pal. Haven't even flipped it yet." He flipped.

Jeremiah said, "Still heads."

Wilmington revealed the coin. "Heads again. Two zero."

Josiah was on the edge of his seat, smiling, eager for another shot at the flip.

Wilmington flicked the coin. "Tails," said Jeremiah.

His father revealed the coin. "Tails it is. Somebody is on a winning streak."

Orion said, "We should take him to the track and place us some bets on some bangtails."

Wilmington flipped the coin, and again Jeremiah guessed correctly, as he did on the next four flips, shouting out his answer the instant that coin left his father's thumb and showing little doubt as he did so.

Jeremiah was now on the edge of his chair, so engrossed in the coin-flip game that he'd knocked his baseball glove from the table to the floor and not even noticed. He rubbed his hands together like he was trying to create warmth.

Down eight to nothing, Josiah's smile began to wane as Jeremiah's continued to grow. Orion scratched his head. After two more correct guesses, Wilmington glanced at Josiah. "He's bound to miss any time now, Josiah, so get your guesser ready."

"No guessing to it," said Josiah with a sharp edge to his tone. "Jeremiah already knows the answers, Daddy. He's a cheater."

"Seemingly." Wilmington held up a finger, and Jeremiah noticed it was shaking. "Seemingly, but not possible."

Jeremiah laughed. "It's called power, Josiah."

Wilmington shot Jeremiah a warning glance, as if telling him to temper himself and not get big-headed.

Josiah shook his head, smelled the leather pocket of his glove, and said, "Well, go on then. Flip another, Daddy."

Wilmington flipped four more times in quick succession, with Jeremiah correctly predicting every time, without a second's hesitation. Jeremiah was now eyeing the coin like it was a golden nugget, rubbing his hands together faster and faster like a dice roller on a hot streak. After four more correct flips for Jeremiah, Wilmington pocketed the coin, ending the game prematurely, and suggested they play something else.

"Game's not over," said Jeremiah.

"It is for today," said Wilmington, with a sternness they saw only infrequently.

Orion stood, smiling large with a handclap, one of those gestures of happy emotion that sometimes seemed so forced. "So who's ready for some dessert?"

"It's breakfast," said Jeremiah.

"Today we'll make an exception," said Orion. "Ice cream?"

"Yes, ice cream it is," said Wilmington with a smile obviously geared toward cheering up Josiah. "Chocolate or vanilla?"

Josiah mumbled, "Chocolate."

"Jeremiah?"

"You took my coin, Daddy. Orion said the winner got to keep the coin."

Wilmington paused as if he didn't want to give it up, as if he didn't approve of how Jeremiah was handling his burst of luck, but then he reached into his pocket and tossed it over. Jeremiah caught it, and his eyes grew large.

His daddy asked again, "Chocolate or vanilla?"

Instead of answering, Jeremiah said, "Heads for chocolate and tails for vanilla."

Josiah shook his head.

Jeremiah flipped the coin and revealed it on the top of his left hand just like his daddy had done over and over. "Vanilla it is."

When Jeremiah came to, he was in the same chair he'd been in when he drifted off, except now his feet were propped up on the catty-corner chair and his boots had been removed.

He wiggled his toes and counted his blessings that he still had all ten of them. He'd never gotten a good look at Josiah's foot after he'd shot him days ago. Maybe he'd blown one of those toes off and Josiah didn't want him to know, so he kept it wrapped up. If so, Jeremiah supposed they were all even now and he'd gotten what he deserved.

Jeremiah felt like he'd been given a jolt of energy from that reverie, the memory of the coin-flip game on that rainy day inside the Bentley. One day years later, Josiah had told him that was when it all started.

"When what started?"

"You thinking yourself bigger than it all."

"Bigger than what all?"

"Never mind."

Josiah had turned away, the first sign of the wedge coming down between them. Just a chip though. The drinking, which Jeremiah had begun way too young, would drive that wedge a little deeper, but it wasn't until the *arrival* that the wedge got hammered home.

Jeremiah couldn't help feeling, although he couldn't put a finger on it, that it had started long before that—like before he could even walk. The coin had been just some kind of conduit. And something told him Wilmington might have thought so too, which was why he'd never approved of Jeremiah flipping that coin to make his decisions, even as a kid.

"Jeremiah?"

Rose's voice brought him back. He shifted in the chair, and a bolt of pain shot down his left side from shoulder to hip, as if he'd caught fire. *How long was I out?* The sun was already setting purple outside the window.

Why was there a long-needled syringe on the table?

And then Rose stepped into view. "Give it a minute to get into your bloodstream."

"Give what a minute?"

"The morphine." She pulled a chair beside him and sat in it. "Found some at the hospital. The sisters were much like what we saw with your family—worse off than some of their patients. Lying on cots and mostly unresponsive."

"Were the patients like the rest of the town?"

"Actually, they didn't seem as bad. They were coughing because of the dust in their lungs and the sickness."

"But none of them were out when the Black Sunday duster hit." He shifted in the chair again. Pain stabbed his shoulder, but it didn't bother him like it had moments before. The morphine acted fast and his head suddenly felt lighter, like it was attached to some string tethered from the ceiling. "That building is pretty tight, keeps out the dust. That's why they picked it for the hospital when the earth started peeling."

Rose looked distracted.

"What is it?"

"Just something I saw that I'm having trouble unseeing." She stared blankly out the window toward Main Street. "When you were out, I took a walk around town—you know, to check on things. That auto repair shop by the Baptist church."

"Deacon Sipes owns it." Jeremiah did his best to focus, but the morphine was muddling his brain. "He can be mean."

"I didn't see him," she said. "But the door to his shop was open, so I took a look inside." Her eyes glassed over. "There were so many of them, Jeremiah. A hundred at least."

He blinked hard through the opiate. "Hundred of what, Rose?"

"Jackrabbits." She motioned with her hand. "Hanging from the ceiling by their feet. He'd skinned them all. Gravity had stretched them longer than any jackrabbit I've ever seen."

"That's what we live off, Rose. Times are hard."

"I know that, but . . . they rustled, Jeremiah. Those rabbits. Even dead they rustled. The breeze moved them like muted wind chimes." Her chin quivered. "Can't unsee it, is all." She took a slug from the bottle of Old Sam on the table and gulped. She coughed and patted her chest.

Jeremiah laughed. It was the morphine's doing, because nothing was funny.

Rose laughed too, wiping moisture from her eyes. "Not usually much of a drinker."

"Desperate times," he said softly. His vision wavered, and Rose became blurry.

She got up from her chair and returned a minute later with a blanket. She covered him with it and ran the back of her hand across his forehead, feeling for a fever like his mother used to do before she'd died. When he and Josiah found her dead in her bed, Jeremiah had done the same to her. Except her skin had been cold.

Jeremiah heard Peter on his typewriter in the back room.

He fell asleep to the rhythm of those keys.

Amanda Goodbye had eyes like a summer sunset, and when she smiled her entire face lit the room. She gathered Jeremiah on her lap, smelling of piecrust and peaches. She was pale and impossibly thin from the cancer, and her breath came out in thin wheezes, but she still insisted on cooking, taking breaks every few minutes to sit down and rest.

Wilmington had remarked later that it took her all day to finish a pie, but he'd looked proud when he said it, not angry. "But I'd give anything to have those days back," he'd added. "Your mother died too young, Jeremiah. Death ain't picky when it comes to things like that. It takes you when it takes you and then leaves you to cope without the least bit of instructions on how you're supposed to do it."

Jeremiah should have been too young to remember his father telling him that, which was probably why Wilmington said it. He'd needed to let those words out. Just as his mother did when she placed him on his lap and said, "Now Jeremiah, you're probably too young to ever remember what I'm about to tell you, but it's more for me than you."

He did remember. Come to think of it, the first thing he'd ever seen was his mother's eyes on the day of his birth, and that memory hadn't left him either.

"You're a special kind of child, Jeremiah," she'd said. "We thought you'd never come out, and when you did, well, perhaps one day I'll let your father tell you about that. But I'll go to my grave knowing that those night scares you have, they all stem from what happened after you were delivered. I'm telling you, only the strongest of the strong could overcome what you did."

She laughed, and her eyes grew wet. "You know what I think? I think life and death were wrestling over you, Jeremiah. Or maybe it was good and evil. Yes, that's how I look upon it now. And you were just too darn stubborn to give in without a fight."

After a pause, she added, "Too bad you didn't share some of that fight in the womb."

Jeremiah had been drifting, half-asleep, dreams mixing with thoughts and memories in his mind. But now he awoke with a startle. His feet fell from the chair where they'd been propped, fragments of his mother's words still drifting through his mind.

Josiah's got fight. I've seen it. He felt defensive on his brother's behalf. As if his mother had been talking down about his twin, her firstborn son, who had been born so easily and never given them any trouble. Besides, Josiah had only been three years old when Mother died. How could a boy that young be expected to fight?

Apparently Jeremiah had.

"Welcome back." Rose placed a rifle on the floor next to the far wall. Beside it was another rifle that looked like Wilmington's along with a handgun, a set of knives, two hammers, an ax, and a loose bundle of rope.

Jeremiah's shoulder throbbed. Spots of red bled through the bandages. "Expecting a bombardment?"

"Just a precaution," she said. "They're all from your father's house. With what happened with Josiah and that gun going off, I gathered up anything possible they could accidently harm themselves with."

Jeremiah nodded. It was a smart thing to do. Hopeless people weren't always careful. And if they got too hopeless?

He didn't even want to think of it.

"What were they doing when you went in?" he asked.

"Sitting at the kitchen table, staring."

"At each other?"

"No, not really. Just staring." Rose finished stacking what she'd taken from the Goodbye household. "They didn't even look at me the entire time I was in there, searching room to room. I snapped my fingers right in front of their faces, Jeremiah. And nothing. But at least at some point they'd moved from the beds."

"Do we need to go in and get that little boy?"

"I thought of that," she said. "But Ellen somehow still seems to be caring for him. I was afraid if I tried she'd . . . well, let's just say

I was afraid to take a mother's child." She stood beside him with her hands on her hips. A strand of hair had fallen loose from the bundle atop her head, so she positioned it behind her ear. "Will you be okay here tonight?"

"I've survived much worse than this, Rose," he said, hoping she'd stay. "But will *you* be?"

"I'll be fine. I've got some writing I want to do back in the room. I'll check in on Orion."

Jeremiah smirked.

"What?"

"Just that you've only been here a few days, and you already act like one of us."

"Just trying to find my place, Jeremiah."

"And you picked the dust bowl?"

She smiled, patted his leg. "Or maybe the dust bowl picked me."

She was a few paces from the door when he said, "I flipped the coin on William Worst."

She froze, then returned. "Go on."

He nodded toward the chair. "Have a seat."

She did.

He wasn't sure if he was ready yet to tell the story of what happened to William, but now that she'd taken a seat, he realized how desperate he was for her not to go.

He told her about the coin-flip game Wilmington had taught them as boys on that rainy day inside the Bentley. About the power he felt as he continued to predict that coin, flip after flip, until ultimately the coin became his. But while it had been his and Josiah's custom to spend whatever money they managed to accumulate on candy at the food store, this quarter he never spent. He'd begun to let it make his decisions for him—most of them favorable—and Wilmington had been against it from the start.

"Not so much the coin flip itself," he told Rose. "But the power I began to feel from flipping it and always getting it right. The look in my eyes bothered him, I think. It was like he feared it. Because no one should be able to control fate, right?"

"Of course not, Jeremiah."

"He thought there was something wrong with it, and maybe there was. But to me, everything about it felt right, necessary even. I once asked Father why he feared it so much."

"And?"

"He wouldn't answer. He looked away. His jaw started trembling, which is why I know he was hiding something. Otherwise he wouldn't be so sensitive to the notion."

"Hiding something like what?"

Jeremiah shook his head. "I don't know for sure. But I've had plenty of time to reflect on it, especially of late, and I just have a feeling it all comes back to my nightmare. The recurring one." *Not the one I've started having of that man made of dust.* "Like somehow maybe he knows about it. Knows why I have it."

Rose didn't have her papers in front of her, but she looked to be recording notes mentally. She blinked, and Jeremiah found himself mesmerized by how long her eyelashes were. She put her elbow on the table and rested her chin in her cupped palm. "William Worst?"

Jeremiah exhaled two puffed cheeks' worth of air. "William was about our age but bigger and stronger. He used to beat on Josiah. Josiah would try to fight back but never had any success with it." Jeremiah straightened in the chair, winced as pain bolted down his arm. "So I confronted William one day. We fought; I won. And I don't know why I did it, but I cut him with a pitchfork. Just a little nick on his arm."

"Like you did with one of those buried bodies?"

He nodded, not proud, because it sounded so irrational—trying to see what evil looked like on the inside. "Well, I had William Worst on the ground. And then I flipped the coin on him."

Rose leaned forward, gripped his hands. Normally he wouldn't let anyone do that aside from Ellen, but the touch felt right. "What happened next?"

"I just did it to scare him. But truth be told, flipping the coin—and it didn't even have to be the same coin, you see—had started to take me over. I wanted to see how far I could go. Told him if it was heads, which I knew it was, then I'd kill him."

"And did you?"

"No. Of course not, Rose. What kind of a question is that?"

"The kind that needs to be asked."

"Let's just say I took it too far."

"He died anyway?"

Jeremiah nodded. "Two days later he was riding his father's John Deere. Back when the town didn't look like this, we had a run of elm trees. It was a windy day, sunny. A branch had fallen from one of the elms beside their wheat field. The wind picked it up, and it sailed across the wheat field and got stuck on the engine of that tractor. William leaned up from his seat to grab it and toss it aside. Me and Josiah were watching from our field. William hit a bump, and he went tumbling forward." Jeremiah looked away. "The tractor, well, it . . ."

He stopped the description when Rose held her hand up and closed her eyes. When she opened them again they looked sorrowful, but Jeremiah couldn't tell if it was for him or for William Worst, who, despite being a bully, had died before he should've.

"It was an accident, Rose. A freak accident. But I couldn't help feeling responsible. That's when my drinking started to get out of control." She let go of his hands and leaned back in her chair, as if pondering things. He said, "I'd like to know what you know about those four men I buried. But not tonight."

She wiped her face, which had gone a shade pale, and then stood again.

"You want to know why I cut one of those bodies before I buried them in the silo?"

"You said you wanted to see what evil looked like on the inside."

He nodded, but showed her the scars up and down his left forearm. "I always wondered if I had that evil in me too, Rose. These cuts on me, they weren't just to relieve the pressure." His hands trembled now, so he didn't even attempt to button his shirt at the wrist. "I went to jail for murdering those four men, and I think I deserved to."

"But you didn't murder them, Jeremiah. I can prove that."

"Might as well have murdered them. I knew what I was doing. I knew what I'd somehow done to William Worst, and I wanted to see if it would happen again."

"Freak accidents, Jeremiah. All of them."

He shook his head. "I've come to learn one thing, Rose. The coin never lies."

"You don't sound convinced of that."

"Well, ever since Old Sparky, I just don't know anymore."

They remained silent for a moment. She kissed the top of his head, and he gripped her forearm.

"I'll stop by in the morning," she said, wiping her eyes. "We'll talk more."

"Yes."

She pointed toward the table, where an inch-tall stack of white paper and two spools of ribbon rested. "I forgot. While you were asleep, I went back and fetched some supplies for Peter. For his typewriter. I had extra. Thought maybe he'd like to see his efforts produce some fruit." She fingered one of the folds of her dress. "Good night, Jeremiah."

"Good night, Rose."

She closed the door. He stood from his chair with a grunt and watched her out the window. She covered her face with her hands and hunkered into the airborne dust, breeze-blown from the surface. Once she disappeared into the Bentley, he looked toward the Goodbye house for any signs of movement. The sheet covering the window shifted. It could have been the wind. Or it could have been Ellen watching.

Just in case, he waved, and then felt foolish for doing so.

"Peter," he called. "Come in here."

Peter walked in with his hands buried in his trouser pockets.

Jeremiah nodded toward the paper and ribbon on the table. "Rose brought you a gift. Do you know how to put the ribbon in?"

Peter nodded quickly, then tucked the supplies under his arm and headed back down the hallway. He never said a word, but something about the way he responded to the gift made it seem as if he'd been expecting it. Or at least was wondering what had taken them so long, because typewriters obviously need paper and ribbons.

"You're welcome," said Jeremiah to himself. He watched his childhood home some more.

From Peter's room, after five minutes or so, he heard the sound of paper winding through the typewriter carriage. Another pause, then eight distinct clacks of the keys. And then Peter stopped typing. The paper slung through, and Peter showed himself in the hallway, holding something in his hand. One of those pages, folded in thirds.

The boy approached Jeremiah, who sat back at the kitchen table because he'd started to feel woozy again. Peter handed him the folded paper and returned to his room.

The door closed.

Jeremiah opened the folded paper, and on it were two words in black ink that still looked a bit wet:

Thank you.

Jeremiah's eyes puddled wet. He wiped them away with his sleeve, wondering how long it had been since he last cried. He tried to remember but couldn't. It had been long enough for him to wonder if he still could produce tears. The answer to that now trickled down the beginnings of a full beard.

Those two words, simple as they were, touched him like his mother's hugs used to—unwavering and without judgment.

For the first time in he didn't know how long, Jeremiah carried a smile back to bed with him.

And he slept all night, free of any nightmare.

EIGHTEEN

It took every bit of strength Ellen had to get out of bed. Had it not been for James lying in his crib all still, she would have stayed put. Her bones ached, and her brain was heavy like a bowling ball. She found it hard to hold up lately, which was why, if a table was near, she rested it on the surface.

James was breathing. That was good, she supposed. If she wasn't so numb, a wave of relief would have swept over her. The boy had lost weight, as she had. As they all had. James stared at the wall and didn't blink much.

There was dust in his lashes. She left it there.

The kitchen was quiet. She wondered if Josiah and Wilmington were still alive. The front door swayed inward, got stuck in a drift, and stayed open, giving her a triangle of vision to the street, to a sliver of crooked porch on the Worst house. *Jeremiah's house now. Jeremiah and his new woman and that boy who looks just like mine should have. Well, he can have her.* Even as she thought it, Ellen realized she didn't care anymore. Exhausted from the walk down the hallway, she sat alone at the kitchen table and rested her heavy, dirt-filled head on the surface, on an inch of dust that puffed when her left cheek hit it.

Her breaths were shallow. Maybe today they'd stop altogether and put an end to all this nonsense. Her stomach cramped a little from hunger pangs. For days now it had been growling, as if begging for food, but even those sounds had waned of late. Perhaps her stomach had given up too. She thought that was funny but didn't have the energy to smile.

A memory came and went. Her first kiss with Josiah. With Jeremiah she'd felt her body light on fire, but with Josiah she'd laughed. Not because it wasn't good, but just because. She feared he'd taken it the wrong way, her laughing, but it hadn't stopped them from kissing again and again, back when things were different. Now she didn't even like him. It wasn't anything personal against Josiah. She didn't like anyone anymore.

"From dust to dust," she whispered, drooling into the dirt against her cheek. Something brushed her hair, and then a long finger moved strands from her ear. But it was only the wind coming through that swaying front door. A door she didn't have the energy to close.

Too bad that Rose woman had removed all the guns and knives from the house, along with the hammers and nails and saws and axes. How would they protect themselves? And from what? *From ourselves.* That made no sense.

She heard Rose's voice in her ear, from when she'd come in early, invading their home where the front door was wide open to the elements. Wide open because Jeremiah had blown the lock clear off. *"You need to eat, Ellen. Here, drink this water."* She remembered letting it trickle down her chin like she was an invalid, but truthfully she hadn't felt like swallowing.

"You're going to waste away to nothing."

Rose again.

Ellen nodded against the dusty tabletop. What would it feel like to waste away? Like a dried-out cornhusk?

No, she didn't have time to eat. Not when she needed to rest.

Josiah walked in from another room where he'd been sleeping nightly on the couch. He pulled out a chair, sat across the table from Ellen, and then let his heavy head thump to the surface, except he rested his on his forehead. She craned her neck and saw the top of his head. Looked like he hadn't washed that hair in weeks. Almost looked bald in spots.

Better not be going bald.

She didn't have time for that.

Wilmington walked in a few minutes later and sat on the floor with his back to the stove. He tilted his Stetson down over his eyes and went back to sleep, his rumbling snore the only sound in the room. Ellen had never known he snored that loud, and she hated him for it.

But instead of doing anything about it, she closed her eyes and took a nap.

"Ellen."

Her eyelids fluttered.

What was Jeremiah doing here? And snapping his fingers in her face? *Yes, I can hear you. I can hear you fine.*

"Say something."

Don't want to.

He stood straight and wiped his face like he was prone to do when he was concerned. She used to like that stubble on him but now wished he'd shave it. Made him look too much like

Wilmington, and she didn't like him anymore because he snored. *And he may have had an affair with my mother.*

She felt lightheaded. *Where am I? Where'd the kitchen table go?* Jeremiah's eyes grew big, like he'd just noticed something he hadn't before. *Why am I on the floor? Sideways.* The chair had toppled. *Where'd all that blood come from?*

"Ellen, what did you do?"

Took a nap. Must've fallen out of the chair.

Jeremiah motioned toward the door. "Rose, go get another sheet and rip it into bandages."

Jeremiah studied her forehead like it was bleeding, which it probably was, hence all that concern. The reporter woman ran from the house. Ellen blinked in slow motion. Wilmington was still propped up against the stove front, staring at nothing. Josiah's forehead was like a deadweight on the table. If he'd noticed her fall from the chair and her subsequent head knock against the floor—she assumed now that's what had happened—he'd certainly showed no urgency in helping her up.

Jeremiah shook Josiah and called his name and then did the same to Wilmington over by the stove, but although they still breathed, neither man moved.

Jeremiah knelt in front of Ellen again. "You're bleeding pretty good, Ellen. Stay with me now."

But she couldn't.

Her head felt like a heartbeat, and her ears were runny.

Peter was there too, pressing his hands to his ears. His mouth was wide open, and his eyes were pinched closed like he was screaming.

Why can't I hear him?

And she passed out again.

When Ellen came to, the sun had shifted in the sky, cutting a dividing line of light and shadow across the kitchen table.

Her head was bandaged, and that Rose woman was trying to pour water down her throat. *Trying to kill me.* Ellen swallowed some of it. Choked some of it up, as if her stomach had rejected it. *Why are you still here? I told you I gave up.* The thought amused her, and this time she managed a brief crooked smile that prompted Rose to ask her what was funny. Ellen ignored her, though. Her and her pretty face and pretty eyes and pretty dresses. She let the rest of the water trickle out the corners of a mouth she couldn't seem to close all the way.

Josiah was sitting up now, grinning like a goon, his eyes following Jeremiah's every move, probably looking at that bullet hole he'd accidently put in his shoulder. They made quite a sight— Jeremiah with his bloody shoulder, Josiah with that blown-off toe, Wilmington with the bullet in his head. And now Ellen, who somehow had fallen out of the chair and gonged her noodle and had no recollection of doing so.

Jeremiah paced like he didn't know what to do, which wasn't like him. *Flip the coin.* Her lips moved, but no words came out. But Jeremiah didn't flip it. He acted like he didn't even consider it an option. *What's wrong with you?*

"Jeremiah." Rose pointed out the front door. "Someone's coming."

Ellen could see out the window. A brown cloud approached up the far road leading into town. Not a duster, but a car—maybe two.

Jeremiah joined Rose at the doorway. "It's the law," he said. "They found me."

NINETEEN

Jeremiah left the front door open a crack—just enough for an eye to show—as the police car puttered to a stop outside the Bentley Hotel. The chains behind it spun up a cloud of loose dust.

His rifle was back at home, which was where Peter had gone once he calmed down from seeing the blood running down Ellen's cheek.

Rose was already down the porch and approaching the car. The lights atop it were caked with mud, and one lone tumbleweed clung to the bumper like it was holding on for dear life.

The car door opened. A man in a brown hat got out, but he wasn't a lawman. He wore civilian clothes, dusty and weather-beaten. The back door on the driver's side opened, and a boy about Peter's age jumped out as if he'd been suffocating. Two suitcases, a pillow, and a washboard slid out behind him onto the dust. The boy squinted in the sunlight and then shielded his eyes with a cupped hand.

Rose stopped. *Must have noticed it wasn't the law.*

On the far side of the car, a woman emerged, black hair tousled and blowing in the breeze, shaking her head at the sight of the town. Two more kids, both younger than the first, stumbled out, and then a shovel and what sounded like a crate of dishes fell out to the dust.

Must have fit their entire house inside that car.

Rose had now engaged them in conversation, and by that time Jeremiah recognized who they were: Reginald and Emory Rochester, with a brood that had grown since he'd last seen them. They'd probably had those two little ones when Jeremiah was behind bars.

"Okies come back home to roost," he said to himself, opening the door to step out onto the porch. He'd always liked the Rochesters. They were good, honest people who had moved to Nowhere at the beginning of the twenties. Emory had taught alongside Ellen at the schoolhouse. But then they'd left town.

Without thinking of how the Rochesters might react upon seeing him, Jeremiah approached their car with a welcoming smile.

Reginald said, "Hello, Josiah."

Jeremiah didn't answer, but he did stop about ten feet away, close enough for the Rochesters to get a better look, and when they did, Emory hurried to corral her kids and hide them behind the far side of the car.

Reginald stumbled back against the hood and fell to the dust.

Rose made a move to help him up—by the inward slope of both cheeks, the man looked exhausted and starved, as did his wife and kids—but Reginald held up a hand and told her to stay back. "Both of you." He stared at Jeremiah. "How'd you get out?"

"I busted out, Reginald. But you've got nothing to fear from me. I mean no harm."

Rose said, "It's true what he says, mister."

"And who are you?"

"I'm Rose Buchanan. I'm a reporter from New York."

"What are you doing here? Where is everybody?"

She ignored the first question and deferred to Jeremiah for the second one.

"Something's happened to the town, Reginald."

The man's eyes darted from house to house, fidgety. "What'd you do with your family?"

"They're inside. Safe." Jeremiah took two paces forward, and then a third, offering his hand to help the man up.

"Then why don't they come out?" Reginald stared at Jeremiah's outstretched hand. "I was preparing for Wilmington or Orion to come out with their rifles and tell me to go back."

"Why would they do that?"

Reginald finally took Jeremiah's hand, but quickly let go and wiped it on his shirt once he was on his feet. "They weren't happy when we left in the first place. Called us cowards."

Emory spoke over the top of the car, her voice not nearly as soft and sweet as he remembered. Life as an Okie would do that to you. "Ellen wasn't too pleased with me either for going." She gulped, still clutching her two youngest—a boy and a girl, probably twins. "Leaving her to tend to all those kids by herself. She still upset at me?"

Jeremiah surveyed the town. One of the swinging doors inside the Bentley swayed in the breeze, and a tumbleweed blew by. "I don't think this town's feeling much of anything anymore."

"What's your meaning?" asked Reginald.

"Let's get you and your family some food, Reginald. I'll explain as we eat."

215

They all gathered around the table inside the Worst house and ate beans and drank well water.

Rose managed to get the stove working enough to boil three near-rotten potatoes she'd found in the cabinet. The Rochesters were ravenous, clinking forks off their plates like they were in a race to clean them. Starving like the town, but certainly not by choice. Not much was said until they finished, and by the glances Reginald and Emory were giving as they chewed, they still weren't comfortable sitting at the same table as the infamous Coin-Flip Killer.

So Jeremiah did the talking while they ate, explaining the best he could about the Black Sunday blizzard and what that dust had done to the town folk—in particular, the three stages he'd noticed everyone going through. "First they turned mean. Then they turned quiet."

"And then what?" Reginald wiped his face with a napkin. "You said there were three."

Jeremiah and Rose shared a glance.

Rose said, "They've given up, Mr. Rochester."

The man looked up from his second plate of beans. "Call me Reginald. And how so?"

"They don't hardly move anymore," said Jeremiah. "It's like they don't even have the will to survive."

"Or the energy," Rose added. "They've stopped eating. We're doing what we can to get fluids into them, but most don't even have the power to swallow."

"They aren't actively trying to do themselves in, but . . . that's exactly what's happening."

Emory covered her mouth, but too late to mute her gasp. She gave her husband a look that said, *You see? I told you we never should have come back.*

Jeremiah said, "You can go from one house to the next, and you'll see. They're still alive in the sense that their hearts are beating, but mentally . . . they're gone."

"What are you going to do?" Emory asked. "I mean . . ." She covered her mouth again, and tears welled in her eyes.

"We haven't quite figured that out."

Peter was typing in the back room. Even with the bedroom door closed, the clacking echoed. The Rochesters had periodically looked back toward the sound as they'd eaten.

"Peter," Jeremiah yelled. "Come out here."

The clacking immediately stopped. The door opened, and Peter showed himself in the hallway. He wasn't wearing his typical smile. The boy had turned solemn ever since he witnessed the blood running from Ellen's forehead.

Emory said, "Who is he?"

"Name's Peter Cotton. He's a bit of a question mark, but he's a good kid."

"Who does he belong to?"

"He's mine, I suppose."

"Yours?"

"I took him on," said Jeremiah. "Found him out alone." He didn't feel like explaining that he'd accidently bought him.

Rose took the lull in conversation as a good time to place a hand on his injured shoulder and say, "He's a changed man. He's not what the newspapers called him."

Reginald looked at his kids and then focused on Jeremiah. "You didn't kill those men like they say?"

Jeremiah shook his head. "No, I didn't. I buried their bodies, but I didn't kill them." He swallowed hard, an involuntary movement he hoped wouldn't be a tell, because he did believe he'd sent those men to their graves. He put his elbows on the table and changed the subject. "Why did you bring your family back . . . to this?"

Emory started crying, and Reginald did his best to console her, but something told Jeremiah that the two of them had been fighting about life for a while now. "Life's no easier on the road. I'll just say that."

"There's signs up everywhere in California," Emory blurted. "They say No Okies Allowed. They don't want us. Nobody wants us. We're no different from the Indians and the blacks and the Mexicans." She paused as Reginald rubbed her back, but she wasn't finished. "They put us on the same signs. The same signs." She looked down at the table and sobbed. Reginald tried to rub her neck, but she told him to not touch her.

He rested his hands on the table. "We took our chances in leaving. We decided we'd rather die here, Jeremiah. So we came back."

"You don't have to justify yourself to me, Reginald. In times like this, there are no right and wrong answers. Just the decisions we've gotta make."

Reginald nodded. He looked to be on the verge of crying too, but was staying strong for his kids. He looked down the table and gave them a forced smile.

Peter stood there, taking it all in, showing zero interest in getting to know the Rochester kids as Jeremiah had hoped. He shuffled his feet, clearly wanting to be elsewhere. So Jeremiah waved him back to his room, and seconds later he began typing again.

Reginald got every last bit of bean juice up with his fork and slid it into his mouth. A quick smile emerged, sudden, like he'd just remembered something.

Jeremiah eyed him. "What is it?"

"Just that not all my memories of you are bad." He looked at Rose. "He tell you about what he did at the auctions?"

Rose shook her head. "There's a lot he hasn't told me. We only officially met a couple days ago."

"That so?" Reginald raised his eyebrows. "You just looked more familiar with each other than that." He wiped his face with a napkin and leaned forward like he'd been wanting to tell somebody something for a long time—anybody who would listen. "Anyway, it took several months for the Depression to hit us out here in the plains. Our banks hung in a little longer. Then money stopped moving. While the rest of the country was starving, our threshers and silos were still full of wheat, but it was stacked to the clouds almost with nowhere to go, on account of how low the prices had dropped. You remember the foreclosures, Jeremiah?"

Jeremiah nodded. *How could I not?* Too many families had gone bankrupt on what turned out to be shaky loans—cars and tractors and appliances and farms with payments due and no way to pay. They'd all had more wheat than they knew what to do with, but it was near worthless, and people couldn't begin to pay for what was owed. So foreclosures had been daily happenings, along with auctions where the banks took back what was theirs because nobody could even afford to bid.

"So Jeremiah here comes in and starts bidding at those auctions with the coins he collected, putting pennies and dimes on each one just to keep those properties alive and in the hands of whoever lived on them. What'd they start calling them?"

"Ten-cent sales," said Jeremiah, unable to conjure the same enthusiasm.

"That's right. So Jeremiah puts in those really low bids, then he tells the judge he'll put a bullet in his belly if anyone even tries to outbid him—especially any of those out-of-towners coming in trying to make a run on some cheap property. So Jeremiah wins the auctions, then he gives the property back to the people that were foreclosed on."

Rose smirked. "Kind of like Robin Hood?"

"That's it—like Robin Hood, except with coins and a pistol. And then there was the day the bank closed. You remember, don't you, Emory?"

"I remember. But Reginald—"

"You see, everyone in town had turned on Mr. Russell, who owned the Nowhere Bank. They assumed he was getting fatter than he already was. But then we walked out one morning and there was a sign outside the bank that said—" Reginald snapped his fingers. "What was the word?"

His wife said wearily, "Insolvent."

"Yes. Insolvent," said Reginald. "The bank just up and closed, with all the town's money gone. Just gone. Backed by nothing except Mr. Russell's word, which turned out not to be worth even a—"

"Get on with it, Reginald," Emory said.

"Well, we were out there chanting that Mr. Russell was a thief and a coward. Somebody even threatened to knock the doors down if he didn't come out. We knew he was in there because we saw the curtain move. But what we didn't know was that his car was already puttering out back. He was fixing to sneak out the rear door and drive off unnoticed. But Jeremiah didn't let that happen. He put his arm through a window—cut it up bad too—and unlocked the door. And next thing you know he's dragging Mr. Russell out by his collar, and Mr. Russell is begging for his life. Because back then . . ."

"Back then what?" asked Rose.

"Well, Jeremiah already had a reputation . . ." Reginald glanced at Jeremiah and looked like he was ready to backtrack. But after an affirmative nod from Jeremiah, he went on. "A reputation for not exactly following the straight and narrow where the law was concerned. I remember Josiah tried to stop him. But Jeremiah, right on the steps of the bank, pulled a coin out and flipped it. Let it land right on Mr. Russell's chest too, and he unholstered his pistol while that coin was in the air. He covered the coin with his palm and told Mr. Russell the rules while the whole town watched. He said, 'Heads, and you'll lose yours. Tails, and I'll let you go with yours slinking between your legs.'"

Reginald shook his head, reminiscing, almost in awe. Jeremiah wasn't proud of the story, but it felt good to see somebody smile in the telling of it. And in hindsight, it hadn't turned out as bad as it once seemed. "Mr. Russell liked to have soiled his pants right there on the steps. He was sweating like a pig under that bright sun. Anyway, the coin turned up tails, but Jeremiah here pulled the trigger anyway and said 'Bang.'" He looked at Jeremiah. "You knew there wasn't a bullet in that chamber, didn't you?"

Jeremiah nodded, ready for the story to be over. His shoulder throbbed, and he needed more morphine.

"So he lets Mr. Russell up, even brushes off the man's lapels, and tells him to get on out of town and never come back. And *then* he pulls the trigger again and fires that next bullet up into the sky." Reginald slapped his leg. "I'm telling you—Mr. Russell jumped higher than I'd ever seen a man jump and took off running for his car. I swear it wasn't five minutes before he was out of town."

Jeremiah stood from the chair. "You best get to unloading that car out there."

Reginald gently gripped his wife's arm. "I suppose so." He digested Jeremiah's tone clear enough. Story time was over. "I rode by our old house," he said. "It's still standing, but we'll have our fair share of cleaning to do."

Rose stood with them, but Jeremiah couldn't help but notice the glance she'd given him after hearing the story. Like she was in awe too.

All I did was let a man live.

A man the entire town, at the time, probably wanted dead.

"We'd be happy to help get your house in order," Rose told them.

Emory shook her head. "Thank you. But this is our cross to carry."

Jeremiah said, "It don't need to be like that."

"Maybe tomorrow will be different," she said as Reginald gathered the family to leave.

Before they reached the door, Emory faced Jeremiah. "You think later this evening, Ellen would see me?"

Jeremiah nodded, and thought, *She doesn't understand.*

"I'll take you there myself," he said. "But she probably won't even remember who you are."

A duster hit midday but only lasted twenty minutes, arriving just after the Rochesters had finished unloading the police car they'd found abandoned days ago.

After the dust stopped blowing, Jeremiah and Rose walked to the Goodbye household and found Wilmington asleep in his bed, covered in a fine layer of dust. Josiah sat on the couch with his eyes closed and, although he breathed normally, was unresponsive to their nudges on his shoulder. His stomach was growling, begging almost.

Ellen was on her bed, sitting up against the headboard with her eyes open. Jeremiah wiped dust from her nose, but the touch barely registered. James was cradled in her lap, as lethargic as she was, but with a diaper and trousers that were so soiled they'd soaked a large patch of Ellen's dress as well.

Rose eased the little boy from Ellen's arms, rooted through a broken dresser for clean clothes, and changed James on the foot of the bed. She hugged him and kissed the top of his head, then gave Jeremiah a what-do-we-do-now look.

He thought at first they should take the child with them and started to suggest as much. But then he noticed the look in Ellen's eyes. A tiny shift. She was staring at James in Rose's arms. Perhaps he was the anchor still keeping her tethered to shore, the last reason to hold on to her sanity.

Ellen mouthed two words: "My baby."

Rose saw it too, and walked the boy back to his mother, positioning him in her arms as close to the way he'd been as possible. James settled back, coughed three times, and closed his eyes.

"My baby."

Jeremiah promised Ellen he'd be back but got no response, so he and Rose exited the house. The sun was inching down over the horizon, a smear of pink and purple that could have been beautiful under different circumstances.

Down the road the Rochesters had their windows and doors open and were whisking out clouds of dust that created eerie nimbuses in the light cast from oil lanterns.

"They won't finish by nightfall."

He and Rose nodded to one another, knowing what they needed to do, despite Emory insisting they would dig out on their own. They crossed to the Worst house to gather shovels and brooms. Before going, Jeremiah walked down the hallway to Peter's room, where the typewriter was busy. The door was closed, and the boy didn't respond when he knocked, which shouldn't have been a surprise. Jeremiah turned the knob and peeked inside. Peter sat at the desk, clacking away with his two index fingers.

"We're going down the road to help the Rochesters dig out," said Jeremiah. "You can come if you want."

"Down the road," Peter said, never looking up from his work. "Help the Rochesters dig out." He pulled a typed page from the machine and carefully folded it in thirds like he'd done with the note he'd given Jeremiah the other night. He placed it on a pile of similarly folded pages beside his typewriter, immediately loaded another, and started right into what Jeremiah assumed was a sentence of some sort. "Come if you want. Down the road," said Peter. "Rochesters dig out. Peter, Peter, pumpkin eater." He grinned.

What are you up to?

"What are you up to?" Peter mumbled.

Jeremiah scratched his head, wondered if he'd said those words aloud instead of thinking them. He closed the door and left the boy to his typing.

The Rochester house was a dust cloud. The entire family had masks on, even the two youngest, who swept at the dust with their feet. Jeremiah and Rose knocked on the open door but didn't wait for an invitation to enter. They just started shoveling and sweeping. Eventually the four adults and the older Rochester boy managed to choreograph their efforts into a systematic pattern of dust removal, starting high on the cabinets, light fixtures, and counters, then allowing it all to settle before starting on the floor. Jeremiah suggested working from the back of the house to the front, and Reginald agreed. Before long, Rose and Emory were discussing how things might be arranged and repainted, if they could get their hands on any paint. Both women looked relieved to have another woman to talk to.

Jeremiah killed ten tarantulas with his shovel while Reginald clobbered eight, the two of them making a sport of it. Behind the mask, Reginald showed the hint of a smile. Without prompting, he told Jeremiah how they'd come by that cop car. Theirs had short-circuited out somewhere in western Kansas, and they'd taken off on foot, carrying what they could. But they hadn't even gone a mile before stumbling upon the cop car, complete with a man in uniform behind the wheel. The cop had died due to what Reginald assumed was suffocation: his face and mouth had been so covered with dust. So they'd buried him in the dust, marked the grave with a couple of boards they'd fashioned into a cross, and then driven back to get their belongings.

Jeremiah leaned on his broom and smirked. "Gave me a scare seeing that car drive into town."

Reginald looked confused, like in the middle of all their cleaning he'd forgotten that the man in his house was wanted all across the country. Then he nodded. "I suppose it did." Reginald was quiet for the next few minutes, giving Jeremiah space.

The sun was down, and with no electricity—there was no telling when the poles would be fixed, if ever—their only light was from candles and kerosene lamps. They were about to give up for the day when a gunshot sounded, echoing in the dusty streets. All four adults paused to look out into the night, as if waiting for another shot.

"What was that?" asked Emory.

Jeremiah said, "A gunshot."

"I know that, but . . . ?"

Jeremiah pointed to his shoulder. "The other day, Josiah had a rifle in his hands. To make a long story short, he shot me."

"It was an accident," Rose quickly added, after seeing Emory's hand flash to her mouth to stifle a gasp.

Jeremiah said, "But sometimes accidents can be prevented. We need to search all the houses, Rose. See who that was." He shook his head. "We should have done what we did at Daddy's house."

"What?" asked Reginald.

Rose said, "Secured all the weapons."

"Better late than never," said Jeremiah. "Come on."

Reginald said, "I'm coming with."

"No, you're not," said Emory. "You're not leaving me here alone with the children in the dark."

And that was that.

Jeremiah found a wagon they'd once used to haul wheat to the silo. He dusted it off and said it would do for holding whatever weapons they took from the homes. The wheel spokes were rusted and caked with hardened dirt, but after a few revolutions clumps fell and the wagon was easier to pull.

Rose carried a lantern and together they ventured through darkness. They started on the north side of town and worked south. Many homes were unlocked, and the owners did little more than stare as they confiscated knives, handguns, rifles, and other potentially harmful items. Doors that were locked, Jeremiah kicked in.

One man sat in the dark with a loaded rifle on his lap. Jeremiah slid the weapon from his slack grip and moved on.

At each house they attempted to give water to the residents, but very little water got in. Most trickled down chins and throats and wetted shirt collars. After an hour they dumped what they'd confiscated into the shed in the Worsts' backyard and then went out for more. They'd yet to find a body to go along with the gunshot they'd heard. After an hour they began to wonder if they'd even heard the shot at all.

They found Mr. Mulraney in his kitchen with an apple on his lap and a knife in his hand. He had a small cut on his right thumb, and a tiny chunk had been taken from the apple, like he'd had a notion to eat but just couldn't make it happen. Rose cut the apple and offered him a slice, but Mr. Mulraney, although his eyes were open, was unresponsive. Jeremiah wondered how long he'd been sitting there. The spot on the apple that had been open to the air was brown, and the blood on his thumb had clotted.

Leland Cantain sat at his dining room table holding a butcher knife. Rose took it from him, and Cantain muttered, "From dust we come, and to dust we shall return."

Jeremiah told him to go to sleep, and Cantain closed his eyes.

In the hospital, Sister Moffitt sat cross-legged on the floor while her patients slept. She held rosary beads and muttered something that could have been prayer.

Sheriff McKinney stood outside his house next to a ladder that stretched to his roof. He seemed frozen though, as if contemplating, and then he mumbled something about getting the dust from his gutters before the weight ripped them clean off. Jeremiah walked him back inside and sat him down on a dust-covered sofa. As McKinney mumbled nonsense, Jeremiah emptied the house of weapons, and on his way out he folded up the ladder and placed that on the cart for good measure.

The cart had gotten so heavy by now that it took both of them to pull it. Jeremiah used one hand to hold the lantern and on they went, making another drop-off back home.

They found Richard Klamp balled up inside his Buck stove, trying to start a fire with a Zippo lighter that sounded dry as the land. He kept mumbling that he was cold and "was just trying to get a fire going." Rose walked him back to his bedroom, tucked him in, and told him to never try to do that again. Richard said, "Okay, then," and started sucking his thumb.

Ned Blythe was lying on the floor in his food store, covered by a pile of canned goods and bottles of smoked rabbit. He'd fallen over while taking inventory on what few canned goods remained, accidently knocking an entire row of shelving onto himself. Jeremiah pulled him out, walked him home, and confiscated everything he saw, even the can opener resting on the counter.

They found Phillip Jansen sitting atop his kitchen table, holding on with one hand to an empty mailbag he'd somehow latched to the overhead light fixture. He said he'd been trying to change the lightbulb but couldn't find his ladder. Three more empty mailbags rested on the table around him. Jeremiah and Rose weren't sure what the mailman was going to do, but he put up no fight when they ushered him down from the table and searched his house for anything potentially dangerous.

Father Steven was in church, lying atop the altar with a small wooden cross in his hand. It looked too sharp for Rose's liking, so she took it. They walked him to the front pew, where he stretched out and went to sleep.

Dr. Craven had returned to the spot on the floor where they'd found him yesterday. At first they thought him dead, but then his chest rose and fell, and a small push of breath moved dust across the floorboards. They carried his slight weight back to the bedroom and placed him atop the bedcovers.

"From dust to dust," he whispered.

Moses Yearling was in bed inside his Bentley Hotel room, clutching one of his TNT rockets. He had enough explosives to bring the entire hotel down, so they cleaned his room of it all, replaced the rocket he'd been hugging with a spare pillow, and then tucked him in.

Orion's door was locked. Jeremiah heard him snoring but kicked the door in anyway. Orion's eyes opened, but he didn't move from his fetal position in the middle of the floor as they searched his dresser. Instead of moving him to his bed, Jeremiah slid a pillow under his head and then covered him with a blanket.

Four hours into their mission, they entered the house where the boy William Trainer, who everyone in town called Windmill, lived. Rose's lantern blew out, so she took a minute to relight it. William's parents were asleep in their bedroom, but not on the bed. His mother lay on the floor holding a pair of scissors. It looked like she'd been trying to cut her own hair; the right side was still long, while the left had been hacked off above the ear. The father snored in a chair beside the window with a deck of cards and a bottle of hooch in his lap. That was no surprise; the man was a known gambler and drinker. Jeremiah attempted to give him some of the booze, but Mr. Trainer wasn't having it. It trickled out of his mouth like the water they'd been trying to force down everyone's throats.

They entered a narrow hallway, where another door swayed as if windblown. The hinges creaked when they opened it fully.

Windmill was inside, sitting on a rocking chair that faced the window, slowly rocking.

"Windmill," said Jeremiah.

No response.

Jeremiah stepped closer. A rifle rested beside the rocking chair. Windmill's limp left hand hung inches away from the barrel. There was a hole in the ceiling, directly above the chair, and dust sifted down from it. "This was the gunshot we heard."

Rose agreed.

William blinked. "Ain't no boy."

"Windmill, can you hear me?"

"Saw me a rabbit," he said. "Tried to shoot it."

"Windmill?"

"Ain't no boy." Windmill rocked faster. Spoke faster. "Ain't no boy, Ellen. Ain't no boy." Louder. "Dust to dust. Ain't no boy."

Jeremiah lifted Windmill from the chair and held him in his arms, hugging him like his drunk father probably never did, and Windmill slowly began to settle.

"Ain't no boy," he said softer. "Saw me a rabbit on that ceiling. Tried to shoot it."

Jeremiah looked over Windmill's shoulder to Rose. "He was lucky."

They walked Windmill to his bed and pulled the cover up to his neck. Rose kissed the boy on his forehead, and they left the house with their arms full. Outside the moon showed bright against a dark purple sky scattered with stars. It felt good to get out of that house, where the air had been thick with whatever ailed the town.

The temperature had dropped while they were inside. Rose took deep breaths of the crisp outside air and exhaled plumes of vapor. She hugged her arms while Jeremiah held the lantern. Twenty feet away was Deacon Sipes's repair shop, where Deacon and his pal Toothache lived in two separate apartments above the garage. Rose hesitated to go in after what she'd seen hanging in there the day before. Jeremiah told her he'd go in alone, but she shook her head and insisted she'd follow.

"Reporters report, Jeremiah." She grabbed the lantern and led the way.

From a window on the front side, a ray of moonlight cut diagonally across the shop, revealing hundreds of jackrabbits hanging from the ceiling, hovering over rusted car and tractor parts, old tools covered in dust, and a cluttered desk that probably hadn't seen honest work in months. The ropes holding the rabbits shifted in the breeze, spinning the jacks slowly from the ceiling beams, and Jeremiah looked away to avoid their eyes. The whole place smelled of death.

Jeremiah and Rose shuffled instead of walked, as if the dust-covered floor could give way any minute. Jeremiah ducked beneath some of the lower-hanging jacks, sidestepped to avoid others.

"Deacon?"

The lantern went out.

Rose sucked in a breath, fumbled to relight it.

A dead rabbit brushed Jeremiah's shoulder. He swallowed hard, closed his eyes, and imagined collapsing into his bed back home, wishing they hadn't saved this place for last.

Something moved in the dust around his feet.

Rose's lantern glowed again. It shook in her outstretched arm. "You seen enough?"

"Deacon?"

No answer. They heard nervous breathing across the room.

The floor shifted, a quick tunnel of movement, and then it disappeared into the shadows.

It was a rabbit. A live one, skittering around that cold dark place.

The lantern went out again. The smell inside the shop was getting to them both. Rose relit the lantern, and Jeremiah shuffled on toward the back of the room, where the breathing was louder. Then he saw them—Toothache and Deacon both sitting on the floor, backs against the wall, each holding a rifle and pointing it at one another from only a few feet away. Their breath was visible, jetting from their nostrils and parted lips.

Maybe the two men had been trying to shoot that rabbit and ended up freezing with the barrels keyed on each other. Or maybe they'd gotten paranoid and frozen right in the middle of shooting one another. Whatever happened, they seemed to have forgotten it. They stared past each other into the dark corners of the room.

Jeremiah called their names, but neither man responded. He hurried to remove the weapons from the two men's slack grips, counting their blessings that the triggers hadn't been pulled, because both weapons were loaded.

Deacon's grimy hands stole Jeremiah's attention.

Grease and grime beneath the fingernails.

Jeremiah suddenly dropped to one knee, dizzy—something from the past churning in his mind.

Those hands around somebody's neck.

He opened his eyes and stood, weak-kneed. "We gotta get out of here, Rose."

"Jeremiah, what is it?"

He hurried from the shop and she followed, oblivious now to the rotating rabbits brushing their arms, shoulders, and heads as they ran.

Once outside, Rose doubled over, hands on her knees, breathing as if she'd been holding it in since they entered the shop moments ago. She looked up. "What happened to you in there?"

He was breathing as rapidly as she was. He'd brushed up against Deacon years ago, and his mind had just given him a glimpse of the vision he'd seen back then—back when he saw visions. A reminder that Deacon Sipes was not to be trusted. Had he really killed a man?

"Just a bad feeling, Rose."

"It was more than that. The blood rushed from your face, Jeremiah."

He couldn't answer what he didn't fully understand himself.

Jeremiah stood straight and held her like he'd done Windmill, and she released herself to his embrace. Her chest rose and fell against his stomach. As he rubbed her back, the sharp angles of her shoulder blades reminded him of bird wings beneath the cottony fabric of her dress.

They stood that way under the moonlight until he could feel both of their heartbeats slowing. He rested his chin atop her head. "I don't know what story could be more interesting for you, Rose. Me or the town?"

"I think at this point they're one and the same, Jeremiah."

As much as he couldn't fully explain it, he couldn't deny it either.

They pulled that last load back to the Worst house and secured it all in the shed.

On the front stoop he said, "You writing tonight?"

She grinned. "No. And I'm not staying in that hotel either. I think I'm asleep on my feet, and your couch in there has my name on it."

They went inside, physically and mentally exhausted, but Jeremiah was hopeful they'd done the right thing. It was the only thing they could think of to keep the town safe from itself. He only wished they'd taken more of the water they'd tried to give them. Bodies can't live without water.

He didn't let Rose sleep on the couch. He insisted she sleep on the bed he'd been using, and she didn't argue. She was snoring softly three minutes after her head hit the pillow.

He closed the door and walked down the hall toward Peter's room, turned the knob, and ducked his head inside. They'd been gone for hours, but the boy didn't look like he'd moved from the chair. And he didn't look up from his typing either. More folded pages had been added to the stack he'd already accumulated.

Jeremiah was too tired to ask questions. He closed the door and found the couch in the living room much to his liking. He blew out the lamp, and the room fell to a darkness so thick that even the moon struggled to penetrate it.

He drifted off to sleep minutes later, to the sound of that typewriter clacking.

Had there been any trees left for the birds to nest in, perhaps it would have been a morning fit for birdsong.

The windows were open throughout the house, and a fresh breeze circulated.

On the couch, Jeremiah rubbed his eyes and swung his feet to the floor. Rose stood by the living room window. Coffee steam enveloped her face as she drank.

Had last night been a dream? A nightmare of a different sort?

Visiting all those houses in the darkness? Minutes before he roused on the couch, he'd heard that dust man laughing. But now the blue morning sky looked stolen from a painting.

He stood from the couch, glimpsed all the dust still covering the land, and realized that last night had been as real as the hard life they were all now living. And that morning blue could at any minute turn black and unbreathable.

"Morning." Rose nodded toward another coffee mug on the table behind her. "Come look."

"At what?"

"Out the window." She sipped more coffee, grinning.

He joined her. "What exactly am I looking at?"

"The mailboxes."

Jeremiah saw the Worsts' mailbox and then all the other boxes up and down and all around the town, the mailboxes Wilmington and Orion had crafted, all with their tiny yellow flags pointing upward like flowers reaching for sunlight.

Jeremiah didn't hear the typewriter. "Where's Peter?"

"He's on his bed," said Rose. "Deep asleep."

"You think he did this?"

"I do."

Down the road, the doors to the Bentley swayed open, and out stepped Orion in blue pajamas and slippers. He moved in painful slow motion, but he was moving nevertheless. He paused on the porch, surveying the town with all those yellow flags raised. Orion stepped over a dust drift and used the handrail to navigate the dust-covered steps, favoring that injured shoulder from when he'd fallen days ago. Eventually he made it out to the hotel mailbox. He squatted down and stared at that yellow flag like he doubted it was real. How long had they gone without mail?

Orion checked his surroundings like he was about to do something he shouldn't have been doing, and then he slowly lowered the face of the mailbox.

He reached his arm inside and pulled out a trifolded paper.

Then he opened it right there in the street and read.

TWENTY

How many days?
    How many days since what?

Ellen's brain struggled to keep up with her own thoughts. *How many days since you've changed your clothes?*

I don't know.

How many days since you've eaten a meal?

I don't know that either.

But the questions had at least gotten her moving, a barefoot shuffle down a hallway covered in dust. James rested lazily against her shoulder.

Don't drop him.

Okay.

Since the day the world turned black, they'd had a duster every afternoon, and they'd yet to dig out from any of them. The inside of their house was a wasteland, worse than pictures she'd seen from war-ravaged Europe. It looked like it hadn't been lived in for months.

Just make it to the kitchen table, Ellen. Her feet pushed under the accumulation of dirt like she'd done with sand on a beach as a little girl. Her legs were heavy, like they were made of iron—anchors connected to hips that had rusted over. *Just make it to the kitchen table.*

She stopped five feet away when something out the window caught her eye.

A tiny spot of yellow in all that brown-black dust outside.

The flag on her mailbox was up, something Phillip Jansen had always done after he'd put mail in there and closed the lid.

How long has it been since we got mail?

I don't know.

She faced the window and took a step, this time lifting her foot above the surface of dirt. Jeremiah was out there. The yellow flag on his mailbox—the Worsts' mailbox—was up too. She took another step, and another. Every flag up and down the street had been turned up.

Is this a cruel joke?

Maybe. But maybe not . . .

Orion was out there too, sitting on the street curb next to the Bentleys' mailbox with a paper in his hands. He was reading something, maybe something he'd just pulled from that box. Except he'd left the flag up. The rule had always been to put the flag down once you'd retrieved your mail.

Just make it to the kitchen table, Ellen.

Instead, she made her way to the front window. The yellow flag had grabbed her.

"What's going on out there?" she asked James. He blinked with his head on her shoulder, probably surprised to hear his mother's voice again, just as she was to hear her thoughts turn audible.

Jeremiah wasn't alone. That reporter woman was with him, standing right by his side as he read whatever note had been left inside his mailbox. *Rose. That's it. But why is she there with him now? Did she spend the night?* Jeremiah wiped his eyes as if fighting back tears, and Rose put a hand on his shoulder. It was rare to see Jeremiah Goodbye show emotions like that.

What's written on that paper? She wanted to see what was in her own mailbox, but she refused to go out there with those two making a scene. So she stood there and watched.

A minute later Jeremiah folded the note, slid it into his pocket, and pushed that yellow flag down like he was supposed to do. He gave the Goodbye house a look, which startled Ellen's heart into a gallop, and then returned inside the Worst house.

Rose watched him go in, and then she quick-walked toward the Bentley, holding her skirt up from the dust like some princess. She paused next to Orion, who showed her his note—not what was written on it, but the mere fact that he'd gotten something in the mail. That somebody had cared enough to write something and put it there. Then Rose hurried inside those swaying doors of the hotel and was gone.

Ten houses down the road, the mailman himself stood halfway between his house and the mailbox. Phillip stared at that yellow flag like he was as surprised as Ellen to find it turned up. *But if he didn't do it, who did?* Phillip took slow, cautious steps toward the street, and Ellen found herself inwardly cheering him on, when just minutes ago her thoughts would have most assuredly grown more morbid, wishing some ill will on the postman who no longer brought them mail.

But maybe it wasn't his fault?

Of course it wasn't his fault.

Just make it to the kitchen table, Ellen.

Instead she moved toward the front door.

She placed James on the dusty floor and told him to stay there until she got back. But that mailbox looked miles away. *Could be an all-day venture.*

Phillip Jansen was still down the road, inching closer to his mailbox. His hips were probably rusted over like hers. It was just so hard to move, so hard to convince your brain to tell your feet to move one step and then another. But she did it, and then next thing she knew she was opening the door and stepping out onto the porch. Her foot sank into the dust to just below the knee, and she had to hike her leg up high to walk, but the more she moved, the more that rust chipped away, and the less her legs felt like anchors.

She paused for a deep intake of fresh morning air, then closed her eyes briefly and imagined fields of green grass and even more golden-tipped wheat instead of all this dust.

Just make it to the mailbox, Ellen.

She opened her eyes and urged herself onward.

Leland Cantain had made it out to his porch. He leaned against a column as if to catch his breath, but then carefully navigated down his own dust-covered steps.

Another door opened down the road, and out stepped Nicholas Draper. He moved faster than the rest. He hadn't been taken in by that Black Sunday dust, and Ellen knew why. Jeremiah had covered him up. The Coin-Flip Killer had protected him, saved his life just as he'd saved that boy Peter. Like he'd saved that banker Mr. Russell from the town mob that was most assuredly fixing to lynch him for swindling them out of all of their money.

Nicholas hurried to his mailbox, opened the lid, and reached inside. He read what was on the front and then ran toward the house yelling, "Momma, you got mail."

Suddenly Ellen found herself ten paces from the road. Her legs felt lighter with every step, as if Nicholas's energy had somehow been passed to her.

Just make it to the mailbox, Ellen.

And she did. After taking another deep breath and nodding toward Orion, who'd just waved at her like he hadn't seen her in years, she opened the mailbox and reached inside. She found three separate papers, all trifolded, each with a different name typed in block letters on the front.

One for Ellen Goodbye.

One for Josiah Goodbye.

And one for Wilmington Goodbye.

She thought about leaving the other two in the box but then ended up grabbing all three. It was the right thing to do. She lowered the yellow flag carefully, then started toward the house. Her heart raced faster and faster the closer she got to the porch, until she couldn't take it anymore.

Right there in the middle of the dusty yard, wearing clothes she hadn't changed in three days—yes, she remembered now it had been three days—Ellen unfolded her letter and read with hands that shook as if palsied.

Dear Mrs. Goodbye,

The first time I looked upon you, I saw smiles in your eyes. I knew right away that you were the kind of mother any boy would want to have. When you hug me I feel safe. I get that feeling right after a good meal when I know I won't go hungry, or sitting by a fire that warms me during the cold. You say you've seen me before. Well I think I've seen you too. Because sometimes angels fall to the earth and walk as normal people.

Sincerely,

Peter Cotton

A lone tear smeared the page even before Ellen realized she was crying. Her heart was a great big lump in her throat, and she had to swallow hard to get it to go back down where it belonged. She turned toward the Worst house and wondered if that boy was in there and, if so, what he was doing now.

She folded her letter, tightened her grip on the other two, and put one foot in front of the other until she was inside with the door closed.

James was on the floor, sitting in the same spot where she'd placed him minutes before, but now he was pointing toward the kitchen. She followed his finger. Josiah and Wilmington were up, and they'd overturned the kitchen table. Wilmington had popped one of the legs off and was rubbing the padding of his thumb over the sharp point of an exposed nail. He exchanged a nod with his son and choked out a few words toward Ellen. "Table leg was loose."

Ellen sat on one of the kitchen chairs and held out the two letters toward her husband and father-in-law. Both men stared at her like they didn't understand. But then they each took their letter, and she wiped her eyes, which felt cleansed from her tears.

"Go on," she urged them. "Read."

Josiah read his letter once and refolded it.

He stared at Ellen with a glow in his eyes that reminded her of why she'd agreed to marry him in the first place. He was a kind and gentle man. An honest man. He unfolded his letter and silently read it again, his lips moving along with the words, which got Ellen to wondering what had been written.

Wilmington gulped and wiped his face. He folded his letter and slid it into his shirt pocket. The top of the letter still jutted out, reminding Ellen of when he used to wear those red roses in his lapels. Wilmington stood with a grunt and looked out the window over the sink. He exhaled two full cheeks of air and headed for the front door.

Maybe the rust was wearing off him too.

He moved like a man who was about to do something that made him uncomfortable, like he didn't want to do it but knew he should. He took his hat from the rack beside the door, blew dust from it, and then placed it atop his head.

Ellen watched Wilmington from the window. Josiah had sidled up beside her, so they watched together as Wilmington walked across the road in the direction of the Bentley Hotel, where Orion still sat on the curb.

Orion pushed to his feet when he saw Wilmington coming, and then the two men slowly approached one another as if preparing for an Old West gunfight. They stopped about five feet apart, and as much as Ellen could tell, neither man said a thing.

But then Orion moved closer, and Wilmington did the same.

Wilmington extended his hand and Orion shook it, the grips of two strong men who'd made fortunes and lost it all. Then they hugged in the middle of the street as if all things said in the days prior had been forgiven.

Ellen's breath caught, looking on. Then she felt a touch. Josiah was rubbing her back.

And Ellen's tears started all over again.

In the afternoon a duster rolled in, a sturdy one that lasted nearly ninety minutes and threatened to break windows.

If dusters could talk, Ellen imagined this one saying, *How dare you?*

The heaviness in her legs returned, and although she thought about it, she couldn't muster the energy to dig out when it was finished. No one did except Jeremiah and Peter and Nicholas Draper. Dust flew from their doors and windows like they'd taken on the energy of the entire town. And down the road it looked like Reginald and Emory Rochester were digging out too. *When did they get back?*

Ellen also noticed that every one of those yellow flags had been turned down. All over Nowhere, folks had at least gotten out of their houses long enough to retrieve what had been placed inside their mailboxes.

And that evening Ellen smiled as she lowered her head onto the pillow.

Reading that letter had triggered something. It had turned ugliness to a smile like one would flip a light switch. She lay in bed that evening with James by her side, wondering if in the morning she'd find that yellow flag turned up again.

She hoped so.

Not every car turned over on the first try. Her daddy said that sometimes it took several cranks on that engine.

Tomorrow maybe she would try another crank.

Just when she was about to give in to slumber, Josiah appeared in the doorway to their bedroom. He said, "Good night, Ellen."

"Good night, Josiah."

He nodded, then disappeared down the dark hallway to go sleep on the living room couch.

TWENTY-ONE

Jeremiah checked on Peter first thing the next morning.

The boy had been up all night again, writing more letters, and was now asleep on his lumpy mattress with his arms and legs spread out all akimbo and intertwined with the bedsheet.

Even before fixing himself a cup of joe, Jeremiah looked out the living room window. Just as he'd figured, every mailbox flag in Nowhere was standing at attention.

Again.

Jeremiah had seen the reaction on Ellen's face yesterday when she read her letter in the yard, and he still wondered what Peter had written on it. He'd saved both of his own letters so far—the first one, which said just plain "Thank you," and yesterday's, which had brought him to tears. That one said, "I wish you'd been my father from the get-go."

Jeremiah smiled even now just thinking of it. His heart galloped in anticipation of what currently rested inside that mailbox. But then his eyes caught something he didn't think at first could be real—a bright spot of red amid all that dark dust and those yellow mailbox flags.

He looked again, and the red remained—right in the middle of the road between the Goodbye house and the Bentley Hotel.

Red no bigger than a baseball.

The coffee could wait. He stepped outside and approached the road with a bit of caution. He walked past his mailbox and decided that whatever was in it could wait too. He'd get today's letter on his way back inside.

The closer he got, the brighter the red became, until he stopped three feet away and realized it was a rose. A living rose with a single leafy green stem and thorns. A rose that had no earthly business growing there right in the middle of all that dust—and in the middle of the road to boot. And didn't roses usually grow on bushes, not single stems?

Jeremiah scratched his head.

The red petals were unfurled and strong, glistening as if they'd recently seen water.

He squatted down for a closer look. He blew on it and the petals moved, proving the flower was real and not some imagined impossibility. He started to reach for it, but a voice stopped him.

"Don't touch it."

Jeremiah looked over his shoulder, and there stood Ellen a few feet away. "Morning, Ellen."

"Morning, Jeremiah." She stepped closer, her eyes fixed on the flower.

Jeremiah said, "What do you think it is?"

Ellen looked at him funny. "It's a rose."

"I know that, but . . . where'd it come from? Nothing blooms from dust."

She didn't answer, but he noticed she held a folded paper in her hand. She'd apparently taken her letter from the mailbox on her way out to the road.

"You read it yet?"

She shook her head no.

Orion was on his way out of the Bentley, and behind him came Rose, wearing, of all colors, a yellow dress to match those flags.

Her name now seemed oddly coincidental. Dizziness swept through Jeremiah, and he had to close his eyes to make things right. He stood from his crouch and recalled the way his father had hugged Rose on the evening she'd arrived in town. For some reason that embrace no longer seemed strange to him.

A door banged closed, and Wilmington and Josiah stepped from the house, both men squinting like they hadn't seen sunlight in days, which was probably true. Jeremiah shared a glance with Josiah, and then both brothers looked away.

And now, one by one, the rest of the town was emerging from their homes and making their way toward the hotel. Some stopped by their mailboxes to check what was inside. Others chose to wait. Sister Moffitt read her letter as she approached the gathering crowd. She walked with a hand clasped to her mouth. She could have been hiding a smile or holding in a cry, but the show of emotion was apparent. She was a different woman than the one they'd seen mumbling through that rosary the other night.

Five minutes later it seemed everybody in town had gathered, two rows deep, standing in a circle around that perky red rose. Whispers ruffled through the crowd, but mostly everyone just stared, transfixed by the bright, luscious color of that flower. Sheriff McKinney opened his letter and read it to himself while standing there, clenching his jaw as he did so, as if to stifle some show of emotion he didn't wish the others to see. Phillip Jansen had opened his letter too, and read with a smile.

Peter had joined them, yawning into his fist. His hair was

tousled, and his dimples were so deep they could have been holes. The people were watching him as much as they were watching the rose, and Jeremiah read the question in their eyes, the same question that had him wondering: *How does he know so much about me?* But more than one person said a silent thank-you to Peter as he stood there, eyes fixed on that red rose—a red rose that Jeremiah now felt the boy had something to do with, perhaps unknowingly. Did the boy understand what he'd done—or had begun to do— to a town so close to the brink? Jeremiah had a feeling he did, yet Peter hung back in a shy way that showed he wanted no credit.

Glancing back, Jeremiah saw that Wilmington and Orion had inched their way forward until they stood on opposite sides of the rose, eyes locked. Jeremiah wondered how many people had seen the two of them embrace in the middle of the road yesterday at just about that same spot.

What did it mean?

The two town founders looked to be asking the same question of each other.

The rose had sprouted where there'd been an outward display of kindness and forgiveness—not in the exact spot, but darn close. But Jeremiah sensed more in that look they shared, something that had to do with the past even more so than the present.

Then Dr. Craven stepped forward out of the crowd, frail and pale and wrinkly-old, but alert enough to share that same look with Orion and Wilmington. The three of them stood there together for long time, even after the town folk started to return to their homes.

Finally Wilmington, too, turned away, but he didn't follow Josiah and Ellen into the house. Instead he moved to the place beside the house where a deep drift covered what had once been the Goodbyes' rose garden—where Jeremiah's mother was buried.

Wilmington grabbed a shovel and started digging—slowly at first, and then faster, crunch by crunch, biting into that hill of dust that had grown the size of a tractor.

Orion crossed the road with a shovel and joined in the effort. Jeremiah went back home, retrieved a shovel from the porch, and came back to help. A minute later Josiah stepped outside with a shovel and a garden rake. Ellen held James and watched from the porch, covering the boy's mouth and nose to protect him from all that dust they were bringing up.

Thirty minutes later Dr. Craven shuffled over, a half-eaten apple in one hand and a shovel in the other. Jeremiah warned the doctor not to push himself, but Dr. Craven wasn't hearing it. He insisted on shoveling side by side with Orion and Wilmington, as if the threesome of town founders were some kind of team reunited.

Three hours later they finished. Or at least Wilmington stopped, which was a sign that *he* was not only finished, but satisfied. Jeremiah wasn't sure exactly what Wilmington had hoped to find under all that dirt, but he was thankful that bullet had never moved during all the physical activity.

They'd more or less just leveled the area out, exposing hard-pack underneath the dust that had been gathering there for years now. They had also uncovered the rainbow-shaped slab of concrete that marked Amanda Goodbye's resting place. But there was no trace of the rose garden that had once adorned it.

Wilmington leaned his shovel against the side of the house and went inside, having moved a ton of weight off his shoulders.

And the rest of them did likewise, glancing over at that lone rose in the middle of the road as they went.

TWENTY-TWO

When Ellen was a little girl, she had wanted to live in a castle.

So her father, before he moved the family west to the Oklahoma panhandle in search of riches, had set out to build her one.

It was a small castle with one turret no more than ten feet tall on the front left corner—a glorified playhouse, really, and a hurricane had knocked it over a year after it was built. That had prompted Ellen's mother to say to her husband, "Should have built it sturdier." To which he'd shrugged and said, "At least she got to be a princess for a year."

It was true. Ellen had gotten twelve months of play out of the little castle before those winds turned it to rubble. Every day she had been out there slaying dragons and felling knights—more of a warrior princess than the kind that waits up in a window for a knight in shining armor. But she had seen how long it took for that tiny castle to be built and how hard her father had worked to build it, so she was determined to make the most of it.

"Brick by brick, Ellen. Stone by stone," he had reminded her every day when he ventured out after a hard day's work to add to the walls of that castle. "That's the way anything worthwhile gets finished. And you know what every stone does, Ellen?"

"What, Daddy?"

"Every stone adds to the strength of that castle. It fortifies it."

Ellen now stood by the window staring at all the dust covering Nowhere. Such a desolate place compared to the windswept coastline of her childhood. But she held the latest letter from Peter in her hand, and in her mind she compared it to the stones her father used to build that castle.

The letter was a brick. The letter was a stone.

She was convinced now, especially with how peaceful and content the second letter had made her feel, that these letters circulating throughout town were, in a sense, stackable like stones in a castle wall, the effects cumulative. The first letters had opened their eyes and got their hearts beating again, and the second letters had added fuel to the fire. Moments of despair still reverberated in people's hearts. But at least now, with each breath taken, life seemed more of an option in the midst of all this dust and misery.

And that rose.

With that strong green stem and those lush red petals, it was still out there in the middle of the dusty road, breeze-blown and swaying, but appearing stronger than any castle her father—*God rest his soul*—had ever built. She imagined clutching onto that thorny stem and pulling and pulling, the green coiling upward like rope but never ending. That's how sturdy that rose looked, impossible as it seemed.

Wilmington and Josiah sat at the kitchen table, exhausted from all that shoveling beside the house. Josiah ate beans with James on his lap, while Wilmington just sat there grinning. A minute ago he'd reread the letter he'd pulled from the mailbox earlier.

Stone by stone. Letter by letter.

She told the two men that she was going out for a walk.

They nodded. James said, "Bye, Mommy."

Outside, she walked slowly past the rose, eyeing it like it might jump out and grab her. Jeremiah's door was closed, but there was light inside. She wondered what he was doing in there and if the reporter was with him. The air was crisp, and many of the windows in town were now open, so sounds carried. Peter Cotton was inside that house clacking away on his typewriter. Brooms whisked across floorboards in other houses, and somebody, a woman, was singing. Typewriter sounds came from the Bentley Hotel as well, which was where Rose was probably holed up now, punching those keys as if in competition with Peter across the way.

Ellen's eyes wandered as she walked. To the blue sky and floating white clouds. To the clear horizon that seemed endless, pretty now but always on the brink of peeling up and lifting away. To her fellow town folk who, like herself, were venturing forth.

Richard Klamp waved as he shoveled out hills of dirt in front of his clothing store. Philip Jansen was out there with him, helping move the dirt with a garden hoe. Sheriff McKinney cleaned off his patrol car, which was buried in the courthouse lot. He called out and asked Ellen to wait, so she halted as the chubby man huffed over the dirt toward the road. Although he tried, he couldn't seem to look her in the eyes, so he watched the ground as he spoke.

"That rose," he said. "Something else, ain't it?"

"It sure is, Sheriff." She waited through the lull. "What is it I can do for you?"

He scratched his head and chuckled. "Just something I need to get off my chest is all. It's no secret that I've always thought of you as quite a looker. And I've always secretly carried a torch for you, Ellen, which I know ain't right, you being a married woman and all and me being a somewhat ugly man. I believe in times past I've said some things I shouldn't or probably stared to the point of making you uncomfortable, and for all that I am sorry." He offered his hand, and after a moment's hesitation to get over the suddenness of it all, she shook it.

"Good day, Sheriff McKinney."

"Good day, Mrs. Goodbye."

He returned to his car, and she went on her way, wondering what could have possibly been written in his letters to make him apologize like that. Either way, the warm feeling inside her was welcome. "Stone by stone," she whispered, walking on, hoping that the sheriff's change of heart meant he was no longer intent on turning Jeremiah over to the authorities.

Then again, maybe that was why he was cleaning off the car in the first place—so that he could put a handcuffed Jeremiah Goodbye in it and drive him back to prison like he was a prized turkey. But something in the way Sheriff McKinney was now whistling as he worked told her that wouldn't be the way of it.

Letter by letter.

Ellen hadn't set out with a conscious destination in mind. But seeing as how she ended up standing on the Rochesters' front porch and knocking on their door, perhaps subconsciously she'd had one. After all, in today's letter, Peter had mentioned that Emory Rochester was sad and in need of reassurance. He hadn't needed to add any more. Ever since Emory's arrival in Nowhere, she and Ellen had been best of friends, and their relationship had only solidified once they decided to run the Nowhere schoolhouse together. The two women had been a team for years, joined by their shared goals of educating every boy and girl in town, until times had gotten tough and the Rochesters had up and went and Ellen had said what she said.

She couldn't even remember exactly what she had said to Emory, but it had been something about being a coward, and it had made Emory cry right there in her living room as Reginald loaded the final suitcase into their overstuffed car.

Ellen knocked again. When the door finally opened and Emory stood there on the threshold, the words were out of Ellen's mouth even before she'd properly formulated what to say. "I'm sorry, Emory. And I still love you like a sister."

Emory put a shaky hand to her mouth. Her eyes melted, and out came tears. The two women hugged right there in the doorway and held on long enough for Reginald to walk by and ask if somebody had just died.

"Only thing to die is old grudges," said Ellen.

Josiah cooked a meal that evening.

He made the same thing they'd been eating for months now—rabbit. But a meal was a meal, and back when things were better they'd done most of their talking over supper.

Wilmington was tired and went to bed early. The sun was going down, and so, Ellen noticed, were people's spirits. It was like the power the letters held waned at dusk, right about the time darkness took over. She could feel it herself, that urge to close her eyes and let the lethargy take over.

It's like a tug-of-war, Ellen thought as she chewed through tough meat. She hoped for another letter in the morning. It'd been awhile since she'd sat alone with Josiah like this, and the air between them felt stilted.

And then all of a sudden, without looking at her, Josiah said, "I'm sorry, Ellen."

He didn't need to say what for, because she already knew. There were years of gunk backed up to that apology. And after another bite and swallow of salt-flavored rabbit meat, she said, "I'm sorry too, Josiah."

They ate in silence for another minute.

Josiah wiped his hands on a cloth napkin he'd set beside their plates before they'd started. "Envy has been the downturn of plenty of men, Ellen. And unfortunately I am not immune to the nuances of that particular sin." He balled up the napkin and placed it on his plate, his eyes focused on the whorls in the wooden table. "I called the authorities in on my own kin. I spied Jeremiah burying those bodies in the silo, and I assumed the worst. I also saw an opportunity to get him out of our way, and I took it. I feared he'd turn you crooked. I loved you then and I love you still, Ellen. If I need to apologize for that, then I'm sorry twice in one night." He finally looked at her. "But some things I need to know."

"Like what?"

"Would you have married him if he'd asked?"

Ellen blinked. "Does it matter?"

"I'd like to think it does."

"I don't know, Josiah."

He nodded, looked around as if contemplating something, and then nodded again. He stood from his chair and wiped a weathered hand across his mouth. He made as if to walk into the other room, but then he moved around the table and gently kissed the top of Ellen's head.

"I think it might be Easter," he said. "I'm not sure of the days anymore. But I know how much you like Easter. That's how come I cooked dinner."

"Thank you, Josiah."

He walked back around the table and stopped before the entry to the living room. "The other day, you asked me about Jeremiah's nightmares. How I used to hold his hand every night when he'd have them, you know, to help get him through. You asked me when I stopped doing that."

"Yes?"

"Well, it was the day you moved into town."

Ellen lay in bed, listening to her son's subtle snore across the room.

She was tired but couldn't sleep.

Josiah had stopped holding Jeremiah's hand during those nightmares because of her. It had been more than two hours since he'd said those words before retiring to bed on the living room couch, but the pain from them still lingered. Those words had hurt her, as the truth sometimes does. But even now as she dwelled on them and on the monotone way Josiah had said them, she honestly didn't know if it had been the dust making him mean again or Peter's letters luring out what needed cleansing. Or maybe it was just Josiah being Josiah—kind of monotone by nature and a little cryptic.

Safety and contentment. She had known what she was getting when she took Josiah's hand, and if she'd expected that to change, then it was on her head. But choosing between them, between those two brothers that she loved, had not been easy, because they were so different, and each had offered her something she craved.

Jeremiah, of course, was anything but safe. She knew him as a confident young man who backed down from nothing. A daring young man who was never afraid to spill blood if that's what it took to protect those he loved. A young man who drank a lot—too much, she'd soon realize—and even more so the longer she knew him, in order to mask the pain he kept hidden. A young man so tough no one dared challenge him, yet so fragile the nighttime could melt him like butter. A young man, despite all, who when he'd kiss her left her trembling until her knees went weak. That was the only Jeremiah she knew.

But Wilmington—and Josiah sometimes too—had told her Jeremiah hadn't always been like that. That as boys Josiah and Jeremiah had been more similar than not, both quiet and guarded in their own ways and, despite their different coloring, not easy to tell apart. Until it got easier. Until Jeremiah started to change.

Now, after what Josiah had said, she realized that she'd unknowingly been a wedge driven between two twins who had once been, in Wilmington's words, inseparable. She knew she wasn't responsible for the changes in Jeremiah. Those had been due in large part to the nightmare and the drinking and what ultimately happened to William Worst. But she was part of the reason he and Josiah had lost one another. And perhaps that loss, that alienation, had been the hardest blow of all for both of them.

Maybe a teenager was too old to do such a thing as holding a brother's hand, even in the protected confines of their childhood room. But did Josiah let his brother down? Without the comfort of his closeness, had the nightmare become unbearable for Jeremiah? Was that the reason behind what he became?

Josiah probably wondered too. His words to her earlier had been laced with guilt.

He had stepped away from his brother. From his twin. Because of a girl.

Because of me.

TWENTY-THREE

A duster raged through town overnight.

Jeremiah couldn't sleep with so much dust tapping the window, so he walked down the hall to check on Peter, who was busy at the typewriter. Jeremiah invited himself in anyway and pulled a spare chair next to the desk, wondering to whom that particular letter would go come morning.

"Peter?"

"Peter?" said the boy, punching the keys.

"Can you stop for a minute?"

"Stop for a minute." He finished a sentence, pulled the page from the typewriter, folded it in thirds like he always did, and then looked up.

Jeremiah had his attention, but he hadn't thought of exactly what to say, so they stared at each other for a bit.

Peter smiled.

Jeremiah smiled back. "Don't go repeating what I say, okay?"

Peter nodded.

"I have a question for you."

Another nod.

"How do you know?"

Peter stared at him.

"I mean, look what you've done here. How do you know what to say to all these people?" He pointed to the desk. "In those letters. Do you understand what I'm saying?" Peter nodded but didn't answer. Jeremiah scooched forward on the chair and pointed to his chest, where he could feel the rapid beating of his own heart. "You're touching people right here. The town was on the brink of killing itself, Peter, and we had no answer. The dust turned everyone mean and ugly and then took away their ability to care. And what you're doing is . . ."

He scratched his head, searching for the words, because even now it didn't seem possible.

That rose. Those letters.

Peter loaded a sheet of paper into the typewriter and quickly punched out four words:

Killing it with kindness.

Jeremiah rubbed his chin. "Yes you are. That's exactly what you're doing. But how do you know? How do you know what to say to each and every person in Nowhere?"

Peter turned in his chair, faced Jeremiah, and pointed to his eyes.

"You watch?"

Peter nodded, then pointed to his ears.

"You listen."

Peter nodded, then pointed to his head.

"You have hair?"

Peter laughed, shook his head, then typed again:

I'm a writer. I pay attention to detail.

Jeremiah laughed and on instinct ruffled the boy's hair. He leaned back with his arms folded and watched the boy. "I think you've changed me, Peter."

Peter shook his head, then typed,

You changed me, Mr. Goodbye. My father left us when I was five. He always said I was strange and wouldn't ever amount to anything.

Jeremiah leaned over, pulled the page from the typewriter, and crumpled it into a ball.

"Peter, your father was never more wrong about anything in his life."

Jeremiah awoke the next morning at the kitchen table, leaning back with his feet propped up on the seat of another chair. The sun was bright and the air summery warm.

He vaguely remembered taking a seat at the table last night after his conversation with Peter. He'd nodded off to the sound of the boy typing his letters from down the hallway. And maybe he'd dreamed it, but at some point during the overnight duster, something had slid under the front door and into the room and taken the shape of a man who sat across the kitchen table from him—a dust man with no eyes or mouth or nose, but somehow still watching.

But Jeremiah had watched right back. *I know who you are. You've had a hand on me my whole life. Taking the form of dust don't change things. Except now I know how to get rid of you,* he remembered telling the shape that might or might not have even been there. *I sat in that electric chair and died long enough to cast you out. That jolt only made me stronger. And you can't get back in.*

The dust man's voice was a whisper in Jeremiah's head, from his nightmare, because he now knew that's all it had been. *From dust we come, and to dust we shall return, Jeremiah. I took her. And I nearly took you too.*

What do you mean you took her?

He remembered the dust man collapsing at that point, scattering into millions of motes that floated in every different direction.

Take whatever form you want, Jeremiah remembered saying. *I won't let you back in.*

And now the sun had replaced the night, and he doubted last night had even happened. He stood from the kitchen table and approached the window, feeling an urgent need to see if that rose was still out there in the middle of the road.

It was. His yellow mailbox flag was up too, as were the others all over town. But that wasn't what had dozens of people outside right now standing and staring in shock.

Jeremiah opened the front door and stepped outside for a better look. Then he was staring too. For while yesterday had brought that one lone spot of red in the middle of the road, today brought a dozen at least.

Red roses had sprouted all over town.

One bloomed in the middle of the courthouse lot. Sheriff McKinney stood next to it scratching his head. Another grew from the dust that had gathered on one of the Bentley Hotel's porch rails. Another sprouted in the middle of the road where he'd seen Sheriff McKinney and Ellen shake hands yesterday. Another adorned the dusty sidewalk leading to the opera house. And yet another rose grew from the Goodbyes' dirt-covered driveway, not too far from where they'd all shoveled dust the day before.

His first estimate of twelve turned out to be eight roses off. By the time he'd cased the town and discussed the situation with others—Rose was out taking notes—it was agreed by one and all that nineteen more roses had popped through that dust overnight. That made twenty in all.

They studied them like they'd studied the lone rose the day before. Orion bent down next to one and, after getting a nod of encouragement from Wilmington, touched one of the petals. The roses were real, all right, each one as sturdy as the next, and they smelled like springtime was supposed to smell.

Like wet blooms and life.

Wilmington shook his head and stood watching as Rose took notes across the way. Then he went inside while all the others stayed out.

"There's something he's not telling us."

Jeremiah turned to find Ellen beside him. "Morning, Ellen."

"Your father," she said. "He's holding back." Her eyes were wet, fresh from tears, the good cleansing kind. She held Peter's latest letter in her hand. She must have just read it. "He knows more than he's letting on about all this. I think Orion does too. And Dr. Craven."

"You might be right."

They watched the town folk move about. Some walked from rose to rose. Others read their letters, while even more were sweeping and digging out from last night's duster.

"I'm sorry, Jeremiah."

He looked at her. "About what?"

263

She didn't answer, not verbally, but her glance toward Josiah, who was kneeling next to one of those roses across the way, gave him a hint as to what she was thinking. Was she talking about him and Josiah? His eyes flicked toward his twin, and she answered his question with the lowering of her head.

"Don't blame yourself for us two drifting apart. You hear me?"

She nodded but kept her gaze on the dust.

He lifted her chin with an index finger and caught her eyes. "You were right the other day, Ellen. About what happened years ago. I did flip a coin on me and you. I know it sounds nonsensical, but that's what I did. Just like you surmised."

She nodded, squinted into the sunlight. They shared a look. He was trying to guess her thoughts like he used to but things seemed fuzzy now.

"I loved you, Ellen. I wanted more than anything to be with you."

"I know." She smiled, and the smile was genuine. "But it just couldn't be, right?"

"I didn't flip the coin when you think I did."

She looked at him again.

"That hurt you showed the day before my arrest," he said, "when I told you I couldn't be with you and to marry my brother—I relived it every day I was in jail. Took it with me to bed every night I was behind those bars. Took it with me into that electric chair, even. I didn't flip the coin that week Josiah proposed to you, Ellen."

"When, then?"

"I flipped it the day you drove into town," he said. "I had to know."

"And it told you yes? That you and I would be good together."

He didn't answer, exactly, just looked down at the dust.

So it was no. She nodded and wiped her eyes.

"But it was real, Ellen, every secret day of it. So real I was willing to test it."

"Test what?"

"Fate, I guess. I'd learned early on that the coin was never wrong with me. But with you I wanted to give it a go. I carried a torch for you, and I wanted to see how long it could burn."

She nodded, clear-eyed. "You think that's why our baby didn't survive?"

He looked to the ground again. "Can't say I haven't had the same thoughts, Ellen, but I'm not sure that's the way of things. I suppose it just wasn't meant to be."

"I suppose so." She wiped her eyes and smiled up at him. She held out her arm, bent at the elbow. "I was on my way to the schoolhouse. Emory and I were going to clean it out today and get classes going again. Would you mind accompanying me?"

He linked his arm with hers, and they began walking.

She laughed.

"What's funny, Ellen?"

"Just that life is sometimes ironic once you allow reality into it."

"I reckon so." His eyes fished for more, because what she said made little sense.

"I was an only child, Jeremiah," she explained. "I'd always begged my parents to go out and get me a sister." She smiled up at him again as they strolled. "But I suppose a brother-in-law will do."

TWENTY-FOUR

It took most of the day to get the schoolhouse to Ellen's liking, but by the time the sun began to drop across the blue sky, the desks smelled of fresh cedar oil and the floors had been mopped clean enough to dine upon. Ellen knew she'd have to clean again as soon as the next duster rolled in, but for now it gleamed, and that was enough.

Most of Ellen's pupils had joined in the effort, eager now to get back to learning, and Emory Rochester had been happy just to be around them again. Peter had even shown up after a while. He had mostly observed, but the other kids had seemed to be warming to him. They weren't giving him those queer looks they'd thrown him when he first came to town. In fact, they treated him with a bit of awe over what he'd done.

Nicholas Draper, who beamed because he'd finally gotten his mother to eat that morning, inched over to Peter and showed him how to shovel dirt across the floor with the instep of his shoe. After a few tries, Peter took right to it. James was there too. He imitated what Peter was doing, and the two of them acted as a team.

Jeremiah, despite the wounded shoulder, had been a big help, doing most of the heavy lifting and dirt pushing once they'd piled it too high for the kids to budge.

Windmill showed up a couple of hours into the cleaning. He didn't say anything to Ellen as he grabbed a broom and got right to work, but she sensed embarrassment in the way he kept his head lowered. Bravery was more like it, showing up despite what he knew she'd said about him.

They'd created a system of dirt removal that proved efficient—shoveling heaps of it onto blankets and sheets and then either carrying or pulling those right out the door. One blanket got way too heavy for the kids, so she made a point to call both Jeremiah and Windmill over.

"Let's let the two *men* remove this one," she said to the kids, winking at Windmill, who blushed, smiling as he helped Jeremiah remove the heavy dirt-filled blanket from the schoolhouse.

Rose Buchanan stepped inside ten minutes later, waving her hand through floating dust and asking how she could help. After a few seconds of sizing the reporter up, Ellen handed her a broom and said she could start in the back corner, which Rose did without hesitation. *Did she even notice I gave her the corner with the most dust and grime?* If she did, she said nothing about it, just got right to work despite her fancy dress. She also brought the news that Josiah and Wilmington and some others had gathered to help Orion clean out the Bentley Hotel. When they finished there, the plan was to move on to the courthouse.

"Stone by stone," Ellen murmured, dusting off one of the desktops.

"What's that?" asked Jeremiah.

"Oh, nothing." She hadn't realized she'd said it aloud and hadn't known Jeremiah was working right behind her. She'd been too busy spying on Rose across the room. "She's pretty, by the way."

"Who?"

"Miss Fancy Dress over there." And then, "You flip a coin on her yet?"

"No." And after a beat, he said, "Should I?"

Ellen chewed on it. "I don't know yet. Maybe we should see if the law ever comes for you first."

He grinned. "That the only reason I should wait, Ellen?"

"Of course." She looked away and resumed working, dealing with her emotions the best she could. It took time to remove stones too, and these particular ones had acted as boulders for way too long. She had a notion to go on over and help the reporter with that corner of the room, an olive-branch attempt to help bridge the unsaid. She probably would've done just that had the rumble of thunder not moved everyone in the room to silence.

Ellen laid her dustcloth on the desk and hurried outside. With thunder could come rain. The others followed, and as a cluster they faced the western horizon, where the noise seemed to be coming from. A great big cloud approached, wide and moving and buzzing.

Buzzing?

Jeremiah said, "That ain't no thunderboomer."

The cloud approached, not as black as the typical duster, but it buzzed like an electric current ran through it. The people began to stir, uneasy, looking around now in every direction.

"It's no duster either." Ellen looked for her son. "James?"

The cloud got closer and wider, loud and crackling, buzzing loudly enough for some of them to hold their ears. And then, with little warning, it was upon them.

Peter started shrieking.

"James?" *Where is he?* Ellen turned, frantic.

Jeremiah had James in the crook of one arm. He swooped Peter up with the other as a wave of grasshoppers poured over Nowhere like a tidal wave, millions of hopping insects, swarming and landing and munching everything in sight.

Now that James was safe with his uncle, Ellen took charge of the schoolchildren. She and Emory rushed the panicked kids back inside. They closed the doors and windows, but large numbers of grasshoppers still made it inside, banking off the walls and bouncing off the chalkboards, covering the handles of the brooms and shovels, gnawing on the wood, on the desks, the wooden door frames.

Ellen gathered the kids in a cluster and had them kneel next to the back wall and hunker down. More grasshoppers poured in. And outside was an insanity she could simply not fathom, a plague of biblical proportions. First the drought, and then the dust storms and the jackrabbits. And now this.

The grasshoppers covered her dress. She swiped at them, but they kept coming. Jeremiah protected Peter and James, doing his best to shield the terrified boys from the tumult like he'd done with Nicholas Draper during the big black blizzard. Windmill swung a shovel side to side in front of them, smacking dozens of hoppers with each movement, screaming as he did so, daring them to come at him.

Rose stood frozen in the middle of the schoolhouse, her face pale as hundreds of grasshoppers danced around her feet and ankles and clung to the skirt of her dress, rising upward as one munching collective.

"Rose," screamed Ellen. "Over here." The swarm of hoppers wasn't as thick where the kids were.

But Rose wouldn't—or couldn't—move.

Ellen ran to her, grabbed her arm, and pulled her from whatever trance had left her stuck in the middle of the room, and together the two women hurried toward the kids, who were screaming and crying, yet unheard because of the sheer power of sound coming from the sudden plague of hoppers. The ground outside reverberated. The walls shook.

Ellen gripped Rose's hand. They lowered their faces to the floor, but the hoppers were everywhere—over, under, and on every side of them, hopping and munching and buzzing, and Ellen wished it over, but no one was listening. The hoppers clipped her face, danced off her hair, and hurtled across her ears. She squeezed her eyes shut, clenched her teeth, and held on for dear life.

An hour later the sound dissipated. They lifted their heads from their hands and slowly stood from their hunched-over crouches. They walked across the room, where at least three dozen hoppers still jumped around.

Ellen ran to James and hugged him so tight he started coughing.

Jeremiah stood by the window. Ellen and Rose joined him, looking out on a bleak landscape. The starved grasshoppers had eaten everything they could find and were now a dark cloud rolling southeast toward Texas. Thousands remained though, hopping at wild tangents on every outside surface. But at least the dust was visible again.

The good old dust.

Ellen had never imagined she'd be happy to see it.

"They're gone," said Jeremiah.

At first Ellen assumed he was talking about the grasshoppers, but upon closer inspection she realized it was something more.

The roses were gone.

Eaten. Every one of them.

Thorny stems and all.

TWENTY-FIVE

Just before sundown another duster hit. And after the dirt moved on, everyone in Nowhere stepped outside to assess the damage. Dead grasshoppers, smothered by the dust storm, crunched underfoot. The wind died down, but not before it blew over Orion's mailbox, weakened from the hoppers snacking on the wooden post.

Jeremiah felt too many eyes on him—everyone dust-covered and weary—like they blamed him or they just didn't know what to say or do anymore. He turned in a slow circle as the town gathered. "It's testing us."

Deacon Sipes spat brown juice to the dirt, then wiped his mouth. "What's testing us?"

"The land."

"Why should we trust you?" asked Deacon. "Ever since you come back to Nowhere, we've had nothing but trouble. That Black Sunday duster, pushing us to the brink. And now a plague of grasshoppers?" He stepped closer and spat again. This time it landed on Jeremiah's boot.

Wilmington said, "Those dusters had been blowing in daily for months before Jeremiah showed. You know that, Deacon. He's got nothin' to do with it."

Ellen said, "If anything, he's kept us from killing each other—him and Peter. You saw those roses just as we all did."

Jeremiah walked toward his porch, grabbed a shovel, and returned to the circle. "Way before any of us were even thoughts in our parents' eyes, Indians and buffalo roamed these lands. And now the dirt is stained with their blood. They were killed at the hands of white men so that we could take what was theirs. Then we plowed up what was sacred to them—turned over what wasn't meant to be turned. And now the land's fighting back. It's not me." He took in all the eyes on him and said again, pointing to his chest with the wooden shovel handle, "Not me. Give in if you want. But I'm not sleeping on dust tonight."

Then he stalked back to his porch and started digging out from the duster.

The town watched, listened to the crunch and hurl of four full shovel tosses over his shoulder. Then Josiah headed for the Goodbye house. At first Jeremiah assumed he was retiring inside, but then his brother reappeared with a shovel and started digging their porch out too. Next, Peter grabbed a broom and went to work whisking the porch boards.

One by one the town folk walked to their homes and followed Jeremiah's lead. As the sun disappeared, lanterns and candles were lit, and the inside of every home glowed with light. When one house was clean, folks moved to the neighboring house and helped them, until the only one in town remaining idle was Deacon Sipes, who watched from the lean-to outside his automotive shop, where all those rotting rabbits still hung from the ceiling and had begun to smell like a slaughterhouse. Even Toothache was out and about with a shovel in one hand and a broom in the other, cleaning other homes because Deacon wouldn't let him clean theirs.

"Deaconwontletmeinthere," he said. "Heaintrightintheheadno-more."

By dusk a group of men, led by Father Steven, had reposted Orion's mailbox in the ground out in front of the Bentley. Throughout the day, the folks had watched Peter as they swept, dusted, and shoveled, probably wondering if the boy was going to go home and start writing more letters. Around ten o'clock that night, he retreated back into the Worst house and got to work. And once the clacking echoed from that back bedroom, the citizens of Nowhere found their second wind and began to work faster, sweeping deep into the night, anticipating the words they would find inside their mailboxes come sunup.

By midnight every house had been cleared. The accumulated dust had been swept away, along with thousands of dead grass-hoppers. But before the town was able to turn in for the night, Orion's bell chimed from inside the Bentley. People paused and waited. Occasionally, over the years, Orion had accidently rung it in passing. But once the bell sounded for a second and third time, the weary town folk started filtering into the hotel and taking seats in a lobby that now shone from a fresh coating of cedar oil.

Jeremiah was about to leave Peter to his typing and walk to the Bentley alone, but upon that second ringing of the bell, Peter's bed-room door opened and he emerged with his typewriter, carrying it like it was attached to his belly. He led the way across the town square toward the hotel. Jeremiah followed, lagging behind a little as people filed by him, answering Orion's summons.

Not Deacon Sipes, though. He leaned against a darkened streetlamp, arms folded, eyeing Jeremiah as he approached.

Jeremiah had gotten close enough to Deacon the other night inside the repair shop to get that feeling he'd always gotten when someone bad was near. And that in turn had rekindled the memory that had startled him at Deacon's shop—the memory of brushing by Deacon years ago, before he'd gone in to do his bit in the big house. In that instant he'd gotten a brief glimpse of something, the way he sometimes did. He'd seen Deacon with crazed eyes and his hands around another man's neck.

Right now all Jeremiah got was the bad feeling. The rest was radio static. But he still had the memory, and he doubted Deacon had changed.

"You've killed a man," he blurted before he could think it through.

A strange, panicked look crossed Deacon's face. He covered it up fast with a sneer, but he couldn't mask the guilty quiver in his voice. "Says who?"

"Says me."

"What, the one that killed many? The one now preachin' fancy. So what if I have?"

"Then maybe I should do something about that."

"What if I say it was self-defense? Or what if you're wrong?"

Jeremiah shrugged, then spat to the dust. Peter had stopped outside the hotel. Jeremiah told the boy to go on into the Bentley and secure them a table. Once the boy cleared away, Jeremiah reached into his pocket and pulled out a quarter. He ran it in between his knuckles like a magician would, warming up for a show.

Deacon eyed it. "Go on, Coin-Flip Killer. I ain't scared. Flip it."

"You *are* scared, Deacon. 'Cause you don't know."

"Don't know what?"

Jeremiah looked deep into Deacon's eyes. "What does evil look like on the inside?"

"What kind of a question is that?"

"The kind I'm asking."

"Flip the coin."

Jeremiah held the coin in his palm, stared at it for a beat, and then stuck it back into his trouser pocket. "Not today."

The Bentley's church bell rang for the fourth time, and he followed it.

Inside the Bentley Hotel, Ellen rubbed her tired eyes, then James's back as he slept against her shoulder. She leaned toward Wilmington. "What's this about?"

Wilmington shrugged.

Josiah was sitting next to his father. "I suppose Orion's got something to say."

It was well after midnight by now, and after digging out from the duster, everyone was exhausted. Only in an emergency would Orion ring that bell this late at night. Ellen struggled to keep her eyes open. She caught a glimpse of Jeremiah and Peter across the room, sitting at their own table.

Once the room was full, Orion stood. "I'd like to thank everyone for coming. I know it's late, and we're all tired. But I'd like to invite the newest guest of my hotel up here for a few important words."

No one clapped. Tired eyes followed Rose Buchanan as she made her way to the front of the room with a bundle of papers in her hands. Her dress didn't look so new anymore, and she'd begun to take on the look of the town. Rose cleared her throat and glanced at Ellen and her table as if what she was about to say was in large part for the Goodbyes.

"I won't talk any longer than I need to," said Rose. "But as I said in this very room days ago, I came to Nowhere with a purpose in mind, and that purpose was to complete an article I was writing on Jeremiah Goodbye, the so-called Coin-Flip Killer. An article pleading a case for his innocence, just seeing what dust a woman could stir up in a profession dominated by men."

Ellen smiled despite her fatigue. The woman was growing on her.

Jeremiah looked uncomfortable in his seat across the room. He and Rose exchanged a glance, and Rose went on. "I was side-tracked by the somewhat unbelievable goings-on in this town of late, which has pushed me toward another story altogether. I'd be naïve now to think that these two stories aren't somehow related, and my parents didn't raise me to be naïve. But the reason I wanted to speak tonight has to do with the truth, and I see it as my responsibility to bring it to light, especially because Jeremiah himself would probably never do so."

Jeremiah's head lowered. Ellen had a notion to comfort him but stayed put.

"As you know, Jeremiah went to prison because four men were found buried inside Nowhere's grain silo," said Rose. "He never denied putting them there. I've grown close enough to Jeremiah over the past week for him to explain exactly why he did this, and without breaking what was told to me in confidence, I can say it all stems from the nightmares that have plagued him since birth. He was always a man with a tortured mind searching for answers."

She took a deep breath and focused on the pages in her grip. "I want to tell you about those four men the law found in that silo: Jarvis Kingsley, age forty-seven; Brent Bagwell, thirty-three; Toots Moran, fifty-eight; and Linus Carlbridge, twenty-nine. It is true that Jeremiah came into contact with all four of these men. He had confrontations with all four as well, on four separate occasions, all within a four-week span. It is also true that he did what he's become known for—he flipped the coin on all four of them. All four came up heads. And all four died after that. But he didn't kill them. He didn't shoot them as he'd threatened."

She looked at Jeremiah. "And why not?"

Jeremiah eyed the crowd, hesitant, but spoke anyway. "Because I knew they'd die on their own."

Shocked murmurs ran through the crowd inside the Bentley. Rose raised her hands to quiet them. "The day after you flipped the coin on Jarvis Kingsley, he had a massive heart attack while milking one of his cows. And Brent Bagwell, on the night of your confrontation with him inside the Butcher's Block Saloon in Liberal, became intoxicated, drove off the road and into a ravine, and drowned. Who pulled him from the water?" She nodded toward Jeremiah. "Jeremiah Goodbye. He'd followed him. And he'd also been spying on Jarvis Kingsley the day he had his heart attack. He was the first to get to him when he stumbled off the milking stool and lay shaking in the dirt. I've found witnesses willing to testify to the way these men died."

She held up a finger. "Toots Moran. The night after he and Jeremiah scuffled inside the Watering Hole outside Boise City, Toots was fixing a leak in his roof. The boards were rotten beneath the shingles, and the roof collapsed. He broke his neck and died. Jeremiah saw it happen from the surrounding field and then went in to help. And again, there were witnesses."

Ellen found herself shaking by this point, and Josiah's eyes were wet. He wiped at them with hands that shook. Wilmington had gone pale. Ellen gripped his hand as Rose went on.

"And lastly, Mr. Linus Carlbridge. Jeremiah got into a heated argument with this man inside the Foxtrot Saloon in Guymon. They fought. Jeremiah flipped the coin on Mr. Carlbridge's chest as he lay on the ground wiping blood from his nose. It was heads, and Jeremiah moved on. The next morning Mr. Carlbridge was out feeding his horse. Something spooked it, and up the hind legs went, delivering a blow to the head that killed Mr. Carlbridge instantly. Jeremiah saw it from a line of trees."

Sheriff McKinney stood from his table and faced Jeremiah. "If all this is true, Jeremiah, why'd you bring those bodies back here?"

Jeremiah looked at Rose and then answered. "I don't know. I was drinking heavily at the time, Sheriff. My mind wasn't my own, and I wasn't thinking clearly. I didn't kill those men, but I knew I wasn't innocent. And witnesses had seen me scuffle with them. And threaten their lives."

Josiah spoke through a cracked voice. "But those were accidents, Jeremiah. Anybody would've seen that. You shouldn't have brought them back here and done what you did to them."

"I know." Jeremiah's voice trembled. "Like I said, I wasn't thinking clearly. And I felt responsible, because I had flipped the coin." He clenched his jaw. "Those were bad men, Josiah. When I brushed by them, I . . ."

"You what?"

"I saw into their souls. I got glimpses of the bad things they'd done. It was—I don't know why, but I've always been able to do that. To see and feel . . ."

Whispers spread across the room at that—people looking at each other with varying levels of shock and disbelief. Rose silenced them and read again from her paper. "Jarvis Kingsley." She swallowed hard. "He was a secret Klansman. Even his wife didn't know.

He'd killed more men than I can count on all my fingers and toes—and all because of the color of their skin. And Brent Bagwell—I investigated him just as I investigated all of them. I talked to too many of his victims not to believe what I'd heard. Female victims. Jeremiah sensed it right when he brushed up against him that night, and what's done is done." Rose's voice grew stronger, her words gaining steam. "Toots Moran was a gangster of the most sordid kind, hiding out on the plains because of murders he'd committed during Prohibition. Well, he'll never kill again. And Linus Carlbridge—if he robbed one bank, he robbed two dozen, under at least five different names, stealing money from hardworking folks like you and not caring how much blood was shed in his wake."

Wilmington buried his face in his hands and cried. Ellen rubbed his back. Her heart thumped faster than a wave of jackrabbits during a summer drive.

"Thank you for listening," said Rose. "This man was not responsible for the deaths of those men. And he shouldn't be strapped with that burden any longer." She returned to her table.

The room stayed quiet.

Ellen stood and faced Jeremiah across the room. "If this is all true, why didn't you fight harder at the trial?"

"Because I knew what the power of that coin had done to me. I didn't think I had the right, Ellen, no matter what those men had done."

"What right, Jeremiah?"

"The right to play God."

TWENTY-SIX

"Ellen."

She opened heavy eyelids.

Wilmington sat at her bedside, leaning close enough that she could smell coffee on his breath. Morning sunlight cut across the bed, highlighting her father-in-law's freshly shaved face.

"Morning, sunshine."

She leaned up on her elbows and rested against the headboard. "Morning, Wilmington. Where's James?"

"Josiah's got him. Look, I've got something I need to say." Wilmington cleared his throat. "It's about what Orion said the other night. About your mother and me."

Ellen sat up taller. "Queer topic to wake up to first thing in the morning, Wilmington. I don't know if I want to know."

"Your mother was a beautiful woman, Ellen."

"Stop." She clamped her hands over her ears like a child.

"And although it may be true that she at one time had feelings for me, she never strayed from your father." He grabbed her hand and held it on the bed. "And I never strayed from the memory of my Amanda. I've only ever loved one woman, Ellen."

Ellen looked deep into Wilmington's eyes and feared she saw what had brought this sudden conversation about. She wondered if that bullet was fixing to move, if he could feel it in there starting to rustle and twist. She brought her other hand around and held his. "I drove a wedge between your sons long ago, and for that I am sorry."

He grinned. "Never seen a divide that couldn't eventually be bridged, Ellen. There's things about Jeremiah that happened long ago that you don't know about. Things I swore I'd take to my grave and still plan to."

"Tell me."

"Just know that you didn't cause Jeremiah to take the turn he did. He's been battling it from the start." He stood from the chair and kissed her forehead. "You're my daughter, Ellen. I couldn't ask for a better one. Nor would I." He gave her hand a gentle tug. "Come on. There's something outside you need to see."

She sat up, feeling something was different, but unable to put her finger on it. She thought she heard voices outside and something tapping on the roof that had a flatter, less abrasive sound than dust. She slid her feet from the sheets and stood hand in hand with Wilmington. "The reporter, Rose? Wilmington, the way you embraced her when she arrived into town. It was as if you knew her . . ."

"No more questions on this fine morning, Ellen."

"What's so fine about it?"

"You'll see in a minute."

"More letters?"

"I suppose that's part of it."

She allowed him to lead her outside to the porch, each of them reveling in the childishness of it. She even closed her eyes briefly, recognizing the feeling as similar to when her own father walked her outside as a child to show her the fully finished castle he'd built for her overlooking the coastline.

A warm breeze coated her face with moisture as she crossed the threshold. The air was thick with it. She inhaled a scent both foreign and familiar—something almost forgotten. Then she opened her eyes, and what she saw falling down all across Nowhere made her heart skip.

Rain.

A soft gentle rain.

Not one of the sudden downpours that would flash-flood entire houses away because the ground was packed so hard, but a misty soaker that held down all that dust and trickled down rooftops and dripped into recently cleared gutters and downspouts.

She covered her mouth with the hand that wasn't clutching Wilmington's. The rain wasn't the only thing that had come overnight. The red roses that had been eaten by the grasshoppers had all returned, and then some. Hundreds of red roses, all sturdy-stemmed and strong, stuck up from the wet dust all over Nowhere. Some sprouted in bushlike clusters, like roses were supposed to grow, and some bloomed on climbing vines. On all of them, red petals glistened as if they'd recently been watered. Perky red roses drank in that rain, petals open like mouths to take it all in.

Ellen looked at Wilmington. "When did it start?"

"About ten minutes ago. We were all out looking at the roses, and then it clouded up beautifully. Then Moses came out."

He nodded across the street at Moses Yearling, who sat on the porch of the Bentley Hotel, crying and clutching one of his TNT rockets like it was a baby.

"As soon as it clouded," Wilmington continued, "Moses hurried in and got one of his rockets. He fired it right into the belly of those gray clouds, and a minute later the rain started. Pretty good timing—even though I doubt the rocket really had anything to do with the rain. Ain't no such thing as a cloud-buster."

As a teen, when the rain would come, Ellen would hunt for an umbrella or hurry to shelter. But now she couldn't wait to stand outside in it, to let it soak her hair and dress, to revel in the chill it put on her skin.

Apparently the whole town felt the same. It looked like all of Nowhere was outside—standing, walking, some staring downward at the hundreds of red roses, others with their necks craned upward toward the pregnant sky. She waved at Josiah, who stood in the yard holding James. They waved back and smiled, both of them soaked to the skin, a big smear of mud on her baby's face. Had he ever even seen rain?

Wilmington led Ellen down the porch steps and then finally let go of her hand as she gazed around in wonder. The roses were everywhere. In places they grew so thick they looked like private rose gardens, but mostly they'd popped up as singles, anywhere and everywhere, one making no more possible sense than the next. But she did have a feeling that the kindness instigated by those letters had something to do with it. Kindness had brought about that beauty.

Kindness had made roses bloom from dust.

The Bentley Hotel—where the entire town had gathered last night in what turned out to be a clear session of healing by truth— was completely surrounded by roses. One had even sprung up from the angled gutter on the hotel's façade, another from an old flowerpot resting on a windowsill. Next to that window, two roses had sprouted from the dust-clogged engine of Orion's rusted tractor.

Josiah and James held their hands up toward the sky and laughed as they tried to catch rain. Most of the schoolkids ran the streets, play-fully dodging the roses while at the same time trying to get hit by as many raindrops as they could. Orion watched from his hotel porch, smiling with a cigar nub angled in his mouth, his thumbs hooked under his suspenders.

Sheriff McKinney stood next to his mailbox reading his latest letter, as did Sister Moffitt down the road.

Jeremiah was out with Peter, staring skyward in disbelief.

Richard Klamp was overcome with emotion, down on his knees in the dirt and mud, trying to get hold of himself. Windmill held a bucket in two hands, catching rain to save for later. Ned Blythe had retrieved his wheelbarrow from the food store and was using that to gather the fresh rainfall. Phillip Jansen walked the street with an empty mailbag over each shoulder.

Mr. Mulraney walked his two skinny cows down the road, and the two animals looked to be drinking straight from the air. Leland Cantain stood on the porch of his opera house the way he used to do years before, when lines of people would funnel into his theater to watch his shows. Father Steven grabbed Sister Moffitt's hand and the two of them danced innocently right in the middle of the road, dodging roses as they sidestepped and shuffled. Toothache held a coffee mug up to the sky, collecting raindrops and drinking and then doing it all over again. Nicholas Draper had walked his blind mother outside, and she smiled as her face soaked in the rain. The Rochester family stood clustered in the middle of the road, one just as wet and amused as the next.

Ellen dared another duster to come, because she knew now that the town would meet it head-on, shovels and brooms ready. The people of the plains had been beat down, but they weren't finished. *Stone by stone. Letter by letter.*

She said to Wilmington beside her, "You know why these roses are popping up, don't you?"

Wilmington grinned, winked. "I have an idea, yes."

"And you won't tell?"

"Not today."

"Tomorrow?"

"Don't know if you'd believe me if I did tell, Ellen. But who really knows what tomorrow will bring."

And then, suddenly, the rain stopped.

All was quiet as everyone stared upward, waiting to see if it would start again.

One minute turned into two, and the skies began to clear. A sliver of blue shone between two cottony clouds.

Toothache said, "DoitagainMoses. Dothatthingwiththerocket."

"Fire another one," yelled eleven-year-old Rachel Finnigen.

After several more shouted requests, Moses Yearling hurried toward the road with his rocket. He looked up toward a patch of sunlight and, probably figuring that it wasn't the best spot to bust a cloud, he moved west about twenty yards, quickly setting up there. But as he fumbled to get the rocket lit, Deacon Sipes showed himself in the middle of Main Street.

Unlike the others, who seemed refreshed, Deacon still looked tired and beat down by the years of dust and drought.

"Jeremiah Goodbye," he yelled.

Ellen sensed trouble right away. Deacon staggered as he walked, like he was under the influence of booze, or even worse. And the look on his face was pure hate.

The next few seconds unfolded in slow-motion. Deacon pulled a pistol from his trousers, aimed it at Jeremiah, who turned right toward it.

Deacon said, "Dust to dust, Jeremiah. Maybe you should've flipped that coin."

And then he pulled the trigger.

The bullet whistled.

And then thunk.

Jeremiah spun, dropped to one knee in the middle of the road. Screams sounded. Unaware of what had just happened, Moses shot his rocket into the sky, and the explosion sent everyone down to the ground in shock. Toothache ran at his friend and tackled him at a full sprint. Sheriff McKinney dropped his letter and hurried toward Deacon as well, pulling hand shackles from his belt.

"No!" Ellen screamed, sprinting toward Jeremiah on the ground.

Rose, too, ran toward the growing circle forming around Jeremiah, who rolled onto his back, blank eyes gazing upward toward the rapidly clearing sky. Blood pumped from an entry wound on his right side, just below the rib cage.

His face grew pale, his lips bloodless. His shoulder was still bandaged from where Josiah had shot him days ago. And now this. He couldn't afford to lose much blood. He was only starting to get his full strength back.

Sister Moffitt was on her knees, pressing a handkerchief against the wound. It was already soaked. Ellen grabbed a shirt someone had removed from his own back and handed it to the sister. "Stay with us, Jeremiah," she pleaded. "Stay with me."

His body got to trembling as fear set in. His hands flailed as if fighting off shadows. His eyes closed. *What's he seeing in there?*

"Don't let it get me," he whispered. "Josiah . . ."

And then out of nowhere, Josiah was there, boots sliding in the mud. He dropped to the ground, found Jeremiah's hand and squeezed hard enough to turn their fingers white. Jeremiah's other hand still flailed, fighting whatever it was they couldn't see, whatever it was he saw behind those closed eyelids. Then Josiah gripped that hand too.

He knelt over his brother's body and told him to hold on.

"I got you now, Jeremiah. You hold on now! I ain't never letting go."

TWENTY-SEVEN

While Toothache and Sheriff McKinney dragged Deacon Sipes down the road to the jailhouse, Josiah and Father Steven carried Jeremiah into the Goodbye house and placed him gently atop a pallet of blankets Ellen and Rose hastily put together on the kitchen floor.

Ellen propped his head on two pillows while Dr. Craven and Sister Moffitt cleaned the wound, working like the dickens to get that blood to stop spilling. After twenty minutes of constant pressure it slowed. The fact that Josiah would not let go of his brother's hand made it hard to maneuver, but Ellen wasn't about to ask him to move.

Luckily the bullet had passed clean through the left side of his abdomen. Sister Moffitt cleaned the entry and exit wounds the best she could, tossed aside that blood-soiled shirt, and said she hoped no fabric was left in there to fester into an infection. But at least the bullet was out of the picture, aside from it now being lodged in the wood on the front side of the house.

An hour later Jeremiah's side was packed tight and wrapped and the blood had begun to clot. The shot he'd taken to the shoulder days before had been a graze in comparison. Ellen had never seen Jeremiah so pale. Sore now from her efforts, she finally rested back on her heels and let time take over. She watched his chest rise and fall. Rose had joined her on the floor, and for the moment the reporter felt like the sister Ellen had always wanted.

Jeremiah was in his brother's hands now, literally—Josiah had yet to let go of his right hand. And Josiah talked nonstop, telling stories of their childhood, year by year it seemed, just to keep saying something. Behind those closed lids, Jeremiah's eyes moved, like he was trying to open them but couldn't. Like he recognized the voice and was rooting for more.

"Keep talking, Josiah," Ellen said. "He can hear you."

Wilmington had pulled a kitchen chair close to where Jeremiah's head was positioned. He ran his hand over Jeremiah's hair and demanded he stay alive.

After two hours, Peter got on the floor and gripped Jeremiah's left hand. Peter mumbled what sounded like that nursery rhyme, the one he'd been named from, and Jeremiah seemed to respond. His head rocked slightly.

Color returned to his cheeks.

Ellen put her hands on Josiah's shoulders.

Josiah must have realized then that he'd stopped talking in order for Peter to get his words in, but there wasn't any time for taking turns. Josiah dug right into more stories—about the two of them working the wheat fields together, fishing the river when it was full, shooting rabbits and flipping that coin. Josiah laughed about the day Ellen came to town and how he'd said he'd marry her and Jeremiah had said, "Only if I let you."

"You remember that, Jeremiah?" Josiah wiped his eyes and rocked slightly like Peter was doing. He squeezed his brother's hand and looked up at Ellen. "He just squeezed me back."

"Keep talking, Josiah. Bring him back."

Wilmington continued to run his hand over his son's hair. "There's some warmth returning."

Josiah bit his lip and paused for a few breaths like he'd run out of things to say, but then he went on, his voice cracking. "I needed you when you were gone, Jeremiah. The town needed you." Josiah's jaw trembled. Full tears streamed down his cheeks and dripped to the floor. Ellen rubbed her husband's back, as she sensed where he was going. And then he said it. "The cattle, Jeremiah. I needed you when they came to kill those cattle."

Never had Ellen been more proud of Josiah on that day when the government came to kill Nowhere's cattle. But she'd also never been so scared of him. The way he'd gone distant for days after, weeks even. So silent and stoic she feared he'd never bounce back. And come to think of it, perhaps he never did.

"Go on," she urged him. "Tell him what it was like, Josiah."

"He knows what I done."

"But *you* need to tell him. And he needs to hear it from you."

Her husband nodded, conjured strength. Wilmington was crying now, and that only made things harder. Wilmington had never really gotten over that day either. It was when he'd started sneaking behind the house for a secret cry every night.

Josiah said, "It was nobody's fault, Jeremiah. Those cattle were starving. Skin and bones and dust. They were used up, with hardly any meat on them. The milking cows had long since gone dry."

Wilmington said, "The town needed money. That money got the economy moving in Nowhere again, at least for a time. We had no choice." His voice softened. "The cows were gonna die anyway."

"A dollar an animal was better than nothing," said Josiah. "Better than nothing. Roosevelt was doing the right thing. It's just that those government men that come weren't good about it. They didn't take into account our feelings for those animals, what they meant to us. Probably numb from having killed too many already."

"They were gonna die anyway," Wilmington repeated, closing his eyes. "Jeremiah, your brother was a hero."

Josiah bit his lip, composed himself. "Did what I had to do."

Ellen rubbed his shoulder. "Let it out, Josiah."

And he did. "Got tired of hearing those animals crying. All that anguish from the owners as the government gunned them down one by one with no remorse. I looked at all the town folk. And I did what you would have done, Jeremiah. You hear me? I did what you would have done." He looked up at Ellen. "He just squeezed my hand."

"Go on," she urged.

"The cattle needed to go out proper, Jeremiah. So I took my pistol and as many bullets as I could muster. Those government men told me to stay back, but I said no. If someone was going to shoot those cows, it was gonna be someone who knew them. I threatened to shoot those government men, Jeremiah, just like you would've done. And you know what? They listened. They backed away and said, 'Be my guest.' So I did. One by one I petted those cows between their eyes and whispered them calm. I said sweet words to accompany them to the afterlife, and then I pulled the trigger. Told each one of them I was sorry for what I had to do."

"They were gonna die anyway," said Wilmington. "The town was desperate for the money."

Josiah never broke stride. "If I didn't know the animal's name I'd call the owner over. They'd tell me, and then I'd move on to the next one. It took me six hours, Jeremiah, but I did it. I did what you would have done. For the town."

Jeremiah's eyelids fluttered. They all stopped talking and watched. A minute later the whites of his eyes showed, and his lips opened a crack. He found his twin brother and a weak smile emerged. "You done good, Josiah. You done good."

Josiah finally let go of Jeremiah's hand. He exhaled and stood, then took a slow walk around the kitchen to compose himself. Ellen had never seen him so emotional, but knew it was needed—not so much the emotion, but the willingness to show it.

Peter stood from the floor, let go of Jeremiah's hand, and left the house without telling anyone where he was going. He returned a few minutes later with his typewriter. Josiah helped him get inside the door with it and set up on the kitchen table. By then Jeremiah had propped himself up on his elbows and asked why everyone was huddled so close.

"Give him some space," said Wilmington, which they barely did.

Peter loaded a sheet of paper into the typewriter and clacked out a few quick words. He rolled the paper out and carried it over to Jeremiah, who chuckled weakly.

Ellen took the paper next and read,

Quit getting shot, Jeremiah.

She smiled and passed the note around the circle, because everyone was eager to read anything Peter wrote.

The atmosphere was jovial again, not too unlike what it had been during that short burst of rainfall, but then a quizzical look passed over Jeremiah. "What's wrong?" Ellen asked.

Jeremiah looked up at his father. "I sometimes have memories of Mother."

Wilmington went quiet, as did the room.

Jeremiah said, "Memories of things I should have been too

young to remember. But with me, they stick. She used to tell me things, probably thinking I wouldn't remember, or understand."

Wilmington's jaw quivered, and his eyes pooled.

Jeremiah grunted, asked for an extra pillow to prop him to a sharper angle. "It's time we talk and make sense of some things, Daddy."

"Like what?" Wilmington asked, fishing to see what all Jeremiah knew.

"Like the day me and Josiah were born." Wilmington stared at the floor, but then he looked up when Jeremiah said, "I know there's something you aren't telling us—you and Orion and Dr. Craven. I think you know exactly why these roses are blooming from dust."

TWENTY-EIGHT

Wilmington kindly asked those who weren't family to give them privacy. But when Rose grabbed Peter's hand and began to walk him to the front door, Wilmington stopped them. "No, I need you both to stay."

He motioned for Rose and Peter to sit at the nearby kitchen table. Peter grabbed a chair like he'd been born a Goodbye instead of bought at a dugout, but then he changed his mind and sat on the floor next to Jeremiah. "And Ellen, if you could go across the street and fetch Orion, I'd appreciate it."

Turned out Orion had been watching through the porch window anyway. Ellen needled him for staying outside, and he told her the sight of blood made him queasy. But when she told him he'd been summoned by Wilmington, his face showed that he had an idea of what this was about. The two town founders shared a glance, then a nod, as he stepped over the threshold, and then they all pulled chairs closer to Jeremiah's pallet—Wilmington and his two sons, Orion and Rose, Ellen, Peter, James, and Dr. Craven. They were afraid to move him just yet, so they'd made him as comfortable as possible with pillows and blankets.

The three older men sat together and exchanged nervous looks.

Wilmington poured himself some Old Sam corn whiskey and downed it in one shot. He placed the bottle on the table and let out a deep breath. "Do you all believe in miracles now?"

Jeremiah said, "As it pertains to those roses outside, yes I do."

Wilmington began. "You are astute as always, Jeremiah. Well, I'm going to tell you about the miracle that happened when you were born.

"It was a hard pregnancy from the start. Your mother began to show much sooner than her lady friends thought she might, and the guessing started right away. 'You're gonna have twins, Amanda.' 'Triplets,' another friend would say. 'Quadruplets,' even.

"She'd laugh along with them, but as that belly grew, it became harder for her to sleep at night. Harder to breathe as well. Even as a child she'd had problems sometimes catching her breath, and it had only worsened with age. The doctor thought the air out here on the plains might could help, so when we heard about this new town called Majestic, Oklahoma, we jumped on a train and headed west.

"I noticed a difference in your mother right away. But as Orion and I have told the story many times . . ." He trailed off, wiped his face.

Orion said, "There was no Majestic."

Wilmington smiled, reminiscing. "It was your mother's idea to name this town Nowhere—'cause that's what it was. We'd been dumped out in the middle of nowhere."

He moved the empty glass from hand to hand, showing nerves Ellen was unaccustomed to seeing from him. "The town came together quickly. We set up windmills and started pumping up water from the ground. Started tilling and dropping seed right away. Lived in dugouts at first until we could get real houses up."

Orion said, "Remember those centipedes?"

"You could hear them nesting in the walls," said Wilmington. "Scratching all night and into the morning." He laughed. "Your mother would take a flatiron to the walls and crunch them."

Orion said, "For insulation we used to put newspapers on the walls. I remember reading them by candlelight sometimes when I couldn't sleep on account of not being used to the winds yet."

"Boy, we lived through some stuff, didn't we?"

"We sure did," said Dr. Craven. "Prairie fires. Flash floods. Thunderboomers and roof busters with hail twice the size of a baseball."

"But we started making money, and soon your mother was ordering appliances from those Sears and Roebuck catalogues."

Orion nodded. "Built my first house from a kit ordered from there."

Ellen scooted forward in her chair. "Wilmington. The birth?"

Wilmington sighed and poured himself another shot of whiskey. This time Orion took one as well. "Soon after the town got going and weeks before she was to deliver, Amanda started having these nightmares." He glanced at Jeremiah. "Not exactly like yours, but perhaps similar. She'd wake up sometimes and cry out that he was trying to take her babies. Even then, all the needling from her friends aside, she knew she was carrying more than one."

"But who was *he*?" asked Josiah. "Who was Mother talking about? Who was trying to take us?"

"That I don't know for sure." He looked at Jeremiah. "Do you remember that day when you were a boy? It was soon after you started flipping that coin to make your decisions. You remember what you told me?"

Jeremiah nodded. "You told me not to speak of it again."

Josiah looked at his brother and father. "What?"

Wilmington said, "I asked him why he flipped that coin to make all his decisions. He said he had an angel on one shoulder and the devil on the other and he could hear them both whispering in his ears."

Jeremiah shifted on the floor like he was uncomfortable, like the discomfort involved more than just the physical pain of the bullet wound.

Wilmington said, "I didn't approve of his flipping. But I told him to go on with it if that's what he did for fun, but to speak no more of that angel-devil nonsense."

Jeremiah said, "It wasn't nonsense at all."

Wilmington gulped, wiped his eyes. "I know that, son. But the unexplainable is just easier when buried. Or at least that's what I thought at the time." He looked at Josiah. "So now that that's out, the *he* your mother spoke of—I can only assume she was talking about the devil."

"Or not," said Jeremiah. "In my nightmare, I felt both sides."

It went quiet, as it appeared the three older men had lost track or were afraid to go on.

Josiah broke the silence. "I was born first?"

Wilmington nodded. "Your mother was slow to get about on those days before. And when she started having contractions, I called Dr. Craven in here right away. It was raining hard that day, fattening up our wheat fields as we watched. We got your mother fixed up on the bed. Orion was here with us, more to support me than anything else. We waited in the room adjacent. The rain on the roof was so loud we could barely hear each other."

Dr. Craven said, "I was practically yelling, the rain was so loud. Called Wilmington into the room because I needed help. He came running."

Wilmington looked at his two sons. "You were the first babies ever born in Nowhere." He closed his eyes as if to remember it all. Orion reached over and patted his arm and Wilmington's eyes oozed back open. "You did come out first, Josiah—easily, just like we've always said. Crying and healthy, with lungs strong enough to register over the tumult against our roof."

Wilmington glanced toward Jeremiah, who winced as he sipped from a glass of water. "Jeremiah, you came next. But your birth wasn't a struggle like we always said. That happened after you came out." Wilmington wiped his eyes and stared at the floor between his boots.

Orion took over. "I heard your father scream, so I came into the room."

"What happened?" asked Ellen.

"Jeremiah was dead." Orion took in every set of eyes around where Jeremiah lay on the floor and found them all rapt. "He was blue. Wasn't breathing at all. Dr. Craven was working on him, but . . ."

Dr. Craven chuckled. "Truth be told, I didn't know full blown what I was doing either. Delivering babies was something I had to learn to do."

"How long?" asked Jeremiah. "How long was I dead?"

Wilmington said, "To keep myself sane, I watched the hands of that grandfather clock tick and tick as I hoped and hoped."

"And then all of a sudden you gasped for air," said Orion. "Like you'd been underwater for too long and were desperate for what was above the surface."

Jeremiah said, "You said you counted the ticks, Daddy. How long was I out? How long was I not breathing?"

Wilmington watched both sons. "A minute and fifty-one seconds."

Ellen's heart raced.

Josiah wiped his face, and his eyes got big. "Same as the nightmares."

Jeremiah nodded. "Exact same, Josiah."

"Those weren't nightmares." Josiah faced his brother. "Those were memories."

Jeremiah nodded. Wilmington watched them both like he didn't completely understand. Jeremiah said softly to everyone gathered around the table. "It makes sense now. The angel and the devil trying to make me their own."

Ellen felt her lungs deflate. "They fought over you."

Jeremiah looked at his daddy. "I always saw a pinprick of light in all that darkness. Swirls of light and dark. Every nightmare was the same at the end, and I'd open my eyes gasping for air. But they were memories. I was pulled through . . ."

He hesitated, a strange look on his face as realization hit. "But somebody . . . somebody wasn't."

Wilmington stared, eyes red but dry. He nodded. "I used to stick a red rose in the lapel of my coat every morning. Every morning without fail." He offered no more.

Orion said with caution, "Dr. Craven . . . while we were all stunned silent by Jeremiah gasping for air . . ."

Wilmington nodded for his friend to go on, and so did Dr. Craven, like he wasn't ready to tell it either.

Orion said to Jeremiah and Josiah, "Dr. Craven focused his attention back on your mother, who was pale as a clean bedsheet but lucid enough to know . . . to know that there was another baby. A third baby."

Wilmington smiled. He glowed like Ellen hadn't seen him glow in years, like a tremendous weight had been lifted. "It was a girl. And unlike Jeremiah, she didn't make it. But something amazing happened. As soon as she was delivered, that rain stopped." Wilmington snapped his fingers. "Cold. Stopped just like that, like the weather froze. The clouds opened up and the sun shone so bright we had to squint against it."

He looked over at Rose. "I named her Rose. We'd had names picked out for boys, and Rose was the name we'd picked for a girl."

Ellen now understood why he'd embraced Rose the way he did when she'd first entered the Bentley Hotel days ago. Rose teared up as she listened.

Wilmington said to her, "I know we are of no relation whatsoever, but the instant you walked into that hotel lobby my heart grew warm. How old are you, dear?"

Rose said, "A year younger than your sons."

Wilmington nodded, smiled, reached across the table, and briefly gripped her hand. "You see, I was never able to see my Rose." He looked at both sons. "Neither was your mother. It's just not something you did when a baby comes out stillborn. I didn't see you either, Jeremiah, not until I heard you crying."

A little choking sound escaped from Ellen, and she covered her mouth to stifle it. Josiah reached over to rub his wife's shoulder.

Wilmington said, "Dr. Craven wrapped her up, and me and Orion buried her beside the house. I begged him to tell me what color eyes she had, and he said blue. He told me not to ask any more questions—that she was beautiful and that was that. But before I covered the hole with dirt, I took the rose from my lapel and placed it atop the bundle."

He took in all the eyes around the table. "I can't explain it, but I wasn't sad. I cried as we shoveled the dirt back on top and marked it with a cross, the sun beating down on our shoulders. But they were happy tears. I know it sounds strange, but I felt we'd been given a gift, however brief it had been."

Orion said, "It's true what he says. I felt hope permeating. A sense of optimism such as I've never felt before. I hugged your father, and he hugged me back, and we stared at each other like we couldn't even begin to explain what we were feeling."

"It was kindness."

They all looked at Peter, who'd just uttered those words unprompted. He said no more, even as they all stared at him. His expression showed he was as startled by the words as they were.

"Why didn't you tell anyone about Rose?" asked Ellen.

Wilmington shook his head. "I don't know. Maybe because of what happened the next day."

"What was that?"

"Amanda was tired and sore, but I walked her outside with me. Made her see what I was seeing, so I knew I wasn't losing my mind. A rose had grown up from the ground right above where we'd buried our daughter. At first I thought the one I'd buried with her had somehow sprouted, but no, this one was different. I gave it a tug and found it rooted strong. The one I'd pulled from my lapel had already begun to wither. We sat there together, me and your mother, and stared at that rose. Never seen one grow up from the ground like that. As a single instead of off a bush."

"Until this week," Ellen said softly.

He looked up as if he'd forgotten they were all there. Then he nodded. "Until this week. Anyway, when the town folk stopped by to see the twins, they saw us sitting beside the house watching that rose and asked if we'd just planted a garden. We looked at each other and said that we had, never mentioning what really happened. And then, since we didn't tell initially, it became harder to tell in the future. Especially the next day, when we went back outside and found that not one, but three, roses had sprouted. We sat there and smiled, in awe of the color."

He looked around the table as relief washed over him. "I never planted a rose garden. All I did was bury your beautiful sister." He looked at both of his boys. "Some things can't be explained, so you don't even try to."

Ellen looked out the window to all those roses sprouting across Nowhere. "Yet the truth still finds a way."

TWENTY-NINE

That night, despite the warnings for him to take it slow, Jeremiah insisted on getting up and walking. Even with the pain, he craved fresh air. So Josiah set up two chairs on the front porch and helped him out. From there they sat overlooking the town like they used to when they were kids.

The sky was still overcast, so the moon offered little more than a fuzzy purple blur, but their eyes had long since adjusted to the dark. Still mostly dust and tumbleweeds out there.

And roses.

Hundreds of them, sticking up sturdy and strong now well into the night. But who knew how long that would last. The short morning rainfall they'd had would more than likely be an isolated event. Didn't mean the drought was over. Probably far from it.

Jeremiah said, "You think we'll ever see green grass in the plains again?"

"Maybe someday," said Josiah. "I hope so, for Daddy's sake."

"You think if we stayed out here and watched all night, we'd see more roses actually pop up?"

"You want to?"

Jeremiah shrugged. "Nah, I suppose not. Sometimes if you wait too hard for something it never happens." He winced and grunted as pain resonated around his stomach wound.

"You need to head back in and rest."

"Rest ain't never helped me, Josiah. You know that."

Josiah smiled, and Jeremiah found the smile contagious.

"That story in there." Jeremiah glanced at Josiah. "That mean I'm technically your little brother?"

"It's the way I've always looked at it. That story didn't change the fact that I came out first."

"You know how I can feel it when I'm around someone bad? Well, it goes both ways. Like two sides of a coin."

Josiah looked over. "What are you saying?"

"Just that every time I got around you I felt something good. When you'd hold my hand when we were younger, during those nightmares, I'd know it. I'd feel it in my heart."

"Okay."

"I'm just saying, you must've had a little of what our sister had." Jeremiah patted Josiah on the shoulder. "Sorry about that toe."

Josiah laughed. "And I'm sorry about that shoulder."

Jeremiah stood slowly, limped down the steps, and turned. "I don't want what's yours, Josiah. I hope you know that."

"I do, brother. I do."

It took Jeremiah longer to reach the Worst house than he expected, but he made it. After resting for a little while and drinking a glass of water, he checked in on Peter and found the boy typing away like he had a deadline. He closed the door and left him be. Then he made his way back outside and breathed in the night air.

He knew which room was Rose's inside the Bentley Hotel. Her light was on. A shadow moved behind the curtain and then settled. Even from the Worst house he could hear the clacking of her typewriter. Rose was hard at work just like Peter.

How long would she stay in town? The way she'd left the Goodbye household after Wilmington's story made Jeremiah think it would be shorter rather than longer. Rose was an ambitious woman who'd come into town with a goal in mind and a job to do, and truthfully he'd think less of her if she were to stray from it.

At least for now.

Especially since her work could one day mean his freedom.

Still looking toward the hotel, he pulled a quarter from his pocket and started to flip it in the air. His side screamed in pain and he dropped the coin on the dusty porch. He stared down at the result for a few seconds and then left the quarter where it lay. Thinking about what the result might could mean, he moved slowly down the road toward the jailhouse, knowing he wouldn't be able to sleep until he confronted Deacon Sipes.

"You sure you should be out? You don't look so good." Sheriff McKinney shook his head, but didn't object to letting him in for a quick visit.

"Wasn't but a few days ago that you were intent on putting me inside one of these cells, Sheriff."

Sheriff McKinney said, "Still might."

Jeremiah couldn't tell if he was kidding him or not. So he moved on toward the cell that held Deacon Sipes and found the young man sitting in the corner shadows with his knees raised and his elbows propped on the shelves of them.

Jeremiah gripped the bars and leaned with his forehead against them. He hadn't come with anything particular to say; he'd just wanted to come. And he saw right away that some of that meanness was gone from Deacon's eyes.

The dust no longer weighed as heavy.

Deacon was the first one to talk, which was what Jeremiah had hoped. "I've done some bad things in my life, Jeremiah. How'd you know I'd killed a man?"

Jeremiah shrugged. "Saw it years ago in my head. Gift and a curse, Deacon."

"I'm sorry for shooting you. I didn't want it to get out. Now the town hates me."

"I don't hate you, Deacon."

Deacon chewed on it. "If you seen it years ago, why didn't you flip the coin on me? Like you done with them other four men."

Jeremiah laughed.

"What's funny?"

"Piece of candy saved your life."

"How so?"

"That day I brushed up against you and saw what I saw, I'd just given the quarter in my pocket to one of the schoolchildren wanting candy."

"So you didn't have a coin to flip."

"Not at that particular moment, no."

Deacon digested it all. "Then why didn't you flip the coin on me the other night, when you told me what you seen? I could've killed you, Jeremiah."

"Never too late for lesson learning."

"For me or for you?"

"Both, I suppose."

A door latch echoed, and Father Steven entered the cellblock. The priest waited by the door until they were finished.

"Thought maybe it was time to confess some sins," said Deacon. Jeremiah grinned. "Send him my way when you're finished."

Ellen couldn't sleep.

The reasons were multiple, and none of them were bad. She just couldn't get the story Wilmington had told them out of her mind. As much as those roses out there could make sense, for her they now did.

Perhaps Wilmington had felt that same connection with Rose as she'd felt with Peter upon first sight.

Wilmington had left her bedroom ten minutes ago, and her forehead still felt the touch of his lips from when he'd leaned down to kiss her good night. He wasn't accustomed to doing that. In fact, the more she thought on it the more finality that gesture carried, to the point where she'd almost gotten out of bed twice to check on him. Maybe that bullet hadn't moved over the past three years because he wasn't ready for it to move. He still had a story to tell, and now that he'd told it . . .

She swung her legs from the bed, checked on James, who was asleep in his crib, and then tiptoed down the hallway to Wilmington's room.

She was satisfied for now to hear him snoring. She closed his door quietly and started back to her room, but instead of going in she continued on down the hall toward the kitchen to pour herself a glass of water. *Quit stalling, Ellen.*

She knew why she couldn't sleep. Wilmington's story had righted a lot of ships, or at least kept them from tipping, but it hadn't righted them all.

She drank the water and watched out the window and wondered what Jeremiah was doing walking home from the jailhouse. He had no business being out of bed, really. She watched him go inside the Worst house and close the door behind him, and she poured herself another glass of water.

She chuckled softly after she drank it, recalling the first time she'd kissed Josiah after secretly kissing Jeremiah so many times behind that barn. How she'd laughed after she'd done it. How Josiah had pulled away and said, "What?" like he'd done something wrong. Before he'd had time to turn red from embarrassment, she'd planted another one on him, this one good and lasting until she felt both of their hearts racing.

She knew now why'd she'd laughed.

She was prone to do that when she was happy.

She finished the water and placed the glass quietly on the counter next to the sink. She walked through the kitchen and into the living room, where Josiah was asleep on his back, snoring with his mouth barely open and the knuckles of his left hand grazing the hardwood floor. She laughed at him and then shook his shoulder.

"Josiah," she whispered.

He grunted but didn't awaken, so she kissed his mouth, and that got him. She laughed again when his eyes shot open, and she wanted to say, "You were always the one I was supposed to marry," but didn't feel like she needed to.

"Ellen?"

She shushed him, gripped his hand, and pulled him from the couch. Next she led him through the kitchen. They quietly moved down the hallway, and she kicked the bedroom door closed behind her with the heel of her right foot.

They were both giggling now, like they used to when they'd first married and tried their best to be quiet with Wilmington down the hall.

"You sure about this, Ellen?"

"Never been so sure about anything, Josiah."

Jeremiah gave himself a small dose of morphine after returning from the jailhouse, and it sent him under for three hours of deep sleep.

When he awoke, rested but groggy and feeling as if someone had taken a sledgehammer to his abdomen and shoulder simultaneously, he heard Peter typing down the hall. That wasn't a surprise. Peter stayed awake most nights writing those letters. Letters that had transformed the town, the messages and notes more contagious than any disease Jeremiah had ever come across.

Kindness breeds kindness.

But when Jeremiah knocked on the door and let himself in, Peter handed him a trifolded paper and watched as Jeremiah sat on the bed and opened it.

We've done what we came to do, Mr. Goodbye. Now it's best we move on.

Jeremiah looked up from the note. In a way, it was as if the boy could read his mind. He'd been thinking about leaving Nowhere sometime soon. Though the dusters might have kept the law away for now, it wouldn't keep them forever. But he'd figured Nowhere would still be the best place for Peter to live. As much as he'd miss the boy, Jeremiah wasn't sure he'd been cut from the fatherly mold like Josiah. Ellen and Josiah would be good parents for Peter, and Wilmington the perfect grandfather.

But now, for the first time, Jeremiah saw that there might be another option. "Where would we go?"

Peter turned toward the typewriter and punched a series of keys.

Jeremiah moved toward the chair next to the desk so that he could watch Peter type. It's how they'd begun to communicate.

To the next town.

"I'm a fugitive, Peter."

So am I.

"No, you're an orphan."

What's the difference?

Jeremiah laughed. The boy was stubborn and too smart for his own good. "What about Nowhere? Don't you like it here?"

As much as anyone can like all this dust. Yes, I love it here. But Nowhere's not going anywhere, and we've got business to do.

He paused to think, then punched the keys again.

They're safe now.

"How do you know this?"

Same as you. The dust man moved on. And we will too.

"What dust man?"

The one you've been seeing in your dreams, Mr. Goodbye. Some of the town folk are starting to talk about him. I mentioned him in some of the letters.

"But how do you know what's in my dreams, Peter?"
Peter grinned, typed.

You talk in your sleep, Mr. Goodbye.

Jeremiah laughed. "I talk in my sleep, huh?"
Peter nodded, typed.

There might not be these roses where we go next, but they'll need us just the same.

Jeremiah stared at the boy in awe. "You mean they'll need you."
The boy smiled large as he typed.

"Without you there is no me."

He paused.

If I can call you Daddy then I'll no longer be an orphan.

Jeremiah couldn't have hid his grin if he'd wanted to. "Reckon that'd be okay, son."

That night when Nowhere slept, Jeremiah and Peter delivered the letters together.

Peter let him read what he'd written to each one of the town folk, and as usual his finger was right on the pulse of what mattered most. And although his words hinted toward a departure, it was also made clear that he'd be back after his work was done. In the meantime, it was time they wrote letters to each other now—if not with words, then with deeds and actions.

They needed to just keep on spreading that kindness.

Jeremiah watched the ground as he delivered each letter, taking pride in closing the mouth of each mailbox and turning those yellow flags upright as Peter did the same on the other side of the street.

But as carefully as he watched, no new roses popped through. Must be like watching for a weed to grow. They don't do anything while you're spying, but as soon as you turn your back they grow like the dickens.

Ellen woke the next morning with the pleasant weight of Josiah's arm draped over her shoulder.

His breath touched the nape of her neck, and for the first time in a long time she felt safe.

She eased herself out from beneath his arm and put her bare feet on the floor, which was gritty with dust. She looked back toward the bed and saw the outline of where her head had been etched by dust on the pillow. A duster must have rolled in overnight. Or maybe the dust that constantly permeated the air had just settled.

In the kitchen she looked out the window. Her mailbox flag was up. More roses had sprouted overnight—one right there on the railing of their porch.

But no more rain.

She recalled Wilmington's story from yesterday, and cold chills covered her skin. The look of relief and contentment on his face when he'd gone to bed last night had warmed her heart, but now it unnerved her. She'd been hoping he'd be up by now.

Had that look she'd seen on his face meant he was ready now? Ready for that bullet to move and take him the rest of the way? To Amanda and his daughter, Rose?

Next thing she knew she was running through the kitchen and down the hallway and opening Wilmington's bedroom door in one long breath. He lay motionless on the bed, covers tucked over his shoulder.

"Wilmington?" She knelt beside the bed. Sunlight paled his face. His eyes were closed.

She placed a trembling hand beneath his nostrils and couldn't tell if she felt anything. So she gently shook his shoulder and started crying. "Wilmington, don't do this. You might be ready, but we aren't." She shook him again. "Wilmington?"

And then he opened his eyes, and she fell back on her rear end.

"Ellen, what in the world? I was having a good one for a change."

She covered her mouth, stifled a chuckle. "I thought . . ."

"You thought what?"

"Thought you were dead," she said, feeling her face flush red. "I thought that bullet moved."

He leaned up on an elbow and felt the scar, the entry wound that never did have a proper exit. "Sometimes I think you *want* that bullet to move."

She shook her head. "Of course I don't."

He sat upright and felt the slightly concave entry above his ear. "I do feel a duster coming, though."

She smiled, patted his bony knee. "That we can handle."

At five minutes after ten in the morning, a week and a half after Jeremiah stepped down from Old Sparky with his heart still beating, the lawmen finally came.

They came in four cars and with enough men to bring down four Coin-Flip Killers if they had the need.

Jeremiah waited by the window of the Worst house as car doors closed and boots touched dust. The wind blew. Tumbleweeds tumbled. Guns cocked.

"Jeremiah Goodbye," shouted one of the lawmen. "I know you're in there. Come out with your hands up."

Part of him hoped they'd come in after him. The other part . . . He glanced across the room at Peter and thought, *Perhaps in another life.*

"Jeremiah Goodbye," the lawman shouted again, loud enough for all of Nowhere to hear and flock to their windows and doors. "Come out with your hands up."

Jeremiah looked out the window. Four dusty cars, eight men total, all armed with rifles and wearing hats and badges with titles on them.

The one doing the talking just happened to be the biggest. His badge dappled in the sunlight and he kept his eyes fixed on Jeremiah's door.

The other lawmen seemed distracted by all the roses—like they were trying to make sense of them and at the same time stay on task. Bringing in the Coin-Flip Killer was no small one.

Peter approached Jeremiah with a rifle in his hands. The boy's arms shook; it was against his nature to even hold a weapon, let alone urge someone to use it. But if he could have typed out something right quick, Jeremiah imagined it would have been something about desperate times.

Jeremiah shook his head and told Peter to put down the gun. He knelt and hugged the boy like he'd never see him again. "You stay with my brother and Ellen. They'll watch over you proper. No tears."

Peter did his best, but the tears still came.

Jeremiah turned toward the door and stepped out onto the porch with his hands up. He walked slowly down the steps. Peter stood in the doorway.

"That's close enough, Peter."

"Keep 'em up," said the head lawman, stepping away from his Model T, both hands on his rifle, finger on the trigger.

"To whom do I have the pleasure on this fine morning?" asked Jeremiah.

"Agent August Livingston," said the tall one. "I'm with the State Bureau of Criminal Identification and Investigation." Up close his face wasn't fully shadowed. He had a mustache, brown and thick like the hair beneath his hat. "Your little vacation is over, Mr. Goodbye. Keep your hands up where I can see them and approach slowly." He spoke out the side of his mouth toward the agent next to him, a chunkier man with still enough size to do damage if it came to it. "Get the bracelets ready, Charles."

Charles unlatched a set of cuffs from his waistline.

Livingston's eyes shifted from Jeremiah to all the roses. "What's with all the flowers? Roses don't bloom from dust."

"Seems they do here," said Jeremiah. "It's a long story. And you wouldn't believe me anyway."

"It's a long ride back. You can tell me on the way."

"Won't be a ride at all," called Josiah, stepping down from his porch with a rifle aimed at the agents.

"That's close enough," shouted Livingston, motioning for two of his men to aim their shooters toward the other Goodbye.

Josiah took four more cautious steps before stopping near the street.

"Put down the weapon," said Livingston. "We don't want bloodshed."

"It'll get bloody if need be," said Josiah. "Law ain't taking my brother again."

Jeremiah turned toward his twin. "Josiah, put the rifle down. I'm gonna get in the car with these gentlemen and go. I won't cause any more trouble."

Josiah spat. "You're staying put."

Orion appeared next, slowly approaching from the Bentley Hotel with a rifle aimed.

"Halt," shouted Livingston. "Put the rifle down."

Orion stopped about twenty paces away, but he didn't lower the rifle. In fact, he seemed to have Livingston in his crosshairs.

Livingston hissed at Jeremiah. "Get in the car. Put an end to this."

Jeremiah took a step with his hands still up.

Josiah said, "Stop, Jeremiah. I mean it. I'll start felling lawmen one by one."

Just then Wilmington stepped from the house with his rifle and made it to about three paces behind Josiah before Livingston shouted for him to stop too.

Wilmington said, "If you take my son, it'll be with a bullet in your back."

"You just threatened a state officer," said the chunky one holding the cuffs.

"Yes I did, tubby."

Ellen walked out from behind the house and knelt behind a drift of dust. She had a rifle as well. She leveled steady, finger on the trigger.

Livingston's eyes darted from rifle to rifle. He looked over his shoulder, as did his fellow lawmen, when they heard footsteps approaching in the opposite direction.

Sheriff McKinney approached with a rifle aimed—not at Jeremiah but at the agents.

Livingston said, "Sheriff, tell them to stand down. Tell them to lower those rifles, or I'll take them all in."

"I'll do no such thing, Agent Livingston."

Livingston chuckled.

"What's funny?" asked Sheriff McKinney.

Livingston turned in a slow circle. "What kind of a sheriff are you?"

Sheriff McKinney said, "The kind who knows more about all this than you do."

Rose had just emerged from the Bentley Hotel in a dress and holding a rifle. She stopped beside Orion's tractor, where another rose had sprouted from the engine overnight.

Livingston faced Jeremiah again and clenched his teeth. "Get in the car."

Josiah said, "Don't move, brother."

Jeremiah said, "Josiah, don't do this."

Livingston regained his focus and pointed his rifle directly toward Jeremiah. "This man was supposed to be dead already. He escaped Old Sparky, but he won't escape me. He's guilty of taking the lives of at least four men."

Josiah said, "He didn't kill those men."

"I can prove it," shouted Rose. "I'm pushing for a new trial. Only thing he's guilty of is having a conscience."

By now, windows had opened all over town with rifle barrels poking through. Doors opened and guns were cocked. Toothache stepped from the shadows with a rifle in each arm. Leland Cantain propped his atop his mailbox. Moses Yearling, from the porch of the hotel, pointed one of his rockets toward the agents. Phillip Jansen pulled a pistol from his mailbag and pointed it.

Father Steven and Sister Moffitt were unarmed, but their intentions to intimidate were clear in their straight-backed postures. Pastor Johnson stood a few steps behind them, frowning.

Minutes ticked by, and the agents grew skittish.

More of the town folk stepped from the shadows and around house corners and parked cars with pistols and rifles aimed. William "Windmill" Trainer held a shotgun. Ned Blythe gripped a pistol in both hands like an Old West gunslinger.

Jeremiah grinned as he took it all in, but still he said, "Josiah, put a stop to this."

Josiah said, "Close your head, Jeremiah. For once you're listening to big brother." He took two steps toward Livingston. "Ever heard of Tombstone, Arizona, Agent Livingston? The shootout at the O.K. Corral?"

Livingston spat to the ground. Sweat dripped from his brow. "What do you think?"

"By the looks of that sweat dripping, I think you have."

"You're no Wyatt Earp."

"And he was no Goodbye."

Livingston scoffed, his eyes darting toward all the aimed rifles. "You don't have the sand."

"Maybe not." Josiah took another step. "But I've had my share of dust. And I'm prepared to make Tombstone look like a tea party if you and your badges don't go back where you come from."

Livingston eyed his men, straightened his hat. "You won't do it."

Josiah shrugged. "Try me."

"I'll come back with an army. You know that, don't you?"

"Figured as much."

"And I'll bring you in with him."

"Figured that too," said Josiah, jerking the agents a nod. "But not today."

Ten minutes after the lawmen's cars left in clouds of dust, Ellen sat trembling on the porch step.

Josiah sat beside her and kissed the top of her head. "It'll be all right, Ellen."

She gripped his hand and squeezed. Somehow she could tell by his touch that it would be all right. The law would return, but by then Jeremiah would be long gone. He and the boy were packing inside the Worst house now.

The door closed behind them, and Wilmington walked out to the porch holding James's hand. Ellen opened her arms, and the boy came running. He'd shown more energy of late and less of that croupy cough.

Rose was fixing to leave town as well. She stepped from the Bentley Hotel with her bags packed and approached an idling Model T on the street.

Jeremiah must have seen her. He hurried from the house and met her in the middle of the road. They talked for a minute and even spent a few beats of it laughing. She covered her mouth as if he'd said something to make her blush, and then Jeremiah kissed her hand.

Rose said her good-byes, which included a firm hug and a wish of good luck from Ellen. Then she got in the car and drove away.

Jeremiah stood next to Ellen and Josiah until Rose's car was the size of a thumbnail and then disappeared. He looked at his brother. "Would you have really pulled the trigger and started a gunfight earlier?"

After some thought, Josiah said, "Yep." He nodded toward the road, where Rose had gone. "She going to get you a new trial?"

"Gonna try to," said Jeremiah. "Woman's determined."

Ellen said, "I've been seeing how you look at her, Jeremiah. And how she looks at you."

"And how's that?"

"Like there isn't enough to go around." Ellen folded her arms. "I can't believe you just let her go like that."

Jeremiah grinned out toward the distant road.

"What?" asked Ellen.

"She'll be back, Ellen. I'll see her again."

"And how can you be so sure?"

Jeremiah winked.

"You didn't?"

"'Course I did."

Twenty minutes later the entire town had gathered around the packed car, and Jeremiah leaned against the open driver's side door.

He said to Josiah, "Thanks for the wheels. I wasn't looking forward to carrying that typewriter on foot."

"When they come back, I'll say you stole it."

"Punched you and stole it."

"Even better."

The two brothers embraced. Wilmington was next. Then Ellen held Jeremiah and looked up into his eyes. "I know why you have to go, but I wish you didn't."

"A thought come to me last night, Ellen. I figured all this time it was chasing me."

She didn't need to ask what was chasing him. The nightmare. His gift. It was all one and the same. "And now?"

"I think I've been the one chasing it. And I ain't done yet."

She stepped away from Jeremiah, then knelt down and hugged Peter tight. "You promise to come back and visit?"

"Come back and visit," said Peter. "Peter, Peter, pumpkin eater."

Figuring that was as good of a verbal answer as she'd get, she stood and wiped her eyes.

Jeremiah knelt down, and with his pocketknife cut a red rose from the dirt. He smelled it and then stuck it in the pocket of his button-down so that the working end showed bright.

The gesture clearly made Wilmington proud.

Jeremiah pulled a quarter from his pocket and prepared to flip it, but then stopped. Instead, he handed it to Peter. "You do the honors. Heads we go west. Tails, east."

Peter flipped the coin in the air with pride and let it puff to the dirt.

Jeremiah plucked it from the ground and dropped it back into his pocket.

"West it is."

AFTER

Dusters raged for years after Jeremiah left town, and the rains continued to stay away. More grasshoppers came along with the rising temperatures and more rabbits too.

But Nowhere lived on.

After each duster, they clung together and dug out with shovels and brooms at the ready, daring the next one to come along too, and the Bentley Hotel played music and hosted gatherings almost every night in defiance.

Those mysterious roses eventually wilted and died, but what they represented didn't.

Kindness continued to permeate the daily doings.

That seed wouldn't be so easily plucked.

Back in the summer of 1935, Jeremiah and Peter helped transform five more towns throughout the southern plains dust bowl with all that letter writing. But eventually, after they'd spent nearly seven months on the lam, Agent Livingston picked them up in Somewhere, Colorado.

At least that's where Jeremiah later said he was caught, because he couldn't remember the name of the town. Or maybe he was just trying to be funny.

But by then, the near showdown in Nowhere months before had garnered enough attention that half the country was rooting for Jeremiah to continue evading those lawmen.

Rose Buchanan's newspaper articles had made their way all over the country too, shedding light on the truth behind the notorious Coin-Flip Killer. Jeremiah Goodbye had gone from infamous to famous overnight, it seemed. After the arrest, Agent Livingston was kind enough to drop Peter back in the town of Nowhere, just as Jeremiah requested, so that he could live with Ellen and his brother, Josiah.

Josiah Goodbye, by then, had begun to gain notoriety as a gunslinger. He never asked for it. He only wished for rain and green grass and wheat fields again so that his children could grow up in something other than dust. But rumors spread quickly about that sunny April morning when the lawmen first tried to carry Jeremiah away.

Josiah hadn't yet gained the status of Doc Holliday or Wyatt Earp, and he didn't want to, but with the way he'd backed Agent Livingston down with that rifle and told him he'd make Tombstone look like a tea party, well, each story told got him closer to just that.

Jeremiah only did six more months in jail anyway.

Rose Buchanan and her newspaper articles had developed enough steam to drive a train right toward a new trial. With the new information those articles set forth, Jeremiah had become somewhat of a national celebrity, and he got off with time served. What he'd done burying those bodies was one thing, but killing them was another. The judge dismissed him, and told Jeremiah just before he left the courtroom that "perhaps it wouldn't be a bad idea to give that coin a rest."

Jeremiah tipped his Stetson and told the judge politely that he'd consider it, but he "wasn't sure that could be the way of things."

Days after Jeremiah Goodbye was declared by the judge to be a free man again, he was reunited with Peter in Nowhere. By then, Ellen was large with the twin boys she'd give birth to a few months later.

Jeremiah and Peter took up residence in the Worst house, picking up right where they'd left off. The people of Nowhere were already calling it Jeremiah's house anyway.

Those magical roses didn't come back, but Wilmington had restarted his rose garden beside the house, and he tended to it daily like he used to. With enough well water, it turned out, even ordinary roses could bloom in the dust.

Peter kept to his letter writing, and eventually, three weeks before his eleventh birthday, he restarted the Nowhere newspaper. He called it the *Desert Rose Tribune*, and Deacon Sipes, who was good at fixing things, got the printing presses up and running again.

Peter and Jeremiah delivered them to the town's mailboxes every morning at sunup.

After Jeremiah's return, it was hard to find a day gone by where someone didn't arrive in Nowhere with luggage and hole up inside the Bentley until housing could be claimed.

"Just heard there's no better place in the plains to be," most of them would say, despite all the dust.

Some came from those towns where Jeremiah and Peter had made a mark before his arrest. They'd come with saved letters Peter had written back then, hoping for more, and soon the town began to grow again.

Large portions of the southern plains never returned; the earth had been abused and chewed up so badly. But gradually, over the years, the rains came back, and after a decade of trial and error, so did some green grass.

Wilmington, following President Roosevelt's big idea, planted trees fit for the climate, and after a while shade returned. He eventually put more wheat in the ground, but took care to rotate the crop, treating the land with the gentleness of holding a newborn.

Wilmington Goodbye was seventy-seven when he died, with seven grandchildren to his name and green grass aplenty. And as far as Ellen knew, that bullet Jeremiah had accidently put in his father's head back in the summer of 1932 had never moved. It was a heart attack that finally did Wilmington in, and Ellen, eventually a grandmother of two of her own, had been warning him about it for years. Too much meat and greasy food had thickened him.

"Went too many years near to starving, Ellen," he'd tell her. "I could eat until I'm ninety and still not catch up."

"Well, you don't have to do it all in one day," she'd tell her father-in-law.

Wilmington Goodbye's seven grandchildren didn't all belong to Josiah and Ellen. Only four of them came from that union. They'd had a girl two years after the twin boys.

The other three belonged to Jeremiah.

A year and two months after the judge declared him a free man, he was up on a ladder in Nowhere cleaning dust from the gutters.

A car puttered into town, fancy and new, and it pulled to a slow stop in front of the Bentley, where Orion stood on the porch smoking a cigar.

Out stepped Rose Buchanan with two suitcases.

Jeremiah was down that ladder so fast he nearly fell. He met her in the road and took the luggage from her.

"Hello, Jeremiah."

He nodded with too much enthusiasm. "Rose."

She smiled, pretty as the day he'd first laid eyes on her. "Figured it was too awkward to tell a Goodbye good-bye for good."

Jeremiah didn't know exactly what she meant, so he laughed, and she did too. All that mattered was that she was standing before him again.

"Coin never lies," he said.

She grinned, playfully. "You flipped a coin on us, Jeremiah Goodbye?"

"No. Maybe. Yes, I suppose I did."

"It's a good thing too," she said. "I knew there was a reason I was turning down all those suitors my parents were bringing by." She slid her arm inside his as they walked toward the Bentley.

Three months later they married inside that same hotel. Ellen and Josiah stood up with them. And a year later Rose was pregnant.

Wilmington said she looked as big as Amanda had when they'd first arrived in town. "Liked to never fit her in that train car."

Josiah told his daddy it wasn't polite to talk about how big a woman looked when she was in the family way. Besides, she wouldn't have been *that* big when they arrived.

Wilmington just shrugged that off. That bullet in his head sometimes made him say funny things. And then Wilmington leaned in and asked Rose, "Did I ever tell you about Majestic, Oklahoma?"

She laughed.

Jeremiah knew she'd already heard the story, but she allowed him to tell it again.

And then, a couple of months later, Rose gave birth to triplets.

Two boys and a girl.

They named the girl Amanda.

Amanda Rose Goodbye.

And when Wilmington first held her he cried.

DISCUSSION QUESTIONS

1. There are some flawed characters in this story. Discuss how redemption plays a role in the novel, specifically with Jeremiah and Josiah Goodbye.
2. The Dust Bowl was a terribly bleak time in our country's history. I've always been a half-full kind of guy. Think of some instances in the story where a character shows optimism and hope when all seems lost.
3. Discuss the aspect of fate in regard to Jeremiah flipping that coin. Discuss fate vs chance with some examples throughout the book.
4. As twins, in what ways are Jeremiah and Josiah Goodbye similar? In what ways are they different? How does their relationship go from broken to whole again?
5. Peter Cotton is an observer who doesn't verbally say much, although his actions and smile speak volumes. After he gets the paper and ribbon for the typewriter, how is his written word ultimately transformative?
6. In the story, Peter's letters aren't just letters. Discuss the power of the written word.
7. While writing this story, the phrase "killing it with kindness" popped into my head. The kindness in Nowhere ultimately trumps meanness. Can kindness really be contagious?

8. I always try to have my characters transform throughout the course of a novel. Which character changes the most from the beginning of the novel to the end? How and why?

9. Give examples of how forgiveness plays a role in the novel.

10. In many of my books, beauty can be found beneath the dirt and grime of life. Only in fiction can red roses bloom from dust. In the novel, what seeds, planted now or in the past, helped bring this miracle about?

11. The Bentley Hotel is more than just a hotel in this story. What role does the hotel play in this town?

12. In many cases, you can't judge a book by its cover. Discuss how Jeremiah Goodbye was often misunderstood.

ACKNOWLEDGMENTS

I might sit at my computer and do all the typing, but books aren't written alone. *What Blooms from Dust* had a quick deadline, and luckily—except for the month I had to take off to sub seventh- and eighth-grade math (and I'm not good at math)—this book flowed like a rain-swollen river, practically writing itself, the first draft finished in less than three months. Because of the timing, I wasn't able to hand the early pages out to my normal stable of readers, so I leaned heavily on Aldan Homrich, who offered to read quickly and brainstorm; he came through big time—and thank you 3rd Turn Brewing for hosting us with some mighty fine porters! Karli Jackson's expert editorial touch on the novel was spot-on, as always—thank you for everything! And to Kimberly Carlton for championing this story to the end. Anne Buchanan for the spectacular line edit. To everyone at Thomas Nelson who had a hand in the process, from the amazing cover design to marketing—I'd attempt to name you all but would probably have nightmares of leaving someone out. I watched several videos on the Dust Bowl, from the History Channel to Ken Burns on PBS, but my go-to was the truly wonderful book, *The Worst Hard Time*, by Timothy Egan;

it flows like a novel and was one of the most interesting history books I've ever read. To my wonderful agent, Dan Lazar, as always, job well done—because of you I'm still getting paid to make stuff up. To my parents and siblings, cousins and friends—you know who you are—thank you for your unflinching support. John, this would be the perfect book to use that blurb from Stephen Kang! Ryan and Molly, you continue to impress and inspire; and Tracy, your role in this entire process is more important than you'll ever know. It's easier to run and chase dreams when you know there's steady ground beneath your feet. Patience is certainly a virtue. And finally to you, loyal reader, for doing what you do!

James Markert
Louisville, Kentucky
November 2017

Discover the secrets of the Bellhaven Woods . . .

Where evil can come in the most beautiful of forms.

ABOUT THE AUTHOR

James Markert lives with his wife and two children in Louisville, Kentucky. He has a history degree from the University of Louisville and won an IPPY Award for *The Requiem Rose*, which was later published as *A White Wind Blew*, a story of redemption in a 1929 tuberculosis sanatorium, where a faith-tested doctor uses music therapy to heal the patients. James is also a USPTA tennis pro and has coached dozens of kids who've gone on to play college tennis in top conferences like the Big Ten, the Big East, and the ACC.

Learn more at jamesmarkert.com
Facebook: James Markert
Twitter: @JamesMarkert